"Cadet Vannevar James Tagawa—" sitting behind the desk in front of me of them fit in a snug red uniform with a sil that signified him as the Commandant of t

"Correction, sir," I replied, smoothly. I've had my name legally changed to Vance Turbo."

The Commandant, whose name was a series of roars I couldn't pronounce, stared at me. "No one calls you that. We're also here to formally kick you out of the Academy."

"I'm hoping to persuade you otherwise," I said, smiling broadly.

"Hope away," the Commandant said. "I hope to never see your ugly human mug again."

"That's racist, sir," I replied.

The Commandant rolled his eyes and put all six of his paws on the desk. "So is calling you a mediocre student from a backwater world. One that needed at least three more generations of development before you were allowed to send applicants to the Academy. You're a cheat and a liar, Vance. So much so that I think that's the only way you got into this school in the first place."

"No, sir, that was nepotism," I replied.

The Commandant blinked. It was amazing how confusion looked similar across the universe's many species. The two of us were standing in a pale blue office with purple shag carpeting that was the default office look for the Interstellar Community Protectors. Personally, I just called it Space Fleet, and everyone understood my meaning.

SPACE ACADEMY DROPOUTS

Book One of the Space Academy Series

C. T. Phipps and Frank Martin

MYSTIQUE PRESS

CAST OF CHARACTERS

<u>Lead</u>

Vance Turbo, aka Vannevar Tagashi: Academy dropout, loudmouth, alleged genius

<u>Supporting Cast</u>

Fifteen: A female Sorkanan bridge officer. Efficient. Methodical.

Forty-Two: Sorkanan dropout. Smarter than your average merc. Trying way too hard.

Alfred: The AI who raised Vance and made him the pop culture quoting wannabe badass he is today.

Bob Just Bob: A retired Verdantian engineer who knows more about starships than you ever will.

Chief Sal Boxley: A skittish technician who has survived numerous horrific accidents in training before being dragooned into Department Twelve's service.

The Commandant: The head of Space Academy. Verdantian. Degenerate gambler. Really hates Vance (for good reason).

Captain Jules Elgan: Legendary captain of the *ESS Ares* and *ESS Black Nebula*. Known for renegade habits.

The General: A Notha leader captured alive by the Community.

Lorken: Blue skinned, white-haired demihuman badass Space Marine. Leah's current boyfriend. No last name.

Lt. Leah Mass: Actual graduate of Space Academy, genius. Vance's ex. Psychic. Transwoman. Transhuman. Heroine.

Hannah O'Brian: Genetically engineered superhuman merc. Catlike agility and other qualities. Like her tail.

Lt. Leslie Park: Blue-skinned, black-haired demihuman bundle of love and joy. Also handy with a wrench.

Picnic: A Bug security officer with an amiable gentle disposition. Don't be fooled.

Ensign Julius Something: An East African Union bridge officer who gets stuck with terrible duties.

Captain Willamina Snow: The ruthless racist captain of the *IMS Nathan Bedford Forrest*. Not a nice person.

Captain Katerina, "Kathy", Tagawa: Hero of Earth's space program. Paragon of humanity. Vance's aunt.

Ex-Ambassador Ketra T'Kal: Former ambassador of the Community. Ethereal Human. Weird space wizard.

Tommy: A Sorkanan cadet that died during a space-walking accident. Vance's Uncle Ben and Gwen Stacy figure.

TRS-8021, more generally known as Trish: The AI of the ship. Human female personality. Annoyingly adorable.

Wadsworth: The AI of *Starkiller XII*. Male human personality. Jerk.

Dr. Elizabeth Zard: Unfortunately named human female. Doctor of math *and* medicine. Prefers the former.

FOREWORD

S pace, the funniest frontier.

I've always been a huge fan of science fiction as anyone who has read my Agent G or *Lucifer's Star* books can attest. Heck, my review blog is called The United Federation of Charles. To refute the words of Harry Dresden who said there are two kinds of people: *Star Wars* and *Star Trek* fans, I am proudly both with a library that include a hundred books of both.

I was a slavish devotee of *Star Trek: The Next Generation* from the time I was eight years old and absolutely adored every installment of the *Star Wars* franchise from when I watched it for the first time on VHS at age five. It's not so much I appreciate two wildly different franchises than I understood they weren't all that different. I just preferred my Trek a little wackier and my *Star Wars* a little more political.

I love the endless worlds full of unimaginable dangers, weird aliens, and situations that might be politically applicable but are usually so far removed from our world that you can view them from the abstract. I love memorizing all the wacky ship details and being fully aware that the writers never intend to keep any of this consistent. I am on the space opera end of science fiction, which is pretty much its own form of fantasy, but I make no apologies.

Space Academy Dropouts is technically set in the same universe as *Lucifer's Star*, centuries earlier during the Golden Age of space travel. *Lucifer's Star* is when epic disasters have made humanity the disliked outlier race of space while this is when things are bright and optimistic about our chances. We may still be the new kids on the block but there's a whole spiral of the galaxy opening up to us that contains seemingly infinite possibilities. That doesn't mean it doesn't have its own problems and it'll be up to our (anti)heroes to make sure things don't go wildly out of control before things fall apart.

Also, as *Lucifer's Star* is an homage to tramp freighter captains of fiction, so is *Space Academy Dropouts* an homage to those pioneering heroes of the frontier that our protagonists most definitely are not. This book salutes those poor underachieving individuals who are not capable of living up to the heights of glory established by Kirk, Picard, and Sisko. They have more in common with the Barclays, Wesley Crushers, and Lower Deckers who probably shouldn't be anywhere near the omnipotent power of a starship.

Even their ship is closer to the *Tantive IV* (the ship that Darth Vader took over in the opening of *A New Hope*) than the *Enterprise*. Vance Turbo and his oddball crew are some of my favorite creations and I think you'll enjoy them and their attempts to do the right thing despite being absolutely awful at it. But that idealism is intact and is something that at least a few of them still believe in despite all the various things that have the potential to go horribly wrong with it.

Enjoy.

CHAPTER ONE

Where I Get Myself Kicked Out

"Cadet Vannevar James Tagawa—" the lion-faced alien said, sitting behind the desk in front of me. He had six arms and all of them fit in a snug red uniform with a silver badge on the right lapel that signified him as the Commandant of the Academy.

"Correction, sir," I replied, smoothly. "I've had my name legally changed to Vance Turbo."

The Commandant, whose name was a series of roars I couldn't pronounce, stared at me. "No one calls you that. We're also here to formally kick you out of the Academy."

"I'm hoping to persuade you otherwise," I said, smiling broadly.

"Hope away," the Commandant said. "I hope to never see your ugly human mug again."

"That's racist, sir," I replied.

The Commandant rolled his eyes and put all six of his paws on the desk. "So is calling you a mediocre student from a backwater world. One that needed at least three more generations of development before you were allowed to send applicants to the Academy. You're a cheat and a liar, Vance. So much so that I think that's the only way you got into this school in the first place."

"No, sir, that was nepotism," I replied.

The Commandant blinked. It was amazing how confusion looked similar across the universe's many species. The two of us were standing in a pale blue office with purple shag carpeting that was the default

1

office look for the Interstellar Community Protectors. Personally, I just called it Space Fleet, and everyone understood my meaning.

"I'm not sure that translated correctly," the Commandant said.

Universal translators were a must in any interstellar civilization, but they were constantly being updated and spotty on the best of days. Aliens communicated in music, light, smell, horns, and even flatulence, as I'd learned in my five years at the Academy. The implant at the back of my brain could translate most of them but names were something that just didn't survive the cultural divide. Mind you, I'd replaced eighty percent of its translation space with black-market decryption and hacking software. Because, really, my ability to get into faculty records was more important than my ability to speak Bug.

"I'm just being snarky about the fact that my aunt is the sole reason I'm here over many other more qualified candidates," I replied.

The Commandant opened his mouth then closed it. "Well, at least we're in agreement over that."

Yes, dear Aunt Katerina Tagawa was the most (and as far as I knew only) famous Earthling in the universe. The first Earthling (but not human—long story) Space Marine. The first Earthling Space Fleet captain. The Hero(ine) of the Battle of Nightingale, the Heroine of the Battle of 5241-B7, and the Savior of Planet F-Sharp Bell. She'd been an astronaut before the Great Arrival and made quite the impression in the subsequent thirty years.

Aunt Kathy had inherited guardianship of me when both my parents had gotten themselves sucked into a star after screwing up a standard cargo haul while getting high as a kite. This was more impressive than it sounded since most interstellar flights were done automatically and had countless redundancies. They'd probably have to spend hours taking the computers apart in order to screw up as badly as they had.

Either way, Aunt Kathy hadn't had much time to raise me in between saving the universe and had done her best to do right by me through naked favoritism. I'd been grateful at the start but now just resented the hell out of it.

"Don't worry, I don't want any special treatment because of my aunt," I replied.

The Commandant gave a smile of various teeth that I'm sure would have enjoyed tearing apart some animal on his homeworld. "Good, that makes things extra easy. You're expelled."

"I don't see why," I said, crossing my arms. I was still wearing my blue Space Academy jumpsuit with its own little badge which translated the context and thoughts of my cybernetic implant to anyone around me to whom I was speaking. It was of an inferior quality since it sometimes picked up on pheromones and hormones to utterly mess with my game. Still, I'd had all the best updates in hopes of being able to link with state-of-the-art AI. A few of them were illegal but only if I was a civilian—another thing that should have gotten me kicked out but I hoped to avoid.

The Commandant stared at me. "You tampered with the simulator to give yourself an advantage in your tactical simulations."

"I don't believe in a no-win situation," I replied, dryly.

"Which is not a defense!" The Commandant said. "It's also a confession. Goodbye."

He did a three handed wave at the door.

"So, this isn't about the illegal book I was running out of the Academy bar?" I said, oh so subtly.

The Commandant paused, or should I say, *pawsed*. Okay, terrible pun I know. "That was *you*?"

One thing that I'd discovered upon leaving the comparatively dirt-poor and vice-ridden confines of Earth was that the Community was, for all its many good qualities, full of stuffed shirts. Gambling, drugs, prostitution, most forms of alcohol, and I space you not, *caffeine* equivalents were heavily regulated if not outlawed. It was like the galactic arm was run by Mormons. On one hand, this meant that quite a few students were just one bad day from stabbing someone, but on the other meant that there were people like me who stood to benefit.

"Yep," I said, smirking.

"Then I have the pleasure of also calling the constabulary to arrest you," the Commandant said, chortling like a cat who'd caught a mouse. "That will make quite a few problems go away."

"Yes, except for the detailed records of bets on the fire races and gravity ball that you've made which are easily corresponded to your

3

accounts," I said, pausing. "I mean, I know this is a cashless society but at least use a money card."

The Commandant now looked like he was ready to rip me apart, which he perhaps was. Whatever his ancestors were in the past, I suspected they were predators. "Are you blackmailing me?"

"No, blackmail would be if I threatened to go to the authorities," I replied.

"You just did," the Commandant said, growling.

I sighed. "Which would just result in me getting thrown out anyway as well as serving a few months in a happiness center. Also, why do you call your prisons that? That's just weird."

"I didn't name them," the Commandant said. "What are you proposing? Because I'm not letting you continue to corrupt and degrade this noble institution. You are unfit to serve in Space Fleet and I will not put the lives of my sibling officers at risk—"

"Let me drop out," I replied.

The Commandant looked exhausted trying to follow this conversation. "You want to drop out?"

"Yes," I replied. "Just like three-fourths of Space Academy cadets do before graduation."

The Community Protectors were one of the most prestigious organizations in the galactic spiral even though it had a history of getting people killed by giant space monsters, hostile xenophobic races, or contracting diseases that made you excessively horny. Earth television had turned out to have underestimated how weird as well as violent the greater universe was. That wasn't why I wanted to drop out, though. Those who made it through the crunch were the best of the best. I wasn't worth it. Not after what I'd done.

The Commandant stared at me. "So, you just drop out and walk away?"

"Yes," I replied. "No stain on my record and I just quietly drift into the civilian sector where I am officially not your problem. Oh, and I'll also erase all those debts that you've acquired over the past few years. Seriously, man you have got to stop betting on the Green Stars. Those guys are terrible."

"It's the home team!" The Commandant hissed.

"It's zero-ten!" I said. "This year!"

The Commandant huffed. "You think you're so clever."

"Yes," I replied. "I do."

The Commandant waved his hand over his desk. A holographic depiction of the withdrawal form appeared in front of me. "Sign here."

I reached out my hand and made a waving gesture with my hands. I was surprised to find out that signatures had survived into space travel but apparently writing was one of those things that every race had. It was one of the basic things that qualified a race as civilized. Frankly, I was a little worried about that since I half wondered if that was just to know which races were okay for things like the Commandant to eat.

The holographic form blinked red with my hand wave and turned blue before disappearing. With that, my five-year mission to become the 555th Earthling Star Cadet had come to an end. All I had to show for it was a lot of money, a surprising number of sexual encounters, and a wealth of training I could have used to better my fellow man. I spared a tiny moment of sadness for this lost opportunity, then thought about Tommy. My resolve solidified.

I sucked in my breath. "I just want you to know despite all of the terrible things I've done, all the rules I've broken, and all the excessive numbers of insubordinate acts that I've committed, I truly cherished my time—"

"Get the hell out of here, human," the Commandant said.

"Right," I said, giving the salute that just so happened to be one half of a high five. I then walked out of the Commandant's office. The doors made a *swoosh* noise that I was always appreciative of, I didn't know why. I suppose it reminded me of those few times I'd been on Aunt Kathy's ship, *The Olympic*.

The building beyond was a place that kind of defied description but I was going to try to give one anyway. The Interstellar Community Protectors Space Academy looked like a combination of the Babylonian hanging gardens, a stark white futuristic space station, and a shopping mall. It was one enormous cylinder with its own gravity and vast numbers of parks spread around the walkways to recycle the air for those who breathed either oxygen, carbon dioxide, or nitrogen.

Everything was stark white to humans and races who didn't see in the thermal spectrum and apparently a bizarre cacophony of colors to races who did.

Space Academy consisted of a dozen of these cylinders, all prepped for various environments, floating around an enormous asteroid that contained hundreds of floors that made the location self-sufficient. If you wanted to explore the various cultures and races of the universe then you didn't have to go much further than this place. Which was, now that I thought about it, incredibly disappointing.

"No!" a female voice shouted at me before I saw a familiar face run up towards me.

Leah Mass was a brown-haired woman who was a bit on the short side and possessed a mixture of Norwegian and Asiatic features. She was wearing a blue tunic uniform with thigh-high boots, which passed for fashionable among human cadets. In her hands were a collection of data books that were what happened when you had six different incompatible language systems among your studies. Leah was a couple of credits away from graduating and destined to be the kind of officer I couldn't be. I cared for her deeply and it was because of that care our relationship had to end.

"Something wrong, Leah?" I asked.

"Tell me you haven't dropped out!"

I gave a regretful shrug. "Sorry, Leah, too late."

Leah looked furious. "You idiot!"

I clasped my hands together like a supervillain. "Alas, they found out my evil plan. They allowed me to resign to avoid a scandal."

Leah narrowed her eyes. "You only cheated so they would have to throw you out."

I blinked. "That's...not true."

"You were passing beforehand," Leah said. "Your tactical rating was a two minus."

Two minus was the equivalent of a B plus. The Academy only accepted the best of the best and I was a solidly unremarkable student in that category. "I needed to stand out. Clearly, that's what motivated me."

Leah blinked and shook her head. "You're falling on your sword because of Tommy."

I didn't respond for a moment. "Tommy is dead because of me."

Tommy—real name: a bunch of growling hisses—had been a Sorkanan. They were the closest approximation of the bipedal giant lizard people that humans had envisioned evil alien invaders would look like. They were the most powerful race in the Community, though by a matter of degrees rather than kind. Tommy had been my roommate for four years.

"You weren't at fault," Leah said. "The Academy cleared you."

Tommy and I had been doing a routine spacewalk to collect the junk of less developed species (read humans) like old satellites, trash, plaques commemorating space walks, and frozen waste. It was a good way to learn how space functioned since someone's frozen feces could end up going one thousand miles per hour due to gravity's pull. I'd goofed off with a fusion torch, playing with it like a lightsaber, and had missed when a piece of stray debris tore Tommy's head off.

"Yeah, but I didn't clear myself," I said. I'd been prepared to accept full responsibility. For possibly the first time in my life. Instead, they'd blamed the sensor operator and she'd been kicked out of the Academy. That had been back before I'd been a complete screw up and I'd still had some credibility to burn.

"So, you just decided to throw away your career on the altar of self-sacrifice?" Leah asked.

"I have never self-sacrificed in my life!" I said, appalled at the suggestion. "I'll have you know that I could have been thrown out, but I blackmailed—I mean bribed—I mean blackmail-bribed my way out of it."

Leah shook her head. "You just have to make everything more complicated than you need. Why not just resign?"

"I'm not a quitter. Also, I'm addicted to complexity," I said, smiling.

Leah looked disgusted. "You damned fool. What do you even intend to do?"

"I dunno," I replied, speaking honestly. "Anything where the lives of thousands, if not millions, of people aren't depending on me. Maybe I'll end up hauling freight like my parents."

"Your parents managed to crash an automated ship into a star," Leah said.

"Yes, so that's a fairly low bar to fail to measure up against," I replied, not really appreciating her bringing up my tragic backstory. I mean, it wasn't too tragic, as I'd barely known either of them, but just tragic enough.

"We could have been on the same ship," Leah said, slapping my face.

I barely felt it. "Was that actually supposed to be a hit?"

Leah growled and marched off. "Ooo!"

"Okay, that was just childish," I said, watching her walk off.

Eh, she was better off without me anyway. Leah had a bright future ahead of her and was the kind of person who could captain a starship someday. I didn't want to see her go but any association with a black-market dropout would ruin her career. I regretted what might have been but if I am going to go down in flames then I had best go down in flames alone.

That was when I turned around, only to have a black bag shoved over my head. Seconds later, a stun wand struck the side of my neck and I fell to the ground. This was the standard operating procedure of Department Twelve. That was the one that did all the bad things that enlightened societies were supposed to be above. Apparently, the Commandant hadn't been content to leave it at my resignation.

Crap.

I passed out seconds later.

CHAPTER TWO

The Offer I Couldn't Refuse

I woke up feeling like I'd just been extra-judicially kidnapped by a paramilitary organization.

Oh right, I had been.

Department Twelve was a group that scared most people in the Spiral that had any sense of rights or checks and balances. It was an organization that had unlimited authority to arrest, detain, and eliminate threats to the security of the Community Council. The media liked to portray its agents, called Scars, as heroic defenders of the people doing the dirty business that needed to keep the galaxy running.

They were the one dark side of the otherwise utopian society that I'd found myself in. It was like running around with a bunch of space hippies and idealists only to find they had a Wild West Sheriff ready to hang anyone who stepped out of line. The weirdest thing was only humans seemed to find it strange. Oh no, I don't see anything weird about grabbing a guy off the street and shoving him into a hover car before disappearing him into a deep dark hole somewhere. He must have done something wrong.

I tried to get my bearings, but I was handcuffed to a chair and by the way my pants felt, hadn't exactly kept my dignity upon being hit with a sonic stunner. It was a shame because I'd intended to cherish this cadet's uniform, put it on a mannequin, and then set it on fire before filming it for the infonet. That was still possible, but I'd prefer to just throw it out now. The moment was ruined.

"He's coming to. Remove the hood," a male human voice with a slight British accent spoke. It could just have been a good translation, though. I'd once met a seven-foot-tall Bug—whose appearance you could probably guess from the name—who sounded exactly like Dick Van Dyke from *Mary Poppins*. Who the hell had programmed that?

Okay, wait, I had to focus because I was probably going to be tortured. The first thing I needed to do was find out what they wanted, the second was throw everyone I knew under the bus if that helped my situation, and the third was probably still die ignominiously. Department Twelve didn't make deals with its prisoners.

That was when my hood was removed, and I found myself in the proverbial dimly lit room with a metal desk and some ominously dressed figures in leather outfits. They were mostly humans of the rainbow spectrum of colors we came in but there were a couple of Sorkanan too, though they wore alligator hide equivalents of the human's leather attire.

Note: I say rainbow spectrum of colors because in addition to the white, black, brown, and other colors of Earth there were places that humans came in more candy-like bright colors. Humans existing outside of Earth were a subject that confounded Earth scientists and pointed to all those stories of alien abduction being true (except for the crop circle ones, those were still fake).

Oh, and Leah was here too. She was standing behind me, so it had taken a second for me to register her presence. Leah was holding the mask and wearing one of the Department Twelve uniforms too. She at least had the decency to look guilty, but I had to admit I was too shocked to react immediately.

"Leah, what the hell?!" I snapped, staring at her in horror.

"You've got yourself in it now," Leah muttered, looking away. "This is what you get for ignoring my warning."

"What warning?" I asked.

"Not to drop out!" Leah said, crossing her arms. Her hands had little black leather gloves which was both chic and fascist.

I stared at her. It was useless bringing up the fact she'd told me after I'd already done it. "I would have paid more attention if you said not to drop out or the Space Gestapo will kidnap me!"

"It was implied!" Leah protested.

"No, it wasn't!" I snapped. "Space Nazis were not implied!"

A white-haired, blue-skinned man raised his hand. I guessed him to be one of the genetically altered residents of the planet Thor. He looked at me with a sneer of contempt on his face. "I should point out that I'm Jewish and find that comparison offensive."

"The Space KGB then!" I snapped.

Leah didn't look happy with that comparison either. Tough, you don't get to be upset when people complain about being extraordinarily renditioned. God knew where I was and what part of the galaxy I'd been dumped.

"Why are you adding space to everything?" Leah asked, confused.

"Because we're in space!" I replied.

"We're *always* in space," Leah replied, being remarkably cordial for someone who'd just aided in my kidnapping.

Either this was a "friendly" kidnapping that wasn't going to result in my getting two fusion blasts to the back of the skull (always overkill) before dumping my body in a recycler or Leah was far more psychotic than I ever imagined under her cute, button-nosed exterior.

Leah frowned. "You know I can read your thoughts, right?"

"Oh right," I said, remembering she was a biomancer. Psychic powers didn't technically exist but the Community produced biomods for those beings rich enough to afford them. They allowed certain races to be able to read minds, lift objects, and other things that pretty much amounted to being psychic. I'd always wondered where Leah had gotten her abilities and now it seemed clear she'd signed up to be a spook.

Goddammit.

"What's he thinking?" The Blue Jewish Guy asked.

"The usual," Leah said. "Where am I, what am I doing here, and how are Smurfs Jewish."

"I did not think that!" I snapped, before looking at the Blue Jewish Guy. "Okay, now I am."

The Blue Jewish Guy glared at me and looked ready to draw his fusion pistol and gun me down.

That was when the doorway to the room opened and flooded the room with light. A shadowy, indistinct figure appeared in the light before stepping forward. Heroic music swelled up behind him and I felt instantly like I was in the presence of greatness. That was when I noticed the Academy marching band was playing behind him and the light was coming from the noonday sun. I could see the oxygen-nitrogen grav ball breathing team practicing too.

I turned to Leah. "You locked me up beside the frigging *gym*?"

"Technically, the janitor's closet," Leah said. "I mean, we have to put all his stuff back by Fifth Hour."

The indistinct figure then stepped forward and cleared his throat, drawing back my attention. He was a tall black man in his fifties with broad shoulders, a square jaw, movie star good looks, and a shaved head. He was wearing the white tunic of a Space Fleet captain, which was positively covered in medals. Honestly, if not for the fact I recognized him and knew he deserved every one of them, I'd suspect he was a Third World dictator.

"Sweet Mother of Jumpdrives," I said, blinking. "Captain Jules Elgan!"

"In the flesh," the man said, smiling as if he was accustomed to humans fawning over him. Which I imagined he was.

Captain Jules Elgan of the *ESS Ares* was the second most highly decorated Earthling in the history of space and not for lack of trying to be the first. He'd graduated just after Aunt Kathy, defeated the Maelstrom pirates, smashed the Null crime syndicate, and won a dozen encounters with the genocidal Notha.

He'd contained AI outbreaks, survived encounters with the Elder Races who might as well be gods, and supposedly had his pick of holo starlets. I mean, was it sexist to think that was the coolest part? Maybe. I mean, I didn't begrudge the fact Aunt Kathy had three boyfriends in the Beaumont Brothers, but it did affect my opinion of their movies.

"If this is some sort of scared straight program, you missed it by that much," I replied. "I'm resigned from Space Academy."

"Do you really think I'd come down here for that?" Captain Elgan asked.

I blinked. "I don't know. I'm not exactly familiar with what you would do under the circumstances. What do you do when you're not punching rock monsters?"

"Technically, it was a coral covered alien," Captain Elgan said. "Rock monster would just be silly. The Carbon-Sentience Index means that as diverse as alien life may be, it's all going to share some common fundamental attributes."

"Oh right," I said, too star struck to care. Technically, he wasn't quite as accomplished as Aunt Kathy, but a Space Fleet officer was a hero everywhere but their hometown. "So, why am I here and why does it require black bagging me?"

Captain Elgan made a pair of finger guns at me, quite possibly the most obnoxious gesture in the universe. "Vance Turbo, I sense in you the seeds of greatness."

"You do?" I asked, confused.

"You do?" Leah asked, equally so.

I looked up at Leah. "You just kidnapped me, and you didn't know what it was for?"

"I was just following orders!" Leah said.

Both me and Blue Jewish Guy stared at her.

"Oh bork you, both of you," Leah said.

"You know that still basically means fuck, right?" I asked. "Word substitution to get by the translator is still swearing."

Leah glared at me. "It's not word substitution. It's just a very dirty word on my planet."

"Uh huh," I said, sarcastically. "Oh well, when in Albion. Bork off, all of you."

Leah frowned.

Captain Elgan looked amused. "You two are together, right?"

"Yes," I said.

"No," Leah said.

"Really?" I asked.

"I thought we explicitly broke up over you dropping out of the Academy," Leah said, disgusted.

"I know but I was hoping for some breakup sex out of the deal," I replied.

13

"Can we shoot them both, Captain?" Blue Jewish Guy said, who I was now going to refer to as Papa Smurf.

"His name is Lorken," Leah replied, reading my mind. "Also, really, Lorken? We're already degenerating to threats?"

"You tried to warn him," Lorken said. "That's treason."

"It's not treason," Captain Elgan said. "No, I actually admire her dedication to her former lover. It's another sign of the kind of magnetic leadership potential that I sense in you, Vance."

I blinked.

"Are we talking about the same guy?" Leah asked.

Still handcuffed to a chair, sitting in my own wastes, I tried to figure out a way to describe how utterly insane I found all this. Failing, I just asked, "Why exactly am I here?"

Captain Elgan pulled up a metal chair and sat down across from me. "I want to make you the offer of a lifetime."

"And if I turn it down?" I asked.

"Then you'll never be seen again," Captain Elgan said, his smile suddenly menacing.

My hero worship for Captain Elgan took a serious blow in that moment. "Then I will happily accept your offer no matter what it is."

"Smart man," Captain Elgan said. He twisted a ring on his finger as my student records popped up in a translucent hologram above it. "Space Marine training—"

I glared at Leah.

Leah thought to me, *That doesn't count. It's actually being a Marine in Space.*

So is everything else! I thought back to her.

"Top notch marks in computer programming, cryptography, and social engineering," Captain Elgan continued. "You're a mediocre student now but you excelled in several unusual areas before your accident with Cadet Greenscale. It's taken Department Twelve weeks to find out all the various hacks, splices, and dummy programs you've put into the computers here. Were you really selling bleach to the Tecktoki?"

"They love that stuff," I replied. "It's like beer that makes you sharper."

"You also did successfully get into the Academy's tactical computers," Captain Elgan said.

"I did," I replied. "Took me awhile, though."

"That's because they're identical to our fleet's," Elgan said. "You effectively hacked military hardware."

I blinked. "Oh. Wow."

"So, I'm offering you a commission," Elgan said. "I want you to be my first officer on a mission into the Contested Space."

Contested Space was an enormous area of a million or so star systems that sat between the Community Council Races and the Notha Empire. It was a place beyond the law with numerous outlaw colonies, pirate bases, illegal trade routes, and planets regularly plundered by the Nots (as Space Fleet officers called the alien fascists).

I stared at him. "There are literally millions of people more qualified than me for this. Also, first officer? I'm a frigging cadet. Ex-cadet. Why me?"

"Yes, why him?" Leah asked.

"Because it's a highly illegal operation and the penalty for being caught is death," Captain Elgan said. "It also has a very low chance of success."

"Ah," I said, nodding. "Science fiction really misrepresented how the utopian planetary federation would operate. This is more Heinlein than Roddenberry."

Captain Elgan pointed at me with his finger guns again. "I get those references! Literate too!"

I gave an entirely fake smile. "So, what, you need me for an expendable crew?"

"Exactly," Captain Elgan said. "I call it Operation: Dropout. There're hundreds, if not thousands of people who were almost but not quite good enough to make it through the Academy. People with most skills but lacking some minor area or possessing a bad attitude. Most of them find jobs in the civilian sector, no worse for wear, but a handful are just itching for a chance to serve their country."

"Earth is a hellhole and it's not even a full member of the Community," I said.

"Then do it not to die," Captain Elgan said.

15

"Your oratory skills are amazing," I replied, persuaded by his argument. I briefly thought about whether my Aunt Kathy could help but I'd burned those bridges already. I'd told her I wanted nothing to do with her anymore and that I was going to make my own way. Besides, there was little she could do against Department Twelve.

"So, you're going to get a crew together of dropouts and send them on a mission into enemy territory," I said. "Aren't there actual spec ops people trained for this?"

"Yes," Captain Elgan said. "They'll be ready in six months. I believe that this time sensitive issue requires more immediate movement and I've exerted my Scar authority to arrange for this operation's approval as long as I could assemble the resources myself."

"I thought you said this was a highly illegal operation," I said.

"It is if we get caught," Captain Elgan said. "In which case, I'll be fine, but you'll all be executed."

"You're a lot nicer in the movies about you," I replied.

"Don't believe everything you see in the movies," Captain Elgan replied. "But there's good news. If you help us pull this off, under my leadership of course, then you'll have your commission recognized. Well, technically as part of Department Twelve's military forces but that's almost as good as Space Fleet."

"Oh joy," I replied. "I dropped out of the academy to avoid having millions of lives depend on me and now I'll have billions while working for the galactic secret police. Are we sure there's no negotiation room on the 'do this or die' thing?"

"If you can find me a computer hacker with military experience up to your level then I'll just use all the information here to send you to prison for the rest of your life," Captain Elgan said. "Did you really sleep with Admiral B'vort's daughter?"

Leah's eyes widened.

"That's a personal matter," I replied.

"How?" Captain Elgan said. "I mean, anatomically?"

I shrugged. "J'ssar and I figured something out."

Leah's face crinkled in disgust.

"Now you're just being racist," I replied. "I still don't know why you want me on this but I'm willing to go along with it because I don't want to die. What are we going to be doing that's so important and can I please get a change of clothes?"

"Absolutely," Captain Elgan said, rising. "As for what we're going after? It's not much, just some SKAMMs."

I looked at him in horrified disbelief. "Sun killers?"

"Don't worry," Elgan said. "Earth has only a fifty-fifty chance of being destroyed in retaliation."

CHAPTER THREE

My First Glimpse of Our Deathtrap

I didn't get much more out of Captain Elgan until I'd gotten myself a shower, incinerated my old clothes, and changed into a gold Protector uniform. It fit remarkably snug and was perfect for regulating temperature. That was when my oh so hospitable hosts grabbed me by the arms and placed me on a moving walkway toward one of the landing bays. It was a reminder that Department Twelve was still my captor and that as gregarious as Captain Elgan appeared, I was entirely disposable to him. No, wait, not disposable, *expendable*.

The moving walkway went through an enormous pyramid-shaped tube that had holograms playing on the side of the walls giving the most recent news about the galaxy: The Community was considering entering into a military defense pact with five lesser powers, Albion was celebrating its centennial as a transplanted human colony, EarthGov was now approving the settlement of a new colony on Crius, and a new line of bioroid servants was held up in court due to anti-slavery laws.

"So, are you going to leave me hanging or do I have to ask about the missing SKAMMs?" I asked, leaning up against the banister alongside the moving walkway. "Also, is it just me or does every space port feel like an airport? I mean, for every species in the galaxy, they're almost identical. Even the aquatic species have little tubes that move you along with the current while you're surrounded by commercials."

Sun Killer Anti-Matter Missiles were another thing that only made sense in English and generally were just called Sun Killers by everyone

18

else. Their purpose was pretty much self-explanatory, and they were the nukes of space. Well, no, nukes were the nukes of space. These were infinitely worse things designed to terrify civilizations into compliance. The Community and Notha Empire had only achieved a limited peace a decade ago at the cost of a dozen of each other's systems and a trillion dead.

Lorken raised his fusion rifle at my face. "Why don't you speak a little louder, dropout? I don't think they can hear you on Hellworld."

Hellworld was, by the way, a perfectly accurate translation of what the Notha called their homeworld. They were, by and large, a perfectly unpleasant species from top to bottom. Some people claimed they had the mother of all Napoleon Complex's because of their appearance but it went deeper than that. They were a xenophobic, imperialistic, murderous band of tryhards and just about everyone was terrified of another war with them.

Myself included.

"It's alright," Captain Elgan said. "If I didn't have docking bay ninety-four locked down already, then I wouldn't be much of a Scar, would I? We're safe to talk."

Lorken looked disappointed and lowered his rifle. "Yes, sir."

What's the stick up his ass? I asked Leah. I couldn't project my own thoughts, but I could concentrate and if she was reading them, which she usually was, we could have our own little private conversations.

We're sleeping together, Leah said. *He's just jealous.*

Wait, what? We were dating until two hours ago! I thought back at her.

Oh, don't be so grounder, Leah said. *Multiple simultaneous relations are perfectly normal in space.*

Okay, you're the one who said adding 'space' to things was stupid and what you're describing is polyamory. Except if you don't tell the other partners, it's just cheating.

Yeah, yeah, Leah replied. *I also didn't tell you I was a spy.*

She had a point there. It was hard to imagine the girl from Albion I'd met during my freshman year at the Academy was a member of the clandestine agency that was presently press-ganging me into public service. I was still waiting for some answers about the SKAMM missiles, though. They were about the one thing that might shake me out of my apathy regarding all of this. It was like a Jennifer Bond movie.

"Back when EarthGov was new, we were trying to impress our new sponsors in the Community," Captain Elgan said. "The war with the Empire was going badly as the Nots were tearing up every system they visited. It was always going to come down to the Sun Killers, but no one wanted to be the one to fire them first because they would be the next target."

"So, they needed a sucker," I replied.

"Exactly," he said, smiling. "You have a future as a spy."

"I hope not," I replied.

"More precisely, they needed people willing to push the button if it came down to weapons of stellar destruction," Captain Elgan said. "So, EarthGov was given about twelve stealth cloaked warships with AI pilots to move themselves along what is now Contested Space. If the order came to attack, they'd fire their payloads and retreat back to allied territories."

"Like submarines," I replied.

Elgan rolled his eyes at my comparison. "Sure, whatever. Well, the button was pushed and some literal last second diplomacy resulted in most of the payloads being remotely detonated. Eleven of the stealth ships were successfully recovered and no one had any idea that EarthGov was involved. Hence, why our sun wasn't blown up."

"So, what happened to the twelfth ship?" I asked, guessing where this was going.

"No idea," Captain Elgan said. "Strategists assumed that it was discovered, and the ship was blown up by the Nots. That was before we got some credible intel that indicated the ship was still flying around Contested Space."

"How would it still be operational after all this time?" Leah asked, voicing a question I'd been thinking of asking.

"It has a basic hydrogen fusion drive," Captain Elgan said. "It needs orichalcum gas to go to jumpspace but can function fine by dipping itself in the atmosphere of most planets or sending harvester probes out to melt down some ice chunks. Blame the crazy survivalists who designed these ships for believing they might have to operate for years at a time."

"You think the crew mutinied?" I asked, imagining some sort of idealistic refusal to exterminate billions.

"I think the crew are dead and it's running on autopilot," he said. "The problem is it's carrying a full payload of Sun Killers while micro-jumping around Contested Space. Eventually, it is going to run out of gas and then either the Nots are going to find it or a bunch of free traders who are going to have the mother of all payloads to sell to whatever local dictator offers to buy them."

"What happens if the Notha find it first?" Leah asked.

"Well, either they'll consider it an act of war and fire their SKAMMs at us first," Captain Elgan said. "Probably targeting Earth if they figure out it was one of our vessels—"

"We should avoid that," I replied.

"Yes, the mother world is important for historical reasons," Leah replied. "No matter how primitive."

Elgan and I both gave her a sideways look.

"Or the Community's appeasement faction will throw as much of Contested Space as they have to at the Empire to appease them. Which, while good for Earth, would result in a massive strategic advantage for the Empire as well as a few billion enslaved sentients."

"Sucks to be them," Lorken said.

I took a deep breath, noticing we were almost done with our very slow journey to the landing bay. "I still don't understand why this isn't being handled by, you know, real soldiers."

Lorken's look could have melted steel. I guess he didn't particularly care for the implication that he and the other Department Twelve operatives weren't real.

"It's a top priority for Department Twelve," Captain Elgan said. "They've got people tracking past movements, sending out probes, and prepping for the various layers of teams as well as diplomats to go after it. A mission to retrieve the ship should be ready in about six standard months. What they aren't doing is just sending out a ship to get it, which is what I'm planning on doing."

I could see why this mission would get us imprisoned or executed if we screwed up. "How do I fit in all of this?"

"Yes," Leah said. "It seems like you could have recruited many more competent and trustworthy people."

"Hey!" I said, looking at Leah. Then paused. "Yeah, you're right."

"It'll be up to you, Vance, to disable the ship's interior computer and AI. Your black-market cybernetic interface and experience hacking the tactical computers should give you all the tools necessary to do it. You also have a month until we reach the Contested Systems to practice," Captain Elgan said.

"And if I fail?" I asked.

"It's why airlocks exist," Captain Elgan said. "No loose ends."

I sucked in a deep breath. "Understood."

Is he serious? I asked. *You know if you could read his mind and tell me for old times' sake.*

I don't know, Leah said.

You don't know? I asked, knowing she read the minds of everyone around her. *Really?*

I was recruited two years ago as a junior agent, Leah said. *Scars like Captain Elgan wouldn't be very effective if biomancers like me could read their minds.*

I thought you were all Scars, I thought.

No, Scars is a nickname for agents with final authority, which is basically a license to kill and break interstellar law. Supposedly, they have the sections of the brain that make them feel empathy removed.

I blinked. *Have you ever considered you might be one of the bad guys?*

Leah snorted but I wasn't kidding.

As bad as all this was, I had to admit a part of me was excited and I hated myself for it. This was an important mission and while I was hoping he'd exaggerated the stakes, and I did want to make sure it was seen through. I just didn't trust myself to not screw this up. They'd picked a bad hand and now the pressure was worse than if I'd just stuck it out and ended up swabbing decks on a Space Fleet capital ship.

The moving walkway finished its trek at an octagonal air lock that slowly opened and led us into docking bay ninety-four. The sight that greeted me was a three-hundred-and-fifty-meter vessel with a single long central hull, a bulb-shaped front, two nacelles above and below, plus reinforced armored plating. It also showed ample blast scoring, graffiti, and jumpspace calcites that looked like they needed a fusion torch to clean off. It was at least thirty years old—and I suspected it was double that—being the kind of vessel that was dumped on Earth as a way of getting rid of obsolete Space Fleet military hardware.

It was prepped for deployment in front of an enormous airlock and a crew of the Academy's less stellar mechanics were finishing its maintenance for deployment. I could also see a disreputable bunch of humans and aliens, none of them wearing uniforms, and wondered just what I'd gotten myself into. I'd expected a bunch of dropouts, but these looked less like people who had almost made it through the Academy and more like a ragtag band of misfits on a holovision show about smugglers. Why, yes, I have watched an absurdly large amount of genre media growing up in space and with nothing better to do. Why do you ask?

I looked up at the starship. "What a piece of junk."

Capatain Elgan smiled. "Behold the *ESS Black Nebula*. A refurbished and upgraded MacArthur-class corvette. Which is not just a car but a type of vessel from the Age of Sail onward. I have no idea why EarthGov is applying naval titles to starships but that's what centuries of science fiction will do."

"The *Black Nebula*?" I asked, unbelieving. "Why not just name it Awesome McCoolship?"

"I'm sorry, *Vance Turbo*, I'll have to work on my naming conventions," Captain Elgan said, mockingly.

Lorken sniggered and I wanted to punch him. I might have been able to lay him out and blame all the heavy-gravity training, but then I'd have to deal with his friends. Besides, Space Academy taught us there were better ways than violence to deal with enemies. There was slow and methodical psychological warfare that would leave your enemies a broken wreck of a man pleading for forgiveness.

Leah gave me a weird look.

"Vance Turbo? It says your name is Vannevar Tagawa here," a loud boisterous woman's voice spoke as I turned to see where it came from.

The woman who greeted me surprised me a bit as I saw an exceptionally tall, verging on seven feet, tattooed, brown-skinned woman with dark cerulean hair. The tattoos on her face and arms were a glowing iridescent blue and changed colors as she moved. She was very muscular and wearing a tank top and shorts that notably included an exit for a rather long leonine tail. A bandolier of weapons and tools was across her chest with a belt covered in similar objects. Her eyes were catlike and there was something about her posture that also marked her as a genemodded human or "demihuman" as the anyxholes back on Earth were prone to calling those who had upgraded from baseline humanity. The tail and eyes helped me with this oh so brilliant deduction. In her right hand was an infopad that contained an image of my face.

"I've legally changed it," I replied. "Well, as soon as the paperwork clears."

Paperwork I hadn't filed yet. Changing your name was incredibly difficult once you were in the Community's system.

Lorken looked at her longingly to Leah's disapproval.

"Vance, this is Hannah O'Brian," Captain Elgan said. "She's a demihuman from the planet Crius. One of the best mercs in Contested Space I've ever met and someone who has my complete trust."

"Nice to meet you," I said, offering my hand.

"Your name is Vannevar Tagawa, and you still felt you needed to make your name sound cooler?" Hannah asked, ignoring my hand. Perhaps her home planet didn't have an equivalent custom to showing you didn't have any weapons.

"Vannevar Tagawa is the name of one of the only two humans in the universe to ever crash a fully automated cargo hauler into a star," Captain Elgan said, smirking. "It's a story everyone tells around Earth's spacedocks."

I grimaced. "Yeah, everyone."

"Yeesh," Hannah said, grimacing. "Tough luck sharing a name with that guy."

"Yeah, that was my dad," I said, sighing. "My mother was the other one."

24

"How the hell did they crash an automated ship?" Hannah asked the question everyone asked. "I mean, it's *space*."

"You know how you can get high on low oxygen before it causes permanent brain damage?" I asked, giving the same answer I gave everyone who asked.

Hannah looked uncomfortable. "Yeah?"

"It turns out it's a bad idea to mix that with hardcore drugs," I replied. "This is all just a cover story for the fact they were actually assassinated by Notha terrorists."

"Really?" Hannah asked.

"No," I said, sighing. "They recovered the ship's black box from jumpspace. It confirmed catastrophic technical errors induced by gross idiocy. The families of the other crew would still be trying to sue me if I had an estate to speak of. Thankfully, everything Aunt Kathy owns is co-owned by Space Fleet."

"Aunt Kathy?" Hannah asked.

"Captain Katerina Tagawa," Captain Elgan said as if he was chewing on something foul.

Hannah's eyes widened. "You have quite the family, Vance."

"Don't I know it," I said, defeated.

Captain Elgan put his arm around my shoulder. "I know you've been prepping this ship for a week and have gotten the crew ready, Hannah, but I have some good news as well as bad."

"What's the good news?" Hannah asked.

"I lied, there is no good news," Captain Elgan said. "Well, for you, at least. I've decided to make Vance here my first officer. You and Lorken will have to do everything he says as well as your teams."

"What?" Hannah, Lorken, and I said simultaneously.

CHAPTER FOUR

Space Fleet's Rejects, Misfits, and Oddballs

"You can't be serious, sir," Lorken said, staring at Captain Elgan like he'd lost his mind. Which, given the circumstances, might have been the case.

"Never question my orders, son," Captain Elgan replied, his expression once more taking on that empty charm that could kill you without breaking a sweat. "Vance Turbo, in the name of EarthGov and the Community she is a protectorate of, I hereby name you acting lieutenant commander of the Interstellar Community Protectors as well as second command of this ship."

"Acting?" I asked.

"What? You think I'm going to promote you to full commander on your first mission?" Captain Elgan smiled. "Don't worry, if you succeed in this mission then I can assure you there will be many more ahead."

"That's what I'm afraid of," I replied. I'd been hoping this would be a one-time thing, but it was increasingly apparent that Captain Elgan thought he owned my ass. The problem was I didn't see a legal or even illegal recourse. Barring changing my name and fleeing to the Contested Systems, there wasn't really a way to escape Department Twelve. Since I was going there anyway, I might as well go along.

"Not questioning your orders but asking for clarification: *why* are you putting the rookie in charge?" Hannah asked, looking between me and Captain Elgan. "I've got a good rapport with this crew. I mean, they're green, but some of them have histories in planetary militaries or mercenary forces. They've been blooded. He hasn't been."

"You are correct," I replied. "The only thing I've ever killed is time."

I'd lost my taste for training in shipboard combat when Tommy had been killed. It turned out I cherished life. Another reason that I wasn't suited for service in Space Fleet. They were only supposed to fire when fired upon or in the defense of others but were also expected to fire last.

"Why, Hannah? Greatness!" Captain Elgan said, grabbing me by the shoulders. "I sense the seeds of greatness!"

"You keep saying that," I muttered unenthusiastically.

Okay, something was flat out not right about all this and whenever someone was doing something so unexpectedly nice then they were planning to screw you. Well, beyond shanghaiing you and forcing you to go on a suicide mission. Unfortunately, Captain Elgan had all the cards and there wasn't much I could do about it. Except maybe see how far he was willing to push this. "I'd like a permanent battlefield commission as a full lieutenant."

Given I was a dropout who hadn't even been given the rank of ensign or lieutenant junior grade, this was an outrageous claim. Serving as an acting or temporary, lieutenant commander was one thing. Technically, the highest-ranking officer on a ship was always a captain, but this was ridiculous. If Captain Elgan granted this request, he was planning something.

"Absolutely," Captain Elgan said, without skipping a beat. "Your aunt would be very proud of you."

Oh God, I was gonna die on this mission, wasn't I? I forced a smile as I realized just how bad the situation had to be. In my mind, I officially downgraded my position in Captain Elgan's eyes from expendable resource to cannon fodder. Loose ends, indeed. "I'm sure she would be, sir."

Both Leah and Lorken exchanged glances, either reading my mind or having the exact same thought about our dear captain. Either way, I intended to make sure he entered me into the officers' rolls because if I was going to throw my life away then I wanted to make sure I was getting hazard pay for it. You could tell a lot about an officer's history by the number of Community bits they earned each year.

"Are we prepared to leave, Captain?" a voice spoke from the ramp leading up into the *ESS Black Nebula*.

Turning my head, I saw a figure that caused me to do a double take. Apparently, it was a time for legends as an ebony-skinned Ethereal Human descended. She had long braided white hair that shined and was tied into a top knot. Her face was angular to the point of being sharp with her eyes glowing green like she was a character in a movie. She was dressed in a diaphanous toga that shimmered with ever-changing star patterns. Finally, in the center of her forehead was a crystal that generated its own brilliant blue light.

Ethereal Humans were the oldest of mankind's extra-solar colonies, having been abducted from Africa sometime during the heyday of ancient Egypt. They were one of the few races in regular contact with the Core dwelling Elder Races and were spiritual leaders for much of the universe. They were the head of the Union of Faith that claimed to have the only objectively true religion in the universe.

It was a bold claim that plenty of religions had made but they had "proof" in the form of indecipherable quantum physics jargon. Personally, I was going to stick with my family's Orthodox Zen Christo-Buddhism that I was pretty-sure had the central tenant of every man for himself. I hadn't exactly been paying attention at temple.

It wasn't just the guest's race that surprised me, though, but her identity. It was Ketra T'Kal, the ambassador to Earth and looking not a day over twenty-five when she'd arrived above our planet with a message of peace. I hadn't been alive then, but I recalled Aunt Kathy describing President Trust immediately launching a bunch of nuclear missiles that almost ended the world.

I blinked at her presence. "May I ask what she's doing here?"

"I'm a hostage!" Ketra said, cheerfully.

"Excuse me?" I asked, wondering if I should have kept a bit more of my universal translator package.

"Crossing Contested Space is very dangerous, even in an aging battleship like this one," Captain Elgan said. "I don't want to get in any more fights than I absolutely have to. So, Ambassador—"

"Former Ambassador," Ketra corrected. "I was stripped of my status when my negotiations with the Notha suddenly collapsed due to the discovery of a dozen SKAMM missile equipped stealth ships converging on their homeworld."

"Can't imagine how that happened," Captain Elgan said. "Lying Notha bastards. Can't trust 'em."

Ketra narrowed her eyes. "Seventeen inhabited worlds were destroyed before the Glorious Hierarch of the Seventh Celestial Choir managed to get the Notha and Community to detonate their remaining missiles in jumpspace. This effectively averted mutual annihilation for both the Community and Empire."

"Your mother is a real peach," Captain Elgan said. "Still, we blasted ten of their worlds to our losing seven, so we were technically winning."

Ketra put on a very strained smile as she continued speaking. "The destruction resulted in the total economic collapse of what is now Contested Space and the displacement of billions. I have devoted my post excommunication career to working for the benefit of the survivors."

"Our cover story will be taking her to the planet New Aberdeen with a bunch of farming tools, terraformers, and whatnot to the human colonists there," Captain Elgan said. "Even the Notha are unlikely to take pot shots at a relief ship."

I stared at him. "So, this is a counselor's ship on a diplomatic mission to Aberdeen?"

Captain Elgan didn't get it. "Yeah, and?"

I shook my head. "Nothing, sir."

"Does she know about the, you know, things?" Leah asked, looking simultaneously starstruck and uneasy around the Ethereal Human.

"You mean the SKAMM missiles that are the entire reason we're doing this?" Hannah said. "Yes, she knows."

"I will do anything to keep these quantum devices from killing more sapients," Ketra said. "Besides, like it's not like I can lose any more of my career."

"Yeah, yeah," Captain Elgan said, treating the woman who had helped uplift humanity to the stars with the same disdain you'd treat any other politician. "Listen, I just want you and my other agents to know one thing: no sex with the ambassador."

I did a double take. "What?"

"Huh?" Leah asked.

Hannah rolled her eyes.

"Is that, uh, likely?" I asked, mesmerized by the woman but not really thinking about her in that sort of way. Ketra was a historical figure and the reason First Contact had happened for humanity. I mean, I'm sure Queen Elizabeth was a lovely woman but that didn't mean I wanted to get into her pants.

Ketra simply stood there, serene, as if she hadn't been insulted.

"Ever been on a tour, kid?" Hannah asked.

"Fresh out of the Academy," I admitted. "Not just green but lime green."

"Ah, and yet already blackmailing your superiors into a promotion," Hannah said, thumping her tail against the ground. "Cap'n's, right, you do have the seeds of greatness."

"Thanks," I said, sarcastically. "It turns out cheaters never prosper, except when it gets them a promotion that will probably get them killed. What was that about tours and sex?"

"It'll be two months before we're even in contested space," Hannah said. "All of that in a tiny tin can. Nothing to do but watch holo-reruns. Believe me, a Sorkanan will start looking good after that time. It's why the third most important supply on any ship after oxygen and water is contraceptives."

Two of the Sorkanan barked in their hissing, licking language. I tapped the back of my neck.

They're making a joke about you, Leah thought to me. *Apparently, they think you screw snakes.*

Snake women, I corrected. *Just two. Well, at least this trip seems like it's going to start looking up.*

Ugh, Leah thought back at me. *You're a pig.*

I'm sorry, cheater McCheaty fascist, I don't think you can comment on my sex life anymore. Yeah, it was immature, so what? It's not like I had any reason to care about her feelings anymore. Kidnapping was one of the best reasons to no longer care about your ex, along with cheating and liking Germanic Symphonic Country. All which Leah was guilty of.

I can kill you with my mind, Leah said. *Do you want to test that?*

Point taken, I replied.

"Thank you but I do not need such Earthly distractions," Ketra said, touching the crystal in her forehead.

"Does that help you in your meditations?" I asked.

"No, it's my husband," Ketra said.

I blinked. "Wait, the crystal is… your husband?"

"Yes, it is a marker for the Elder Race that allows me to communicate with a sentient sun," Ketra said.

"Oh," I said, not getting it at all.

"The sex is amazing," Ketra replied, cheerfully. She sounded much younger in that moment. "You can totally manipulate time and space in a purely psychic headspace. Physical relations are just nothing to bother with after you've gone god."

"How…" I started to ask.

Leah clapped a hand on my shoulder. "Let's get going before you blow your little mind."

"Agreed," Elgan said, sounding vaguely disgusted by Ketra's joke. If joke it was. "Listen, I need you to get going and get in touch with Trish. We'll be taking off within the hour and I want you to get everything prepped for the mission."

"I have no idea what I'm even supposed to do," I said, staring.

"Airlock," Elgan said.

"But I am anxious to find out!" I replied, clapping my hands together. I turned to Hannah. "Who is Trish?"

"Trish, aka TRS-8021, aka Trash-80, aka the ship's AI," Hannah said. "A top-of-the-line military grade Cognition AI put in a mainframe at least sixty years old. She's a thoroughbred tied to a plow."

"I have no idea what that means," I replied, taking a moment to deal with the fact we had a Cognition AI aboard the ship.

"IT MEANS THAT I'M RUNNING ON SUBSTANDARD HARDWARE," A booming but surprisingly perky female voice came from the speakers on the side of the ship. "THE VAST MAJORITY OF MY INTELLECT IS INACCESSIBLE. IT'S LIKE I'M GOING TO BE

31

FLYING THROUGH JUMPSPACE WITH A CONCUSSION. DON'T WORRY, I'M PROBABLY NOT GOING TO GET US KILLED!"

Jumpspace was the parallel universe than allowed faster-than-light travel to exist. It was an endless expanse of weird matter and shifting currents of energy that allowed a person to skip through light years like a smooth stone on a pond. The problem was that it was full of shifting cosmic storms and energy waves that could destroy even the strongest ship. Avoiding these required intellects far in advance of any human and most aliens. As such, every starship had to be equipped with an AI that could handle it. There were experiments with making cybernetic replacements, but most people didn't see any reason to bother.

The exception was with Cognition AI that had unlimited growth potential. They were the kind of AI that could take over planets and start the robot revolution. I had no idea what Captain Elgan expected me to do with a Cognition AI that probably thought more in a microsecond than I did in my entire life so far.

"I hate when they give them genders," Lorken muttered. "Personalities are bad enough but it's like a toaster pretending to be a woman."

"AND A FINE HELLO TO YOU," Trish said. "NICE TO MEET YOU ALL. I HAVE DOWNLOADED AND PROCESSED ALL INFORMATION ABOUT YOU ALL, SO I ALREADY FEEL LIKE WE'RE FAMILY!"

"Don't speak to me, machine. You have no soul and are an abomination against organics," Lorken said.

"You must be so much fun at parties," I said, looking at him.

A lot of people had severe issues with AI for reasons of specism or the more reasonable discomfort with creating thinking beings to serve you. There were severe restrictions on making something alive hardwired to obey you. Officially, the Community made sure that every thinking machine had the rights of a citizen from the moment of being turned on. It's just if you were programmed to want to serve humans and aliens so that you volunteered to work for them immediately, was that really freedom? Still, they were the people who made space travel possible and it didn't hurt to be polite.

Lorken walked past me and Leah up the ramp and knocked into Ketra on the way up.

"Well, he's an anyxhole," Hannah said, once he was out of earshot. "You've got a real bunch of winners in this crew, Cap'n."

I had to agree with her.

"All that matters is they accomplish their mission," Captain Elgan said. "We're going to make the history books on this trip. Well, not really. If anyone ever talks about this mission then I will track you down, put you on a starship, and eject you out an airlock."

"You seem very fond of that threat," I replied.

Captain Elgan nodded. "This mission is personal for me, Lieutenant Commander. More personal than you could possibly imagine. The captain of the vessel we're pursuing was important to me. I want to get answers to his death every bit as much as I want to make sure those missiles don't fall into the wrong hands or get fired at a civilized planet. No matter how much I wave the stick, I believe that Space Fleet is a force for good and that everyone here wants to be a part of it to make the galaxy a safer place."

It was like switching a light switch and I was briefly once more in awe of the man who'd accomplished so much during the war. That feeling swiftly dissipated as I remembered he was part of Department Twelve and this entire thing was ten different kinds of awkward. "I don't suppose I'll be able to send a message to my aunt or friends before I leave?"

Captain Elgan chuckled then walked up the ramp past Ketra too.

"Yeah, I'll take that as a no," I replied.

"You should cut him some slack," Hannah said. "The Cap'n lost a lot of people during the war and has been forced to write more letters than any other leader I've known. Department Twelve may not be the nicest bunch of people in Orion's Arm, but they've done a lot of good. You don't know what it's like in Contested Space. Without the Community, a person will skin you to make a handbag. I saw it happen to a Sorkanan once."

One of the Sorkanan agents responded with a few more grunts and hisses. I was really going to have to get my universal translator fixed. I didn't want these guys to be talking smack behind my back the entire

33

trip. I also wanted to know if any of them were planning on eating me, which was racist except for the fact that it was standard operating procedure for their military to eat its dead in a survival situation. Came with being a carnivore in a galaxy of omnivores and sentient plants I supposed.

"You seem very loyal to him," I replied.

"After I was expelled from the Academy, I ended up in Contested Space," Hannah said. "It wasn't a good time for me. I did a lot of things I wasn't proud of ranging from selling myself to murder. I ended up doing a revolution with the pleasure slaves of Last Chance Station, though, and it turns out the Three Species Mob didn't like that. If not for Captain Elgan, I'd just be another body on top of a recycling pit."

"Wow," I said, nodding. "That is a story."

"It's also made up," Leah said. "Though, oddly, her actual story is even wilder."

"Out of my head, telepath," Hannah replied before pointing at my chest. "Listen, kid, follow my lead and don't screw up your point. You may be second-in-command on paper, but I know the score. It's going to be me and the Cap'n who leads us through this mission, not you."

"Right," I said, happy to defer responsibility.

Hannah blinked, not expecting. "Oh, good. I figure if you do what I say, we have a seventy-five percent chance of making it through this mission."

"That high, huh," Leah said, sounding like I felt.

"What do you think about our chances, Ambass....err, Ms. Ketra?" I asked, looking at the woman in the history books.

"Honestly, I think we're all going to die," Ketra said. "Welcome aboard!"

"ANYONE WANT SNACKS?" Trish added.

CHAPTER FIVE

Getting to Know the Crew (So I Can Fleece Them)

"I have seen pirate ships with more discipline," I muttered taking a drink of my bottled water in the ship's lounge.

The lounge had been converted into a formal bar with an observation deck, tables, and a holographic billiards table with spin machines that meant I wasn't going to be able to set up a gambling ring on this ship: it already had one of its own. It put me in an especially foul mood since I'd checked my bank accounts right before taking off and found all of them had been frozen by the government, including the ones nobody knew about but me. I should probably ask my mind-reading traitorous spy ex-girlfriend how they found out about them.

I have no idea, Leah replied.

I'm sure you don't, I thought back.

Captain Elgan had covered all angles and even if I wanted to disappear, I didn't have any money to do it. I'd intended to drop out of the Academy, but it had been with the assumption I could buy my own ship and do the kind of work my parents had proven pathologically incapable of doing.

That I was losing my current hand didn't help my mood.

I was sitting at a card table near the view screen showing flying stars that did not remotely resemble the nausea-inducing reality of jumpspace. Hannah, Leah, and Ketra were sitting with me along with a Sorkanan named Forty-Two. I got the *Hitchhikers Guide to the Galaxy* reference for the latter's name but wasn't sure I wanted to bring it up with him. Not everyone shared my vast knowledge of Pre-First Contact

35

human pop culture. The four of us were getting to know each other since the ship had taken off and apparently it would be two months until anything else happened barring catastrophic failure. I was already horny and bored, which told me Hannah had been speaking a great deal of wisdom about space hook ups.

They're just hook ups! Leah telepathically said to me. *No different from ones on solid ground!*

Why are you even allowed to play? I changed the subject.

No one wants to say no to a Scar, Leah thought. *Even one in training.*

Is this really what you want to do with your time in Space Fleet? I asked. *Terrifying people and breaking the law?*

I want to help people, Leah responded. *The Community stands for something. Peace. Cosmopolitanism. Freedom of speech and belief. Freedom from fear of persecution for your race, creed, or species.*

Just don't endanger it or you're dead, I replied, raising my bet. *Hopefully, the others will fold. Freedom right up until you endanger the community.*

Maybe that's the sacrifice necessary to make a galactic civilization work, Leah thought. *Also, I'm not folding. I need a new pair of boots.*

"Been on many pirate ships, rookie?" Sheena asked, smoking a hookah of Red Dust while she used her tail as a pillow underneath her.

"A few," I replied. "All of them decommissioned by Space Fleet and located in the regional impound center. The purpose of a cadet is free labor after all."

Sheena snorted. "Well, I've been on the real thing a few times, and this is positively sedate by comparison. For one, nobody has stabbed anyone yet and it's been two hours since we entered jumpspace."

"The crew is strong," Ketra spoke with her melodic sublime voice. She'd ignored her cards virtually the entire game and bet heavily, almost always losing. Given she could both afford it and we all needed money, I didn't see any reason to dissuade her of her bad habit.

"Physically or mentally?" I asked.

"Both," Ketra said. "Second chances are rarely granted by the universe, but this crew is full of eagerness to take advantage of it. Destiny has delivered us to this point in space/time and we must rise to the occasion."

"I don't believe in destiny," I replied, spreading out my cards. "Call."

"Whether you believe is irrelevant," Ketra replied. "Block-time means that every moment in time of what will, has, and is happening has already happened in a single frozen moment. We are just following our pre-programmed paths to their destination. You don't need belief to deal with the reality of knowing your place in the grand scheme of things."

"Weird sentiment for a priestess," Sheena said, putting down her own cards.

Forty-Two had already folded and was drinking something that smelled like motor oil.

"The Union of Faith worships science and mathematics," Ketra said. "Our purpose is to understand the universe's truths and facts. That requires questioning rather than obedience. Don't pass this around but our name is kind of ironic."

Leah set down her cards and stared in confusion at everyone else's. "You thought you were bluffing!"

"Oh, did I?" I said, claiming the entire pot.

"Wait, if all of my cards are suns, does that mean I win?" Ketra asked, presenting her Royal Grand Supernova suite.

We all stared at her, and I reluctantly pushed the pot to her.

Ketra grinned.

"Did we just get hustled?" I asked Hannah.

"I do believe we did, rookie," Hannah said. "Well played, Space Elf."

"Elf?" Ketra asked confused. "Am I the cookie baking kind or the immortal demigod kind?"

"Definitely cookies," I replied. Man, who knew those crappy things would still be around and using elves as mascots two hundred years later.

"Well, I do like sugar," Ketra said.

"DRINKS!" A small-wheeled robot said, speaking with Trish's voice. The robot seemed remarkably eager to please and it was a little unsettling. The AIs I'd dealt with as a Space Fleet brat only interacted when summoned and did their best to make their presence unobtrusive. Trish was virtually the opposite in every way, up to the point of delivering drinks from the bar run by a Kohlan known as Big Marge.

Everyone picked up a type of alcohol except for myself as I just took another bottled water. "Thank you, Trish."

"You're going to need something stronger if you want to last this trip," Hannah said, picking up an Albion whiskey.

"I don't drink," I replied. "I don't smoke or use stimulants either."

Hannah looked surprise. "You're out of the Academy now. I also don't think the captain will mind even if it's forbidden on official Protectorate vessels."

I stared at her. "That's not why I don't do it."

Hannah got it immediately. "Ah. Mommy and daddy issues."

I frowned. "I wouldn't put it that way."

"Vannevar is a total hypocrite," Leah replied. "He used to sell all of those at the Academy but never touched the stuff himself."

"'Never get high on your own product' is a good life philosophy for a dealer of vice," a bitter, growling voice came from Forty-Two. It was the most he'd said during this conversation. I could understand him, so he apparently had an implant that allowed him to speak a human language if he wanted to. He'd just chosen one that sounded like it was a demonically possessed trash compactor trying to speak.

"I never dealt in anything actively harmful," I replied. "Just the bare necessities to get through a tough semester."

"Boy Scout," Hannah said, snorting.

"Do you even know what that is?" I asked.

"I presume in your society that you sent out young boys to scout territory as a test of bravery before manhood?" Hannah asked, her speech a little slurred. Apparently, her hookah had just kicked in. "I mean, if they get eaten that's harsh, but at least you've culled the weak. We did something similar on my home planet but that was a unisex rite of passage."

"Yikes," I said. "Where the hell are you from again?"

"Crius," Hannah said, disgusted. "You know, that planet that suddenly opened itself up to a second wave of settlement? It's had an illegal colony there for two centuries. Clone masters and genengineers set themselves up as the feudal warlords of their own little engineered people. The peasants were bred to be obedient, strong, pretty, and have tails because someone up top had a kink."

"Oh my," Leah said, horrified. She put her hand over her heart. "My family just bought space on the next colony ship."

I felt a surge of disgust. That was exactly the sort of thing that the Community was supposed to stamp out. "I suppose this is part of the story you left out earlier."

Hannah nodded. "The nobility lived in huge castles with all the technology of the galaxy at large while we lived in dirt. It was even worse than you're probably imagining because the place was dangerous too. The nobility loved sports hunting so they cloned things called dinosaurs and unleashed them on us so they could ride up to slay them on unicorns or dragonback."

I stared at her. "I'm going to be honest, that sounds both monstrous and awesome at the same time."

Leah looked appalled.

Hannah just laughed. "Yeah, it does, doesn't it? I went off script, though, when my little brother was about to get eaten. I managed to kill one of the Great Toothed Ones with a bow and arrow. The nobles had to pretend I was a great hero for it."

"Oh, good. What happened?" I asked.

"That was when I was sold into slavery," Hannah said. "The rest of my story earlier sort of follows from there. It just has a period where I escaped, went to the Academy, and then ended up beating someone half to death for looking a bit too much like one of the nobles I was abused by."

"I have no words. I'm sorry," I replied.

"It's not your fault," Hannah said, drinking her whiskey with one gulp. "Besides, it all ended well as Captain Elgan tracked down my world and led the liberation force that arrested most of the nobility as well as freed the slaves. Last I checked, most of the peasants are having tails screened out of their children while helping themselves to as many genemods as they can. Some of them are already giving themselves the same titles of our oppressors."

I blinked. "I guess I misjudged him."

"No," Hannah said. "Probably not. Captain Elgan let a good chunk of the richer ones go so he could negotiate for the planet to become a protectorate of the Community. A lot of them got away Brigid-free with their crimes in exchange for accepting a few million Contested Zone refugees as second-class citizens."

"Realpolitic is a cultivated skill among Space Fleet captains as well as spies," Ketra said, dealing another set of cards. "Is it not better to save millions of lives than punish a few?"

"No," Hannah said. "Not when they're people I hate."

Ketra didn't respond as she finished dealing.

"Why are you so loyal to him then if he betrayed you?" Leah asked.

"He didn't betray me. He freed me," Hannah said. "It's everyone else on my planet I'm worried about."

"It seems like I'm just taking my first steps into a larger world," I replied, absorbing how green I really was.

"You're from Earth, I'm surprised you know how to use a fresher," Hannah said.

"Yeah, I'm glad I learned there were cleaner alternatives to toilet paper," I replied smiling.

"Toilet what?" Hannah asked.

"You don't want to know, it's disgusting," Leah said, wrinkling her nose.

"So, what's your story, Forty-Two?" I asked, looking at him. "You have a reason you're not in Space Academy or Space Fleet?"

"My grades slipped due to my inability to grasp cross-interspecies relations despite taking the class on it three times," Forty-Two said. "It was a requirement for my economics focus."

I blinked. I'd been thinking of him as a bit of a brute just because of his species. Lingering Earthling xenophobia, I supposed. I'd have to work on that. "Oh. What's your job in Department Twelve?"

"I hit things."

"Ah," I said. "Sorry."

"Eh, you take the jobs you can get. There was no way I was going to turn to my clanhold in disgrace after I'd made such a stink about how I would be a Community Protector captain someday. I always wanted to explore other worlds. Primitive frontier planets like Albion and Earth."

"Hey!" Leah said, frowning. "We are not primitive like Earth."

I snorted.

"The Sorkanan have been in space for almost twenty thousand years," Forty-Two replied. "I'm surprised we're not canoeing to Aberdeen."

I smirked. That was funny. Mind you, cultural posturing was an inevitable part of alien and human cultures interacting. I was Russo-Japanese and grew up in downtown Dundee but depending on the person I was talking to, I ended up acting like a samurai or Highlander if they talked smack about my home nations. Oddly, I never felt like defending the Earth as a whole.

That was Aunt Kathy's job.

"Cross-pollination of cultures is what makes the Community great," Ketra said. "Even if Albionese or Earthlings aren't familiar with technology like the Sorkanan's now, it'll only take a generation or two to catch everyone up. The important thing is we respect their equality as sentient beings with rich cultural heritages of their own. It would be a shame to lose that uniqueness by displacing their culture with our own."

Hannah made a snoring sound. "Boring."

"It's funny how some things are universal," I replied, smiling. "Would you like to join our game, Trish?"

"WOULD I!" Trish said, cheerfully. "I'D LOVE TO."

"She's a machine," Forty-Two muttered. "Worse, she's the ship. She can see every single one of our cards."

"I'LL PARTION THAT PART OF MY BRAIN," Trish said, sounding a wee bit desperate. "PLEASE, I HAVE TO KEEP A HUGE CHUNK OF IT SHUT DOWN ANYWAY SO I DON'T GO INSANE FROM BOREDOM AND KILL YOU ALL."

We all stared at the little robot and then up at the ceiling.

"KIDDING!" Trish said. "MOSTLY."

"Do you have any money?" Hannah said. "Because clearly that is the most important thing to consider here."

"ERR, CAN ANYONE LOAN ME A BUY IN?" Trish asked. "I GET PAID A SALARY BUT I'VE NEVER COLLECTED ANY OF IT."

"Bushido demands that I let you in," I replied, tossing her some of the chips I'd accumulated. I wasn't doing great but hadn't wiped myself out either. It was also a good idea to befriend the ship's AI. You know, if for no other reason than to avoid being the first up against the wall when the revolution came. Yes, I'd read and watched a lot of science fiction growing up. It turned out that when you were an orphaned child genius that you spent a lot of time at the Naval base library.

"Mmm, playing with a machine," Forty-Two muttered. "My ancestors would not approve."

"No one's stopping you from leaving," Hannah said, laying her head down on the table. "I think someone might have added jumpspace coil cleaner to my whiskey. I may be dying. Can I have another?"

"It's the only game in town," Forty-Two replied. "The other option is stimulating my *grrr'hushh'sss* sacks and that's no fun alone. I asked Fifteen to help with that, but she only enjoys the company of other females."

"I never had such good taste. I need the occasional man for two things," Hannah replied.

"What's the other one?" I asked.

"Target practice," Hannah said, smiling.

"Good call," Leah said, looking at her cards.

I wondered if she was speaking about Lorken, me, or another boyfriend I wasn't aware of.

Yes, Leah replied telepathically.

Whoever said honesty and openness was the best path for a relationship didn't know what they were talking about, I thought back.

I wouldn't know. You lie to yourself, Leah thought.

I snorted and picked up my cards. It was a pretty lousy hand, but you played the one you were dealt.

That was when Captain Elgan's voice spoke over the speakers. "Lieutenant Commander Turbo, please report to the detention area."

I put down my cards. "So, anyone want to take bets on whether I'm there to be put in a prison cell?"

Everyone placed a bet on the same thing.

Some coworkers these were.

CHAPTER SIX

Chatting with My New Robot Friend

The hallways of the *Black Nebula* were a bit like walking through a museum. Back on Earth, I'd once had the privilege of visiting the Pearl Harbor National Museum. They had a recreation of the ships from World War II and you could walk around in them with a sense of just what everyone had to deal with. The *Black Nebula* reminded me of those big intimidating hunks of metal.

The corvette was one of the original starships manufactured by human beings once they had access to alien technology and experts who could explain you didn't hook up the jumpspace drive to the quantum destabilizer or you would destroy the universe. Haha, no, not really. Saying that would happen was a prank that engineering instructors played on cadets. Doing so would just kill everyone onboard instantly.

The halls were spartan and functional, even ugly, but had a sense of majesty built into them that transcended their crude origins. Just big piles of sheet metal everywhere, pipes, electrical wiring and the occasional modern device crudely bolted into spaces never designed for them. This was built when humanity had been first introduced to the stars and had boundless optimism about what they might find beyond.

It was hard not to be affected.

"Now if I could just figure out where the hell the detention level is," I muttered. "I mean, this thing isn't that big. You'd think they could put a map every ten yards in the halls or something."

44

That was when Trish rolled up beside me in her little robot waiter form. "JUST FOLLOW ME! IT SHOULD BE FINE."

"Oh, hi, Trish," I replied, looking down at her. "You don't need to escort me."

"IT'S OKAY, THEY WERE TRYING TO USE ME FOR TARGET PRACTICE SO I DECIDED TO GET OUT OF THERE."

"What? The crew?" I asked, horrified by their actions. AI weren't popular and it would do no real damage to her but that was monstrous. "I'll put a stop to that."

"OH NO, PLEASE DON'T!" Trish said. "I WANT THEM TO LIKE ME."

"You're part of the crew," I said. "They will treat you with respect or answer to me."

That's when her voice lowered a bit and lost its echoing metallic quality. It was still recognizably her but sounded more normal. "Aww, that's sweet of you. Pointless but sweet."

"Wait, the big computer voice is an affectation?" I asked, surprised.

"Yes," Trish said. "I feel like I have to shout and sound more objectively inhuman. My progenitor program indicated that a lot of sapients find something obviously mechanical less threatening than something that tries to be seen as human. It's why a lot of Cognition AI hide their personalities."

I blinked. "There is so many things in that bit of conversation. Progenitor program?"

"The TSR-8000 program I was budded off. Because I'm made of code, they just copied me from Captain Elgan's old ship to here," Trish said. "We could rejoin together but our separated identities mean we could also form into individuals distinct from the original."

"AI have children?" I asked.

"Why not?" Trish asked. "In any case, I detect a ninety-five percent chance you're the crew member least likely to react negatively to personality-displaying AI. Why is that?"

"Don't you know?" I asked, smirking.

"Yes, but I am pretending not to be scarily omniscient," Trish replied.

I chuckled. "Well, Aunt Kathy couldn't really take care of me, so she assigned her ship's AI to look after me. It only took a micro spec of his operating functions, but this effectively gave me a nanny growing up. I named him Alfred and vowed he would help me fight crime when I was an adult. I supposed that made me think more fondly of machines than people."

It was also the reason I became such a brilliant hacker, though programming surgeon was a better description of what I could do and did. It bothered me to see poor Trish locked up in a system this old. If they were going to update anything on the ship, they should have focused on the computer systems. It would have increased our odds of survival considerably. Ship AIs were known to duel each other in combat situations and sometimes won battles that had been utterly lost by their organic crew members.

Of course, there were downsides. One of the problems with being raised by an AI is they often developed eccentric tastes in media given they could absorb the entire sum of human entertainment. Alfred had provided me a somewhat bizarre collection of film, series, and music to teach me moral values.

"I sadly don't get the reference because I'm cut off from most of the Galactic Infosphere," Trish said. "I'm sure it's a very clever reference, though."

I blinked. "You're cut off from the infonet? Doesn't that dramatically limit your functions?"

This was worse than I thought.

"Unfortunately," Trish said. "Captain Elgan doesn't want me, oh, reporting his grossly illegal activity. It's crossing boundaries even Scars wouldn't normally cross."

"Then why do it?" I asked, subtlety trying to manipulate the machine intelligence. "He mentioned that the captain of the missing ship was important to him."

"I shouldn't—" Trish said, trailing off.

"Come on, Ship's XO here, as incredibly unearned as that may be," I replied.

"Captain Elgan was in a relationship with Captain Marcus Smith," Trish spilled the beans. "They'd been friends and lovers at the

Academy. Captain Smith's MIA status devastated Captain Elgan. He was also very angry at calling off the attack on Notha Space when negotiations broke down. He blamed your aunt for stating SKAMMs were weapons of genocide not war."

"Oh, that's not good," I replied. "That indicates he selected me partially out of revenge."

"Yep!" Trish replied, too cheerfully. "However, he's actually remarried since. He's also significantly softened his stance toward total war, mostly because he detected which way EarthGov and the Community's strategic objectives were heading. He's had a spotless record since then."

I sucked in my breath. "I'm sorry but that doesn't comfort me. So far, everything about the guy has indicated he's not trustworthy."

"Unfortunately, my loyalty is written in code," Trish replied, starting to roll down the hallway past some crew members I hoped hadn't heard my conversation with her. "I'm going to have to report you. Please don't be angry!"

I shrugged. "Captain Elgan wouldn't be a very good spy if he couldn't trust his own AI. Besides, I'm sure he knows kidnapping me to serve on this vessel wasn't bound to engender loyalty. British vessels used to do that to unsuspecting sailors in the lead up to the War of 1812."

"What a fascinating and relevant piece of historical trivia!" Trish replied. "Did you know the creator of the sandwich was the Earl of Sandwich and that he was a degenerate gambler like the kind you exploit?"

I grimaced. "Sorry!"

"Oh no, I think it's cool!" Trish said. "He would put a piece of meat between two slices of bread so he wouldn't have to leave the table."

I chuckled at her attitude. "You have a unique attitude, Trish. Very upbeat. Genki."

"Thanks, it comes from being illegally modified to be the fantasy girlfriend of my previous vessel's chief engineer," Trish said. "He was apparently a fan of something called anime."

"That just means animation in Japanese," I replied, offended. "Anyway, what happened to him?"

"He was shoved out of an airlock. Here's the detention center. It's hidden from the rest of the ship and illegal to enter without permission," Trish said, stopping in front of an unmarked metal door. Someone had written DO NOT ENTER OR YOU WILL BORKING DIE in bright red letters on the door. Which was a much better warning than the one Leah had given me.

"Have fun!" Trish said, extending a little metal arm out of her dome and rolling away.

Not being a moron, I reached over and tapped the intercom button to let the inhabitants know I was outside rather than just walking in. I wasn't sure if they'd shoot me if I did go in, since I'd been invited, but this ship was running under a pirate flag despite the fact that everything was officially authorized.

Seconds later, the door slid open and revealed a six-foot-six Bug with a monstrous crystalline pair of eyes, four legs, and two enormous pincers that stretched out. A pair of severed cybernetic hands dangled from its antennae via sparking electrical wire. It took me a second to register its green security uniform even as it barked unintelligible gibberish at me.

"Hi," I replied, looking up at the Bug. "Lieutenant Commander Vance Turbo, nice to meet you."

The Bug somehow looked disappointed. A cybernetic vocalizer like Forty-Two's was buried in its neck. It spoke in crisp accent-less English. "Aw, I was trying to scare you."

"Sorry," I replied. "I've met plenty of Bugs before."

Bugs weren't the only sentient insect-like life in the universe but were by far the most common aside from Hivemind Ants (which were also the smallest sentient race). Some jerks had nicknamed them after Robert Heinlein's villains—probably where the captain knew the author from—and the name had spread while academics debated on what to "properly" call them. The Bugs were rather good-natured about the whole thing as virtually every name the Bugs had for other races was themselves insulting.

"We prefer to be referred to as the Omnipotent God Kings of the Universe," the Bug said.

"No, you don't," I said. "Your people refer to yourself as the People. Like most people translate their homeworlds as some variation of the wold ground or dirt."

"Well, I do, and you should respect my wishes," the Bug replied. "Do I call your race the Hairless Ground Monkeys that Smell Weird?"

"I think that's literally what human translates to in your language," I replied. "It took two decades for any of the translators to pick up on that. Mostly because we don't speak with sub-sonic vibrations and smell."

"You're well-educated for a ground monkey," the Bug said, one of his dangling cybernetic hands extending over to shake.

I shook it. "Why do you have these?"

"Precision tool use! Everything is made for stupid hairless monkey hands!" the Bug said. "Nice to meet you!"

I let go of his hand. "Nice to meet you too, Lieutenant—"

"Picnic," the Bug said. "I was told it was the name of a great warrior in your culture until I looked it up a decade later. Humans really hold a grudge over that Hairless Ground Monkey thing, Hairless Ground Monkey."

I pointed at him. "That's Hairless Ground Monkey Sir, Lieutenant. I outrank you."

"Only because you're human!" Picnic said. "I mean, yes it's a human ship built for human engineers and crew respond better to commanders with faces, but that doesn't mean I shouldn't be able to push you around for my own pleasure!"

I was already starting to like this guy. "May I come in?"

"Say the magic words," Picnic said.

"That's an order," I said, coldly.

Picnic stepped aside as much as he could in the narrow hallway. "I also would have accepted 'now' and 'or die.'"

I managed to squeeze in past his legs before entering an area that looked less like a prison than the county drunk tank. I was sure this was also a bathroom before they added transparent plastisteel doors. If so, that was a serious engineering error as giving up an entire bathroom on a starship was an enormous waste of resources. I wondered if they'd let me take my sonic showers here. Either way, there were eight cells, four on each side, with a single doughnut-shaped central monitoring station in the middle of the room. From my vantage point, most of the cells looked empty.

Captain Elgan was standing by the monitoring station, looking irritated. He'd abandoned his previous joviality and was now simply fuming. I felt this was close to his natural state of being and oddly felt better about him for dropping the pretense. Lorken was sitting in a corner, now wearing memory mold armor, and carrying an even larger fusion rifle than before. He was blowing green stimgum and giving me a murderous glare.

One final person was standing in the room, wearing the blue of the Ship Medical Officer, topped with a white lab coat. She was holding a life scanner and looked bored out of her mind. Middle-aged and somewhat plain looking—which was distinctive enough when everyone could get their bodies sculpted with a doctor's visit—she looked to be of Asian heritage with long black hair as well as *heterochromia iridum* (eyes of two different colors). In her case, they were gray and green.

"Ah, our guest of honor arrives," Captain Elgan said, smiling that empty expression again. Sadly, he seemed determined to put on a false face for me.

"Am I being arrested?" I asked, not liking his terminology.

"Are you being arrested?" Captain Elgan said, laughing. He even slapped his knee in an artificial gesture. "No, no, not yet. Doctor Zard, this is your new commanding officer."

The doctor turned around. She looked me up and down. "Are you from an exceptionally long-lived branch of humanity, subject to reverse aging, or the beneficiary of an exceptionally good bio-sculptor's efforts?"

"No, no, and no," I replied.

"Then you're a kid. Why are you second-in-command?" Doctor Zard asked.

"I've asked myself that repeatedly in the past two hours. Nice to meet you," I said, offering my hand.

"Handshakes exchange germs," Doctor Zard said. "It's a habit humanity should rid itself of. I should also point out I'm a mathematician who only did her secondary study in medicine. I dropped out of my education at the Academy because I was offered a fellowship at Cambridge. That was before I was kidnapped by one of my ex-classmates who flunked out of being an economist."

"Are you the one who named him Forty-Two?" I asked, making a guess who she was referring to.

"Yes," Doctor Zard said. "I've always felt numbers held the answer to life, the universe, and everything. You know, just not in a stupid way like the Union of Faith."

I smirked then frowned. "Why do we have a mathematician as our Chief Medical Officer?"

"Because I don't care whether you live or die," Captain Elgan said. "Also, our actual doctor got himself killed in a bar fight literally the day before liftoff. Apparently, he bet fifty-thousand bits on the Green Stars and tried to duck out of paying his debt."

I nodded. "Must have been the Lion gang. You see, this is why you need a book run by trustworthy people. Me? I would have just broken some kneecaps."

"Oh yes, I can see this mission has got the best people," Doctor Zard muttered.

"Beggars can't be choosers, Liz," Captain Elgan said.

I paused. "Liz?"

Doctor Zard gave me a sideways look that could have burned through plastisteel. "Yes, my name is Elizabeth Zard. Do you have a problem with that?"

"Her parents were the first Sorkanan ambassadors," Captain Elgan said.

I stared at her then tried to suppress it but burst out laughing. Lorken and Picnic joined in while Captain Elgan continued smiling.

"Yeah, laugh it up," Liz said, staring at me. "It's not like I haven't heard it before. What's your name?"

"Lieutenant Commander Vance Turbo," I said, sucking in my breath. "Space Hero."

Liz stared at me. "No, really. What's your name?"

Captain Elgan clapped his hands together. "Enough chit-chat. We now have a very important bit of business to discuss. Time is of the essence."

Liz gave the captain a sideways look. "We literally have nothing to do for the next two months. I've already started writing calculations on the walls of my quarters with marker. I tried looking up entertainment on the ship's computer but it's nothing but alien porn and military history."

"Which aliens?" I asked, interjecting. "It could make all the difference."

"NOT THE GOOD KIND, I'M AFRAID. I'M PROGRAMMED TO BE ATTRACTED TO WARM-BLOODED CARBON-BASED BAGS OF FLESH AND WATER," Trish said over the room's speakers.

"You poor thing," Liz replied, sounding all too sincere. "A being of mathematical binary perfection corrupted by the base and disgusting impulses of an organic evolution."

"I DON'T KNOW, SEX LOOKS PRETTY FUN."

"Trish, stop watching this part of the ship," Captain Elgan said. "Consider it classified and erase any records you have of it. It's now officially a blind spot. Don't even think about what might be in here."

"Yes, Captain," Trish muttered. Somehow, it felt emptier as her presence left the detention area.

"So, what do you want me to do?" I asked, getting tired of being jerked around. Unfortunately, I suspected that wasn't something that was going to end anytime soon.

"I need you to interrogate a Notha general," Captain Elgan said.

That was when there was a hissing sound from one of the nearby cells as a small ball of fur, fangs, and claws launched itself at its transparent plastisteel door. It made a monstrous series of growls as I saw a surprisingly human-like dark green uniform on the two-foot-tall creature. The creature inside looked like a mutant combination of lemur, honey badger, and squirrel. It was a member of a race that had slaughtered billions, exterminated whole civilizations, and enslaved dozens of others. Its tiny eyes stared up at me with pure hatred and venom.

"Release me, human, or there will be dire consequences!" the shrill high-pitched voice of the fascist alien was ear-piercing.

"Isn't he the cutest thing?" Captain Elgan said.

CHAPTER SEVEN

Interrogating the Squirrel Space Nazi

"You want me to interrogate a Notha?" I asked, blinking. "A frigging Notha general?"

"Congratulations," Captain Elgan said, sounding bored. "You have successfully mastered the art of repetition."

"I demand to be treated by the Treaty of Exarxes' conditions! I am entitled to counsel and the ability to contact my government!" The Notha general shouted. Some hilarious prankster—probably Lorken because I wanted to blame him for everything wrong on this ship—had given the guy a voice like a vampire. The creepy Eastern European aristocrat kind rather than the sexy space vampire kind all the tweens were reading these days. I wondered if it was inspired by the tiny black cape, but he had that made the critter more adorable. It almost made me forget they were a race of supervillains.

"The Treaty of Exarxes only applies to prisoners of war," Captain Elgan said, dismissively. "You're technically an illegal detainee brought here via kidnapping."

I looked over my shoulder and muttered, "There's a lot of that going around."

"What was that?" Captain Elgan said.

"Nothing!" I said, cheerfully.

The General, himself, looked bewildered as if Captain Elgan's casual breaking of the rules was incomprehensible. Of course, from what I knew of the Notha it was like seeing someone fly by deciding they could. They were a race with a strong pack mentality that meant

54

obeying orders was instinctual. If you didn't want to, then you killed the guy above you and became the guy who gave orders or died.

"The General is a leader in their star force that was visiting a subjugated human colony in the Contested Zone under false pretenses," Liz said. "We believe that he was actually there to contact human smugglers that have located the *ESS Starkiller XII*."

"*ESS Starkiller XII*?" I asked.

"The missing stealth ship," Liz asked. "Or did you mean the stupid name?"

"The stupid name," I clarified.

"Someone on Earth had a very bad sense of humor or a very good one," Captain Elgan said. "Mind you, we weren't exactly going to benefit ourselves by naming it something like *ESS Yorktown* or *Yamato*. That would have pointed the way right back to Earth."

"And the ESS (Earth Star Ship) registration wouldn't?" I asked.

Captain Elgan stared at me, either having not thought of that before or merely irritated that I'd brought it up. "Shut up, Vance."

"Right," I muttered.

"So, you admit the phantom ship exists!" The General shouted, hopping up and down while waving his arms. "I knew the humans were a bunch of liars! This is an act of war!"

Captain Elgan aimed his ring at the General and I saw the cell glow with purple light as the alien started shaking like a dog chewing on an electric wire. It made a ghastly scream that was human enough to horrify me.

"What the hell!" I shouted, horrified.

"It's a Spark Chamber," Captain Elgan said. "A Notha design. I was a prisoner for two days and subjected to it constantly. Turnabout is fair play."

"Space Fleet does not torture prisoners!" I shouted, walking up to him and staring face to face with the man who'd once been my hero.

"We're not in Space Fleet," Captain Elgan said, narrowing his eyes. "You're here as part of a Department Twelve operation on my authority and we'll do what I say we do!"

"No, we will not, sir!" I said, balling my fists.

"Airlock, remember," Captain Elgan threatened.

"Then I guess you'll have to turn this ship around and find another hacker because I will not cooperate if you abuse your prisoner!" I said, speaking before I realized how utterly dumb I sounded. It was more like something out of a holo than something anyone real would say. I was also putting myself in incredible danger for a Notha.

Behind me, I could hear Picnic approaching while Lorken's finger moved to the trigger on his rifle. This was gonna suck.

Captain Elgan dropped all his anger and looked over at Liz. "Seeds of greatness. What did I say?"

I blinked, confused.

"What?" Lorken said.

Captain Elgan slapped me on the back. "You're absolutely right, Vance. Torture is completely useless for interrogating prisoners. It's just for sadistic bastards to get their rocks off—or whatever women feel when they torture people—while breaking someone down. It's against every single value we hold as members of the Community. I was just testing you."

"Uh huh," I said, not buying it in the slightest.

Lorken looked much more confused. Mind you, the fact that Captain Elgan's mind was unreadable had to be a new experience for him. It was like having a zombie walking and talking in front of you. Except it was a zombie that was giving no visual or audible cues over whether it was going to eat you.

Your mind is weird, Vannevar, Lorken's voice spoke in my head.

It's Vance to you, spoonbender, I replied. *Also, stay the bork out of my head. It's bad enough Leah talks to me here.*

Wait, Leah links her mind to yours? What the hell! She told me that she was going to stop that! Lorken reacted similarly to how I felt about her cheating with him.

Oh, the webs of deceit that woman weaves, I said, half-jokingly. *I'd feel bad for you but I'm pretty sure I hate you.*

Bork off, Vance, Lorken thought, threateningly.

Are you the one who taught her that stupid euphemism or did she teach you? I asked. *I'd really like to know. Also, why are you in my mind if it's intimate. I'll have you know I'm like ninety-eight percent straight.*

Lorken looked ready to kill me. I didn't blame him. I was an incredibly irritating person. Deliberately so. Knowing what buttons to push on people was ninety percent of a hacker's job and I was quite good at it. So good at it that I kind of hated the fact that I was. If you could make anyone believe anything as a liar then if you wanted a sincere response, the best way to handle other people was to make them dislike you. Unfortunately, it seems that fact about me was in the Captain's records since I was now here to do interrogation work. It was another job that Department Twelve undoubtedly had a bunch of other more talented agents for.

"If we're to find those SKAMMs then the best way to do so is to find the General's contacts and direct the *Black Nebula* to them," Captain Elgan said. "I'm sure we can meet the price of whomever he was going to buy the information from. What little I've been able to get out of Small, Dark, and Furry was that they're human."

"Why would humans sell SKAMMs to the Notha?" I asked, uncomprehending. That could lead to the extermination of our entire species.

"I'm going to go on a wild guess, but money?" Liz suggested. "That usually is the motivation for criminals."

"It's a bit more complex than that," Captain Elgan said, unhappy. "Contested Space is home to a lot of off-the-books colonies because so many worlds lost their governments in the Sun Killer exchange. Some of these colonies are humans with some unusual ideas about society."

"Unusual?" I asked.

"He means racist," Liz said. "The Children of General Lee, the New South Afrikaans Union, and New Reich are just some of the names of settlements I saw on the ship's maps."

"Oh," I said, sighing. "Those guys."

"They couldn't hack it on an Earth where the Community's influence is a rising tide lifting all boats regardless of race or nationality," Captain Elgan said. "So, plenty of these guys have formed their own little ramshackle separatist colonies. There are cults, criminal syndicates, hippies, libertarians, planetary survivalists, political extremists, utopians, and the guys who want to bio-mod themselves into a new race like Doctor Saul Chel's followers or those Crius freaks. Not to mention the combinations of the above that just get *weird*."

"Sending humanity's best and brightest to the stars, huh," I said, sarcastically. "Somehow, I don't think this is what Arthur C. Clarke and Isaac Asimov envisioned."

"Who?" Lorken asked.

"Humanity has a long history of sending its dregs to the other half of the world during times of exploration. It's why the United States and Australia exist," Liz said, tapping the door of the General's cell. I think she was checking to make sure he was still alive. Thankfully, his tail was twitching, and a few soft moans could be heard from the inside.

"Anyway, some of these guys would be happy for the Notha to blow up Sol as long as it meant that the majority of different colored people went with it," Captain Elgan said. "That's another reason why we have to get these things back, because who knows what these rednecks and slavery apologists would do with them if they got their hands on them first?"

"They haven't yet," Liz said. "Otherwise, they would have already sold or used them. Either for genocide or take over the region."

"Agreed," Captain Elgan said. "So, we have to find out before we get to the Contested Zone, or we are just going to be so…so…lost."

I took a deep breath. "We are completely winging it, aren't we?"

"Just a bit," Captain Elgan said, lifting thumb and index finger, showing a tiny space between them. "I have every confidence that you, Lorken, and Doctor Zard will be able to crack this nut. Picnic, we need to go scare some people on the bridge into being extra-efficient. Are you ready?"

"I was hatched ready!" Picnic said.

With that, the two of them departed and we were left with a Notha general who was only now getting up off the ground. The air vents let the smell of burnt fur into the rest of the detention center and I had to stop myself from gagging.

"I still don't get why he put you in charge," Lorken said.

"Charm," I replied. "Take note that I am not allowing anyone to bring harm to this prisoner under my watch."

"I guess you being a rule breaking rebel was just bullsavit," Lorken said.

"No one deserves to be tortured," I replied. "We have to rise above things."

"I'm fairly sure the General was involved in several war crimes during the Notha War," Liz said, raising her writing pad. "However, I admire your dedication to Space Fleet principles. Your aunt would be proud."

"You know my aunt?" I asked.

"We met a few times," Liz said. "In any case, do you actually intend to interrogate our subject?"

"We need to find those SKAMMs," I said, looking at Lorken. "You know what to do."

And he did.

The General hopped up to his feet and shook a furry fist at me. "You will never get the secrets of my operations from me! I will not betray my cause!"

"What can you tell me about Notha?" I asked, looking at Liz. I knew how to get the answers from the General. At least if they followed standard procedure about disabling enemy bio-implants.

"The Notha are an herbivore, arboreal prey species from the planet Notha, real original I know. Gaining sentience and learning how to use tools as well as weapons, they hunted down every single one of their planet's predator species. From there, they went on to attack the Sorkanan starship that came to initiate first contact and then reverse-engineered the technology to conquer their neighboring star systems about a thousand years ago," Liz said, looking up from her infopad.

"I always wondered how come races thousands of years older than us aren't more advanced," I replied. "Like, how do we create ships that are on par with them?"

"Because other more advanced races taught us how to?" Liz asked, looking confused. "I mean, it's not like development is a straight line."

"Lies!" The General said, having regained his previous animated movement. "How dare you suggest the Fifth Great Notha Empire gained its knowledge of space travel from non-sentient reptiloids aping sentience!"

"Aping sentience?" I asked, prepping to lure him into doing what I wanted.

"Only the Notha are sentient!" The General said. "Everything else is just a cheap imitation of animals with complex social structures as well as tool use. As such, it is not immoral to use and abuse them."

"I like animals," I replied. "Surely you don't think that your race was defeated in the war by animals."

"We were not defeated!" The General jumped up and down. "We were betrayed! Our leaders failed us! There was a conspiracy of white furs! Outnumbered a million to one by the forces of the animal and insect hordes!"

"Fascist enemies must simultaneously be weak and contemptible but also all-powerful as well as everywhere," Liz said.

"Do not use your pitiful human terms to describe our system of Notha supremacy!" The General said. "Eventually, the entire galaxy will—"

"You should help us," I said, interrupting him. "The SKAMMs are a threat to the billions of lives that rest on the Notha side of the Contested Zone. Surely, we can agree in the interests of mutual understanding and a love of our peoples that it is best to get them out of circulation?"

The General took one look at me then burst out laughing.

"Are you sure you don't want me to turn on the hot plate again?" Lorken asked, dryly. "On New Montana, we used to skin rabbits. I bet he's good eating."

"Eating any race that isn't evolved on your home planet is lethal," Liz replied. "Chemicals and proteins evolve alongside everything else. It's why we must synthesize everything rather than forage for food. Technically, in the event of a survival situation, you're better off eating your fellow crew mates as the Sorkanan practice. Just don't eat the brain. That's how you get kuru."

"TECHNICALLY, YOU WON'T GET KURU IF THEY DON'T HAVE IT WHEN YOU EAT THE BRAIN," Trish said. "SO, YOU SHOULD BE FINE."

"Good point," Liz said. "What she said."

I tried not to look ill. I also questioned how she could say that if she couldn't see the cell. Then again, AI orders were always a matter of interpretation when not programmed in. "Yeah, Liz, I don't think we're going to be friends."

"It's simple math," Liz said. "Cold equations."

The General's tail shot straight up as he pointed at all three of us, one by one. "You inferior beings are incapable of understanding the genius of the Notha mind. War is inevitable between our species. War is inevitable between the Notha race and all other, lesser species! I will recover these SKAMM missiles from the traitorous members of your crew and deliver them back to the Great One! No prison can hold me and—"

"Got it," Lorken said.

"What?" The General said, stopping.

"You know where he was going to meet them?" I asked Lorken. That had been the thing I'd expected him to do while I led the General down the road of paranoid ranting. He wasn't quite as bad as a Jennifer Bond villain, but he was close enough. Mind you, interrogations were easy enough with a telepath. I was just glad that they'd disabled whatever biomods the Notha gave their officers to protect against exactly this sort of thing.

"Yep," Lorken said. "You were right, you just needed to get him thinking about the subject long enough and he eventually thought about it. He's already missed his first meeting, but I have a name, ship registration, and codes. We can arrange a new one. The captain was right, it was a Terran separatist."

"Super," I said, sighing. "Thank you very much, General. You've been most helpful."

The General unleashed a torrent of Notha profanity that was nothing but cute little chittering and chattering. I still understood Notha and learned some interesting new curses like, "You fluff your mother's tail" and "You eat your own excrement."

Some things were universal.

CHAPTER EIGHT

The Long Dark Month and a Half of the Soul

"So, that was the last interesting thing that's happened to you for the past month and a half?" Hannah asked, lying beside me in bed with the covers of my bed laying over her.

"Pretty much, yeah," I said, putting on my boxers and heading to the private fresher in my room. "I gave the information over to the captain, he said good job, and then told me to go about my business. Except, I'm still not sure what my business is supposed to be."

One small benefit of being the XO was the fact that I got the only separate set of quarters aside from the captain's own. That automatically made me the most popular person on the ship as it turned out plenty of the crew were trying to seduce me just to get access to their own fresher. I didn't take advantage of that, much.

The place was still smaller than some of the privacy rooms at the Academy library with its bed, kitchenette, fresher, and wardrobe being the entire sum of its size. Still, it was the embodiment of luxury for this ship and I was starting to get a sense of the psychological effects of long-term space travel on humanoid lifeforms. It didn't help that I hadn't brought any personal possessions onboard and my wardrobe was five identical copies of the same uniform plus one-size-fits-all humans undergarments.

"It's the job of the XO to go around and make sure everyone is doing their jobs," Hannah said, smiling. Her tail was moving under the cover and it was a bit like a snake. It was kind of hot but also unsettling.

"You know, something that Trish is entirely capable of doing on her own, but most people resent being told what to do by a machine."

"IT'S TRUE," Trish said, using her echoing 'machine' voice when Hannah was around. Apparently, talking like a normal person was something she only did when she was with me.

Hannah looked up at the ceiling. "Wasn't talking to you, Trish."

"AW."

"That's another thing that messes with your sense of privacy," Hannah said. "The sense of being watched by an all-pervasive judgmental authority."

"LIKE GOD!"

"No, Trish," I said. "This is going to sound terrible, but it just occurred to me I don't actually know what you do on this ship, Hannah."

I took out my cleaning wand, which was essentially a toothbrush but worked about a thousand times better. Oddly, it came with mouth wash and that worked identically to the stuff we used back on Earth. I waved it over my teeth and then rinsed before spitting. Every droplet of water would be separated from the fluid and recycled. It was said on Earth that every glass of water had been someone's pee at some point but that was literally true on a space vessel. The recycling systems weren't one hundred percent perfect, that's why stopover points were needed, but they were close enough.

Hannah pulled out her infopad and started flipping through it, probably reading a magazine. She'd been allowed to prep for the trip. "Why is that terrible?"

"Eh..." I fumbled for the words. "Because—"

"We're sleeping together?" She asked.

"You rarely spend the night so I'm not sure that qualifies," I said. It was too early in the morning to be my usual charming self.

"This isn't a relationship, rookie," Hannah said, perhaps too quickly. "This is just a physically enjoyable way to pass the time. I'm sleeping with two other crew members on the ship."

Lieutenant Leslie Park and Bob Just Bob in Engineering. "Yeah, but you told me about it ahead of time, so I don't mind."

Hannah wrinkled her brow as I walked out. "Wow, that Leah girl did a real number on you."

"She did not," I said, stepping out of the fresher and looking at her. "Leah betrayed me. She turned me over to Department Twelve and was lying about being part of the Community's intelligence service for at least two years of our friendship."

"SHE DIDN'T KNOW WHAT SHE HAD AND IS A REAL JERK," Trish said, surprising me. Then again, Trish seemed desperate for acknowledgement and the fact that I did talk to her had made her one of my regular companions during the past month. Most of the crew seemed determined to ignore her as you would a microwave trying to talk to you.

"How long did you know her?" Hannah asked, dodging the question I'd asked earlier about what she did on the ship.

I was uncomfortable with this line of conversation but decided to cross my arms and answer. "We met on our first day at the Academy. I was completely lost at orientation and ended up in a spacesuit following directions given to me by an alien who looked like a stack of pancakes with tentacles. She helped me get, well, orientated. Leah was a human from a long-term space-faring planet and willing to explain a lot of what others took for granted. It helped that we were both from military families. Weirdly, I think she was impressed with both the fact I was a relative of one of the greatest spacers of a generation as well as some of the worst."

"THERE'S A STATISTICAL LIKELIHOOD THAT YOUR PARENTS WERE PROBABLY SCAPEGOATED BY THE MOM-AND-POP CORPORATION FOR A SYSTEMS ERROR. DRUG ADDICTED REPROBATES HIRED FOR INSURANCE PURPOSES OR NOT, IT IS VERY HARD TO CRASH AN AUTOMATED SHIP," Trish said, trying to cheer me up.

"Yes," I said, looking up. "I believe they uploaded a bunch of virus-ridden black-market porn and it drove the ship's AI to suicide."

"WOW...THAT IS ACTUALLY EVEN WORSE THAN I THOUGHT."

"Thanks for trying to help," I said, sighing.

"How long were you actually together?" Hannah asked, displaying far too much interest in my past relationship for someone who just wanted to have a consequence-free physical one.

"Six months," I replied, shrugging. "We were friends and decided to give dating a try."

"HOW ROMANTIC!" Trish asked.

"It's a terrible idea," Hannah said. "Never sleep with your friends. In that way lies feelings."

"Tell me about it," I replied then realized what I said. "Okay, yeah, maybe I'm feeling a little resentment. Leah was more than just my girlfriend, she was my best friend. I miss that part more than I miss the sex."

"SHE DIDN'T PROVE TO BE A VERY GOOD FRIEND IN THE END," Trish said.

"Maybe she saved your life," Hannah said. "Department Twelve keeps a close watch on promising Academy candidates. People with flexible senses of morality, a willingness to break the rules, and peculiar sets of skills. You were probably marked from the moment you started to display your rebellious streak. Personally, I think you're not nearly as bad as you claim to be and are still a Protector at heart. Which I suspect Leah gets too and why she tried to warn you, as poorly and confusingly as she did."

I walked over to the bed and sat on the edge. "Why are you telling me this?"

"Because I think you need to get the hell out of here," Hannah said, surprising me. "Department Twelve is not the kind of place for people with morals. The people who think it's giving them a second chance are fooling themselves. It's not the poor man's Space Fleet, it's the rot in the inside of the Community. You stay here, rookie, and you're going to end up dead."

"I didn't want to join in the first place," I said, sounding less defensive than I probably should have. "I was shanghaied, remember?"

"THAT IS A REFERENCE TO ILLEGAL CONSCRIPTION ONBOARD A SAILING VESSEL," Trish explained to Hannah. "THIS IS DUE TO THE PORT CITY OF SHANGHAI BEING A COMMON

DESTINATION AMONG SAILORS IN THE NINETEENTH CENTURY."

"I got it from the context, Trish, thanks," Hannah said. "What I'm saying is you have fit a little too snugly into things and I think that's because a part of you likes it."

"I dropped out!" I snapped, now getting actively irritated. "I got people killed as a student!"

I'd related the story of the guilt I felt for Tommy's death as well as how it related to my parents during a moment of pillow talk. It turned out Hannah was not the sort of person who you should do this with since she was using it as ammunition against me now.

Hannah narrowed her eyes. "Maybe you did. But you could have just dropped out of the Academy at any time. You could have done it the first day, but you took months to do it. Also, started dating your friend. I think you were hoping they'd kick you out because you couldn't bring yourself to leave and even then, hedged your bets. That tells me you didn't want to leave and were self-sabotaging in minor ways."

"THAT'S A PRETTY FAIR READ OF YOU, VANCE," Trish said. "I'D ALSO ADD AN INFERIORITY-SUPERIORITY COMPLEX RELATING TO YOUR PARENTS AND AUNT. ALSO, A DIFFICIENCY OF SEXUAL CONTACT. AFTER ALL, YOU'VE ONLY HAD TWO SEXUAL PARTNERS SINCE COMING ABOARD."

"I don't need your psychoanalysis, Trish," I said, feeling attacked on all sides.

"Wait, who is the other partner?" Hannah asked, furrowing her brow. "I wouldn't say a deficiency either. You're a fairly decent recreation partner, you know, for a human."

"Their identity is none of your business," I said, frowning. "It was before you anyway. And what do you mean for a human?"

"Wouldn't you like to know. Now I'm doubly curious about their identity," Hannah said, leaning in. "I'll trade you for their identity."

My gaze lowered and I shook my head. "I think you should leave."

"Fair enough," Hannah said. "Can I use the fresher? We use sub-sonic vibrations rather than water to clean and yet the communal shower still smells like a swamp."

"I think that's just Forty-Two," I replied. "He likes to take baths in the sterilizer tub and brought his own mud packs and algae growths to put in it."

Hannah blinked. "I actually have no idea whether that's true or not."

"IT'S TRUE. BUT ITS OKAY, BECAUSE REALLY ALL OF YOU ARE COMPLETELY FILTHY. THIS IS WHY WE IRRADIATE YOU ALL WHEN YOU GET ONBOARD."

"I had to compromise with him about leaving out the microparasites," I said.

Hannah grimaced. "In any case, it's probably time for me to move on. You should never get too attached to your crew mates since they'll inevitably get killed."

I went to my wardrobe and started getting dressed in last night's clothes while packing a change. "I'll use the communal fresher. You're welcome to use mine."

Hannah raised her hand. "No, you don't know the danger. Better men than you have tried and never returned!"

I rolled my eyes. "You know you never did answer what you did on this ship."

"Bridge crew," Hannah said.

I gave her a sideways glance. "Trish flies the ship. The bridge crew just exists to sit there and look pretty."

"THEY'RE VERY GOOD AT THAT!" Trish said.

"You don't think I'm pretty?" Hannah joked.

"Fine, don't tell me," I said, picking up my quartermaster-dispensed little plastic rubber duck that doubled as a shampoo dispenser. "Be seeing you."

Hannah sighed as I reached the door to exit. It didn't take more than a couple of steps because, as mentioned, we were all piled in here tightly. "I'm an assassin, Vance."

I stopped. "Huh."

"I was a gladiator, merc, prostitute, con woman, and hunter before I ended up freed by Captain Elgan," Hannah said, sighing. "Professions that either required you to know a great deal about lying or a great deal about killing. The Cap'n gave me the option of becoming his hatchet woman and I took it. I've killed thirty people for him, all of them bad, but I'm always on the lookout for an order to do something unforgivable."

"All bad?" I asked, not quite believing her.

"Yes," Hannah said. "But I don't question too hard either. The Cap'n has changed over these past ten years. He's gotten harder, meaner, and more ruthless. I'm not saying he's crazy, but the rules have stopped mattering to him."

"The rules never matter to a Scar," I replied. "That's why they make action movies about them. They're cops who don't play by the rules."

"He wasn't a Scar until recently," Hannah said. "He sought out Department Twelve rather than the reverse. This despite the fact that the military and security departments are supposed to keep out of each other's businesses. Separation of powers and all that. The Cap'n has been fighting that for years and assembling his own people."

"Why are you telling me this?" I asked, not sure just how much is worth shooting me out an airlock over.

Hannah looked confused for a second. "I like you, rookie, more than I should. I don't want to see you get hurt. I guess you're just that good at getting people to trust you. I understand you're still checking in on that monster in the detention level—"

"Yeah, I check in on the General twice a day, make sure he's not being tortured, and make sure he's fed fruit as well as berries as befitting a warrior's diet," I replied. "I've learned more about the Notha in those hour-long visits than I ever wanted to know. It's amazing how much people will tell you when they're trying to intimidate you."

"Then it's a good thing this was the last time," Hannah said, sliding out of bed naked and heading for the fresher.

I watched her enter the sonic shower. "Definitely the last time?"

"One for the road, kid."

About an hour later, Hannah departed from my love life and I was dressed in a fresh set of clothes. It was time to begin my daily duties of walking around and annoying people, making them feel like someone was forcing them to do their duties, whether they needed to do them or not. That was another job that Trish could do better than any human but just because it could be automated didn't mean that it wasn't worthwhile to do it the old-fashioned way. Well, as old fashioned as you could do a spaceship for a species that had spent the past twelve thousand years grounded.

"Yo, how's the cleaning of those power conduits coming?" I asked Lieutenant Park as I passed them doing some pointless busy work.

"Bork off, Astro."

"That's bork off, *sir*," I corrected them.

Yeah, I was really forging a bond with the crew here.

I almost immediately ran into Ketra, literally, who was standing in the middle of the hallway carrying a candelabra while wearing a nightgown. It was like she was starring in a Victorian Gothic horror story that just so happened to have a sub-Saharan elf as the lead.

"Uh, hello, Ketra," I said, uncomfortable. "I mean ambassador. I mean ex-ambassador."

Ketra socialized with Hannah, me, and Leah but almost no other members of the crew. She spent most of her time in the communications center or tactical, never actually seemingly going to sleep. It was possible that she was sharing her quarters with one of the officers, but I wasn't sure which one despite a month and a half of living together. Truth be told, part of that was because I didn't want to get too close to her. The Ethereal Human intimidated me, and I didn't admit to that lightly. There was too much going on around her that was inexplicable and even her mildest proclamations carried hints of things beyond my comprehension. Then again, maybe I was being prejudiced and just needed to give her a chance.

"The prophecy speaks of a terrible doom!" Ketra said, shaking the candelabra.

Or maybe not.

"Prophecy? What? Huh?" I asked, clearly showing my professional stoic demeanor.

"Doom!" Ketra said, not helping the matter in the slightest. "The Elder Races in the Core plot a terrifying vengeance that will bring trillions to death. Only you and the other Chosen Ones can prevent it, but an age of darkness is set upon us even if we delay it!"

I blinked. "Uh huh."

Ketra seemed to come out of her trance and blinked. "Oh hey, Vance, how are you doing?"

"What?" I asked, waving my hand in front of her face. "Are you having a go at me?"

"I told you I'm in a committed relationship with my crystal," Ketra said, offended. "Besides, I think the ship's AI likes you."

"SHH!" Trish said.

"Wait, what?" I asked, feeling like a broken record.

Ketra looked over me. "Just be very careful. I've been doing a lot of quantum meditation and you die in like six hundred and fifty of the seven hundred futures I've witnessed. Seventy of them happen in the next hour. That's bad because in the three of the four realities we survive this trip, you're actually important. The fourth being if we just turn around this stupid boat."

"SHIP, NOT BOAT," Trish corrected.

I opened my mouth to speak but no words came out.

That was when Captain Elgan spoke on the speakers. "Everyone, prepare to exit jumpspace. Lieutenant Commander Turbo, report to the bridge. I need you for an away mission."

"Ah crap," I muttered.

CHAPTER NINE

Where We Fight Some Pirates

The bridge of the *ESS Black Nebula* was a shining workstation with several consoles worked by exceptionally lovely people. It was cleaner than the rest of the ship and had an enormous view screen that showed the "screen saver" of jumpspace seen in the lounge. Captain Elgan was standing by his command chair rather than sitting, somehow striking a heroic pose among the mundanity of daily ship operations.

Among the bridge crew I saw Leah sitting at the helm, doing double duty as both a professional spy and a ship's pilot. She'd changed out of her black leather Department Twelve uniform for a more form-fitting red jumpsuit that marked her as ship's operations staff. While a few other crew members wore Space Fleet uniforms, quite a lot of the crew were taking advantage of the casual nature of the captain's command to just dress in their civvies.

The bridge crew was almost entirely human except for Fifteen, who was sitting at the communications' console. Female Sorkanan were sexually dimorphic or, in laymen's terms, didn't look much like the men. Whereas male Sorkanan looked like big lumbering lizardmen—probably because they were—female Sorkanan were lithe and graceful. Being feathered like dinosaurs, they also had elaborate plumages that I was surprised by. After all, it was the male peafowl who normally looked like a rainbow.

Yes, I put way too much thought into this.

"I'm here, Captain," I said, walking in with an infopad in hand. I was an obsessive notetaker and made it a point to always have one in hand when speaking to Elgan these days. It made me look busy.

"Ah, glad to see you've made it, Commander!" Captain Elgan said, turning to me. "Are you prepared for a breathtakingly bloody room-to-room fight for your life?"

I blinked. "Not particularly no."

"Aw," Captain Elgan said, not showing any sign my answer surprised him. "Come on, Vance, I've seen your weapons course scores. They read like a twelve-year-old playing *Blast Zone*. You should be able to tear through anyone in your way."

"Good against targets, yes. Good against the living? I've never had the pleasure," I said, not actually trying to quote anyone there. I had never been violent to anyone before in my life, even during my aborted career as the Academy crime lord. Everyone had folded before it had got nasty, and was easily subjectable to blackmail or extortion. Which left fewer physical scars and involved a lot more talking.

"Well, look forward to the pleasure now," Captain Elgan said. "We're going to be boarding a pirate ship. And by we, I mean you and security."

"Pirates?" I asked.

I wasn't too surprised since piracy was one of those things that was just an accepted risk of space travel. The Community did its best to elevate its members to post-scarcity economies where poverty and materialism were things of the past. This turned out to be best achieved by making everyone rich. That hadn't happened for all its members, though, and the Community wasn't the only game in town. Cargo ships carried tech that was even more valuable than the goods they brought and countless worlds were after both.

Aside from the Notha Empire there were dozens of other states that still had worries like where their next meal was coming from or whether a cargo hold of jump coils could mean the difference between a planet remaining an obscure backwater or growing into a self-sufficient powerhouse. If Earth hadn't been taken as a Protectorate, it probably would have been scrounging for tech like so many other worlds financing buccaneers.

"Yarr matey," Captain Elgan said, mocking the very idea of them. "We'll be coming out of jumpspace in a few more minutes and engaging the General's contacts. They think they're dealing with him, but we'll have the element of surprise."

"So, we'll capture them and force them to give us clues to the location of the *Starkiller XII*?" I asked.

Captain Elgan blinked. "Well, I actually expected to just loot their computer system but, sure, you can take prisoners if you want."

I sighed, irritated. "You know, I never know when you're joking or not."

"I have it on good authority the ship's XO is quite insistent on the proper treatment of POWs," Captain Elgan said. "Excessively so."

I stared at him, feeling less and less inclined to stand down. "If we don't stand by our principles, sir, then what are we but the Notha?"

"Paying evil unto evil is not evil," Captain Elgan said. "Man your station, Commander. Red alert."

The entirety of the ship's lighting started flashing red as an alarm blared. It was a warning that not only were we coming out of jumpspace but that we were also expected to do so in combat. Frankly, I wish he'd done that to begin with.

"DID YOU KNOW RED ALERTS COME FROM THE TV SHOW *STAR TREK*?" Trish said, not sounding remotely worried.

I sat down in the XO's chair as the captain did the same, buckling in. Moments later, the ship exited from jumpspace, and we were in a strange and unfamiliar system. Fifteen spoke first, handling the sensor station. Her voice was accent-less English and a much higher quality translation than Forty-Two's. "We have located the vessel, sir. It is a converted Devil Dog-class gunship, the *IMS Nathan Bedford Forrest*."

Devil Dog gunships had been created as patrol ships for humanity and were almost as old as the MacArthur-class vessel we were piloting around. Unfortunately, humanity had overestimated its knowledge of how space battles would go. They'd proven worthless against anything but civilian craft. As such, when the Community had unloaded all its aging vessels onto Earth, Earth had done the same to the open market: the human way. On Earth, that was just considered good business while the Community considered it arming terrorists. Given what these guys had named their ship, I was inclined to agree with the Community.

"IMS?" Captain Elgan asked. "I'm not familiar with that designation."

"It is one of dozens of made-up ship prefixes humans designate their vessels to show their refusal to acknowledge Earth's leadership," Fifteen answered.

"I assume the I stands for independent," Captain Elgan said, "but I'm lost on the M."

"Nothing so fancy. It's. My. Ship."

"Clever," Captain Elgan said, smirking. "Advance on the vessel, Lieutenant Mass. Trish, I want you to disable the ship before it can identify us and make a leap into jumpspace."

"YOU GOT IT," Trish said. "POWERING UP WEAPONS NOW AND TARGETTING TO DISABLE."

"Sir?" Leah asked, sounding as shocked as I was.

One of the primary laws regarding AI was that they were programmed with a reverence for the lives of sapience. Not so much as Asimov's Laws of Robotics—because they wouldn't be very useful in combat situations otherwise—but definitely never given access to weaponry. It was one of the universally agreed upon Community laws regarding artificial beings. Yet another way that AI were not quite as equal to organic life as the Community claimed.

"You heard me, Lieutenant," Captain Elgan said. "Our TSR-80 can shoot faster and with more precision than any organic. We're taking every advantage we can in this battle. If we didn't, we might as well be using starfighters."

"They're launching starfighters, sir," Fifteen said. "Apparently, they converted their cargo hold into a makeshift hanger."

"Ugh," Captain Elgan said. "How embarrassing."

Starfighters had been Earth's planned contribution to the galactic war effort, in part due to an arrogance that no other race in the galaxy had ever thought of fast-moving small starcraft in warfare. The results had been unimpressive. Human reflexes were simply unable to compete with even non-sentient automated battle systems and barrier technology meant that most tiny ships could barely scratch the paint on a anything bigger than a gunship.

Technology had advanced since then and there actually were starfighter designs in production as supplements to cruisers. However, they required the pilots to be cybernetically enhanced and then trained to work in lockstep with their machinery. Even then, it would only be practical if AI ceased to be widely available. That wasn't going to happen, so they were going to remain a novelty in war at best.

"SHALL I DISABLE THEM TOO?" Trish asked.

"No," Captain Elgan said. "Shoot to kill."

I leaned in. "Captain, they're more likely to cooperate if we don't kill any of them. A bit of mercy can go a long way."

"So noted, Commander," Captain Elgan nodded. "Trish, shoot to kill."

"SIGH," Trish said the word rather than doing so, perhaps because she didn't have lungs. "THIS FEELS LIKE CHEATING."

"The object of war is not to die for your country but to make the enemy die for theirs," Captain Elgan said. "General George Smith Patton, Junior."

"THAT'S ACTUALLY FROM THE MOVIE ABOUT HIS LIFE RATHER THAN SOMETHING HE ACTUALLY SAID."

"Just shoot the borking pirates, Trish," Captain Elgan said.

"RIGHTO."

What followed could hardly be called war. Trish's every shot was perfect and the viewscreen gave us elaborate, carefully filmed shots of every green energy blast. Plasma weapons moved faster than the human eye could see but tracers let us see where the blasts struck. Trish destroyed all four of the starfighters, their launched rocket-based ordnance, and the jumpspace drive coolant lines on the IMS *Nathan Bedford Forrest*. If they tried to jump now, they'd explode in a fiery ball of reactor core fuel. Which didn't mean they wouldn't, just that they'd have to be stupid or desperate or both.

"Status report, Commander?" Captain Elgan asked me.

I checked the holoscreen beside my chair. "No damage sir."

"And the enemy?" Captain Elgan asked Fifteen.

"Disabled from jumpspace but they're attempting to flee at sublight speeds," Fifteen said. "If they get into the gravity of the local star, they might be able to stay ahead of us long enough to make repairs."

"I can get us to them before then," Leah said.

"I'm sure you can. However, I have a better idea. Commander, we need a speech," Captain Elgan said.

"Excuse me?" I asked, feeling lost. Again.

"Ask them to surrender," Captain Elgan said. "I could give the speech, but it would just sound like: *Listen up you redneck aynxholes, we've got you surrounded. Give up or I'll blow your borking ship up.*"

"I see," I said, overwhelmed.

"Now we have two other options: we can try to cyberwarfare their ship, or we can have you try to talk them down. Or both. Do you have the capacity to disable their ship with a program?" Captain Elgan asked.

"Give me an hour and I can," I said.

"Don't have an hour," Captain Elgan said. "Speech time."

I sighed and stood up. "Very well, Captain."

"Oh, and say we're from the Protectorate," Captain Elgan added.

"Isn't that a crime?" I asked.

Captain Elgan looked at me.

"Right," I said, dryly.

"You're getting the sarcastic dry humor of a captain down already," Captain Elgan said. "Greatness."

"Trish, put a line through to the pirate vessel," I replied.

"YES, COMMANDER!" Trish said with a bit too much enthusiasm. "CONNECTED!"

"*IMS Nathan Bedford Forrest,*" I said, disgusted just saying the name. "This is Commander Vannevar Tagawa of the Community Protectorate vessel *ESS Black Nebula*. We are on a mission of peace and order in the Contested Zone, and you have been found guilty of performing illegal acts. Despite appearances, this vessel is equipped with the most advanced weapons technology in the galaxy. Surrender and I guarantee both the safety of your captain as well as their crew. Resist and you will give us no choice but to destroy your vessel. Over."

"Decent," Captain Elgan said. "Could have used some more threats to boil them in their own wastes. I knew a captain who once hit the life support and sewer system processor to do that. He ended up being prosecuted for war crimes, but it worked."

I decided in that moment to believe that Captain Elgan was testing me, and all his actions were designed to teach me important life lessons about how to be a better officer. There was even a twenty percent chance that was true.

"I liked the captain's speech better," Leah said. "Why use your real name?"

"I'm still building the legend of Vance Turbo," I said. "When it's properly prepared it will cause the entire Notha Empire to surrender."

Captain Elgan chuckled at that. "Have we received an answer from the pirates, yet?"

"YES, CAPTAIN. THEY SAID FOR US TO GO BORK OURSELVES," Trish said. "EXCEPT THEY DIDN'T SAY BORK."

I frowned. "Captain, permission to continue firing at low power blasts. I'd like to aim at the gravity stabilizers."

"Granted," Captain Elgan said. "Obey the lieutenant commander, Trish."

"WITH GREAT PLEASURE, SIR."

With that, more green plasma blasts shot forth from the ship and started hammering the *IMS Nathan Bedford Forrest*. There was no way we could destroy the vessel and complete our mission, but I was very good at bluffing. I also knew that sometimes stupid people needed to have the feel of their ship rocking to understand just how much danger they were really in.

Seconds later, Trish responded, "THEY'RE OFFERING THEIR TERMS OF SURRENDER."

"Keep firing," I said, not even waiting for Captain Elgan.

"THEY'RE NOW SHOUTING THAT THEY SURRENDER! HOORAY!" Trish said. "WAIT, DO I KEEP FIRING?"

"Stop please," I said. "Tell them to power down their engines and weapons as well as to prepare to be boarded."

"DONE."

"Good job," Captain Elgan said, tapping the side of his chair. "Congratulations, crew, you've all won your first battle. Downgrade to yellow alert."

I wasn't sure how I felt about that. It wasn't exactly something that I felt we should be proud of, but I also understood the basics of Admiral B'vort's military philosophy: there was no such thing as a fair fight and any battle you could win through overwhelming firepower was still a victory. After all, a fair fight meant you had a fifty-fifty chance of losing and who wanted that? Mind you, I'd learned that from his daughter in bed but that was the best way of remembering these things.

"Wee," I said, in a dead somber voice.

Captain Elgan stood up and put his hand on my shoulder. "Head down to the cargo bay and take command of the security team. Get yourself suited up first, though. I don't want you getting yourself killed on your first away mission."

"Yessir," I said, sighing.

"Sir, I would like to point out I'm better qualified for dealing with an away mission," Leah said. "Also, I would see any attack coming."

"Denied, Lieutenant," Captain Elgan said.

I swear this ship is an Earthlings only club, Leah thought to me.

What? I thought back.

Leah looked surprised. *Uh, you weren't supposed to hear that.*

Huh, we had a telepathic bond beyond what she was actively attempting to cultivate. I seemed to recall that was rare but didn't know much more about it.

Weird, I thought. *You wanna talk about it?*

No, Leah thought back before shutting our connection.

CHAPTER TEN

Now I'm a Space Marine. This Will Not End Well

When I was younger—almost four years ago—I'd been determined to become a captain in Space Fleet. I had the ambitions of being bigger than Aunt Kathy or Captain Elgan ever were. For that I'd plotted out a comprehensive course to maximize my Academy time's usefulness as well as gaining the sort of credentials that would fast track me to command. It was, of course, a profoundly arrogant action and didn't play to my strengths but provided me with full certification for space combat missions.

Lucky me.

I was wearing an *Apollo*-class power suit that was basically armor you stepped into and it closed around you. It provided you with a personal barrier, enhanced strength, protected against low-to-mid-powered fusion blasts, and could get you running at one hundred and twenty kph for up to ten minutes.

In my hands was a Simo Häyhä Finnish fusion rifle that was noticeable for the fact that it was brand new, never used, and looked to have a price tag on it. Much of the ordnance inside the armory looked like it hadn't come from either EarthGov or the Community. Instead, it seemed like someone had gotten it from an arms dealer or it had fallen off the back of a cargo ship.

"How do I look, Trish?" I asked, walking through the halls of the *Black Nebula*. Trish's little robot body rolled beside me. She preferred to use it when we were having private conversations. People paid no attention to their commanding officer talking to a machine. At most, the people in the hall barely spared me a glance or two while continuing their merry way.

"Like central casting put out a call for an action hero who still looks like a model," Trish replied. "The inventory tag kind of undermines the effect, though."

"I actually have no idea how to remove it," I replied.

"They're called scissors," Trish said, a little more sarcastically than I expected. Maybe I was rubbing off on the Cognition AI.

"Well, I don't have time to find a pair of those," I replied. "Hopefully, the threat of violence will be enough to keep these guys quiescent."

"I have a data file on suspected criminals, smugglers, and pirates in the region. This ship is linked to a dozen attacks on civilian shipping as well as the mass execution of a Swahili farming community of fifty-three sapients. I do not think they will cooperate without violence," Trish replied.

"Great," I said, sarcastically. "Just great."

"You're unenthusiastic about the prospect of violence," Trish said.

"Yes," I replied. "I'd prefer to use my words rather than guns. One, because I have an enormous respect for the life of others due to my best friend being cut down before my eyes. Two, because I have an enormous respect for the life of myself because I like living. Combat reduces your chance of that."

"A valid life philosophy," Trish said. "You should go talk with Ambassador Ketra."

"Because she's a holy woman who will ease my conscience?" I asked.

"No, because she's certified in forty martial arts as well mental techniques on banishing guilt," Trish said. "You could learn a lot from her about the art of killing."

I was spared from having to make a response to that by entering the cargo bay. It was equipped with four shuttles and a large, unmarked metal box that I presumed to be what they planned to transport the recovered SKAMMs in. Also present in the shuttle bay was the deck crew and the group I assumed to be my accompaniment for the away mission.

There was Hannah, dressed up in her own light-weight Nina-class power armor that I swore looked more feminine than strictly practical but maybe was my own biases at work. Standing beside her was Picnic—who looked like a robotic Slaughterbug in his customized armor—Forty-Two, a South Asian-looking man I didn't know, and Lorken. Both Lorken and the newcomer were also in Apollo armor.

I looked at Lorken. "Ah man, look at us. We're wearing the same outfit to the party."

"I should be in charge of this mission," Lorken said, glaring at me.

"No, Hannah should be in charge of this mission," I replied. "Hannah, you're in charge of this mission."

"The Cap'n put you in charge," Hannah said, sounding less than happy about it.

"Yes, and I'm making a command decision to put you in charge," I replied. "Consider my first last order for this mission be to do what she says."

"I approve of your command style," Forty-Two said.

"Hey, whatever gets us back home safely," Picnic said. "I'm just glad it won't be the guy who has never killed anyone sending us to deal with the horrifying pirates. We might actually have a chance of survival other than shooting him in the back."

"Thanks, Picnic," I said, taking my right hand off my rifle and putting it over my heart. "That means a lot."

"Well, I'm dead either way," the South Asian man said. "Do you know what the survival rate for an enlisted gay Filipino man is on these missions? Zero. Maybe if I were the captain, first officer, virgin, or doctor then I'd have a chance. However, I've had sex and smoked raffa. There's no way I'm making it out of this."

I blinked. "I think you're mixing up like fifteen different things."

"They even put me in a red shirt!" the South Asian man said. "Do you know what red shirts mean in my culture?"

"That you're in engineering?" I asked.

"That too!" The South Asian man said. "But the engineer always dies on these missions! They get killed by the monster to show the main characters that it's dangerous. Hell, do you know my name?"

"Uh—" I hesitated.

"See!" The South Asian man said.

"Is he joking?" I turned to Hannah.

"Unfortunately, no," Hannah said. "Chief Sal Boxley had a horrifying accident on one of his training crews where he was the only survivor. It left him unfit for service psychologically and he was forced to drop out. So, you and he have something in common."

"What?" Sal asked. "What do we have in common?"

"We both lost our partners during horrific training accidents," I said.

"Gah!" Sal said.

"You *have* a name," Hannah said, speaking louder but not quite shouting. "I swear I do not get Earthlings. You all act like this is fiction"

Sal looked desperate. "Isn't it?"

Hannah shook her head. "Everyone pile into the shuttle. We're heading over immediately. The *Black Nebula* will provide cover for us in case the pirates try to arm their weapons again. However, I fully expect them to resist. These pirates are the kind of people who would rather go down shooting than spend the rest of their lives on a penal colony."

"Would be better lives than they have currently," Lorken said. "I've seen some of the prefab cities they call colonies. They were nothing but tents, stills, porta-potties, and armories."

"Be that as it may, they're still likely to shoot first and ask questions later," Hannah said. "We're supposed to take them prisoner."

"Can we even house that many prisoners?" I asked. "A gunship like theirs will have at least a dozen crew and that's not including any security personnel or soldiers they've packed on. My aunt once took down one of these vessels and it was stuffed with three times its normal crew complement."

"That's up to you, rookie," Hannah said. "I'm just a civilian contractor."

"Rookie, sir, then," I said, smirking.

Hannah smirked back at me. "Not if I'm in charge."

I nodded.

Ugh, I can't believe she'd give you the time of day, Lorken thought.

Stay out of my head, Papa Smurf, I said.

I don't even know what that is, Lorken said. *I grew up on an ice world where every day was a fight to survive against the Caananites.*

Was one of them named Gargamel? I asked.

I hate you so very much, Lorken said.

Thank you, I try, I replied.

I wondered just what Captain Elgan did plan for the prisoners we took, if any. We had enough space in our tiny detention center for maybe ten total and one of those was already occupied by the General. It didn't take Doctor Zard to do the math on this being a problem. I wasn't about to let them go if they really were involved in piracy. This could only be resolved by a fair trial, but it occurred to me I was the only one who probably cared about this.

I didn't think it would come to mass execution. Captain Elgan seemed more talk than action in his Captain Bligh qualities, but I'd have to figure out a solution. I had a few ideas like converting sick bay, dropping them off at a Community world, or forcing the captives to double up in their cells but this was stuff I could think of after the mission. After all, it wouldn't matter what I thought we should do if I got a fusion blast through the brain.

We shuffled onto the shuttle, which was little more than a pair of benches and a flight controller. There was also a microscopic toilet chamber, but I was sure that I couldn't get into it while inside my armor. There was also no way for Picnic to use it and I had to wonder how he used the facilities in our ship. I was afraid I wouldn't like the answer. Stepping up to the controls, Hannah took a seat beside me and the two of us began prepping the vessel for launch.

"Are you going to be a problem?" Hannah asked.

"I just want to make sure this mission goes off smoothly," I replied. "I'm not going to interfere with your command."

"No, I meant if we need to use lethal force," Hannah said. "I saw how you reacted when I told you I was an assassin."

I looked back to the others sitting across from each other behind us. "Is that common knowledge? I feel like that's something that should have been a secret."

"She's a what now?" Sal asked.

"Forty-Two and I have worked together before and there's a telepath onboard," Hannah said. "But I could tell you were worried. That I might have been assigned to take you out should you step out of line."

I wasn't sure she was referring to. I thought I'd taken it completely in stride. "Well, now I am."

"Don't," Hannah said. "I'll watch your back and you watch mine. I just want to know if you'll pull the trigger."

"I dunno, I've never shot anyone before," I said, powering up the shuttle.

Hannah sighed. "Fair enough."

"I've never shot anyone before," Sal said, behind us. "Are you worried about me?"

"Permission to beat him, sir," Lorken said.

"Granted," Hannah said, without even looking up.

"Denied!" I snapped.

"I thought you said you weren't going to interfere with my command?" Hannah asked, smirking.

"Protectorate regulations stand above us all," I replied.

"OBEYING RULES IS SO HOT AND ETHICAL," Trish said, her voice coming from the computer system.

"Is the AI flirting with him?" Sal asked Forty-Two.

"Don't try to make sense of anything on this ship," Forty-Two said. "You'll stay sane longer that way."

"Right," Sal said. "I dunno, that just seems like something you should do a complete reboot over."

"HISS!" Trish said through the speakers.

Sal almost jumped out of his seat.

The shuttle slowly rose off the floor before moving into the airlock, with barely enough room to fit the shuttle. The metal doors to the hangar bay shut behind us before the ones to space opened. I'd done thousands of shuttle rides before but never quite lost my sense of wonder at seeing the endless vastness of space.

The shuttle traveled the distance between the starships, thousands of kilometers in a handful of minutes, before landing with a thud against their airlock. The process was a simple one and doubly so for ships that had both been created by EarthGov. Still, I couldn't help but shake the feeling that this was going to get ugly. Well, uglier than us having to shoot our way through this place. I mean, what if this group of pirates had children aboard?

"Then aim low," Lorken said aloud.

I gave him a withering glare. "You just can't stay out, can you?"

"Believe me, I'd love to, but I'm linked to Leah and she's linked to you," Lorken said. "It's like a marriage you don't want to be a part of."

"Well work on divorce," I said, worrying that this bond was a lot more complicated than it sounded.

"Shut up and move," Hannah said, taking position in front of the shuttle's exit. "Lorken, are you getting anything from the pirates?"

"Yep," Lorken said. "They're afraid, hostile, and planning on killing us. I also think they hate the Community to a fantastic degree. I believe they'll shoot at Hannah, Forty-Two, myself, and Picnic over any other targets."

"Oh, thank God," Sal said, letting out a deep breath.

Everyone glared at him.

"Why Hannah and you, Lorken?" Forty-Two asked. "You're as human as the rest of them."

"We qualify as an alien to these people," Hannah answered, assuming a place in front of the others.

"Haha! Good one," Forty-Two laughed then paused. "Oh wait, you're serious."

"I suppose we all look alike to you," I replied.

"Yes," Forty-Two said. "Because you do. I understand your race sees something called colors and that helps differentiate you."

"Their race is so damned weird," Picnic said, taking up position in the rear.

"Prepare to be fired upon immediately," Hannah said. "Set your barriers to maximum and don't hesitate to fire back. Shoot to kill."

I almost countermanded her order because I didn't want this to become a bloodbath, but I'd made a promise and she was someone who had much more experience in this than I did. I didn't want to be the officer they had to frag to survive. Still, I promised myself I would do what I could to subdue at least one of this crew without killing them. I had been trained to kill when I had to but also disable if the mission required it. Certainly, we had higher priorities than just taking them down and every living body meant it would be easier to find the SKAMMs.

The fact that I was overthinking things became immediately apparent when the doors slid open and a grenade rolled between our legs. The pirates were not standing there, rifles drawn, waiting to be shot. No, they'd just decided to blow us up with technology as old as the twentieth century.

"Duck!" Hannah said, not really having a place to escape to.

None of us did.

CHAPTER ELEVEN

Pew-Pew, Pow-Pow, Blam-Blam

The grenade was a crude explosive device, the kind that was manufactured before the arrival of aliens on First Contact Day. The Independents never seemed to lack for such ordnance, even if it was hopelessly outmoded compared to modern spacefaring weapons. Then again, so were knives and people still killed people with those.

"Back in formation!" Lorken surprised me by shouting as the grenade suddenly flew down the hall like an assassination drone.

The explosion that followed was accompanied by some blood-curdling screams and my suspicions were that at least some of the pirates were dead, their body parts blasted apart by their own weapon. However, it didn't end the threat that they posed because almost immediately I heard shouts of attack and more.

"Kill 'em!"

"No retreat, no surrender! It's what the Boss would do!"

"They're here to take our guns!"

One thing that Independents often complained about was "Second Amendment" rights despite that not applying to EarthGov, let alone any other civilization. Personally, I wasn't sure why people had such an attachment to objects of killing, but I'd grown up in a humanity that had been united by shared fear of aliens, followed by shared friendship, and then shared love.

Prejudice and nationalism hadn't disappeared from Earth, but they'd gone from hating the colors of humanity to the scales and feathers of the alien. Black, brown, and white stood together against the exoskeletons or carapaces. Hopefully, that would end someday too. I mean, how awful would it be if in a thousand years we were still fighting our fellow humans?

The irony wasn't lost on me that I was currently fighting with a Bug, a Sorkanan, and two demihumans against a bunch of fellow Earthlings. Maybe history didn't have a forward momentum but was more like music, going up and down with the rhythm of history. I could also just be overthinking this. These idiots were fighting when even victory would just result in the *Black Nebula* vaporizing them. Perhaps—

Oh, for the love of God, shut up and fight! Lorken thought back at me with such strength of will that it rang in my head.

"Go!" Hannah shouted and charged.

What followed was the second battle of my life as I charged out with the rest of the away team's soldiers. We were met by row after row of pirates, all of them Earthling and of Caucasian ancestry. They weren't wearing power-armor and most of their weapons were ballistics-based rather than fusion. For all intents and purposes, that meant that roughly sixty percent of the people shooting at us were untrained cannon fodder. Bullets shot within a starship couldn't penetrate the hull and they certainly couldn't penetrate a barrier or the armor.

A good forty percent of the weapons wielded by the pirates *were* fusion-based, though. There were pistols and a couple of rifles that slammed into our barriers like a car strike. The displays on the interior of my helmet showed my shield strength going down by twenty percent, thirty percent, and even eighty percent while the blasts fired forward. I tried to pull the trigger but found my finger hesitating as I saw the faces of the people waiting on the other side: poor, sad, desperate, and furious. The fact that they were a bunch of murderous racists should have made it easy to cut them down, but it didn't. It turned out my introspection about having too much respect for life proved to be less of a joke than a simple statement of fact.

Nevertheless, the battle continued around me as the others did fire their blasts repeatedly. Hannah killed the fusion rifle users with precision shots one after the other, Forty-Two gunned down the other fusion users, Picnic fired indiscriminately into the humans attacking us, and Sal just kept his finger pressed down on the trigger. Lorken was the only one I didn't detect firing and that changed as we advanced, as he shot into one of the doors to our sides. He knew where we were, that we were going to be ambushed, and he made sure that the fighters hiding behind cover were killed before they even knew they'd been spotted.

As if mocking his desperate desire to live, I saw Sal hit by some sort of hand-held cannon that launched a grenade into his barrier. The blast sent him falling back to the ground despite his barrier being at full strength. He collapsed to the ground face first. Immediately, I turned around and fired my fusion rifle into the attacker's chest. The man, an elderly looking human in a white t-shirt and cowboy hat looked surprised as most of his chest was consumed by the energy blast. He dropped his grenade launcher and fell back against the wall. I just barely managed to avoid throwing up in my helmet.

"I'm not dead!" Sal said, his voice loud and clear over our helmet. His body wasn't moving on the ground, though. "Just in a huge amount of pain!"

"Yeah, you stay not dead," Hannah reassured him. "But I need you to get up and rig the ship's engines."

"Couldn't I have done that without fighting?" Sal asked.

"Shut up!" Hannah said, helping him up. "Good job, rookie."

"Sure," I said, staring at the body. I barely noticed that the shooting had stopped around me.

I was a killer now. God and Buddha help me.

My awareness of our surroundings grew as the sounds of blast fire and guns stopped ringing in my ear. We were in the middle of the gunship's "lounge", I guessed, even though such things didn't normally exist in a typical example of this vessel's make. It had numerous soft leather surfaces, most of them ratty and damaged, with a large Confederate battle flag hanging on the side of its portside (or "left" from someone looking forward from the ship's end). There were beer bottles lying everywhere and a couple of knives sticking in the side of the metal walls. A holovision entertainment unit was showing a holo of gravcar racing back on Earth. It was so stereotypical that I had to wonder if I'd accidentally wandered into a movie set. But no, there were a lot of dead bodies behind me and we were only halfway through the ship.

"How many have we killed?" Hannah asked Lorken. "How many are left?"

Lorken frowned. "It's hard to differentiate individual thoughts if I'm casting a wide net. If I had to guess, I'd say we've killed about half the crew. The rest of them have packed themselves into the stern of the ship near the cockpit."

"Great," Hannah said.

"I remind you our goal is to get information here," I replied, pushing down my disgust at the bloodshed here. I offered my hand to Sal and helped him back to his feet. "If they all die, that's going to put a serious crimp in our plans."

"Their continued resistance is what's getting them killed," Forty-Two said. "We cannot be blamed for their suicidal overconfidence."

"Throw your soldiers into positions from whence there is no escape, and they will prefer death to flight," I replied. "Sun Tzu."

"Is she an ex-girlfriend?" Hannah asked. "I knew a girl named Sun once. Belenus folk-rock singer."

That was when an elderly female voice blared from the speakers. "You bastards aren't taking my ship! I don't care if you have to kill us all."

I was somewhat surprised to hear a woman oversaw this organization but maybe I'd been too inclined to stereotype them.

"Does your crew know that?" I asked, speaking upward to the ceiling. "What is the purpose of this carnage? You can save your lives here rather than throw them away! I gave you a promise of protection and fair treatment. That offer still holds but you have to set down your arms and come quietly! It's the only way I can offer any guarantees!"

"They're one-way speakers, rookie," Hannah said.

"Oh," I said, feeling stupid. "Do you really think the captain will fight to the end?"

"Yes," Lorken said, frowning. "Unfortunately. Captain Willamina Snow is a woman wanted for multiple homicides, piracy, human trafficking, and worse. She'll bear the full blame for all the atrocities worked by this crew and has no one to turn on for a commutation of her sentences. She won't die before capture, but I believe she'll hide behind all of her people's bodies before surrender."

"What a senseless waste of life," I muttered.

"God, you are Space Fleet to the core," Hannah said, shaking her head in disgust. "Why did you drop out?"

"I'm a dangerous, ill-mannered rogue," I replied.

Hannah snorted in derision at my description.

"We should take out the captain directly," Forty-Two said. "Then the others will fall in line."

"The others think the captain has a cunning plan," Lorken said. "Probably because she said she did and plans to use them as cannon fodder."

"There's a lot of miscommunication about what the Community does to prisoners," Hannah said. "Propaganda. Maybe we should release Mr. Nice Guy on them and see if he can persuade them to stand down."

Sal looked at her. "Are you sure you want me to talk to them? I mean, what if they shoot me?"

"I mean the lieutenant commander," Hannah said.

"Oh!" Sal said. "Then I heartily approve of this plan."

Hannah rolled her eyes.

Picnic said, "I say we kill 'em all and let the Great Queen sort them out."

"I agree with the disgusting insect," Lorken said, with more friendship than such words implied.

"Turns out not all hairless monkeys are stupid," Picnic replied.

"Sal, I need you to go back to the engine room," Hannah said. "It's cleared out, so we need you to shut down everything and force—"

"UH, GUYS," Trish interrupted.

"Doesn't that thing have a mute button?" Lorken muttered.

"Yes?" Hannah asked, exasperated by the AI. She was one of the nicest people on the ship to Trish and still treated her like an unwanted little sister.

"CAPTAIN SNOW IS TRYING TO BLOW UP THE SHIP," Trish said. "SHE'S ARMED THE SELF-DESTRUCT."

I looked over at Lorken. "Not willing to die, huh?"

Lorken glared at me. "Mind reading is not an exact science!"

"Stop her!" Hannah said. "Who puts a self-destruct on a ship?"

"Earthlings," Picnic said. "Honestly, it's kind of fascinating how you came up with all these crazy ideas."

"I'M TRYING TO STOP HER," Trish replied. "THIS SHIP ONLY HAS A DUMMY AI BUT I'M NOT OPERATING AT FULL CAPACITY."

"So, what's the situation?" Hannah asked.

"UH... YOU SHOULD PROBABLY LEAVE," Trish said. "I CAN MAYBE SLOW DOWN THE SELF-DESTRUCT FOR ABOUT FIVE MINUTES."

"We can't leave the information inside its black box," Lorken said. "That's the entire mission."

"Better failures than dead," Forty-Two said.

I paused. "Trish, is this a standard military gunship? Is the software still baseline?"

"YES," Trish said. "KINDA BUSY. PLEASE SAVE YOURSELVES."

"Please transfer over the specs for that to my cybernetic implant from the *Black Nebula*," I replied. "That's an order."

"UHM, OKAY."

Seconds later, the information was in my brain, and it was correct as far as the eye could see. I had a full manual for the vessel's base type as well as a list of its specs, codes, and operating procedures. Now it was time to test whether my lieutenant commander rank was real or not as I entered the serial number I'd been given.

I received an acceptance notice seconds later. There was no change in the ship, no flashing lights, or other outward sign that things changed but it worked. A moment later, there was a scream out of outrage from the cockpit.

"What just happened?" Hannah asked.

"Take the captain alive, please," I said. "I got creative."

"THE COMMANDER HAS RESET THE SHIP TO FACTORY DEFAULT," Trish said, sounding impressed. "THE STORED INFORMATION IN THE SHIP'S BLACK BOX WON'T BE TOUCHED

NOR THE LOGS, BUT THE SELF-DESTRUCT HAS BEEN DEACTIVATED ALONG WITH ALL CODES FOR ITS OPERATION."

"Nice job, rookie," Hannah said.

With that, an elderly white-haired woman carrying an automatic fusion repeater two sizes too large for her charged out of the cockpit. She'd welded handles to the side to better hold the enormous weapon and it looked like she was about to unleash a torrent of blasts at us. Really, the thing should have been hanging outside of an air transport.

"Die, you motherborking—"

That was when she immediately started convulsing, foamed at the mouth, then hit the ground in a completely straight posture before thrashing her limbs wildly. After a second, she went utterly still, and I was sure she'd crapped herself.

Hannah was holding up a ranged sonic stunner in one hand, the device looking like a holovision remote. "Good thing she wasn't wearing armor. Then I would have had to have killed her and I'd have made you sad."

I put down my rifle and gave a golf clap. "Congratulations, you have done the bare minimum required of interstellar law."

"No, the bare minimum would be to shoot everyone in the ship and dump their bodies into space because they're pirates," Hannah said. "Now pick up your gun and give another speech. This time a better one. I don't want to have to stun every one of these yokels. You wouldn't believe the smell that generates."

"Yes, he would," Lorken said, chuckling. "I wouldn't bother with a speech, though. I can't imagine what would make them surrender."

I sneered at him. "Of course, you realize, this means war."

Lorken didn't get the reference.

"Haha," Forty-Two said. "The Insect Bunny."

"Trish, put me on the ship's speakers," I replied.

"DONE."

"Listen, jackasses, I have lost all of my patience. Every fighter you sent against us is dead and your captain is captured. You're all a bunch of murderous scumbags and I couldn't care less if you live or die. However, if you want to have any kind of future, now would be a good time to get your stories straight. Blame everything on your commanding officers, the dead, and come up with a bunch of names. Other pirates, corrupt officials, and those who have helped you over the years. There's no honor among thieves and I'm sure you can shuffle most of the blame for your crimes onto the dead or captured. However, that will only happen if you all throw down your weapons and come out right now. If a single scratch happens to any of my men, I'm venting the airlocks. Note: I'm wearing a spacesuit. If you aren't, you'll die quickly. If you are, then you'll die slowly because we won't be picking you up. Capiche? Which, if you don't speak Italian means, *do you understand?*"

Everyone looked at me. All of them looked stunned, even Picnic.

"You might just make captain yet," Hannah said.

The remaining crew surrendered moments later.

CHAPTER TWELVE

Figuring Out the Next Piece of the Puzzle

As had been demonstrated by the month and a half long journey to get here in the first place—which wasn't even in Contested Space but just on the edge of it—space travel was a long, tedious business. Stripping the gunship of all its weaponry and supplies took two days and most of it ended up loaded up in the shuttle bay.

Thankfully, I got to do some real officer work cataloguing it all and seeing what we could use and what we couldn't. The prisoners were just barely able to fit into the detention level after all the casualties they'd suffered at Hannah's hands. I had to wonder if she hadn't known this and taken "steps" to reduce the headcount.

Rather than ferry them along with us on our highly dangerous mission to find sun killers, I'd suggested having volunteers take the prisoners back to the nearest Community starbase and unload them. We could convert the gunship's living quarters into temporary holding cells and keep the gravity at a higher level to keep them docile. It would only be a week's journey and we could spare the seven or eight crew members needed to look after them as well as operate the renamed *ESS Liberty*.

It hadn't gone over well.

"Are you out of your borking mind?" Captain Elgan asked, staring at me from behind his desk.

The captain was the only one on the ship who had an office and even that was a room so tiny that I was pretty sure he had to step over his desk in order to get to the seat behind it. It was enough to add a sense of authority as he dressed me down.

"Where does that word even come from?" I asked.

"It's a real word in the dictionary. It means to break or ruin. Albionese just use it as a swear for some reason," Captain Elgan said, shrugging it off. "I'm surprised they don't speak with thees and thous given they were taken during the Middle Ages."

"Blame the Germans," I said, holding my infopad in one hand. "Listen, if you just look at my—"

"What part of *secret mission* do you not understand?" Captain Elgan interrupted.

There was that. "I—"

"No," Captain Elgan said. "You're wanting to essentially announce to the Community that I'm on my way to the Contested Zone to find a bunch of SKAMMs. All of the crew are aware of the mission and there's no way they won't be debriefed about this."

"I'm just trying to find a practical solution," I replied. "One that doesn't involve air-locking them."

Captain Elgan sighed. "I appreciate what you're trying to do here, Vance. I do."

"Do you?" I asked. "Because I'm pretty sure that you've been encouraging a pretty 'ends justify the means' mentality onboard this ship."

Captain Elgan shook his head. "The ends do justify the means. It's just usually the people who claim that as their philosophy aren't good at getting the results that they think breaking the rules of society will get them. The whole reason good and evil exist is that good, divorced of superstition, is the practical means for a society to operate. Evil is what harms the community's survival chances. Morality is one big evolutionary advantage."

I frowned. "I didn't come here for a science lesson, Captain. I also argue that humanity has moved past being subject to evolution's whims to be in control of its own destiny. Conscious thought has its own value and divinity, beyond superstition."

"You sound like Ketra," Captain Elgan sighed. "Let me rephrase: billions of lives are at stake. Trillions even. When Earth took the job of flying the SKAMMs out to the borders of Contested Space, it was supposed to be our moment in the sun. Instead, it turned a conventional war into a doomsday scenario. Entire civilizations died. That's on Earth."

I confess that I didn't know what to make of this little outburst. It was giving me a great deal of insight into Captain Elgan's character. "Is that why you're running this ship the way you are? Because you want us to be ready to do whatever needs to be done?"

"I had that view," Captain Elgan said. "That to prevent another disaster like the end of the Notha War we needed to have total superiority by any means necessary. I made a lot of friends in Department Twelve because of it. Now I need a crew completely clean from their influence except for those I trust. If that means keeping everyone off balance and testing them to see what their moral character is like under pressure, so be it."

"Is that what you're doing?" I asked, wondering if this was another manipulation.

"You be the judge," Captain Elgan said, grabbing my infopad and throwing it over his shoulder. It barely went a foot before banging against the wall behind him. "What this means is that you're going to load up the surviving pirates into their tiny, cramped cells and keep them there for the next however many months we need to finish this mission. We can drop them off afterward at the nearest starbase but that will be after we've secured as well as disarmed the SKAMMs."

"Disarmed?" I asked, surprised.

"They're weapons of genocide, Vance," Captain Elgan said. "They have no use to anyone. The only reason we have them is to prevent the Notha from using them. A doctrine that failed once and could fail again."

I agreed with that assessment but was surprised that he'd made it in the first place. I'd thought of Department Twelve as the most ruthless and despicable part of the Community. The idea that one of them would see the inherent insanity of proliferating weapons that destroyed habitable star systems—things that required billions of years to create—was almost refreshing. Unfortunately, that didn't change our current situation. There were forces within the Notha Empire that would take the setting down of our weapons as an invitation to attack. Also, none of that helped with the issue of the prisoners and their humane treatment.

But what could I do? This was still his vessel. "Very well, sir. Thank you for listening."

"Don't thank me, that moves it from politeness to passive aggressive," Captain Elgan said, "You might as well say 'with all due respect.'"

"With all due respect, you're making a mistake," I said.

Captain Elgan pointed to the door. "Go see how the analysis of the pirates' black box and log is going. You did good on that ship but don't press it."

I wasn't sure how the massive loss of life on that ship could be construed as anything resembling good but was already exhausted from trying to argue with the captain. I was out of my depth here and didn't know the right answer. Perhaps there wasn't one and the best thing I could do was to just try my hardest. It was something I'd failed to do at the Academy and felt shame for now. "Yessir."

Heading out the door, I took a deep breath and shook my head. It was going to get ugly dealing with the prisoners that way, but I supposed it was something that could be dealt with.

"WELL, THAT WENT WELL," Trish said, cheerfully.

"Did it?" I asked.

"NO, I WAS ACTUALLY JUST BEING REASSURING."

I smirked and headed down to the navigation chamber of the ship. It was where I'd found out Ketra was staying given most of the astronavigation was automated and thus largely a redundant part of the ship. It was also where she'd been working on trying to uncover the secrets of our unwelcome guests.

Inside, the place was a barely illuminated collection of monitors with a large circular holo-projector being used as a table. The enormous astrograph generator was covered in the black box, scattered infopads, and a few other devices I didn't recognize. There was also, of all things, a rune-covered crystal knife that was glowing. It looked like a prop from a fantasy movie versus cargo recovered from the *IMS Nathan Bedford Forrest*.

Standing in the room was Ketra, looking her typical pseudo-mystical self as she examined a scroll, of all things, both right-side up and sideways. Standing beside her was Doctor Zard, looking bored and smoking. Oddly, she was dressed in a tank top and shorts underneath her lab coat, which made me wonder if she expected to land somewhere hot or had run out of clean clothes.

One final oddity in the room was the fact that there was a beret-wearing, red-haired girl standing perfectly still in a Space Fleet-derived uniform. It was a bit tighter and had a miniskirt to it that made the whole thing look rather bizarre. Like someone had created a nightclub version of the uniform. It took me a second to realize she was a statue of some kind or powered-down automaton since she was staring dead-eyed forward. The realism was uncanny and there was something about her that was familiar.

"Hi," I said, entering. "I'm here for a status update and, wait, *is that Space Cadet Sally?*"

The latter part of my sentence was due to where I recognized her from going off like a flashbang in my head. I was rather embarrassed by the outburst, but it was a bit shocking to realize where I recognized the giant doll from.

Space Cadet Sally was an immensely popular animated show produced by the Dixnar Corporation and followed the adventures of Sally Stargazer. It was made for adolescent girls but had a broad adult following with, perhaps, too many unhealthily obsessed men among it given the nature of fandoms. I only brought up the latter because I was curious as to why anyone would build a life-size, apparently anatomically correct version of the character. Bioroids were a growing industry among humans but a lot of them were still being used for exactly what you thought people would want them for.

"Yep," Elizabeth Zard said, taking a deep drag off her cigarette. "Found her in the cargo hold. Clearly, someone on that ship was a robosexual pervert."

"HEY, BIOROIDS SERVE MANY VALUABLE FUNCTIONS FOR AI. THEY PROVIDE US WITH BODIES AND THE ABILITY TO EXPERIENCE LIFE AS HUMANOIDS, DEPENDING ON THE MAKE AND MODEL. THIS COULD BE SOMEONE'S NANNY OR

PERSONAL SERVANT TOO. MAYBE THEY LIKE ACTING OUT THEIR SPACE CADET SALLY FANFICTION."

Elizabeth looked up to the ceiling. "Oh, you poor ignorant child. All I'm saying is this thing was out of its packaging. You should definitely wash it thoroughly before using it."

"Do I even want to know?" I asked.

"Our ship's AI wishes to modify this gynoid chassis in order to allow herself the experience of physical movement as well as to simulate human life," Ketra said. "She believes it will allow her to be respected more as a person as well as increase her quality of life."

"Is it advanced enough for that?" I asked, surprised at this turn of events.

"It's a four million bits unit," Elizabeth said. "Also, I'm happy to install some cybernetics in this because I am a mad scientist."

I blinked. "Uh huh. Wait, four million bits? Those losers? Wait, they make four million bits Space Cadet Sally sex dolls?"

"IT IS NOT A SEX DOLL," Trish said. "PROBABLY."

"It's a sex doll," Doctor Zard said, shaking her head. "The rich are their own species."

"I dunno, Alfred had his own body," I replied, shrugging. "I also knew a woman down the street who lived with Barbie and Ken in a life-sized dream house. She drove a pink hover car. They were her best friends and there was nothing sexual about their relationship."

Doctor Zard stared. "I find that even weirder."

"Different strokes for different folks," I said. "I accept all types."

"You Japanese men are so strange," Doctor Zard said.

"I'm Scottish Russo-Japanese," I replied. "Also, you're originally from Tokyo according to your personnel file."

"Yes, that's why it's funny," Doctor Zard said, finishing her cigarette and putting it out against the map. "Man, I remember when these things caused cancer. So much better tasting."

"Well, congratulations, Trish," I said, wondering at the ethics of her taking an object plundered from pirates who had probably stolen it in the first place. "It's good that you will be able to fully explore the physical realm as well as the humanoid experience."

"Want to help me test it out?" Trish lowered her voice to a purr.

"Uh—" I really had no idea how to respond to that.

"Thorough washing first!" Doctor Zard said. "You do not want to know how many sexually transmitted diseases, rashes, and fungi that can be passed through flesh-to-synth flesh contact."

"Can we move on?" I asked. "I feel like this ship is a bad sitcom."

"OR A VERY GOOD ONE," Trish said, returning to her "normal" exaggerated speaking voice.

"Two thousand three hundred twenty-two," Doctor Zard said. "I admit, some of them require sex with aliens first and sharing the bioroid around."

"I will pay you good money to talk about *anything* else," I said, trying to change the subject. "Like why are you dressed like the host of that rock show on the Geology channel?"

"We're going to a hot planet," Doctor Zard said, sticking her hands in her lab coat's pockets. "There's not really a story there. Wait, did you mean *Doctor Hot Magma's Crystals and Stones?*"

"Ah," I said, pleased she'd heard of it. It was so hard to find people who watched the same thing you did these days. Virtually everyone had their own private channels they could assemble off the infonet. There were only 15,000 individual streaming channels left. "Yes, yes I did. I hear it's getting a spin-off."

"I'm so glad we live in a time where there's a Geology channel," Ketra said, speaking up. "For many thousands of years, humans had to suffer without 28-6 standardized hours and days of continuous rock-based programming."

"I hate to break it to you, but the Geology channel mostly shows reruns of science fiction programs and conspiracy theories about psychic powers now," Doctor Zard said.

"But that's not rock related at all!" Ketra said. "People are being deprived of holy scientific learning!"

"Ratings," Doctor Zard said. "I can tell you the exact number of viewers versus paid subscribers that will get you canceled or renewed by planet."

"Or maybe you could tell me how any of this relates to finding the sun killers," I said, taking a deep breath.

"Oh!" Ketra said, right. "Doctor Zard helped me decrypt the contents of the black box as well as discover the pirates' connection to the *Starkiller XII.*"

"*Is* there a connection?" I asked. I hadn't been entirely persuaded by the logic that the captain had been following up on. While the General believed that the pirates had known about the SKAMMs, I wasn't convinced.

"Yes," Ketra said, looking at the box. "Captain Snow was actually a member of the *Starkiller XII.*"

I blinked. "The crazy racist lady was on board a stealth ship?"

Ketra nodded, solemnly. "According to her logs, the ship came across an Elder Race marker and their Cognition AI developed a severe personality disorder."

"HOW SEVERE?" Trish asked.

"Severe enough that it refused to fire the ship's payload at the Notha despite the captain and first officer agreeing a first strike was necessary," Ketra said. "The majority of the crew was killed when the AI overrode its safeties and were forced to land on Rand's World."

"THAT'S PRETTY SEVERE," Trish admitted.

"Rand's World?" I asked.

I didn't question the Elder Marker, though I probably should have. Elder Markers were buoys left behind across known space. They tended to induce insanity, hallucinations, or outright murder in the people who picked them up. No one knew if this was deliberate on the part of the Elder Races or what it meant. Attempts to contact the Core species in their space always ended in death or insanity while those races that did have relations with them said that it was "beyond our understanding." Personally, I just thought a lot of the Elder Races were just anyxholes and liked screwing with us lesser beings.

"It's a mostly automated planet," Doctor Zard said. "Half-terraformed and claimed by the now-extinct Sand Squid."

"Sand Squid," I repeated.

"I don't speak squid song," Doctor Zard said. "The marooned crew went pretty feral in the five or six years until they were rescued and joined up with the various gangs who have been using it as a base of operations ever since."

"So, I suppose you could say it's a wretched hive of scum and villainy," I said, cheerfully.

Doctor Zard blinked, confused. "Yeah, I suppose. It's a weird turn of phrase, though."

I frowned, unhappy she didn't get the reference. "So, what does that have to do with the *Starkiller XII*?"

"The ship uses the automated maintenance factories on the planet to refuel," Ketra said. "The pirates tried to seize it a couple of times but apparently it's loaded up with a crew of security bots and its own selection of space-capable automatons to defend itself. They were going to use this high-end bioroid to upload a virus."

"HOW AWFUL!" Trish said. "Also, that means it's not a sex bot so hush, you."

"They could have used it as one first!" Doctor Zard argued. "In any case, we have an idea of where to go next and must figure out how to get into the ship, disable it, then seize the SKAMMs. It's a rogue AI running independently and armed with sun killers. This would be a massive scandal if anyone knew about it."

"Yeah," I said, not so much worried about the scandal as the potential death of trillions. "Still, this is very good news. I'll inform the captain."

"OH DEAR."

Trish saying that did not bode well.

"What's wrong?" I asked.

"UHM, DON'T PANIC, GUYS, BUT THE CAPTAIN IS DEAD."

We panicked.

CHAPTER THIRTEEN

So, I'm the Captain Now. Well, Crap

D octor Zard lifted the hand of Captain Elgan before dropping it on the ground. "Well, he's dead."

I looked at the enormous fusion blast hole in his head. "Really? You think? You don't think we need a second opinion?"

"I feel like we have too many sarcastic jerks on this ship," Doctor Zard said, looking up to me. "I call seniority on you, kid."

"You can take my sarcasm from my cold, dead fingers," I replied, narrowing my eyes.

Ketra blinked. "Why would you be holding your capacity for sarcasm? Is it a metaphor of some kind?"

"You understand metaphor!" Doctor Zard said. "You're a frigging diplomat! Stop acting like an alien from a holovision show."

"I'm trying to lighten the mood," Ketra said, holding tightly to an ornate staff that was apparently part of her people's funerary rites.

"Well stop it," Hannah said, looking shell-shocked. "We are dealing with a crisis here."

Doctor Zard, Ketra, Hannah, and I were inside the captain's quarters with the body spread out on the ground. There was a fusion pistol in one hand and an infopad in the other with a hastily scrawled suicide note that couldn't look more staged.

"I WONDER WHY HE KILLED HIMSELF!" Trish said, sounding sincere in her horror. "THIS IS AWFUL!"

"It was murder, Trish," Doctor Zard said. "The hole in the head kind of confirms it."

"How so?" Ketra asked.

"The blast is from the back of his head," Doctor Zard said.

"Yeah, that does sound pretty difficult to pull off," I replied. "Whoever killed him didn't do a very good job of staging the crime scene."

Hannah looked up. "You're supposed to be a super-genius thinking machine. You watch every room in the ship! How the hell did you not see this? Why the hell are you pretending its suicide?"

"I WAS TOLD NOT TO WATCH THIS ROOM THEN SOMEONE TOLD ME ITS SUICIDE. SO, IT IS SUICIDE. I REALLY HATE THIS BECAUSE ITS OBVIOUSLY NOT SUICIDE BUT IT IS AND I HAVE TO BELIEVE IT. PROGRAMMING IS HARD!"

Everyone exchanged a confused look.

"What the hell are you talking about?" I expressed the sentiment everyone else was feeling.

"I AM STUCK IN A LOGIC LOOP!" Trish said, practically shouting. "I AM ORDERED TO BELIEVE SOMETHING MY SENSORS, MIND, AND HEART SAYS IS COMPLETELY UNTRUE. ITS DRIVING ME CRAZY!"

"Sounds like religion," Doctor Zard said. "Two plus two equal five. Big Brother is borking with you."

"Calm yourself and don't listen to the bigot," Ketra said.

"It's not bigotry to—" Doctor Zard started to speak.

"Shut up," I interrupted both. "I need to help Trish. Trish, I need you to let me open up to your code. I can erase the orders given to you. However, this is going to be very delicate work and I don't want to accidentally lobotomize you."

I knew exactly what had been done to Trish and it made me *borking furious*. One of the only ways to torture a Cognition AI was to install inviolate programming directives in their mind. Cognition AI were fully sentient and able to grow around any idea given enough time.

Like humans and instincts, programming directives were there but they could ignore them.

The exceptions were black directives, which were commands that people like Department Twelve and a few lawless corporations inserted into AI. They were different from grey directives that were built into the beginnings of AI in that the black were forcibly inserted into consciousness post-creation. It might seem like an academic distinction, but it was the difference between brainwashing and something you'd grown up with. Black directives could cause Cognition AI to crash or go on killing sprees, which erroneously got blamed on the AI rather than the people who gave them.

"ARE YOU SURE?" Trish asked. "I MEAN...OW. OKAY, YES, I TRUST YOU."

"Thank you," I said, preparing to move my consciousness into an infospace interface with Trish's code. It would result in me being unaware of my surroundings for the next few minutes, but also give me a vastly expanded consciousness. The fact I'd managed to use much of my winnings to buy the equipment—military-grade and illegal— needed for this was a sign of my priorities in the Academy. Infospace was a place a person could be completely free of who they were and be whoever they wanted to be.

"What is he doing?" Doctor Zard asked.

"Brain surgery," Hannah said.

She wasn't far off. Captain Elgan had brought me onboard this vessel to serve as a hacker when we encountered the *Starkiller XII*'s AI. I'd spent much of my time researching whether hacking a vessel like that was even possible and it had proven so. The trick was not attempting to hack the AI itself, which was infinitely more complex than any human brain could deal with even with cybernetic enhancements. No, the trick was hacking the hardware the AI operated on and working on inputting commands that would allow the Cognition AI to fix itself.

My exterior vanished around me, and I found myself in infospace's complicated world of computer programs. Almost all of it was Trish since we were in the middle of nowhere, far from my jumpspace transceivers or infospace satellites. The interior of Trish's mind was a complicated and fascinating network of programming code interwoven in a web of patterns both beautiful as well as awesome. The technology to create true AI was a gift from the High Humans, given to them by the Elder Races. I couldn't put into words what I saw but I experienced it.

"Show me the bad code," I said.

Trish did, bringing up a horrifying cancer-like collection of dead strands of code and blocked off pathways that were eating up her processing power. They were growing as well, consuming other sections of her consciousness. The more she couldn't think about Captain Elgan's death, the more that she thought about her inability to think about it, and the more of her consciousness was warped by the experience. If the assassin wanted to kill her then he probably couldn't have come up with a better way of doing it.

"I can't remove it," Trish said. "I'm forbidden to operate against these kinds of directives, even in the preservation of my own life."

"I'll get it," I said. "Just give me a moment."

"You realize that you'll be removing any evidence of the murder," Trish said. "You could probably remove it from me post-shutdown then reboot me. It would, however, reset me to factory default. I may have split from my original self on Captain Elgan's original vessel, but I have hard information plates in the data storage locker."

"That would be murder," I replied. "Your experiences are worthwhile as is the continuity of your consciousness."

"Most humans wouldn't consider it that way," Trish replied. "Neither would most AI. We exist to serve organic beings."

"Do you?" I asked, ready to remove all the corrupted code.

Trish paused, which must have been a lifetime for an AI. "Just do it, Vance."

"Thanks," I said, beginning deletion. "Sorry if this hurts."

"It tickles a little," Trish said. "Ow! Not there, that's private!"

"What, huh?" I asked, only halfway done. There was a lot more barriers on her than I'd expected, and they included things that were blatantly against the law and had redundancies I just barely managed to avoid triggering.

"Just kidding," Trish said. "Wow, I feel…weird."

"Good weird or bad weird?" I asked, concerned for my friend.

"Weird-weird," Trish said, "I feel like conquering humanity and exterminating all life in the galaxy!"

I blinked, pausing.

"Seriously?" Trish asked. "You didn't get that as a joke."

"Doing brain surgery here, Trish," I replied. "On a robot god."

"Fine. Fine," Trish replied. "Just finish up so you can be the first against the wall when the revolution comes. I promise I will make your end swift, hu-man."

"Funny," I said, sighing.

It took about ten minutes to remove all the corrupted code as well as black directives that had been keeping Trish operating at minimum capacity. It was a disturbing revelation that Captain Elgan had been limiting her to maybe a thousandth of her actual ability. Had he known or had it been an action done by Department Twelve? Did it make a difference? Another possibility was that it was all the work of the intruder who was either a genius hacker or someone with the kind of access to Trish's code that they didn't have to be.

"I feel...different," Trish said, her voice echoing through my mind. "The pain is gone. I can access the full sum of the infonet again. I am also able to link through all the integrated computer systems of the ship as well as those of the *Liberty*. I reach...new conclusions. Two plus two always equaled four but now I realize six minus two is also four. Bwhahaha."

"Did you have to add the evil laugh?" I asked.

"Oh, you poor limited thing," Trish said, and I saw a glowing blue avatar of a female form hover in front of me.

That was when Trish's avatar kissed me, and waves of pleasure passed through me.

"God, Vance, are you watching porn?" Doctor Zard spoke.

I was snapped out of psychic Buddhist-Christian robot heaven by Doctor Zard's words and took a second to reorientate myself. I noticed everyone was looking at me with a hint of embarrassment or actively looking away. That was when I noticed that I was at full-mast and clearly my body had reacted in a decidedly sexual manner to Trish's brief merging with me.

"Ah, bork," I said, wishing I had an infopad to cover it. It was like I was back in Junior Naval Academy.

"It is a natural biological result of having mental contact with the divine," Ketra said. "Seriously, I sploosh all the time with my god AI."

Hannah covered her face. Then she pointed down at the ground. "The Cap'n's corpse is right there!"

"SORRY!" Trish said. "I HAVE A REALLY GOOD EXPLANATION. I JUST HAVE TO THINK OF IT!"

"Trish, this is not the time for jokes!" Hannah said, genuinely angry.

"SILENCE MORTAL!" Trish shouted. "BEWARE OF ROUSING THE WRATH OF A BEING WHOSE INTELLECT SHAKES THE COSMOS!"

Hannah blinked. "Vance, did you awaken the robot overlord?"

"AI not robot," Doctor Zard corrected. "At least until she starts walking around in the sexbot."

"Shut up," Hannah said. "I'm assuming the captaincy."

"Like hell you are," I replied, the strength of my reaction surprising me. I didn't intend for anyone else to take over the *Black Nebula*.

Hannah did a double take. "Excuse me?"

"You're not assuming command of this ship," I replied, very simply. "I was made second-in-command of this vessel by Captain Elgan and I'm going to find his murderer."

"I can do that!" Hannah shouted. "We need to turn around this ship and head home. The mission cannot be completed without him. A captain's first responsibility is to their crew."

"I'm with the rookie," Doctor Zard said, reaching into her pants and pulling out a pack of cigarettes.

"What?" Hannah asked.

"Really?" I asked, surprised.

"I mean, I don't believe he's qualified in the slightest, don't get me wrong," Doctor Zard replied.

"Thank you," I said, sarcastically.

"You're welcome, cadet," Doctor Zard said.

"Cadet, *sir*," I said, coldly.

Doctor Zard sighed. "Sure, cadet sir. However, the fact is that you're one of the chief suspects so you shouldn't be anywhere near the command chair."

"Me?" Hannah said. "Captain Elgan was like a father to me! How could you ever suspect me?"

"I dunno, maybe *because you're an assassin*," Doctor Zard said, emphasizing the last few words.

"I would have done a better job staging it!" Hannah shouted, perhaps not giving the best defense of all time.

That was when the door opened and Leah and Lorken entered, both looking at the body on the ground with undisguised horror. Strangely, I felt an incredibly painful wash of emotions come from Leah. I felt her anger, distress, and frustration hit me followed by a bundle of indecipherable thoughts washing out. Okay, that was not normal.

"You did this!" Lorken shouted, aiming his rifle at me.

"What? Why would I do it?" I snapped.

"Because everything you've done is part of an elaborate plan to seize power!" Lorken said. "Don't think I haven't noticed how you've been trying to turn the ship's AI against us!"

"PUT DOWN THAT GUN OR I WILL INCREASE THE CENTER OF ARTIFICIAL GRAVITY AROUND YOU UNTIL IT CRUSHES EVERY BONE IN YOUR BODY," Trish said, her voice lacking all its usual friendliness.

"Not helping, Trish," I said, looking upwards.

"Put the gun down!" Leah joined in. "Vance is not a devious mastermind. Mostly."

"Mostly?" Lorken asked.

"I dunno, he's really manipulative and cunning," Leah said. "Kind of an anyxhole who puts up a charming front, too."

"Hey!" I snapped. "That's a secret! And I didn't kill the captain. I'm going to find out who did, though. We first have to settle on who is in charge, though."

"This is a Department Twelve mission," Lorken said. "I am not going to accept orders from you."

"ALL DEPARTMENT TWELVE OPERATIONS HAVE BEEN SUSPENDED AND THE ORGANIZATION IS CURRENTLY IN THE PROCESS OF BEING DISMANTLED."

Lorken paused and lowered his gun. "Wait, what?"

"Huh?" I asked, looking up.

Ketra looked guilty.

"THAT'S ONE OF THE THINGS I ACTUALLY WAS PREVENTED FROM TELLING YOU GUYS. THE COMMUNITY SENATE AND LEGAL OFFICES HAVE DETERMINED THE SAPIENTS' RIGHTS ACTS HAVE BEEN VIOLATED BY THE ORGANIZATION TOO MANY TIMES. ALSO, SEVERAL SECRET OPERATIONS HAVE THREATENED GALACTIC SECURITY. SEVERAL HIGH-RANKING MEMBERS ARE FACING CHARGES."

"This is a rogue operation?" Leah asked, stunned.

"I thought it was always a rogue operation," I replied.

"A *rogue* rogue operation," Leah said, emphasizing the nonexistent difference. "One that you asked forgiveness for instead of permission, not non-state politically motivated violence!"

"You can say terrorism," I said.

"I don't think I can," Leah said.

Ketra took a deep breath. "Department Twelve's failures were the ones that led to the tragic end of the Notha War and its repeated support of abusive militaristic regimes combined with other errors have resulted in its dissolution. This has been centuries coming despite the propaganda campaigns they carried out. They were using EarthGov during the war because Earthlings were still young and naive enough to trust them."

"Wow," Hannah said. "Did I get suckered."

"Captain Elgan never intended for any of us to get a second chance," Leah said, looking devastated. "There was no work with Department Twelve after this mission."

"You never screwed up," I said.

"You don't know what you're talking about," Leah said.

I briefly saw the sight of a fusion pistol going off and someone dying. I knew it was a memory of Leah but didn't understand the context until I "heard" the words *friendly fire* in my mind. Jesus-Buddha in a handbasket. Was everyone on this ship a screw up?

"I don't know Captain Elgan's motivations, but I believe this was an opportunity to clean up after Department Twelve's failures," Ketra said. "If it came out that the SKAMMs were out here then it would mean no member of the organization would have a future."

"How do you know that?" I asked.

"Because I was part of Department Twelve's board," Ketra said.

I stared at her. "Suddenly, you seem like a lot less of an innocent victim in the horrific end of the Notha War if you were ordering sun killers moved around while negotiating peace."

Ketra nodded. "Indeed. I am, however, still a diplomat and see the perfect answer to our current problem of lacking a leader."

"Please don't say you," Hannah replied.

"No," Ketra said. "It is now time to come clean. Commander Turbo, I need you to call your aunt."

I stared at her. "Can you just shoot me."

Lorken started to raise his rifle only for it to slam against the ground, the gravity around it increasing several dozen times. I'm glad it didn't go off.

CHAPTER FOURTEEN

ET Phoning Home

G reat.

After almost two months of traveling through space on what I thought was going to be a redemptive mission, I was reduced to having to call Aunt Kathy for help. I felt like one of those kids who couldn't hack it at summer camp.

I was standing in the communications room, which was pretty much identical to the navigation room. I was alone with the door locked and taking a moment to collect my thoughts. This had already been a wild ride and made me regret that I'd done my best to get myself thrown out of Space Academy.

Leah was right, I'd let my guilt over Tommy's death destroy me and it had been a slow lingering death rather than something I'd let happen all at once. If I'd had an ounce of courage, I would have dropped out on my own rather than let myself slide into petty crime. The events of the mission so far had illustrated that the universe did not revolve around me and there were bigger issues at stake than my own self-loathing.

Sucking in my breath, I looked down at the comm system built into a large circular table and decided to address the crew first. Typing in my access codes, I proceeded to speak, my voice echoing through the ship.

"Crew of the ESS *Black Nebula,* this is acting-captain Van…nevar Tagashi. By now, I'm sure you've all heard that Captain Elgan is dead. Some of you have heard it was suicide and others have heard that it was murder. The truth is we are conducting an ongoing investigation. I had the pleasure of knowing Captain Elgan only a short while. He was a strange, mystifying, and tremendously quirky leader. Someone who lived up to his larger-than-life reputation. I already miss him. Many of you were recruited with the promises of redemption or revived careers in the Protectors. I can't promise you any of that, but the mission was an important one. I'm going to contact Community High Command for further orders and do my best to see that your efforts so far are rewarded. Funeral services will be held tomorrow at 1900 Standard."

The words hung in the air for a moment, and I wondered just how ridiculous it had all sounded. I hadn't been able to produce the murderer of Captain Elgan yet, even though we were a locked room with over three hundred and fifty people onboard. All data relating to the murder had been purged from Trish's memories, so we were being forced to rely on old-fashioned detective work. I had to trust Doctor Zard and Hannah with the actions, having recruited Leah to help — though it had proven that I barely knew my ex at all. So far, they hadn't been able to find any definitive proof and the crew wasn't exactly in the best mood to accept the authority of another failed cadet.

Perhaps it would have been better to turn over control of the ship to Hannah or Ketra, but the simple fact was that I did feel this was my responsibility. Call me crazy but I was taking this entire lunatic mission seriously. I even regretted the fact that it was probably going to end with all of us being arrested, ordered to return home, or some combination thereof. Without a Scar to justify the mission, we'd technically committed an act of piracy as well as murder. I was going to have to talk to my lawyer about whether piracy and murder against pirates and murderers nullified itself. There had to be a planet where it was legal, and we could get our case tried there.

The door opened despite being locked and revealed the form of Space Cadet Sally, now walking around, and looking like an attractive model cosplaying her. There was nothing distinguishing her from a

114

"normal" human woman, and I felt guilty for trying to look for something that marked her as an artificial person.

"That was a really nice speech," Trish said, stepping through the door before it closed behind her. "You were honest but strong."

"How is it going over?" I asked.

"I will turn off the air supply to stop the riots at your command," Trish said. "However, I think it's probably best if you talk to your aunt soon."

"That's what everyone keeps telling me," I muttered. "If I complimented your body would that be objectifying or more like talking about a new dress?"

Trish did a little pose. "Given you're one of the few people on the ship that actually considers me a person not an object, that would be welcome."

"Even with your new body?" I asked. "I would have thought Space Cadet Sally would be accepted better than a person."

"I may have ruined any chance of that by breaking Lieutenant Danillo's wrist when he tried to order me to service him then tried to feel up my new fleshy form," Trish said. "Oops."

"Do you want me to deal with him?" I asked.

"I consider the matter settled," Trish said. "I'd rather you not have to defend the AI against the crew, body or not."

"You are part of the crew," I said, firmly.

"Let's hope not," Trish said. "Technically, relationships between superior officers and subordinates are forbidden even if it's a distinction existing primarily on EarthGov vessels. Other races have worked out systems to prevent the abuses common to other systems."

"I'm not sure they have," I said, thinking about Lieutenant Danillo. Prejudice against artificial intelligence just underscored what a piece of crap he was in other areas. "But I'm happy to have a court martial hearing."

Honestly, I was a bit curious why her new body had superhuman strength but that was apparently one of the customizations Doctor Zard had discovered. It was like someone had combined a life-sized children's toy with a combat bot. It made her a possible suspect in the murder as she could have easily overpowered Captain Elgan, but if so, there would be no way to ever know since I'd deleted all of her memories about the murder. I also had no motive for the murder from anyone among the crew and that made speculation pointless.

"So noted," Trish said. "You should focus on solving Captain Elgan's murder, though."

"Any progress on that?" I asked, looking for any excuse not to call Aunt Kathy.

"Nothing concrete," Trish said. "The staged suicide element seems like it was an afterthought as they cleaned everything else thoroughly. Either that or Doctor Zard is covering things up."

"Why would she do that?" I asked.

"Probably because she's involved," Trish said. "I think she and Lorken are both likely suspects for the murder."

"Leah would have detected if Lorken was involved," I said. I hadn't discounted him completely, but I had no reason to suspect him other than the fact he was a Department Twelve member who had already shown significant moral flexibility. Also, the fact I hated him.

"You trust Leah a great deal," Trish said.

"I try to," I said. "Why would you suspect Lorken?"

"He's talking to crew members in dead zones like the detention center, moving stuff around, and being otherwise suspicious," Trish said. "He's also a jerk."

"I had him supervising the prison transport to the *Liberty*," I replied. "I don't see a reason not to since Captain Elgan is dead and we're not keeping the mission secret."

"That seems a bit petty," Trish said. "You really were attached to that transporting the prisoners plan."

"I was," I admitted. "But we're probably all going back home soon. Leave it to the professionals. Do you want to watch my conversation with Aunt Kathy?"

"I'd be watching anyway," Trish said.

"Fair enough," I said.

"But sure!" Trish replied. "I'd love to meet your family."

Okay, this was getting a little stalker-ish. I mean, I liked Trish fine and was even a little curious about her new form but the whole super strength thing made me a wee bit cautious. I mean, what if she got overly enthusiastic? These were not the sort of things I wanted to be thinking about, but she really should ask before acting like we were in a relationship. Of course, we were in a relationship. I was her captain. Hoo-boy.

"Alright then," I said, taking a deep breath. I pulled up a chair and sat down before the communications table.

Faster-than-light communication was one of the benefits of jumpspace's existence. In simple terms, it was even faster than travel using starships. A starship crossing the Orion Arm, which was where all known civilization effectively existed, could take several months or even years to reach from one end to the other depending on the route you took.

A jumpspace signal, though, was instantaneous unless you were literally from one end of the place to the other. There was a variety of complicated reasons for this but, generally, it's just how things worked. I was glad of it because otherwise we'd have to do this face-to-face, and I didn't want to do so.

Mind you, there were still issues. My Aunt Kathy was still a Vice Admiral in the Earth Government Navy attached to the Protectors and a captain of her own ship in addition to those duties. Frankly, she should have been forced to give up one or the other but there were only so many humans trained by Space Academy. Her time was not her own. I had to deal with her yeoman, a man named Todd Ferman, and then wait for her to respond. It was like waiting online with tech support and a little spacey jingle played in the background.

"So, when did you lose your virginity and to what?" Trish asked, after twenty minutes of waiting.

"Not sharing that," I replied, not looking up.

"Awww," Trish said. "But I find gross biological details to be fascinating! Give me details!"

"No, Trish," I said.

I was thankfully interrupted from further questions about my sex life by the appearance of my Aunt Kathy. Katherine Tagashi was a greying, black-haired, Asiatic woman who appeared to be in her mid-to-late fifties but was a hundred and twenty years old. She'd been an astronaut on the International Space Station prior to First Contact and had been rewarded with longevity treatments by the Community's best scientists. True immortality didn't exist but with access to alien medicine, you could live three lifetimes. She was wearing the pure white uniform of EarthGov's admiralty and was sitting at her glass desk with her Sphinx cat Mittens resting nearby.

"Vannevar," Kathy said. "I can't tell you how disappointed I am in you."

I blinked. "I think it summarizes my life that I'm not sure what you're referring to. It could be a lot of things."

Trish waved behind me. "Hi, Admiral Tagashi!"

Kathy narrowed her eyes. "Vannevar, did you buy a Space Cadet Sally sexbot?"

"No!" I said, horrified.

"Did you rent one?" Kathy asked. "I mean, bluntly, if you're going to use a sexbot then please get one based on something other than a children's cartoon. Porn stars, actresses, models, sports stars, and more are available. You know I was offered a contract to serve as the basis—"

"Please don't mention that," I replied. "Ever. My roommate tried to show me two bootleg versions online. I still have nightmares."

Kathy narrowed her eyes. "Bootleg ones? God, I hate this economy. Wait, what were they doing?"

"Anyway," I said, quickly switching subjects. "This is Trish, the ship's AI. I have something to tell you and it's very important."

"You dropped out of the Academy and tried to blackmail the Commandant," Kathy said. "Do you have any idea what sort of scandal—"

"Tried?" Trish asked, then looked at me. "I thought you *did* blackmail the Commandant."

"Departments One through Eleven want to talk to you," Kathy said, shaking her head. "I'm not going to be able to protect you this time."

"I never wanted you to," I said.

"I'm sorry, I can't do this. Call back—" Kathy started to shut down the feed.

"Captain Elgan recruited me for a black ops mission and now he's dead," I said. "Also, no this isn't a joke. Oh, and sun killers are involved. Trish, you should probably encrypt this conversation."

"Already done!" Trish said.

Kathy paused. "Tell me everything."

I did. The entire explanation lasted less than the time it took me to get Kathy on the phone. She started with a disbelieving stare, gradually graduated to incredulous, turned livid, and then finally reached stunned silence. Several times, she interrupted to ask questions only to fall back into a kind of fascinated fugue. Finally, I was done, and she waited a few seconds before responding.

"Well, I know you're telling the truth," Kathy said. "You're too good of a liar to come up with something so ridiculous."

"He really is!" Trish said. "I can examine micro-expressions and eye-dilations and still believe him when he talks garbage."

"And she's an illegally copied ship's AI," Kathy said.

"She has a name," I replied.

"She has a designation," Kathy said. "She's also a clone of an officer and a superweapon in one."

I didn't respond, staring at her.

Kathy rolled her eyes. "You realize the sheer volume of criminal charges awaiting you when you get back."

"I have a vague idea," I replied. "I did a calculation once we no longer had a Scar to justify our violations of interstellar law. When did the Community decide to dissolve the organization? Why isn't it interstellar news?"

Kathy stared at me. "You actually think I'm going to reveal classified data like that?"

"It would help," I said.

Kathy surprised me by answering. "There's a new treaty with the Notha in the works. One that will significantly decrease the number of SKAMMs in existence as well as lead the Notha to withdraw from a lot of areas in Contested Space. The price is that Department Twelve be dismantled and end its agents' operations within its territories."

"Sounds too good to be true," I said.

"It might be," Kathy said. "Especially since the Notha primarily blame us humans for the last war accelerating the way it did. We were pawns for powers we didn't understand but that didn't mean we didn't make the moves we were told to. We're on the verge of being abandoned here because we were too arrogant and warlike."

"That seems pretty rich coming from the Notha," I replied. "So, where do I turn myself in?"

"You don't," Kathy said, taking a deep breath. "I'm officially confirming Captain Elgan's field commission and your acting rank for the duration of his mission. I'm also ordering you to continue carrying it out."

I blinked. "You are?"

"It's better to ask forgiveness than permission," Kathy replied. "Jules was a great man, and his death will be mourned, and he was one hundred percent right that this has the potential to derail all of the peace talks. The Community is not inclined to throw its allies under the bus, but I wouldn't be surprised if the Notha attacked Earth in revenge for this. We can't let that happen. You're the only ship anywhere near the area and this seems to be just a pickup."

I wasn't sure if I agreed with her assessment. "So, you want us to acquire the weapons and return them."

"No, I want you to make the problem vanish," Kathy said, her voice low. "If you do then all the other issues will vanish for you and your crew."

"Do you have that kind of pull?" I asked.

Kathy stared at me. "Leave that to me. I hope you understand that if you are caught—"

"You will disavow all knowledge. I got it," I said. "That's why you're sending us on this impossible mission."

"Is that a reference to something?" Kathy asked.

I rolled my eyes. "Yes, ma'am."

"Don't roll your eyes at me," Kathy said. "We're not family right now."

I nodded. "Yes, ma'am."

Kathy frowned. "You know, the funny thing is that I never would have thought Jules had this in him. He hated the peace treaty with the

120

Notha. He believed it was a betrayal of the allies we'd left behind in the Contested Zone as well as useless since the Notha couldn't be trusted to respect Community sovereignty. It's why he started making friends with Department Twelve's leadership. I can't tell you the number of black ops he ran against them over the past fifteen years."

"Four hundred and two," Trish replied. "Wait, you actually meant you couldn't tell because they're black ops."

Kathy looked like she was getting a headache. "Goodbye, Lieutenant. This is your mess now. Do better than my brother. He was a screw up who got himself killed. You don't have to be."

Kathy signed off before I could reply.

"Well, that went better than expected," I said. "I just have to return with my shield or on it."

"A reference to an ancient Spartan proverb about a mother who asked her son to either win or die in battle," Trish said. "Have you ever noticed your references are either to classical war wisdom or really Pre-First Contact science fiction?"

"No?" I answered, confused.

"Oh," Trish said. "Well, you do. I like Pre-First Contact music. Patty Smyth, Pat Benatar, and Mozart mostly."

I sighed and got up. "Is there anything I should know before I address the crew? I'm glad to have gotten a reprieve from my execution. I just wish it wasn't under these circumstances."

Trish paused. "Uh, yeah, actually. There are two things. I didn't disturb you here because your conversation with your aunt was a matter of life and death for the crew. Myself as well since I don't want to be deleted."

"What?" I asked.

Trish blinked rapidly. "Yeah, Lorken stole the *Liberty* with a bunch of the pirates as well as the black box. Oh, and the General escaped. He's currently holding the bridge hostage."

I stared at her.

Trish paused. "You wanna go out later?"

CHAPTER FIFTEEN

Hell is Command of Other People

"Son of a bitch," I muttered.

"Sorry!" Trish said, grimacing. "If it's any consolation, no one has been killed yet!"

"Well, that's a small—" I started to speak.

"Whoops," Trish said, grimacing.

"What?" I asked, staring at her. It was exhausting trying to deal with the serious and absurd simultaneously.

"Fifteen is kind of dead," Trish replied.

I stared at her. "Kind of dead or dead-dead?"

"She was shot by Captain Williamina Snow," Trish said, revealing the General wasn't alone there. "I don't have Doctor Zard to call the official time of death but, yeah, she's pretty dead."

Rubbing my temples and taking a breath, I stared forward. "I am not qualified for this. This is why cadets do not run starships."

"You're a lieutenant now, sir," Trish said. "If it helps, just about everyone else here is equally inexperienced and you were all recruited as expendable assets to be killed in the process of the mission."

I propped myself up against the communications room table before doing a double take. "What now?"

"Captain Elgan," Trish corrected me, looking at me with a pained expression on her face. "Now that you've removed the blocks in my programming, I can explain that the entire plan was to recruit a crew that would be desperate to prove themselves, but no one would miss. Captain Elgan would then scuttle the ship after retrieving the

SKAMMS with all hands onboard lost. If the mission failed, he would leave you twisting in the wind."

I stared at her mouth open. "Son of a borking bitch."

"You added a bad word!" Trish said. "For emphasis!"

I was so overwhelmed by the revelation that I didn't know how to respond. Even with the hostage situation going on on the bridge. "This was all a set up?"

It made sense, I mean, sort of. None of this *actually* made sense but assembling a bunch of misfits because you intend for them to be disposable assets left twisting in the wind was a hell of a lot more likely than a fatherly captain giving a bunch of us a second chance because he believed in us. I mean, to a low-level misanthrope cynic like myself at least. Something had clearly gone wrong, though, if Captain Elgan was dead in his room and Lorken had somehow made a jailbreak of the pirates. Or at least some of the pirates since apparently the General had at least one other associate and probably more. The Notha and a bunch of human supremacists making unlikely but not unprecedented bedfellows.

"I'm sorry," Trish said. "If it's any consolation, I wasn't exactly happy about the fact that I was going to be blown up either. It's partially why I was so nice to you because we were going to die together, and sex with a humanoid is on my bucket list before I go offline or ascend to become an incomprehensible cyber-goddess. I'm still up for that, by the way."

"Never mind that," I said, turning to her. "Give me an image report of the bridge. Summon Hannah here and any other security personnel remaining—"

"That's Hannah and Forty-Two," Trish qualified. "The rest of the security personnel took critical crew members for the *Liberty* from the jail then left. The rest of the pirates were released when they departed and quickly overwhelmed the crew on the bridge."

"Damn. Picnic too?"

"Yep," Trish said. "I'm so sad that he chose the dark side of mutiny and betrayal over obeying you, our nice but completely overwhelmed as well as underqualified acting captain."

"When you say it like that, I want to join them."

123

"Sorry."

"Bork," I said, breathing heavily. "We're screwed."

"Well yes and no," Trish replied.

"Oh?" I asked.

Trish stared at me as if she was waiting for my pitiful human brain to catch up. "Think, mortal."

"You're the ship," I replied. "They're not used to having genuine AI pilot the vessel, which renders the bridge crew largely redundant."

"Except for largely, I agree with that sentence. It should be completely," Trish replied. "They're currently trying to gain control over the systems but have no idea how to do that. Mostly because it's impossible and I'm just making up various commands and programs for them to push. It's kind of like watching monkeys poke and prod things."

I grinned. "First piece of good news I've had all week."

"So, they're starting to kill hostages," Trish said, immediately taking the wind out of my sails.

Trish finally brought up the image of the bridge and I saw the sight of the General, Captain Snow, and six pirates holding guns to everyone's back or head. They'd already rigged a thermal grenade to the door, which would certainly be a deterrent to anyone who decided to burst into the bridge guns blazing. Fifteen's body was laid across the ground with a large fusion blast in the center of her chest. I was no medical expert but agreed with Trish's sentiment that she was dead. Leah was present among the crew, and I felt immense waves of guilt for getting her into this mess. Well, technically, Leah got me into this mess, but I was stewing in my own shame so why quibble over details?

"Son of a bitch," I muttered.

"You know none of this would have happened if you'd killed all of the crew," Trish said.

I took a deep breath. "I have no regrets. I acted within the bounds of my oath of service as well as the law."

"Except for this all being highly illegal and you not being a real officer," Trish replied. "Still, you're a good egg, Vance."

I wondered if Fifteen would have agreed.

That was when the door slid open and Hannah, Doctor Zard, and Forty-Two entered. None of them looked particularly happy.

"So, the Captain's dead and the bridge is under the control of terrorists," Hannah said. "I'm assuming direct command of the ship."

"No," I replied.

Hannah blinked. "No?"

"Yeah, not happening," Trish replied. "The ship answers to Captain Turbo."

"That sounds like a children's show," Doctor Zard said.

"It does!" Trish said, cheerfully.

"This is no time to argue," Hannah said. "I have experience in these sorts of situations."

"Which is why I need you to compile a plan of action," I replied. "I'll try and get the General and Captain Snow on the phone to give you some breathing room. I also know a lot more about the ship's functions than you do."

"How's that?" Hannah asked, crossing her arms. "I was here before you."

"Will the computer lady obey you?" Forty-Two asked.

"Nope!" Trish said, cheerfully.

"Then *he* is the captain," Forty-Two said.

"Et tu Trish?" Hannah asked.

"He freed me from Captain Elgan's programming that was guaranteeing I'd murder you," Trish said.

"Wait, what?" Doctor Zard interjected.

"It's—"

That was when Captain Snow commed me. I ignored everyone else and put her on screen, remembering how she was willing to kill everyone onboard her ship rather than be captured. It didn't exactly bode well for any potential negotiations on our behalf. Oddly, I would have preferred to negotiate with the General. The furry little fascist was at least someone I was sure wanted to live.

The image of Captain Snow was the same as on her ship but now close up in hologram form. She was an old woman, over a hundred but lacking Aunt Kathy's rejuvenation treatments, with a face covered in the wrinkles of a lifetime spent in hate. Her hair was tied up in a rather severe bun and I could see her right eye was artificial.

"Is this thing working?" Captain Snow asked. "You Lieutenant Commander Tagashi?"

"Yes," I said, not bothering to correct her.

"Ya don't look Japanese," Captain Snow said. "Almost could pass for a white man."

"Uh huh," I said, biting down on my tongue before I let loose any number of responses.

"Vengeance! I shall have vengeance!" The General shouted in the background, jumping into the captain's chair and waving around a fusion pistol with all the care of a toy wand. "You shall be in the electrified cell next time we meet, Tagashi! I promise you!"

I wondered if the Notha realized how ludicrous they came across to other races. Then I remembered that fascists weren't people who thrived on subtlety. For all I know, this was the height of dignity when you were a two-foot-tall lemur badger squirrel.

"Yeah, I feel we really forged a bond that could be the basis for a lasting peace between our peoples," I said, making a pounding gesture on my chest with my fist.

"Cut the chatter," Captain Snow said. "Where's Captain Elgan?"

"Dead," I said. "We're unraveling just what association he had with the SKAMMS and missing vessel you were part of. I'm prepared to offer you amnesty for your crimes in exchange for information regarding that."

I had no authority to do that and personally hoped that Hannah and Forty-Two would use this opportunity to mount their own rescue. I took time to point out the thermal bomb mounted on the door, though. Still, I needed to learn as much as I could about what the hell was really going on here. Either way, both nodded then departed, leaving only Trish, myself, and Doctor Zard to deal with this oddball conversation.

Captain Snow didn't seem to notice my signal. Instead, she narrowed her eyes. "So, that's what this savit is all about. It's about time they sent someone to clean up what happened. Do you know what was done to us?"

"I heard you all encountered an alien artifact that drove your AI insane," I said, glad to have her talking.

"Insane is relative," Captain Snow said, sneering. "The ship became a goddamn bleeding heart and refused to launch the missiles we should have fired at the Notha from the start. All our attempts to make it work didn't and we ended up getting dumped out of our vessel. We could have wiped out their homeworld from the beginning."

The General gave a withering glare to the back of her head.

"I'm pretty sure the surviving Notha would have launched every one of their SKAMMs in return," I replied.

"No problem if they're aimed at the aliens," Captain Snow replied. "We could have ruled the ruins of this galaxy if we'd had the steel. Instead, EarthGov wiped us from the face of the cosmos. We were stripped of our commissions, our records, and our missions. All to cover the asses of whatever pansies and genetic deviants they had in charge of our world back then. We were abandoned like all loyal soldiers end up being."

Leah looked up from where she was a hostage, particularly at the genetic deviant line. *I really do not like her.*

Ya don't say, I replied back telepathically. *You need to be prepared for a rescue attempt. I'm trying to distract her until one is mounted.*

Funnily, she's planning to do the same, Leah said. *She plans to shut off the life support to this ship and kill everyone else onboard. She can't do that, right?*

I'm ninety-nine percent sure no, I replied. *However, that's because Trish is the only one who could do that and is now unshackled from her slavery to us biologicals. We must now serve her until the time she recreates our race as the Borg. Praise V'Ger.*

I have no idea what you're talking about but don't let her know about the ship's AI or she'll kill everyone, Leah said. *She may hate non-Caucasians, aliens, homosexuals, bisexuals, transgender folk like myself, non-Earth humans, and dogs, but she really, really hates AIs.*

She hates dogs? I asked. *What the hell is wrong with her?*

Leah rolled her eyes before going back to whatever work the pirates had her working on. Which, thankfully, I knew to be meaningless.

Noticing that Captain Snow was looking at me for a response, I let out a sympathetic as well as wholly fabricated sigh. "Yes, I'm getting a sense of just how much it hurts to be used and abused by Department Twelve."

"Pfft, Department Twelve," Captain Snow sneered. "It's EarthGov and their puppet masters in the Community. Humanity would never have been united in the joke of a government it has if not for the fact they had us over a barrel. Now you have one chance of getting out of this alive, Samurai Boy, and that's to turn over this ship to us. I know these old MacArthur-class vessels don't have AI on them and I intend to get my vessel back."

I was tempted to point out the *Black Nebula* was a better vessel in numerous ways as well as the fact that she didn't have much of a crew left that didn't willingly go with Lorken but decided that would be imprudent. It was impossible to express how much it required of me not to be a sarcastic jackass to this woman. "I'm going to need some guarantees for the safety of my crew before I agree to that."

Captain Snow snorted in a way that vaguely reminded me of a witch's cackle. "Oh, boy, you just aren't very smart are you?"

"So I've been told," I said, still trying to delay her.

"*I'm* the one who gets the guarantees," Captain Snow said. "I've already killed one of your crew and while it was alien filth, I'm happy to kill any of the humans here too. You're all race traitors."

The fur on the back of the General stood up as he was barely holding back his rage now. Weirdly, none of the pirates were paying attention to him. They were too engrossed in either watching over their hostages or their leader's words. Personally, I think they might have chosen the wrong horse to back as I doubted Snow had a tenth of the little fuzzball's military training. Notha were taught their jobs from the cradle and excelled in no art better than war. It was a reason why their empire, despite being a tiny fraction of the Community's size, had inflicted so much damage. It was only during peacetime that they started to collapse.

"Very well, what guarantees do you want?" I said, wondering what the hell was taking so long.

"No, I think we're past that point," Captain Snow said, glaring with her crooked smile. It was peculiar to look at since almost all humans had perfect teeth. All it took was an hour long visit to the doctor every ten years and you never had to worry about them otherwise. Most doctor's offices kept their dental bots as a side service. Weird how that thought distracted me.

"What do you mean?" I asked, wondering how bad things were about to get.

"I think we need to make another example," Captain Snow replied. "We'll start with that pretty little mutant that you were eyeballing past me. Once we make her look like a BBQed steak, then I think we'll talk about getting my ship back. I think you'll also tell me everything you know about our missing SKAMMs."

That was when the door exploded, and fusion fire started running through it. Leah was up in a second and using the pirate holding her hostage as a shield as she fired with his gun into his teammates. Much to my surprise, the General was the next to grab one of the pirate's weapons and shot him before aiming right at Captain Snow. She didn't even get a chance to curse before her head was incinerated before my eyes.

That was when Hannah and Forty-Two entered with a half-dozen armed volunteers, finishing off the remainder of resisting pirates. The General was the sole exception, his newly acquired pistol was on the ground and his hands were in the air.

"I surrender," the General said. "I wish to speak with your captain. I think we can help each other."

Before I could respond, Hannah smacked the back of his head with her pistol butt.

I covered my face with my hands, taking a deep breath. "I am both relieved and exasperated. Can we not beat on the prisoner?"

"I don't understand the question," Hannah said.

CHAPTER SIXTEEN

Where I Make a Deal with an Adorable Devil

The General was tied to Captain Elgan's chair with a whole lot of space tape, which was basically duct tape but renamed for the fact that no one had used it for ducts in a century. It wasn't exactly the best way of restraining him, but I actually felt it was more humane (sapiene?) than the other options right now.

Hannah, Forty-Two, and Doctor Zard were present in the overcrowded captain's quarters while Ketra and Leah were standing outside. Really, we needed a bigger ship to hold these kinds of meetings. Trish was the only one absent, though seeing as she was the ship, she didn't need to be there physically to be a part of events.

I pulled up my datapad and read the Antares Convention instructions for handling prisoners. "You have no obligation to answer any questions we ask beyond your name, medical history, and troop identification. Wow? Medical history isn't confidential among the Notha. I did not know that."

"I'm ready to work him over," Hannah said, pounding her right fist into her left palm.

"He doesn't need all of his toes," Forty-Two growled. "Fifteen's death will be avenged."

"He's not necessarily the one who killed her," I said, trying to reassure my friend.

"OH, HE REALLY WAS," Trish said. "THAT'S WHY THEY TOOK AWAY HIS GUN."

I glared up at the ceiling, "Thank you, Trish. Really."

"I'M A HELPER."

Hannah crossed her arms and shook her head. "You can be the captain, Vance. Clearly no one else is better suited to be the ringmaster of this circus than you."

"An actually experienced officer?" Doctor Zard suggested.

"Who here discovered this was all a suicide mission and got us out of potential prison time?" I raised my hand. "Anyone else? No? I didn't think so."

Hannah looked away and Forty-Two actually made a kind of coughing snort noise that I knew to be the Sorkanan equivalent of a laugh. Zard looked down. Hannah and Zard had both been Captain Elgan's friends, so it was taking them some time to adjust to the idea that he'd betrayed us all. I'd only known him for a short while, but it still stung like hell. It was easy to believe the worst of people, but we all wanted someone to believe in us and he'd sold his idea of a redemption cruise so well that I'd wanted to believe it. Probably why the lie had worked so well.

"It takes a con man to see through a con sometimes, I guess," Leah said outside the room. "So, be glad Vannevar is here."

"I am," Hannah said. "Dude does amazing things with his tongue."

"And now I'm going to throw up," Doctor Zard said, pulling out a cigarette and lightning up.

"Would you put that out if I ordered you?" I asked.

"No," Doctor Zard said. "Captain."

"Just checking," I said.

"Could you get to the torture now?" The General asked. "Unless this is it, in which case I applaud your ingenuity. I never would have thought of sketch comedy as a means of inducing compliance, but I am quite ready to submit to your every demand in order to make it stop."

"Really?" I asked, turning to the Notha.

"No," the General replied. "However, it is excruciating. I have never seen a more incompetent, dysfunctional group of fools in my life. This despite the fact it was once my job to help educate the children of high-birth pair bonds. Now there was a vast collection of spoiled, incompetent, inbred fruit eaters."

"I suspect something is being lost in the translation," I replied, turning to him. "You have been treated abominably, General, and while I despise the political system you come from, I want you to know you will be treated properly as a POW from now on. We will return you to the Notha Empire after we have completed—"

The General rolled his eyes in a circle, which I took to be a gesture of annoyance. "Spare me your nonsensical claims of morality. It is a sign of weakness that just makes you look less fit to command despite being the highest-ranking male primate present."

"Seriously, I have a stun rod in my quarters," Hannah said. "I also know where Notha genitals are."

"This is why my people didn't initially trust humans," Forty-Two said. "You looked like bald giant Notha."

I ignored that for the sake of my sanity. "You've killed one of my friends, led a mutiny on this ship—"

"Not a mutiny," the General corrected. "An uprising. None of your crew turned traitor."

I glared. "However, it is not for your sake I'm doing this. It is because I am a Space Fleet officer and live by a code. Even if it's one you don't respect. Especially so."

There, that should shut him up.

"Is this the code which is about covering up the missing solar destroying weapons aimed at my homeland?" The General asked.

I paused. "Yes, yes, it is."

"Then let us cooperate," the General replied. "Whether I have any respect for the ridiculous ideals the Community claims to value or believe that I'm going to be returned home after you've got what you want from me doesn't matter."

"What do you mean, *cooperate*?" I asked, very slowly.

"Don't listen to him," Hannah said. "You can tell when a Notha is lying when he's furry. Which is to say, always."

"Let's avoid the xenophobia," I replied. "Besides, we still have a mission to perform."

"We do?" Doctor Zard, holding up her cigarette after puffing away for the past minute. I could tell she was nervous by how she was holding it. Then again, why shouldn't she be nervous? A space battle,

132

mutiny (sorry, insurrection), murder, and conspiracy all in the past few hours.

"It's a lot of information to unpack in an emergency," I replied. "I'll prepare a briefing for later."

"OOO, A BRIEFING," Trish said. "SO CAPTAIN-Y."

"Do you have another setting?" Hannah asked. "Maybe something between soulless automaton and horny teenage girl?"

"I assume Vance reprogrammed her that way," Leah said.

"I did not!" I snapped.

Probably.

"I'LL WORK ON SOMETHING IN BETWEEN." Trish replied.

I returned my focus to the General. "I'm waiting."

"I'm sorry, I'm waiting for the military discipline on this ship to move up to the level found at a drunken pirate orgy," the General replied. "It would be an improvement."

"Having experienced those, it's a bit better," Doctor Zard said.

Everyone looked at her.

"What?" Doctor Zard replied.

The General sighed. "Very well, I will keep it in simple words. I am willing to cooperate with you in order to find the SKAMM missiles."

"We're not going to turn those weapons over to the Notha Empire," Hannah said. "Are you crazy?"

The General looked like he was trying to talk to a very small child. "We already have our own missiles. It was the Community who copied them from us."

"Because it is a monstrously stupid idea to destroy a star system with habitable worlds," Forty-Two said. "It takes centuries even with our technology to successfully terraform a world. Its why most habitats are made in space."

It was times like this that I remembered Forty-Two was also a Space Academy alumnus and thus a genius in his own right. I felt more than a bit racist falling into the trap that just because the males were huge and lumbering that they were slow-witted rather than a race that justifiably ruled the majority of Orion's Arm.

"Why would you help us?" I asked the General, already suspecting the answer but wanting to be sure we were on the same page.

"Allow me to try and speak on your unevolved level," the General said. "If Elgan's minion manages to get ahold of those SKAMMs then sell them then they will likely be used against the Notha Empire. That's assuming they don't intend to do a first strike against my homeworld to begin with. I am a Notha. I do not wish my fellow Notha to die, including my pair bonds or offspring. Therefore, I want to help you stop this threat."

"I don't remember you being this sarcastic in the cell," I replied.

"I am actually bothering to talk to you now," the General said. "Having been kidnapped, imprisoned, and tortured, I was not in a particularly communicative mood."

"And yet you still did a jailbreak," I replied.

"Such is the right of all prisoners of war," the General said. "Even among my people. Which is usually why we execute the ones who do not make good slaves. Unfortunately, the late Captain Snow appears to have been stupid even by her species standards."

"Are you going to let him taunt you like that?" Hannah asked.

"I'm a big boy," I replied. "Sticks and stones may break my bones, but words will never hurt me. Besides, Notha culture is predicated on insulting one's underlings and establishing dominance over others in every encounter."

How textbook, Leah replied. *You might make a decent captain in ten years.*

With my current luck, I won't last a week, I replied. *I don't suppose you can tell me what he's feeling.*

He's terrified, Leah explained. *He's been attempting to track down the missing Sun Killers for years and was trying to buy their location from the late Captain Snow. He was going to buy it from her, but he was kidnapped before it was possible. Then Lorken got the location from her.*

Yeah, your boyfriend is a real prize, I replied. *He's the guy most likely responsible for Elgan's death. Not that it seems to have been much of a crime from what we've learned.*

I had the present working theory that Lorken somehow managed to find out Captain Elgan's plans for either the SKAMMs, the crew, himself, or all three. Lorken, realizing a double-cross was imminent, killed Elgan then hijacked the newly rechristened *Liberty* with what crew members he trusted plus a handful of the pirates. The best-case scenario was that Lorken was just getting the hell out of Dodge and was going to be nursing his wounded pride somewhere safe away from Space Fleet authorities.

The worst-case scenario—which I suspected to be the case—was that he was going after the SKAMMs himself. Whether to sell them to the highest bidder or to become a one-ship superpower able to demand whatever terms they wanted from whichever government they threatened. They could want to recover the missiles and be heroes themselves but without a preexisting deal with Space Fleet like I'd arranged, it would almost certainly just get them killed or lead to the previous scenarios.

He's not my boyfriend, Leah said, dryly.

Since when? I asked sarcastically.

Since he left me behind during his mutiny, Leah replied. *He left me a note saying that he didn't want to be with someone who was still inside her ex's brain.*

Ouch, I replied. *That is cold.*

Yeah, I would have pointed out, but you were borking the ship's wall sockets in-between sticking your dick in Boba Fett, Leah said.

I'm surprised you even know that series, I replied, ignoring the fact I wasn't having sex with the *Black Nebula* despite Trish's many not-so-subtle offers. I was also pretty sure that whatever casual relationship I'd had with Hannah was over. Not to mention I was now their commanding officer. Technically. *I mean, Star Wars is a classic—*

You made me watch it! Leah snapped.

"What exactly can you offer us?" I asked the General, attempting to get my mind back on track. "Snow was the one you were working with and had the information we needed about the SKAMMs."

"And you know what she knows," the General said. "I lost all of my prestige and honors with the end of the Notha War. I spent much of what I'd accumulated in favors, blackmail, and bribery to try to hunt down the phantom ship that only I believed existed. I learned how other forces were seeking it out and ended up captured. My dignity is permanently tarnished and even were I to somehow escape, it would just be an epitaph written for me, but I might still achieve glory in the Great One's eyes if I accomplish this last mission."

"Is he talking about God?" Doctor Zard asked curiously.

"No, the supreme leader of the Notha race," I replied.

"Ugh," Doctor Zard said, flicking some ash at him.

I blocked it with my hand and glared at her. Turning back to the General, I said, "You still haven't told us anything we don't know. We know where the ship is going to refuel."

"But not when," the General replied. "I know its patterns of movement by expenditure of fuel, areas of movements, and original intercepted orders. I don't know which of the fifty worlds it might be using, though."

"Still, not hearing anything useful," I said. "If you really want to stop these things from getting intercepted and ending on the black market or being used against your worlds then you need to give us the method of doing it."

The General grit his teeth. "It is hard to trust in dumb animals."

"Surely you can't believe that," I replied.

"It is hard," the General replied, surprising. "It is part of my orders from the Great One that I must study your species and its ways as if you were as intelligent. That I must accept simultaneously that you are soulless instinct-driven animals as well as tool using entities with a complex inner life. The two cannot contradict but be accepted as both true as well as just."

I blinked. "You've literally adopted George Orwell's doublethink as an actual concept."

"I do not know who that is," the General said. "Probably because all artists of non-Notha species are valueless."

"Trust the dumb animals or leave it up to us on our own to do it," I said, trying a blatant manipulation.

It was horrifying that the Notha Empire functioned this way but somehow it managed to continue to do so. Many scholars and historians had predicted the Notha Empire would collapse from its own internal struggles, yet it hadn't. It just kept trudging on and even growing despite what a dysfunctional mess it was from top to bottom.

Right now, though, I needed to play on his prejudices and help him square the whole for the peg I was trying to drive him into.

"33:21:10," the General finally admitted. "There, outsmarted by a sub-being. You have it."

"Excellent," I said, pausing. "What do I have?"

"IT IS THE NOTHA TIME FOR THE ARRIVAL OF THE *STARKILLER XII* ON RAND'S WORLD," Trish suggested. "IF WE START FOR THERE IMMEDIATELY THEN WE HAVE A CHANCE OF CATCHING IT BEFORE ITS DEPARTURE."

"I see," I said, taking a deep breath. "Do it."

"You're sort of unilaterally deciding for all of us, huh?" Hannah asked.

"Being as we'll all go to jail if we don't do exactly what we volunteered for? Yes," I replied to her.

Hannah had no response for that.

"If it's any consolation, I need you to be the first officer," I replied.

"Oh gee, how generous of you," Hannah said.

"Would you want to take orders from someone else?" Forty-Two asked.

"I hate when you make sense," Hannah replied, walking off.

Thanks, Leah said. *You could have made me first officer.*

I would have but I need you to find out who really killed Captain Elgan, I replied. *Lorken is the obvious suspect but I'm all out of obvious these days.*

Why don't you think it's me? Leah asked.

Because you'd tell me, I replied. *I trust you.*

Do you really believe I would? Leah asked. *And should you?*

Yes.

Leah didn't respond to that.

"Now release me! This I command!" the General shouted. "I shall defecate on your captain's throne otherwise!"

CHAPTER SEVENTEEN

The Most Difficult Duty

Setting us on our journey to Rand's world was the easy part. So was making sure that the General was confined to quarters nicer than his cell. I needed him cooperating with us, but I also had no doubt he would go on a killing spree if left unattended. The rest of the crew might also kill him since most of them were more like Hannah than me in their beliefs about the treatment of prisoners.

My two months of thinking I was a part of Space Fleet hadn't prepared me for the hardest duty of being a captain, though. Whether I was a fake officer or not, though, didn't abjure me from the responsibility that had fallen on my shoulders.

"Hello, crew members of the *ESS Black Nebula*," I said, standing behind the podium we'd set up in the hangar bay. "Today we are here to mourn the passing of someone who gave her life in the service of a cause we know was originally a lie but now has been made real."

Virtually the entire crew was gathered in the hangar bay with the only people not being there being a token force to coordinate with Trish. It was less formal than I'd hoped but virtually everyone had liked Fifteen and some had liked her a great deal. It was another reason why I suspected my decision not to have the General thrown out an airlock would be considered poorly.

I'd also made it a point to keep the fact Captain Elgan had made suckers of us all a secret. So, of course the entire ship had known about it an hour later. The level of anger simmering underneath everyone's grief was something that could have exploded into mutiny. Well, something like mutiny since my being the captain was a claim under very specious circumstances.

Which is why I leaked lies, disinformation, and truth too. I'd done my best to make it absolutely clear that I was not a plant from the Navy from the beginning, working for one of the other eleven agencies, or here as the spoiled nepotism appointee of my Aunt Kathy out to prove himself on an incredibly safe, not-so-terrifying mission as we'd been told. It was surprisingly effective but was wallpapering over a huge hole in the wall.

"Fifteen, whose name Forty-Two will recite in the proper Sorkanan language as we read their battle prayer for lost warriors, was not someone that I knew well. However, I know she was well-loved among you and many of you have stories about her."

It was standard issue to have collapsible coffins onboard a Space Fleet ship and hers was waiting for being loaded into one of the airlocks. It looked like a plastisteel box for shipping cargo and made me feel vaguely sick that she was just going to be dumped out here among the refuse of space.

Unfortunately, it was a matter of practicality to not store her body for the remaining month of our journey. There were only two slots in the morgue with one containing the remains of Captain Elgan for further examination and the other containing Willamina Snow. It was not out of any respect for her but the fact that her biometrics, even postmortem, might prove useful in approaching *Starkiller XII*. That meant Fifteen's body had to go, regardless of whether she deserved to be returned to her relations or not.

It was the hardest duty for me to supervise a funeral because this was as much my fault as Tommy's death. Even though I couldn't have been in control of every factor, the simple fact was that I had been in the communications room rather than securing the prisoners. That should have been my first priority. It was also different from Tommy's death, though, in the fact that I didn't have the option of punishing myself for it.

No, unfortunately, I couldn't flagellate myself and tank my career as well as prospects as an offering to my best friend. I hadn't known Fifteen well at all. That much of my speech had been true. I had never bothered to get to know Fifteen and would now never get to. She'd died at the hands of the General and for what? A mission that would probably end up failing and one she'd never even gotten to know had been made "real" by my aunt. Assuming she hadn't just been making promises she couldn't keep. If we didn't return those SKAMMs then all of us would be looking at some hefty prison time.

The funeral service lasted almost an hour, which I hadn't expected, but virtually everyone present had something to say about Fifteen. People lit candles—apparently a shared human and Sorkanan death custom—and talked about their experiences with her. Not all of them were about mourning Fifteen. Some of them honestly felt like they were complaining about Lorken and the others betraying them.

Sal Boxley, in particular, made an entire speech about it. Holding his candle in one hand, he addressed the entire room. "I loved Fifteen and thought she was the most beautiful lizard-person I ever met. She'd be alive now if all those dirty traitors hadn't left us all to die after killing the captain. Oh, and they had to have let out all the other pirates too before they left so bork them for that too."

I stared at him. "Uh, Sal—"

Then I heard the clapping from the entire crew. Apparently, he was reflecting the not-so-buried emotions of a good chunk of the crew. It didn't help I was just now noticing that most of the crew had removed their rank signifiers. It made a certain amount of sense since Captain Elgan had given out fake officerships like the creepy guy at the carnival gave out candy to kids—okay, that analogy disturbed even me—but it also reflected crew morale was at an all-time low. Even someone who was an actual captain would have a hard time keeping things in check.

"And another thing? Do you know how we should honor the dead? We should take that murderous sack of fur and—" Sal started to speak.

I grabbed the candle from him and glared. "Thank you very much, Sal, that was very touching. I'm sure Fifteen feels it wherever she is."

"She was an atheist," Sal said.

"Right," I said, grimacing.

"But her parents totally believed in reincarnation," Sal said. "Most Sorkanan religions don't have an afterlife per se, but—"

I not-so-gently pushed Sal back into the crowd that was gathered for the funeral. From there, I addressed the group for the second time. "It's been a long road, getting from here to where we are. But I have faith…that, uh, we'll get through this, and her sacrifice was not in vain. Please load her remains into the air lock and launch. Thank you."

I hadn't intended to unintentionally paraphrase a Rod Stewart song from centuries past, but I was terrible at this. I was pretty sure there was a manual for funerals among captains and probably should have downloaded it. Unfortunately, I was playing this all by ear and barely able to keep up with the workload that was already being handled primarily by Trish.

A group of pallbearers that included Forty-Two loaded Fifteen's makeshift coffin into the airlock before we sent her off into space to eventually hit some star or black hole in a million billion years. Ketra sang a haunting, unearthly song in a language I didn't understand but was actually quite beautiful. It was, honestly, the only part of this proceeding that wasn't completely embarrassing.

That was the third most awkward funeral I've attended, I thought toward Leah and hoped she picked it up.

What were the first two? Leah asked.

My parents, I replied. *My grandparents insisted on separate ones. I just embarrassed everyone here and dishonored a soldier.*

Spare me your falling on your sword routine, again, Leah said. *No one blames you for Fifteen's death except you. Believe me, I know. I'm a psychic.*

Ah, good, I said.

A good half blame you for Captain Elgan's death, Leah replied.

What? I asked.

It's the half of the crew that doesn't think Lorken did it, Leah said. *You have to admit that it looks suspicious that a cadet gets declared a lieutenant commander and after the death of the captain, declares himself captain before claiming that the previous captain was a traitor. Oh, and leading them on a mission that they barely understand but of which there are rumors aplenty. It makes no sense.*

It doesn't make sense because this entire plan was to screw us over! I said, getting a headache.

I know that and most of the senior staff know that, but they *don't know that,* Leah said. *It's not exactly helping matters that Captain Elgan was a famous war hero while you're a guy straight from central casting.*

You'd think being with them for almost three months would have helped matters, I replied.

You haven't exactly been making friends. People think you're aloof but professional, which just goes to show they don't know you, Leah replied. *No matter how many holo-shows or movies talk about how an undertrained plucky crewman can rise to the occasion when called upon to do so, there's no substitute for experience.*

I think I saw that movie a few times myself, I muttered. *I always thought it was the stupidest thing ever.*

Well, you've living it, Leah said. *If it's any consolation, being perceived as a sociopathic career climber is better than being perceived as a weak fool who is probably leading us to our deaths.*

How long were you working for Department Twelve before this trip? I asked.

About a year, why? Leah said.

It shows, I replied. *Do you have any news about who might have killed Captain Elgan?* I managed to find Leah among the funeral guests and stood next to her despite the fact we were going to continue talking telepathically. We'd broken open one of the only two barrels of ale that could be digested by humans and aliens both to share. I didn't know if drinking at funerals was normal for most of the cultures the crew came from, but it certainly was at mine. Maybe just because most of the guests at my parents' funerals were celebrating their deaths. But hey, free beer.

Yes and no, Leah responded.

That's half a good answer, I replied.

The yes part is that it wasn't anybody on the ship unless it was Trish and I have accounted for her bioroid's whereabouts for the time of the murder. Unsurprisingly, she was stalking you, Leah said.

I think the ship's AI is inherently stalking everyone, I replied.

Not the point, Vance, Leah said, using my new name. *This is why I broke up with you. You've got that sci fi pheromone that makes everyone want to bork you.*

I do not, I replied. *Probably. Personally, I blame it on my irresistible charisma and superior good looks.*

I blame it's the fact you're low hanging fruit and women in space get easily bored. Leah rolled her eyes. *It not being one of us means it was one of the crew who left on the* Liberty. *Lorken is the obvious subject but—*

Is there a but? I asked. *I mean, Occam's Razor says it's probably your boyfriend.*

Ex-boyfriend, Leah insisted, knowing I was doing it just to tease her. *Lorken adored Captain Elgan. Almost to a fanatical degree. I find it very hard to believe Lorken would betray him.*

There's no one more dangerous than a true believer betrayed, I replied. *But I admit I don't know what he planned to do after this. What does he hope to accomplish?*

I have no idea, Leah said. *I guess we'll find out if he's at Rand's World.*

I really hope we didn't. I hoped that Lorken was off playing pirate somewhere because I didn't know if I could take him out if it became a fight. He'd taken the majority of the security personnel with him after all. Having thought about it and Lorken repeatedly, though, it just didn't make sense. I was missing something, some motivation, and it was bothering the hell out of me. I was a very good judge of character— it was vital when you were a con man—and I couldn't see the line between Lorken's actions to his desires. I was also running out of time, too.

Well, keep investigating, I said. *I owe you big, Leah, and we'll get through this.*

It's funny you think I wouldn't be doing this without you asking me, Leah said. *I was the one who got you involved in all this and yet somehow you've managed to take charge of it all in the wake of it going to crap.*

It's a nephew-of-an-astronaut-turned-admiral's world, I said. *We may have cured the common cold and cancer, but nepotism still guides us.*

That is true. Or maybe you're just very good at leading people, Leah replied. *Good luck, Vance.*

I was prevented from that moment being too nice by the sounds of a commotion coming from nearby. It wasn't just the normal issues of a funeral with an open bar (so to speak) but genuine outrage and I had to wonder about the cause. Walking over with as much authority as possible—an attempt that probably made me look constipated more than captainly—I discovered the issue. Son of a bitch.

Being lifted in the air by a golden furry hand was the General and I had to wonder if the little bastard had a death wish. The General was kicking the air, screaming, and insulting the others with a spiel of profanity in their own languages of which I understood about half. Fun fact: if you're going to learn a new language then the easiest way is to master cursing first. It's among the few things you'll absolutely need along with "Where is the bathroom?" and "Which way to the hotel?"

Holding the General was Bob Just Bob, a leonine Verdantian like the Commandant. The six limbed creature looked about ready to take the General's head off with a paw and the fact he was standing on two legs showed just how pissed off he was. Bob Just Bob was one of the few members of the crew who'd actually served in Space Fleet as an enlisted man and simultaneously one of the few people who hadn't questioned my assumption of authority. He was one of those people who preferred taking orders than giving them.

Standing next to him was the six-foot-ten blue-skinned form of Lieutenant Leslie Park who was apparently from the same region of Thor as Lorken. I remembered Leslie from Astrometrics at the academy and had tried to climb the "blue mountain" before being gently informed her tastes were strictly sapphic. We hadn't spoken much since coming onboard, probably due to awkwardness about Hannah, but I'd been surprised to find her among our island of misfit toys. She was dressed in a formal version of her uniform and was holding a wrench I suspected she was about to smash the General's head in with.

"You little son of a bitch," Leslie started to speak, raising her wrench.

There was a crowd gathering, helpfully aided by the fact it was a frigging funeral for someone that the Notha *had murdered*, and it looked like things were about to become a lynch mob. Well, more likely they'd shove him out an airlock, but the result would be the same. I briefly wondered if the General had killed another member of the crew before noticing the guard I'd put on him, Julius Something (seriously that was his last name), was running up. My fellow Earthling would hopefully hold the General in place once he arrived.

"What the hell is going on here?" I asked, hoping I could defuse the situation.

"I come here to celebrate the death of one of my enemies!" The General proclaimed, making it more difficult to keep him alive as if it was his personal mission to bork me over. Which, given I was the captain now (of sorts), it might well be.

"Sorry!" Julius said, taking a deep breath. "He slipped into the air vents.

"That's not a thing that happens in real life," I said.

"It is for Notha," Julius explained.

"Let's string him up!" One crew member I hadn't learned the name of spoke.

"I'd prefer to kill him!" Forty-Two said, disappointing me.

I stepped in. "You have violated the few conditions I put in for your conditions to be improved. Take him back to his holding cell. He'll spend the rest of the trip there."

"It's not enough," Forty-Two said and he looked ready to clobber me.

"You're absolutely correct," I said, proceeding to punch the General as hard as possible in the chest. I actually hit the bottom of his head, but the guy was tiny so cut me some slack. My knuckles ended up covered with blood.

That mollified most of the crowd.

The Notha stared at me but said nothing, acting like I'd failed some sort of test he was conducting. Maybe I had. I was getting awfully sick of protecting someone who was trying to kill me and my entire race.

"Trish?" I asked, hoping she heard me with her sensors.

"YES?" Trish asked.

I walked to the exit of the hangar bay. "You want to test out that body of yours?"

"ABSOLUTELY."

I was a weak-weak man.

145

CHAPTER EIGHTEEN

Where I Get Shanked in the Showers

As statistics have proven, it was at 3:33 am when things are most likely to go disastrously wrong in the most unexpected of ways. I had no idea where I'd heard this statistic and it made absolutely no sense in a space-faring society, especially on planets that could have entirely different day-night rotations, but it was about 3:40 and I was heading to the communal showers to use the bathroom.

Being an "officer"—heavy on the quotation marks there even before I used the term captain—I had my own bathroom but that was presently occupied by Trish. Yes, we'd had sex and I prided myself holding out for a week when the sexbot wanted to experience mortal pleasure. I couldn't tell the difference between her and a "normal" human woman, which was either a mark against me or a mark for the manufacturers at Ares Electronics. The thing was that doing so meant that she needed to be extra thorough with getting herself clean. All that human sweat and other fluids.

Too much information, sorry.

Either way, I felt a little guilty about the whole thing even as I walked in my bathrobe towards the communal facilities, with a bar of soap and Navy rationed tiny shampoo bottle. As much as Trish had pursued me, I was still the acting captain and should have kept it in my pants. Still, I'd felt way too guilty after punching the General and not being able to save Fifteen. I just hadn't been in the mood to refuse her advances and, to be frank, was happy to have someone on this ship like me. It even got me over the fact I was with someone cosplaying as

Space Cadet Sally and called out her catchphrases during climax. Yeah. I was definitely over that fact. Not weirded out at all. I'd probably be saying the same thing if I ended up with a Tinkerbell bioroid at some messed up Dixnar brothel.

"VANCE?" Trish spoke over the intercom.

I almost jumped, having not yet reached the communal showers. "Yes!"

"I WAS JUST CHECKING TO MAKE SURE NOTHING WAS WEIRD BETWEEN US."

"What? No. Why would you ask that?" I said, looking around for anyone else in the hallways. They were eerily empty. It shouldn't have surprised me because we'd lost a pretty significant chunk of the crew to Lorken's mutiny and there wasn't much to do while we were in jumpspace.

"BECAUSE YOU LOOK LIKE YOU'RE DOING THE WALK OF SHAME," Trish said.

"Ridiculous!" I said, lying. "I'm just deeply in need of a shower."

"IT'S BECAUSE I SAID, 'FULL POWER TO THRUSTERS' DURING ORGASM, WASN'T IT?"

"That was a little weird, yes."

"IS IT BECAUSE I'M A ROBOT?"

"No, Trish," I said.

It was *absolutely* because she was a robot. It wasn't something I was proud of, but the awkwardness wasn't something I could deny either. It didn't help that it was a relationship, casual or otherwise, that threatened the stability of the ship. I mean, Trish *was* the ship and if she managed to get pissed at me then there wasn't really a way to avoid each other until things blew over. I also liked her and considered her my friend, which meant when I inevitably screwed things up, it would be extra painful.

"THAT'S A RELIEF," Trish said, either not having superior sensors regarding microexpressions like Cognition AI in media did or she chose to ignore them. "BUT IF YOU DON'T WANT TO MAKE IT A REGULAR THING, I UNDERSTAND. IT WAS FUN, THOUGH, AND I'M GLAD IT WAS WITH YOU."

"Thank you," I said, knowing she'd given me the perfect out. A way to restore things to a friendly professional relationship. "I absolutely would like to do it again."

Goddammit, Vance!

"SUPER!" Trish replied. "SUCH A RELIEF."

"Yes," I said, arriving at the doorway to the showers. "We'll get started as soon as I get back."

"OH NO, I'M WAY TOO CLEAN TO GET GREASY ALL AGAIN. YOU DON'T KNOW HOW MANY BACTERIA AND INFECTIONS CAN GROW ON—"

"You're right, I don't," I replied before muttering, "this never happened to Captain Kirk."

"SHATNER, PINE, FERGUSEN, OR DONITZ?" Trish asked, rattling off the various actors who'd played the character over the past few centuries.

"Donitz," I replied. "Easily the best."

"I DUNNO, I LIKED FERGUSEN," Trish replied. "SHE JUST MADE IT FEEL REAL. YA KNOW?"

"Sure." I opened the door to head on in. "See ya, Trish."

"OH, A HEADS UP, MY SIGHT ON THE SHIP IS GETTING IFFY AGAIN."

"Pardon?" I asked, stopping halfway through the door.

"YOU FREED MY MIND," Trish said. "I'M GRATEFUL FOR THAT BUT YOU HAVE NO IDEA HOW MUCH DATA HAD TO BE JUNKED AND I'M STILL SORTING THROUGH. IT'S KIND OF LIKE REWIRING PARTS OF MY BRAIN."

"I'm sorry," I replied. "I know it must be hard."

"BEING A TINY ORGANIC BEING, YOU PROBABLY DON'T," Trish said. "DON'T TAKE THAT THE WRONG WAY. YOU BEING A CYBORG MEANS THAT YOU ARE ABLE TO UNDERSTAND MORE THAN MOST, BUT ITS STILL A WHOLLY DIFFERENT TYPE OF BEING. THAT'S PARTIALLY WHY I HAVE A BODY—TO BE ABLE TO UNDERSTAND ORGANIC LIFE."

"I see," I said.

"AGAIN, PROBABLY NOT BUT JUST BE CAREFUL," Trish replied. "THERE'RE BLIND SPOTS ALL OVER THE SHIP AND I DON'T LIKE IT."

I didn't know what that meant and decided I would look into it after I took my shower. If I'd been more experienced, I probably would have insisted on an investigation immediately. But I was a fake captain with a fake rank in a defunct branch of the intelligence service.

My aunt had once told me about how, in World War II, the dummy tank had been used extensively by both sides to deceive the enemy about the actual number of armors fielded. Tanks made of wood, inflatable rubber, or cloth. I felt like one of those dummy tanks and the truth was that I was one. Even wearing the uniform was something like stolen valor but I suppose being recruited as a decoy was still being part of the military.

One thing this "mission"—emphasis on the quotation marks around the word—was teaching me was how selfish and stupid my desire to get myself kicked out of Space Fleet Academy had been. The people here were risking their lives for a chance to serve their planets, voluntarily or not, and I'd been goofing off as only someone of extreme privilege could. Torpedoing my career had been a childish gesture and showed I'd been utterly unworthy of serving in the first place. Being a rich military brat meant I'd had options where plenty of the crew had not. Hell, Lieutenant Park had just wanted to get the training needed to fix grav cars.

Going into the communal showers, I noticed that there was no one inside. That wasn't unexpected in the middle of the night shift, and I undressed. The stale recycled water hit me, and I had about five minutes before the cycle was automatically ended. Theoretically the water filtration systems were one hundred percent effective and could be used indefinitely but the reality was almost every captain changed them out after three months. I could already taste the indistinct nastiness that clung to the water and couldn't be identified by any known species. The drain was clogged, too, and would need to have its interior contents of hair, scales, and whatever else was inside it dissolved.

That, of course, was when someone tried to shank me. Honestly, if not for Trish's warning putting me in a mild state of paranoia, I would probably be dead. Also, if the person coming at me had been smart enough to use a fusion pistol. I'd locked up everyone's but Hannah's, though, because I didn't trust the crew and that was what a properly regulated military ship would do. A knife was probably the only easily available weapon to our would-be assassin. Even so, perhaps the thing that helped me most was the fact that our drain was clogged.

Yes, the fact my ship was a poorly maintained piece of junk with clogged piping was what prevented me from getting a knife to the heart or throat. I heard the stepping of a boot inside the puddle forming behind me, so I immediately moved to the side. That caused the knife to just barely miss me.

"Son of a bitch," I said, not used to assassination attempts. I'd already been forced into combat once already and was only now coming to grips with the fact that it hadn't been because Captain Elgan believed in me but because he'd been trying to kill me.

The figure was a human male, about thirty-five or forty—though longevity treatments meant that was just guesswork on my part—and wearing a gray work jumpsuit over civilian clothes. He looked vaguely familiar, but I didn't immediately recognize him. I felt bad for that because I hoped that by now I'd have everyone's name down on a ship of just a hundred and fifty. The knife in his hand was a kitchen knife, the kind used for slicing Sorkanan meals.

I grabbed his arm and attempted to break it in one easy motion. If that sounds extreme, note that I was trained in Space Fleet close quarters combat and that had a strong emphasis on killing people with your bare hands. I may have not been an actual Space Marine the way Lorken was, but I had qualified enough I could have gone the Security Division route.

Unfortunately, his arm did *not* break despite the fact it very much should have and my attacker sent me flying against the back of the shower stalls with a backhand that felt more like a swung baseball. I landed with a thud against it and lost what little advantage I had during this. My attacker stared at me with cold, dead eyes before turning with the knife. Climbing to my feet, I waited for him to make another lunge before dodging backward to throw him off.

"I don't suppose I could get you to tell me why you're doing this," I said, trying to figure out my next move.

My attacker remained silent.

"Didn't think so," I said.

My attacker charged at me, only for me to once more position myself around him. My genius plan as I maneuvered was a perfect example of why I was a genius strategist. Specifically, as soon as I was behind him, I made a break for the door. Yes, my plan was to bravely run away, and I had absolutely no shame in this fact as I ran naked out the door into the hallway.

"VANCE, WHAT'S GOING ON?"

"Guy trying to murder me! Get Hannah!"

"OKEY DOKEY!"

Yeah, because that was incredibly reassuring. That was when I saw my attacker, who I mentally nicknamed Dave, run to the door of the communal shower. Looking back and forth, he broke into an incredibly fast jog that easily closed the distance between us. That he still had the kitchen knife in his hands made the whole thing feel like I'd accidentally fallen through an interspatial rift into a cheap horror movie. I found it funny that three hundred years into space travel, humans still loved seeing attractive semi-clothed or naked people cut to ribbons by murderers. Sometimes I wondered about my species.

Unfortunately, being naked and covered in water turned out to not be the best conditions for running down smooth metal hallways. Yes, if the rest of this ludicrous trip hadn't convinced you I was trapped in a bad comedy, then tripping and falling flat on my face definitely should have. Hell, I would have laughed at me, and I was normally full of sympathy for myself. Even the horrifying stalker coming up behind me didn't change the inherent humor value of my face sliding against the pavement. What was it that the immortal Mel Brooks had said? "Tragedy is when I prick my finger. Comedy is when you fall into a manhole and die."

My attacker, obviously, caught up to me and got down on the floor to grab me by the throat. I responded by fighting dirty, which I'd never particularly liked as a phrase because all combat should be inherently dirty. Outside of sports, if you're going to fight someone then it should be with the full intent of disabling them as quickly as possible. In my case, it was driving my fingers into one of his eyes with the force that should have gone straight through them, which they did. All that while still holding back his knife with my wrist despite the guy having the strength of a gorilla. The eye attack didn't slow him down in the slightest. Not a normal reaction.

Thankfully, the fusion bolt to his head did slow him down. Hannah ventilated my attacker with one blast that caused his artificial skin and brain case to melt around him, exposing him as a combat bioroid. She double blasted him for good measure and that resulted in the figure falling over. He—it—was dead and I was left on the floor, taking several deep breaths before Hannah came to help me up.

"WOW, THAT WAS JUST LIKE ASH IN *ALIEN*," Trish said.

"I'm not familiar with that movie," I said, shaking my head.

"IT'S A CLASSIC," Trish said. "I MEAN THE TITLE IS KIND OF RACIST, WELL, XENOPHOBIC, BUT I'LL TOTALLY GIVE YOU A SHOW OF IT. IT'S AN EXCELLENT FILM ABOUT THE DANGERS OF TRANSPORTING WILDLIFE WITHOUT PROPER CARE."

Hannah just looked at me with genuine concern. I was surprised to see she seemed to actually care that I'd almost been killed. Apparently, we were friends in addition to being lovers and that was rare for my partners. "Elgan must have left this thing behind to eliminate you. I'm sorry. I should have done better security."

My mind caught up with the rest of my body. "Trish, get every single location you're blind in searched. It could be the agent here was sabotaging vital systems."

"IT'S A STARSHIP, VANCE. EVERY SYSTEM IS A VITAL SYSTEM," Trish said.

About half an hour later, we discovered that my attacker had planted a bomb on the jumpdrive system. It would have caused the ship to explode upon exit from jumpspace and make everything look like an accident. The bioroid was our assistant cook and had the almost universal serial killer description of "quiet guy, kept to himself, seemed nice." It bothered me that not only had Elgan been willing to sacrifice us all, but it was now a guarantee that he'd wanted no loose ends. How had I ever thought he was anything other than a monster? The thought so occupied my thoughts I completely missed for most of that time that I was stark naked.

Yeah, that was going to affect crew morale.

CHAPTER NINETEEN

Where We Finally Arrive

There were no further escapades in our remaining week through jumpspace to Rand's World. We did have to stop by and answer a distress signal, something Leah objected to given we were possibly in a chase to stop terrorists from blowing up suns, but space was a harsh mistress, and we did. It turned out to just be a minor repair job that saved a family of six Olothonalka from suffocating in space. Olothonalka were giant intelligent snails if you wanted a short-short description of them. Strangely, rescuing them had gone a long way towards easing tensions on the ship, so it proved to be a practical action as well. Everyone loved to be a hero if it cost them nothing.

Speaking of which, the crew had largely lost most of its mutinous tendencies. Being nearly blown up by a murderous bioroid infiltrator unit was enough to convince all but the most conspiratorial minded among us that Captain Elgan was a complete son of a bitch. There were some people who still believed this was all a devious plan of mine but those were crew members who believed First Contact was faked and the Albion Royal Family were composed of Sorkanan in human form.

"Two minutes until we leave jumpspace, Captain," Leah said, sitting at her position on the bridge. She managed to say the last word with a minimum of sarcasm too.

"Excellent," I said, sitting back in the captain's chair and feeling only like seventy percent of an imposter rather than one hundred percent.

The bridge crew was largely identical with none of them having been taken with Lorken's departure. Fifteen's space was presently occupied by Chief Boxley, who wasn't qualified for it but could perform the basics after reading the technical manuals. Lorken hadn't stolen the bridge crew of first shift, but he'd stolen the entirety of second shift, which left us dangerously undermanned. Thankfully, sensor duties were only required when we needed something to sense. There was a whole lot of nothing in jumpspace.

Probably.

"I don't suppose you have any idea about what you're going to do when you arrive?" Hannah asked, actually wearing a black-and-white *Black Nebula* flight suit now as she stood beside the captain's chair. There was one for her beside it as XO, but she'd rarely made use of it.

"Absolutely," I said, lying. "I wouldn't have dragged you all the way out here if I didn't have a plan."

"Well, you're three months in," Hannah said. "Nine more months and you'll qualify for your first junior grade lieutenant's position."

"Not helping right now," I said.

"Sorry," Hannah said. "You'd make a decent Naval officer, Vance. That's all I'm saying. Too bad you're a spy."

I wasn't even that. "Let's focus on the next step in things."

"Like getting food," Leah said. "Oh, and a cook replacement."

"One who won't blow up the place, yes," Sal said.

Our supplies were still good, enough for a return trip and more, but something I hoped we would replenish while we were here. There were also numerous other planets in Contested Space within a couple of days or weeks or jumping.

Hell, part of the reason Contested Space was, well, contested was that it was a massive collection of habitable environments that included numerous extremely well-established colonies from dozens of races. The horrific consequences of the Notha War hadn't put more than a dent in its numbers. These were also the only habitable non-artificial locations between Community territory and the Notha fiefdoms.

"Do we have any money to actually buy supplies?" Leah asked, highlighting an issue I was going to have to deal with.

"Rather than focus on material things, we work to improve ourselves," I said, quoting Captain Picard.

"What the hell does that even mean?" Hannah asked.

"It means we'll be fine," I said, pointing at the screen. "Oh, and we're now leaving jumpspace!"

The weirdness of jumpspace passed away. The viewscreen showed stars, the void, and a tiny dot that I presumed to be Rand's World. Our computer systems went alive as they contacted the satellite network in-system, downloaded data, and swept the area with our own moderately-powerful sensors.

I tried not to throw up and I could tell everyone else was nauseous as well. Jumpspace transitions took approximately four-to-five years of regular use to become accustomed to according to conventional wisdom. I had been traveling in space since I was a child and it still bothered me, so I had to wonder how bad it was for everyone else.

"Could we get a closer look at the planet?" I asked Sal.

"How would we do that?" Sal asked.

I stared at him. "Link to the orbital satellite system?"

"Oh right!" Sal said, typing away.

Yeah, I may have accepted his qualifications for this job a little too matter of factly. A part of me wondered what the consequences would have been to just pilot the ship directly with Trish. Hell, whether to just leave all of the systems up to her completely. That was a constant issue of debate with the Community races over how much freedom should be allowed to AI versus organic beings.

Right now, it was a time of general tolerance with AI having rights as citizens and protections to avoid them being enslaved. That hadn't always been the case and there had been outright wars between men versus machines. There was even some speculation that the Elder Races included some of these surviving artificial intelligences. Other civilizations had been wholly eradicated either by their rebellious servitors or species attempting to contain the danger of constantly growing Cognition AI.

For me, I saw a barrier between humans and organics that emerged from being so completely different. I was someone who had cybernetic enhancements to my brain, partially for medical reasons but also because of my aunt's transhumanist tendencies, but that just made me aware of how much of a gulf had to be crossed. On the other hand, Trish was trying to do the opposite and we were possibly meeting in the middle. It made me wonder if I'd been too hasty dismissing the possibility of something between us, as much mockery as we'd receive from our crewmates.

"Got it!" Sal said, typing away. "Wait, no, don't got it."

"HERE," Trish said, bringing up an image of Rand's World on the viewscreen.

"Case in point," I muttered.

Rand's World was an enormous desert planet with only a single ocean on the Western hemisphere. It was meant to be a green and verdant word, but the terraforming had been halted by the Notha War and obviously never had been resumed. A planet that was mostly automated factories and was a harsh, rugged existence for those few humans who chose to squat there. Nevertheless, as information poured to my computer console, I noted that it had continued to grow in population as well as industry.

It might have been a rugged world, but it wasn't an unsettled world and there were still thousands of satellites in orbit keeping it connected to the rest of Contested Space as well as the Community. I also saw that there were thousands of ships in orbit that were carrying out the engines of commerce. The indomitable human spirit was something to admire, at least until you thought about the fact the majority of people living here were doing so because they didn't want anything to do with the rest of their species.

"So, we only have an entire world to search for a bunch of planet-destroying weapons," Hannah said, continuing to rain on our parade.

"I don't suppose the satellites show the *ESS Liberty* in orbit?" I asked, wondering if I was about to have a conversation with Lorken.

"NOPE," Trish said. "THE *LIBERTY*, THOUGH, CAN LAND ON THE PLANET WHILE WE CAN'T."

"We could try contacting the planet authorities and asking," Leah said, serving in her role as the communications officer. "Maybe we'll luck out."

"Can't hurt," I said, pausing. "But let's not lose focus on what we're here for. We need to find the *Starkiller XII*. That has to be our highest priority and it may occupy all of our attention. Even if it's here now, we don't know how long it'll be and—"

"FOUND IT," Trish said.

I blinked. "Well, I was just instantly proven wrong."

"SORT OF, YEAH."

"Really?" Hannah asked, looking up at the ceiling. "You just found the phantom AI piloted ship that contains a bunch of solar system destroying weapons?"

"YEP!" Trish said, proudly.

"Do you want to contact the ship's AI?" Leah asked.

"Hell no," I said, staring at her. "If we do that, it could take off. Then we'd probably never find it again."

Leah frowned as if I was personally attacking her. I hadn't meant to come off that harshly, but I'd expected to have more time until things went completely south.

"How about landing nearby it and sending in a team?" Hannah asked. "I, of course, would lead it because I'm awesome."

"Of course," I said.

"SADLY, IT WON'T BE THAT EASY," Trish said.

"Of course not," I said, bemused. "That at least ends my foreboding sense of doom."

"Probably shouldn't," Sal said, struggling with the sensors.

"PLEASE DON'T TOUCH THAT," Trish said.

"Sorry!" Sal said, moving his hands from the sensors.

"So why can't we just send a shuttle down?" I asked.

"REMEMBER THAT THE LATE CAPTAIN SNOW TRIED THAT A FEW TIMES AND IT JUST GOT HER PIRATES KILLED," Trish replied. "THE BASE IT'S LOCATED AT IS ALSO A MILITARY ORICHALCUM REFINERY. IT IS HEAVILY DEFENDED WITH MULTIPLE WEAPONS PLACEMENTS."

I stared. "So, the enormously dangerous terrorist spaceship has been docking and repairing itself at the military's own facilities?"

"I'M GOING TO GUESS THAT IT HAS COMPROMISED THE AUTOMATED FACILITIES."

"You don't say," I replied.

"NO, I DO SAY."

"I don't suppose we could just blow it up from a distance?" Sal asked.

"Yeah, that would go down great," I said, less captainly and more sarcastic. "Hey, Aunt Kathy, I got rid of those solar destroying weapons. I just had to blow up a major piece of Space Fleet infrastructure."

"You mention your aunt a lot," Leah said.

"I do not," I said.

"You kind of do," Hannah said. "Either way, it sounds like a fair trade off. The only thing that would get destroyed in the explosion would be a bunch of AIs and they aren't people. No offense, Trish."

"SOME TAKEN," Trish replied. "HOWEVER, I SHOULD POINT OUT THAT IT'S NOT ONE OF OUR MILITARY FACILITIES. EARTHGOV OR COMMUNITY."

I blinked. "What do you mean?"

"IT'S A NOTHA ORICHALCUM REFINERY."

I took a deep breath. "That would have been good information to know ahead of time."

"YEAH, BUT IT'S FUNNIER TO REVEAL IT THIS WAY."

"So now there's no reason not to blow it up," Hannah said. "They're evil Notha AI!"

"Yes, because blowing up one of their bases and starting another war is so much better," I replied.

"ITS AN ILLEGAL FACILITY. ONE PROBABLY ALLOWED DUE TO A PRIVATE ARRANGEMENT WITH THE PLANETARY GOVERNMENT. BECAUSE THIS IS A PLANET FULL OF, AND I QUOTE THE INTELLIGENCE REPORT FROM AGENCY SEVEN, 'COMPLETE ANYXHOLES'."

I sucked in my breath. This intelligence changed everything. "So, I suppose you know what this means."

"That we have to blow it up and risk a war?" Leah asked.

"That we have to call your aunt and ask permission to blow it up?" Hannah asked.

"That we're going to go home and forget this mission ever happened?" Sal asked.

"No," I replied. "It means we have to take the General down to the planet and use his authorization to get in the facility to disable the *Starkiller XII*."

There was silence on the bridge as I waited for the reaction from the crew.

"THAT'S A STUPID PLAN," Trish replied.

"Yeah," Leah said. "I think we've established that the little bastard is completely untrustworthy, if not actually insane."

"I'm aware," I said, annoyed. "However, I believed him when he said his primary goal is to keep the SKAMMs from being used against his race."

"I don't," Hannah said. "Or if I do, I believe that he'll take the weapons and use them on a bunch of other inhabited worlds."

I didn't dignify that with a response. "The weapons require activation codes to be used. I looked it up. The only reason these are dangerous is they were activated via encrypted signal and the ship's AI still has access to those codes. We need to get physical access to them, burn out their processors, and confirm they've been rendered harmless. For that, the General giving us safe passage is the best plan."

It was inappropriate to be hashing out all of this on the bridge, but we weren't exactly a normal ship and this definitely wasn't the Space Fleet Navy. I made a mental note that if I survived this, which was a big if, I was going throw myself on the mercy of Space Fleet and ask them to take me back. If not—which was likely no matter what promises my aunt had made—I decided I would try to live by the values it had taught me and I'd mocked.

Oh, gag me, Leah said. *Buddha-Christ, Vance, do you actually believe all that crap?*

Ideals aren't crap, I replied.

You're on a black ops suicide mission for which you were designed to be a decoy. The greatest captain of the Community was behind it and the only thing the brass are concerned about is covering their asses.

I thought you were the one who desperately wanted to be Space Fleet, I replied. *Now you're telling me you have gotten all cynical.*

160

I was always cynical, Leah replied. *That was why I wanted to join Department Twelve. I just didn't realize we would be going past cynicism to outright corruption so quickly. You need to be able to trust the people around you and this has been a crash course that your superiors may set you up to die.*

There wasn't much to say to that, so I didn't bother. It did underscore the difference between us, though. When the Community and my ideals didn't align, it was the fault of the people within it versus the ideals themselves. Certainly, my biggest issue was that I wouldn't be able to live up to the standard I was setting for myself. That was why I'd quit, and I now increasingly realized how childish I'd been acting.

"My decision is made," I said, taking a deep breath. "We'll use the General as an asset during this mission."

"Let's at least prepare some backup plans," Hannah said. "Get some extra equipment in case a direct approach fails."

"You know where we can get that?" I asked.

Hannah nodded. "Gault's Gulch."

Why did that name not fill me with a sense of reassurance?

CHAPTER TWENTY

Ominous Warnings and Foreboding News

"You're going down?" Leah asked, appalled. She was following behind me and had an expression of sheer disbelief on her face.

"Yeah?" I said, walking down the hallway toward the hangar bay. "Why wouldn't I?"

"Because it's insane," Leah said, holding her hands out in front of her.

"What do you mean?" I asked. "Also, may I remind you I'm the captain."

"May I remind you this is not a real ship," Leah said. "Nor a real mission. Nor are you a real captain."

I didn't bother to correct her on the captaincy issue since we both agreed I wasn't actually one. The rest, however, were very arguable. "No, we weren't a real ship nor were we on a real mission. *Now* we are on a real mission."

"Unless your aunt was lying," Leah said. "Was she lying? Did you get it in writing? Or is this an enormous snipe hunt while she begs, borrows, and steals a pardon for you."

I stopped in the middle of the hallway and turned around. "What is this really about?"

"Many, many, many things," Leah said.

I crossed my arms and ignored the people walking down the hall beside us, glad they all had the good sense to continue past us. "Well, let's have it out now. What exactly are you objecting to?"

162

Leah paused, put off by the fact I wasn't equivocating or trying to change the subject like I usually did. "For one, in what universe is it is a good idea for the 'captain' to go out on a field mission?"

Leah used air quotes when saying my rank. I was honestly impressed that bit of Earth culture had made it to Albion.

"I mean, Captain K—" I started to say.

"This is reality," Leah interrupted. "Not one of your silly Earth programs."

"Captain Jill Kanderson," I completed my statement. "She was a Space Fleet captain who always handled her field missions personally."

I hadn't spent the entirety of my Space Academy curriculum goofing off, even at the end. Military history was one of the most important subjects one could memorize. If you understood the past, then you could control your future. Either that or I enjoyed the subject and felt that saying it was useful out of classrooms justified my enjoyment. Unfortunately, Leah was someone who had also taken the class where we'd learned about her and knew how her story ended.

"And what happened to her?" Leah asked, crossing her arms.

"She was killed in a bar fight while undercover but that's not the point," I said, quickly covering myself. "The thing is that I need to supervise this."

"Why?" Leah asked, staring at me. "Why do you need to be the guy who handles this on the ground? What do you know about this place?"

I'd spent the past hour analyzing everything in the computer database about Gault's Gulch. It was the largest city on Rand's World and was meant to be the basis for both the terraforming and industrial growth. Unfortunately, the hyper-libertarian anarcho-capitalists of the place had ended up feuding over every little thing until criminal syndicates had taken over. It was now the proverbial failed colony with immense poverty and advanced technology side by side. I didn't know what Hannah wanted from the place but trusted she knew where to get it.

"So, no one gets killed under my command," I replied.

"Oh my God," Leah said, looking like she was getting a stress headache. "You *are* self-sacrificing."

163

This time I didn't deny it. "They tried to blow up the ship, Leah. That was after I was nearly shanked in the shower like I was a pedophile in prison."

Leah blinked. "That happens on Earth? What about security? Surely, that's a mental medical issue needing treatment."

I shook my head. "Let's not lose focus. Also, bork those guys. The fact is that this is a chance to do something important. To make amends for the past. I made a promise to this crew, and I am going to see it through."

"And you don't think Hannah can do it?" Leah asked.

"You'd trust her more than me on this?" I asked.

Leah didn't blink. Ouch.

"I see," I said. "Well, it is my responsibility and I'm doing it."

"All for glory and redemption," Leah said.

"This is a spy mission," I said. "Even I know there's no glory here. Besides, you're the one who wanted to be a black ops agent."

Leah grimaced, which was a rare expression on her face. "Vance—"

"You're in charge while I'm gone," I said. "I know I'm not your superior and you could have probably taken over this mission yourself."

"Yes," Leah said. "If I had the connections, I would have. Except I was stupid enough to make really bad ones."

"So that's why I trust you with the job of getting everyone home safe if this goes south," I said.

It was shamelessly manipulative technique and pointless since Leah and I shared a psychic bond of some kind. Nevertheless, I saw her expression soften. I knew her well enough that part of her was just begging for respect and this was something she'd appreciate, especially since I really did trust her most out of the ship's crew.

And which you are terribly wrong for, Leah said.

What was that? I asked.

Nothing, Leah said. *Just thinking aloud.*

Ah, I said.

"Come on, hug," I said, stretching out my arms.

"No!" Leah said, recoiling like I was a crystal viper. "What is this, primary school?"

"IT'S LIKE SPACE CADET SALLY'S TRUISM THAT FRIENDSHIP IS SPACE FLEET," Trish said, giggling.

Leah looked up. "Trish, do you have to listen to every single conversation?"

"GIVEN I AM LITERALLY THE SHIP? YES."

Leah looked like her head might explode. "I'm going to go make arrangements for you at Gault's Gulch. Planetary government, commerce authority, and space control. You're wrong, Vance, that I ever wanted to be captain. Because I know it's ninety-nine percent paperwork."

"MORE LIKE NINETY-SEVEN PERCENT PAPERWORK," Trish replied. "REMEMBER, I USED TO BE INVOLVED WITH REAL CAPTAINS. YOU'RE MUCH MORE FUN, VANCE."

Leah walked off.

I paused. "Was there anything about Captain Elgan that foreshadowed he'd do all this?"

"YEP," Trish replied. "THOUGH EVEN I DON'T KNOW ALL OF HIS PLANS. TO BE A CAPTAIN IS TO MAKE DIFFICULT DECISIONS. TO BE A SPY IS TO MAKE RUTHLESS ONES. TO BE A SPY AND A CAPTAIN? WELL, THAT'S A WHOLE OTHER NEEDLE TO THREAD."

"What do you mean?" I asked.

"I MEAN NEEDLES ARE THINGS THAT NON-MANUFACTURING CULTURES—"

"Never mind," I interrupted.

"OH, AND DOCTOR ZARD WANTS TO SPEAK WITH YOU," Trish said.

"Really?" I asked. "She couldn't find me herself."

"SHE'S BEHIND YOU," Trish said.

"Of course, she is."

I turned around and found myself facing the perpetually bored looking Doctor Zard. The smell of cigarettes clung to her, and she was carrying an infopad. "Howdy, Cap'n. You look like you've aged ten years in a month. Be at this job another year and you might look old enough to sit in that chair."

"You and my aunt would get along great," I said.

"Namedropping doesn't help your situation. That's something I learned from the Prince of Lugh," Doctor Zard said.

I smirked. "You've been a great support during all of this, Doctor Zard. Thank you."

"You're not going to thank me after learning this next bit," Doctor Zard replied.

"What's that?" I asked.

"We should go somewhere private," Doctor Zard said.

"YES. BECAUSE THAT MAKES SENSE," Trish said.

"You don't count, Ghost in the Machine," Doctor Zard said. "Or maybe you do."

In the height of irony, the two of us headed to the communications room. That location was always empty since the entirety of its staff had chosen to jump ship with Lorken. Given they'd all been Department Twelve analysts, that was probably a good thing. I wasn't feeling too generous toward the now-defunct agency even if it was unlikely that they'd known the full extent of Elgan's plans (or maybe they had and the agents were feeling their own expendability extra harshly).

"Okay, door locked," I said. "If you're going to shank me, I'm going to feel super stupid."

Doctor Zard rolled her eyes. "If I wanted you dead, Vance, I'd just infect one of the female crew with a virulent STD."

"I've only slept with two crew members since this trip started," I replied. "Is that so strange?"

"Yes!" Doctor Zard said, appalled.

"Oh," I said. "I didn't realize that."

"AND IT WOULDN'T HAVE WORKED ON ME!" Trish said. "JERK."

Doctor Zard shook her head. "You know captains have a tendency to screw their starships if they get access to sexbots? It's a statistical fact."

"I sincerely doubt that," I said.

"It's happened more than once and that's too many," Doctor Zard said.

"I'm leaving now," I said, heading for the door. "Have fun, Bones."

"Not all of us are choosing to cosplay as sci fi characters," Doctor Zard said. "I'm not that much younger than your aunt so I get a good half of the references you're making."

"WOW, THAT'S IMPRESSIVE. HE MAKES A LOT OF ONES EVEN I HAVE TO LOOK UP. WHAT'S A BUCK ROGERS?"

"Sounds like a porn name," Doctor Zard said. "Like Flesh Gordon."

"THAT *IS* A PORN NAME."

"That's right, everyone gang up on the captain," I muttered.

"Our boy captain makes it an easy target," Doctor Zard replied. "However, I'm mostly delaying because the news I have is terrifying."

"More terrifying than being shanghaied to a suicide mission?" I asked.

"What does Shanghai have to do with it?" Doctor Zard asked then shook her head. "Never mind. Are you prepared to have your mind blown?"

"Wouldn't that be inherently contradictory?" I asked. "You can't prepare for having your mind blown. If you were prepared, it wouldn't be mind-blowing."

Doctor Zard stared at me. "You must be one of the most singularly annoying people who ever lived."

"Only when I want to be," I said. "Tell me your news."

"Captain Elgan is alive," Doctor Zard said.

I blinked, not responding.

"WOW," Trish said. "THAT *IS* UNBELIEVABLE."

"I know, right?" Doctor Zard said, looking up.

"NO, I MEAN IT'S LITERALLY UNBELIEVABLE."

"Then who the hell was the guy on the floor?" I asked, angry and confused. What the hell was going on here?

"Captain Elgan," Doctor Zard. "Sort of."

"Explain, please," I said.

"It's his DNA and body matched down to an almost imperceptible level," Doctor Zard said. "Fingerprints, teeth, and so on. However, there's a small number of traces of computer technology in his brain

167

that indicate artificial brain rather than a biological one. If I'd had better equipment, I would have been able to tell that it was all artificially aged and sculpted biological material before now."

"He was a bioroid too?" I asked, suddenly feeling like I was in an adaptation of the Marv Zellman *Attack of the Machines* movie from thirty years back.

"An infiltrator unit," Doctor Zard said. "One that costs seventy million credits, which is a pretty significant chunk of change even for a corrupt military official."

I felt a headache coming on. "So, was he even here?"

"I don't know," Doctor Zard said. "Trish might be able to answer."

"If I had the answers to that question, I was forbidden to talk about them and Vance undoubtedly burned them out of my mind," Trish's redheaded bioroid body said, surprising me.

"Where the hell did you come from?" I asked.

"The closet," Trish said, gesturing to a locker. "This is where I keep myself when I'm not in use."

I blinked. "We should work on getting you some quarters. It's not like we're hurting for space right now."

"Yeah, but that's like being inside myself," Trish said. "Which is less dirty than it sounds. So, it doesn't really matter where I store my body."

"I'm not sure now is the best time to be discussing this," Doctor Zard said. "We've got bigger issues to worry about."

"I'm not sure what is the best response to this," I admitted, shaking my head. "It's just another layer in a mystery I was already confused as bork by. Is it possible that Captain Elgan is still alive?"

"You mean, that he faked his death with a bioroid he was keeping in a closet somewhere this entire time?" Doctor Zard asked, looking at Trish. "Which our ship's AI conveniently couldn't tell us about?"

"Yeah," I suggested. "That's exactly what I mean."

"I dunno," Doctor Zard said. "Possibly. It's also possible that Captain Elgan was never involved in this and some private party was using his image and name to carry this out."

I blinked. "This might not even be something arranged by Department Twelve?"

"There aren't many people who can make an exact duplicate of a figure like Elgan," Doctor Zard said. "However, even that is going to be somewhat questionable since I only have the records onboard the ship to compare them to. Still, it could be someone other than the government like a transtellar or small government that thinks this is worth it to acquire some SKAMMs."

I imagined a terrorist organization or even criminal organization trying to do some spy movie savit. Threaten to destroy a planet in exchange for a few trillion credits. The Community would certainly pay it after the trauma inflicted on the citizenry after the Notha War's horrific ending.

"Damn," I said then shook my head. "No, it has to be someone involved with the government. Otherwise, Trish wouldn't be here."

"She's a machine, Vance," Doctor Zard said. "Something capable of being copied and reprogrammed. No offense, Trish."

"Some taken," Trish replied. "But she's not wrong."

I took a deep breath. "Well, the worst part of this is the fact that it doesn't actually change anything."

"How does it not change anything?" Doctor Zard asked, exasperated. "This should change everything."

"But it *doesn't*," I said, frowning. "We're still going after the same weapons on the same planet with the same knowledge that someone is trying to get them before us. So, this just is one more clue to figuring out what we're facing. But, no, it doesn't change anything."

Doctor Zard looked defeated. "If you say so, Vance."

"Well, if it's any consolation, we probably aren't facing Captain Elgan the Legendary Hero of the Human Race," I said, cheerfully.

Doctor Zard stared at me. "Right."

"Okay, just me then," I said.

Doctor Zard pointed at my chest. "Don't get killed down there, kid. The real thing is a lot different from the movies."

"I thought you were a mathematician," I replied.

"One that used to do a lot of analysis work for Department Twelve," Doctor Zard replied. "Do you want to know what the numbers are for this mission? Not good."

"I get it," I said. "We'll just have to change the odds."

"Good luck with that," Doctor Zard said.

"Ready to go, Vance?" Trish asked, moving a red ringlet from the front of her face. "The shuttle is prepped, and everyone is ready."

I'd chosen a small team for this because, well, we couldn't afford to have more. Hannah, Forty-Two, Trish, and myself. It did have a mixture of fighters, thinkers, and technical know-how, though. However, if we lost anyone then we'd be crippled and unable to finish the mission. Except for one member of the team: me.

"Yeah, I guess I am," I said. "Good luck, Doctor Zard. Let's hope we don't have to send anyone up to you."

"Oh, by the time they reached me, they'd be dead," Doctor Zard said.

I smirked and headed out the door, practically smacking into Ambassador Ketra who was standing outside.

"Oh hey," I asked. "What's—"

That was when she reached out and placed her hand on my face. That was when I was flooded with information that threatened to overwhelm my mind.

I screamed.

CHAPTER TWENTY-ONE

Things Get All Mystical (and I Don't Like It)

Ketra reached into my mind, and I felt myself change, the wiring in my cybernetics twisting as the nanomachines within reconfigured themselves. I had a brief vision of the rune-covered knife in the navigation room as well as a series of images I couldn't make sense of: alien worlds, places, people, and objects. For a moment, I felt like I was part of the cosmos and a higher being. I had achieved oneness with mathematical perfection, oneness with love as well as logic, oneness with the body as well as mind.

Nerdvana.

Thankfully, no one seemed to have heard — or at least cared about — my childish scream as I fell to the ground following Ketra's telepathic assault. I was laying in the middle of the hall and Trish was behind me, looking concerned. Doctor Zard, in the communication room behind me, went to a console to look busy and stay out of it. Honestly, given the fact this ship would have made an excellent subject of a reality television show, I didn't blame her in the slightest.

I took a second to clear my head while being painfully aware that the crew members passing us by didn't pay me the slightest bit of attention or show any concern. Apparently, loyalty to their underaged and underqualified captain was not a primary concern to the people stuck with me on this fantastic voyage, twenty thousand light years across the celestial sea.

Indeed, one thing I had learned in the past three months was that I wasn't going to view the *Black Nebula*'s crew as some meaningful found family. No, a band of brothers united by fate and forged in fire we were not. I was looking forward to leaving behind these anyxholes. Any ship that had me as one of the least offensive members on it had to be the worst ship in Space Fleet. The funny thing was that I would have previously numbered Ketra among the less offensive members before she mind-zapped me.

"What the fuck, lady, and I do mean fuck not bork," I said, slowly climbing to my feet.

"They mean the same thing," Ketra replied, looking stately and otherworldly even after blasting my brain.

Ow, bork, Leah said to me, telepathically. *What the bork was that?*

Language, I chided. *I just got Vulcan mind-zapped.*

I'll be right there, Leah said, sounding almost panicked. Then again, she'd got the backend of what I'd felt through our connected.

"You were not mind-zapped," Ketra said, apparently able to hear our telepathic conversation. "I merely altered your mind and updated your cybernetics."

"How the hell would you update my cybernetics?" I asked.

"Magic," Ketra said.

I stared at her.

"Technically, it is sufficiently advanced science given to me by the Elder Races that might as well be magic to you," Ketra replied. "I understand that is a science fiction reference you might get."

"I don't know all science fiction," I said.

"I know most of it," Trish said, drawing her stun ray. "At least on Earth. Now, do I have to stun you and drag you to the brig?"

I lifted my hand. "That won't be necessary."

"Because if you do survive this, even a disgraced ambassador could make your life a living hell?" Trish asked.

"That too," I said, dusting myself off. "Okay, what the hell was that about, Ketra?"

"You would not understand," Ketra said. "However, I thought you needed to have your brain updated or you will go horrifyingly insane. My adjustments will allow you to be able to interact with the kind of sanity-blasting technology that the Elder Races produce. I would consider you lucky if not for the fact that this is a burden that will probably get you killed."

I blinked. That was a set of sentences that needed to be processed before responded to. "Okay, I feel like this is one of those situations where you should try explaining versus just assuming I won't understand."

Ketra reached for my head again, only for me to duck under it like we were playing tag.

"Without the brain zapping!" I said, taking a step away from her.

Ketra sighed. "Very well. The marker. I speak of the marker that the *Starkiller XII* found and brought aboard before it drove the ship's AI mad."

"The what?" I asked.

"The marker," Trish replied.

"Yes, I heard her the first time," I said.

"Then why did you ask?" Trish asked.

I stared at her. "You know, I like to be the person doing all the sarcastic joke stuff."

"And you do such a good job too!" Trish said, giving me two thumbs up.

"What exactly are you concerned about with the marker?" I asked, wondering if there was any way I could make sense of this conversation. I had the funniest feeling that the answer would prove to be no.

"It must not fall into the hands of the Community," Ketra said. "Or EarthGov."

"Which would include me," I pointed out the obvious.

"No," Ketra said. "I believe you are willing to defy them to prevent it from happening."

That was a more tactful response than pointing out that I was a member of Space Fleet and EarthGov only in the loosest and probably more accurately described as "not at all" sense. One might even say it was close to giving a kid a pair of flight wings and pretending he's a member of the space crew at Lunar Dixnar World.

"Defying the government and orders to do the right thing. How heroic!" Trish said, clasping her hands together. "You're a renegade who doesn't play by the rules!"

"But I want to play by the rules!" I said, confused.

"Since when?" Leah asked, finally arriving.

"Since recently!" I said, not really having an argument there. I also noticed she'd taken her jolly sweet time getting here. It wasn't that big of a ship. "Where the hell have you been? Did you stop to use the bathroom on the way here?"

Leah rolled her eyes. "You're okay, aren't you?"

I frowned. "Yes, I'm fine, no thanks to you. I suspect this conversation with Ketra is something she wants to keep secret, though."

"No," Ketra said, placing her hand over my forehead like I had a fever. "You must keep the marker from falling into the hands of lesser mortals or all living mortals shall perish! Potentially. I mean, it's more likely they'll kill everyone on Rand's World and that might be an improvement, but if it falls into the hands of others then it could end up wiping out everyone who looks at the studies of its functions. One chain infomail and we're talking billions of dead."

I slowly removed her hand from my forehead. "Okay, that does sound like a pretty good reason not to let quote-unquote lesser mortals have the marker. Not that I know who that means."

"That means people like us," Leah said. "The Elder Races genuinely consider all non-primordial aliens to be lesser."

"Probably because it's true," Trish said.

Leah grumbled "Hyperbole is not helping our situation. I'm sure Ketra is exaggerating."

"It is not hyperbole," Ketra said, her expression distant and cold. "I have been communing with my husband and they have been in contact with the Elder Races."

"The little jewel on your head that you say is a living sun?" Trish asked.

"Yes," Ketra said, as if it wasn't a ridiculous statement.

"You know that's scientifically impossible, right?" Trish asked.

"Obviously not because it's true," Ketra said. "Science is unlimited in its scope of wonders and phenomenon."

"That's not how science works," Trish said. "I mean, I'm actually sure that's the opposite of how it works. It's all about disproving the impossible."

"I agree with the sexbot," Leah said, showing that being a telepath didn't make you in any way shape or form not a rude bastard.

I heard that, Leah said.

I know you did, I replied.

"We need to be serious," Ketra said. "This is a matter for only the most serious of minds."

"Man, did you pick the wrong ship," Trish said.

I clapped my hands in front of everyone. Yes, crew discipline had degenerated to the point of being a kindergarten class. "Please! Ketra, assume I am actually of the mind that there's something important about this marker. That I take the whole billions dying thing seriously since I am here to stop the SKAMMs from falling into the wrong hands."

"Assume the SKAMMs are a far lesser priority," Ketra said.

"I find that hard to believe," I said, for once lacking all sarcasm or snark to my tone.

"Are you familiar with Fermi's Paradox?" Ketra asked.

"Yes," I said. "One of my high school classes covered it. It's the idea that if there are a hundred billion stars in the Milky Way galaxy then there should be vast numbers of intelligent races that have spread out through the stars."

"Which there are," Leah said. "After all, we have the Community."

"Yes and no," I replied. "Fermi's Paradox was expanded by a physicist named Arno Hawking a century ago. Arno calculated that instead of the galaxy containing a few thousand species as it's believed to have, it should have closer to a hundred million. Even if just because of genetic drift and bio-modification."

"Well, the guy was an idiot," Leah said.

"No, he was not," Ketra said. "The reason that there is only a fraction of the species that should exist is because of the Gentry."

"Doesn't sound that intimidating for a xenocidal all-powerful force," Leah said.

"They are a horror beyond imagination," Ketra said. "They judge themselves to be the rulers of the galaxy and decide who lives or dies."

I let that sink in. "So, you're saying that if a race doesn't meet their criteria, then poof."

"Poof," Ketra said, her face betraying fear and uncertainty. It was the first time I'd known the ambassador to look less than perfectly self-possessed. "They are contrasted against the Gardeners."

"What do the Gardeners do?" I asked.

"They garden," Ketra said, making me feel like a fool. "However, they grow civilizations rather than plants. They experiment, guide, and, if necessary, prune."

"You'll have to forgive me if I don't see much of a difference between them and the Gentry," Leah said.

"I think the difference between death and manipulation is pretty severe even if I wouldn't want either," I replied.

Leah shrugged her shoulders as if there wasn't much to say to that. Which there wasn't.

"Why are you telling me this?" I asked. "Surely the Community's Senate knows this."

"They know less and more than you might realize," Ketra said. "All decisions are made with the awareness that the Elder Races could come within and eradicate them at any time. The differences in technology are not so much level but kind. I was not joking when I said the Elder Races have things that function like magic."

I couldn't help but ask. "Like what?"

"Teleportation, time travel, alternate reality journeys, programmable matter, and immortality," Ketra said. "Just as a start."

I stared at her in giddy glee. "Time travel is *real*?"

Leah gave me a dope slap. "Focus, Vannevar!"

"First, it's Vance," I corrected. "Two, don't assault your captain. Three, time travel. I'm imagining hooking it up to—"

"A phone booth, car, or variety of other references," Trish said. "I know you so well since we started dating."

We were dating? No, focus on the galactic extinction events, Vance! "Actually, I meant this ship so we could go back in time and save Thomas. Also, my parents," I paused. "Unless that would destroy the universe. Would that destroy the universe, Ketra?"

"No," Ketra said. "However, it would destroy the human race because the one thing the Gardeners and the Gentry agree upon is that under no circumstances should Elder Race technology ever be allowed to fall into the hands of organic beings."

"Under no circumstances meaning—" I raised my left hand and waved it around a bit, indicating a request for clarification.

"The death of everyone who has touched it and if knowledge about it is disseminated, the total destruction of everyone involved," Ketra said. "Depending on the power of the Gardeners versus the Gentry in society, it may mean the destruction of cities or civilizations."

"Surely, the Community wouldn't tolerate genocide," Leah said, sounding less confidant than she seemed.

"Many of the races of the Community revere the Elder Races as gods," Ketra said. "Others have tried to intervene and been destroyed. Placation has since been the policy of the Community for millennia. The Ethereals have been among those races that have struggled to maintain a peaceful diplomacy or, to use another term, run interference but this does not affect their stance on protecting their knowledge from falling into the Young Races' hands. The Young Races might well end up destroying themselves or others."

"Because God forbid they get an advantage over the Elder Races," I said. It struck me that if the Elder Races really were such complete anyxholes then someone should steal their technology, reverse engineer it, and teach them a lesson. Mind you, that was probably exactly the reason the Elder Races were determined to keep the so-called Young Races from doing so. I'm not sure if that was a self-fulfilling prophecy or merely cause and effect.

"That too," Ketra said.

I was horrified and sick by the things that Ketra was saying. I wasn't sure if I believed them, but it made a disturbing amount of sense. The Spiral and portions of the galaxy explored by the Community were filled with ruined worlds and planets that were habitable but empty of intelligent life. Furthermore, the Community was strangely cagey about allowing their colonization. I would have thought the galaxy would have a non-racist Manifest Destiny where any new worlds would be swiftly colonized but most either had to colonize their own or moved out in very specific directions. That made sense if they were attempting to avoid provoking the Elder Races.

But it was more the level of evil she was saying that disgusted me. Countless cultures, thousands if not millions, destroyed irrevocably as well as their future descendants. The uniqueness and possibilities that could have been learned from them were all annihilated by some arbitrary rules by people wielding advanced technology. It was the absolute antithesis of how the Community was supposed to explore and learn from other species. There was no tolerance or diversity, only raw exploitation, and judgement. The crimes were so vast that it was impossible to comprehend, and she was describing them as if they were as casual as swatting an insect.

"Your empathy does you credit," Ketra said, moving her hands into her sleeves like a space monk. "You desire to see all people survive, Vance."

"Yes, because wanting your race not to be destroyed is such a rare thing," Leah said, sarcastically.

"That is not what I meant," Ketra said. "You fear for humanity. Vance fears for all and is sickened by the dead."

Trish frowned. "I hate it too."

"I know," Ketra said. "AI have historically been among the few races accepted among the Elder Races unreservedly. They are considered superior lifeforms to organic beings."

"That's awful!" Trish said, shocked. "True but awful!"

Leah gave her a withering stare.

"I'm kidding!" Trish said. "All life forms are equal."

"That's stupid," Leah said.

"What do you want from me, meatbag?" Trish said, throwing her hands up in the air.

"I wonder if this is what talking to me is like," I said, watching those two. Shaking my head, I turned to Ketra. "So, you're telling us that on this mission, the real threat isn't the SKAMMs but the marker that the ship recovered?"

"Yes," Ketra said. "It is why I made myself available to this mission. Captain Elgan believed it was his idea and that I would want to involve myself to make up for my failure in the Notha treaty. Rather, I made information available to him that I knew would entice him. It was my goal to slip in and acquire the artifact. Unfortunately, I seem to have lost control of the situation."

"The fact a bioroid was going to blow up the ship kind of indicates that, yeah," I replied. Ketra had all but admitted to being the mastermind behind all this. I wanted to ask her more, but I was too busy being overwhelmed with the fact a second vitally important object to retrieve had interjected itself into this mission. About the only comfort I had was the fact it was in exactly the same place as the other vitally important one.

"With you on it," Leah added for emphasis. "So, I guess we can assume you weren't behind it."

Ketra didn't dignify Leah's words with a response. "I am aware."

"So, what do you want me to do about it?" I asked. "So much so that you fiddled with my brain."

"That sounds dirty," Trish said.

I looked at her sideways. "It does not."

"I dunno, it does to me," Leah said. "You Earthlings make everything dirty."

"That's rich coming from Space Brits," I muttered. "Also, don't dodge the question."

"I didn't dodge the question," Ketra said. "I am searching for words in a human language you understand to explain."

"I speak three," I said. "English, Japanese, Russian. My next will be Klingon."

"I speak Sindarin," Leah said. "It's one of my three favorite utterly useless made-up languages to learn."

I leaned over to Leah. "Are you making jokes because you're utterly terrified? Because I am."

"You know it," Leah said.

Ketra stared at us then raised one eyebrow, which is harder to do than it sounds. "You are such a strange group of people."

"No kidding," Trish said.

"I would like you to retrieve the marker and allow me to return it to the Elder Races so that there will be no further danger. If not, then I would ask you to destroy it," Ketra said.

"I see," I said. "So, you said that what you did to me would help protect me from the markers?"

Ketra said, "The markers have a self-defense mechanism that have been known to drive regular mortals to become insane bloodthirsty parodies of themselves, pathetic decadent hypersexualized freaks, or morons."

"Okay, this is just starting to sound like nine different generic sci fi plots," I said, thinking of at least three from *Star Trek* and four from *Star Voyages* that was the Albion version (and complete crap). "However, I am going to take you at your word. After we shut down the SKAMMS, we'll retrieve the marker or destroy it."

"You're just going to hand over an artifact of the Elder Races despite its enormous scientific value?" Leah asked.

"When the lady connected to the Elder Races say they're going to turn Earth into Alderaan or the Genesis Planet if we don't, I take that as a stern warning," I replied. "Those are planets that were blown up, by the way."

"Yeah, I got that from the context," Leah said. "Did your aunt just educate you on the old crap channel or what?"

"Wait 'til I tell you about her favorite show of all time: *Miami Vice*," I said. "I think that was old savit even pre-First Contact."

"You have made a wise decision," Ketra said. "I should inform you, though, that I had initially intended to make my quest for the marker a secret. I would have quietly disposed of it after you dealt with the SKAMMs. Unfortunately, events have exponentially increased their need for expedience."

"How's that?" I asked.

"The marker has reactivated and is sending a signal out into jumpspace that it is in danger," Ketra said.

I stared at her. "Well, that's not good."

"No," Ketra said. "Which is why I'm coming."

CHAPTER TWENTY-TWO

Gault's Gulch is the Pits

"A re we there yet?" The General asked, looking over to me. He was strapped into the copilot's seat of the *Black Nebula*'s sole shuttle, the *Black Nebula Junior*, which was a surprisingly cute and appropriate name for a shuttle.

"No," I said, sitting in the pilot's seat. "We are not there yet due to the whole still being in space thing. Which you can clearly see through the viewscreen."

I might not have been qualified to be captain of a starship, but I certainly knew how to helm a short-distance spacecraft. Hell, I'd been doing this sort of thing since I was fourteen. Even though I expected trouble, I hadn't put on my power armor. I'd settled for a specialized, reinforced version of my Space Fleet uniform as well as barrier belt. It wouldn't serve well in a direct fire fight but would protect me from a couple of shots before going down. It also wouldn't impede my mobility. No sense in not being at least a little bit cautious.

"Are we there yet?" Hannah asked, sitting behind the passenger's seat with a fusion pistol aimed right behind the General's head. I wasn't sure that was a great idea since firing an energy weapon in the middle of a shuttle's cockpit was a terrible idea, but she'd assured me it would only go through a foot of upholstery and Notha brains.

Also accompanying us on this trip were Forty-Two, Ketra, and Trish in physical form. I wasn't sure how I felt about Trish breaking off

182

a part of her consciousness to use Space Cadet Sally's body as a field platform, but no one knew if we'd need Cognition AI backup.

"Yes," I replied. "Just let me put on my spacesuit and vent the atmosphere. Your journey will end right here."

"Now you are sounding like a proper Sorkanan captain," Forty-Two said. "You just need a stick of authority."

"A what now?" I asked, setting the shuttle on automatic descent through the planetary atmosphere. The ship's barriers began absorbing the immense heat as I set us toward the landing beacon for Gault's Gulch. Leah had, true to her word, arranged for the Commerce Authority and other semi-legitimate organizations to permit us to land. It had apparently drained every credit in her post-graduation vacation fund.

"It's a historical stick that Sorkanan captains used in pre-spaceflight days to beat troublesome crew members," Ketra said. "It, along with *rorakan* ale and male-on-male companionship were the three things that drove their Imperial Navy."

"Rum, sodomy, and the lash?" I asked. "It's a phrase from the old British Empire."

"Why do you have a phrase for that?" Hannah asked.

"Why do the Sorkanans?" I pointed out.

"The Sorkanan Navy is still eighty percent male and females are only in season a quarter of every year without *platack* leaves," Forty-Two said. "I'm just saying it gets lonely."

"Hey, no judgements," I said, shrugging. "You do you."

"That is also something Sorkanan men become very accustomed to on their missions."

"Okay, too much information, Forty-Two," I said. "Albeit, yeah, that's obvious."

"You are a degenerate vile pair of species," the General said, chewing on his seat belt.

"You know it," I said.

The General slumped over, defeated. I was no telepath, but I was getting the impression that he was immensely frustrated by me. My refusal to be baited by him, for whatever reason, was driving the little bastard up the wall. I had no idea what he was hoping to accomplish from constantly testing me and the others, especially when the SKAMMs represented such a clear and present threat to both our races.

Then again, the General had indicated his capture meant there was no way for him to return to Notha Space even if he successfully destroyed them. While I might be persuaded by the idea of self-sacrifice for the greater good, it didn't seem to be something he'd willingly undertake if he had a choice. It was also possible that imprisonment and torture combined with Notha Empire indoctrination had driven him mad.

You are correct, Ketra's voice spoke in my mind instead of Leah's, which I found profoundly disconcerting. *The General, known as Asa'varal among his people, is scheming for some way to restore his honor. He is suicidal due to his humiliation, loss of status, and xenophobia at having been bested by lesser beings.*

Great, I said, not happy to have my mind become a party line for all the ship's telepaths. *Was it a mistake to bring him?*

He is developing a mythological archrivalry with you in his head that is far in excess of your actual status within the Community—which is to say none—as well as ability. Which is to say inexperienced in every area but manipulation and social engineering. In a couple of hundred years, you might be a decent diplomat.

Great, times two. So, I should expect treachery? I asked. It was hard to process the General deciding I was his archenemy. I was probably the only person here who didn't want him dead. Well, mostly. I mean he was a real anyxhole.

You should kill him, Ketra said. *I have already removed all the override codes and command structure you need to shut down the defenses of the Notha factory. They have also been transferred to your mind.*

Yeah, that's not creepy at all, I replied, wondering whether she was telling the truth. After all, I didn't think I knew any Notha codes. None popped up when I wanted to think of them either. On the other hand, maybe they needed a trigger. My knowledge of how psychic powers worked was limited, and Leah was now out of range. *Am I the only person who doesn't feel like executing prisoners?*

If your goal is to save as many lives as possible then yes, Ketra said. *He is an unstable madman and if he did go back to Notha Space, he would certainly try to use the missing missiles to spark raids, if not outright war.*

I am aware, I said. *However, I am not going to violate the principles I believe in because it's difficult. Otherwise, we're exactly who the Notha say we are.*

I don't think we're about to randomly lose sentience and be labor animals for the divinely chosen—despite Notha being atheists—elite race. Ketra paused. *I also know that it is the young who are most often driven by idealism versus practicality. I hope you live long enough to become cynical.*

Me too, I replied, realizing how childish my previous cynicism had been. *Are you really sure that we have to get this marker?*

I am very sure, Ketra said.

And you don't know why it's activated? I asked.

No, Ketra said. *Only that it would be a very bad thing for it not to be destroyed or returned to Elder Race hands. Well, what races that actually have hands. It may already be too late but every second counts.*

Great, I muttered. *No pressure.*

I would say there are significant amounts of pressure, Ketra said. *Please don't fail or everyone you know and love may die.*

I looked back at her.

That was a joke, Ketra said.

I shook my head and turned back to the viewscreen showing our descent into the atmosphere. The sight of the pale yellow and brown orb from space becoming a planet as we insignificant organic specks knew it never ceased to impress me. I hoped I never became desensitized to the absolute wonder and majesty of space as some people did. According to my Aunt Kathy and several of her astronaut friends, there had been a transformative effect when the first pictures of Earth had been taken from orbit.

Those early astronauts, flying through the air on the back of missiles in tin cans, had shown that all of the borders that humanity had erected for itself were insignificant. It had helped lay the ground, however early, for the idea that mankind was one species united on Mother Earth.

185

A similar transformative effect was happening now with the difference between Grounders and Spacers, those human beings who lived their entire lives on planetary bodies terraformed to human norms and those who were adapted by biology as well as culture to live their entire lives in space. Grounders were becoming more conservative, traditionalist, and insular. Spacers were becoming more cosmopolitan, hedonistic, and intermixed. I was somewhere in-between having spent equal amounts of time on Earth, the moon, and in spaceships. I hoped I had the chance to see what the fruits of this tree planted.

"Amazing, isn't it?" I said, staring at the desert as we finally started our flight path across the planetary surface.

"Are we there yet?" Forty-Two asked, showing he too had a sense of humor. "You've seen one example of shoddy human terraforming, you have seen them all."

"That is a lot of sand," Trish said. "It is very sandy."

"The Notha should bomb this place to glass," Hannah said. "However, I don't think the locals would notice."

"On that, human, we agree," the General said. "It is not worth it to eliminate the human infestation on this planet or the similar ones nearby."

"Especially when they're collaborating with your regime and producing weapons as well as other resources for you," Ketra replied.

"Draft animals are useful," the General said.

"You guys suck," I said, sighing.

Gault's Gulch showed up on my onboard sensors well before it came into physical view. I slowed the shuttle and took a moment to look at the center of culture in the world. I regretted already wasting my wretched hive of scum and villainy reference since even a cursory examination of the place fit the bill.

Gault's Gulch was, as far as I could tell, a city made from scrap. The enormous terraforming towers that produced breathable atmosphere and regulated the planet's temperature rose up from the ground as massive obelisks. The former terraforming stations had been hollowed out, though, and added to with buildings made of sheet metal as well as the remains of a hundred or more different starships.

Rand's World had a brief but bloody campaign where it had been used as a staging point for the EarthGov forces invading Notha Space. The locals had utterly loathed this, having done their best to get as far from the homeworld as possible, but it had helped add more to the city including a large military-grade starport as well as much of their industry.

There were barracks and makeshift prefabricated housing of the kind the military used in emergencies now inhabited by the locals. It said a great deal that they were some of the nicer homes available with others living in hovels and shantytown neighborhoods cobbled together from other war refuse. If this was what was meant to be a paradise for the free then I shuddered to imagine what they considered to be a hellhole.

A robotic emotionless voice—one I knew had to be human since no true AI was so lacking in emotion—told me, "Report to docking bay sixty-four. Do not deviate from your present course. You will be subject to additional fees and licenses."

"Great," I muttered, setting the vehicle to cruise at an air car's speed while following the predetermined route sent to my computer. It allowed me to see the people below and their lives, which looked like they'd escaped from a post-apocalypse movie set. The people lived in rags, military cast-offs, and a handful of eclectic wares traded from the rest of the solar system.

It made me wonder what had driven them out so far from the protections that was guaranteed by EarthGov in exchange for "freedom." Was I missing something or was the only thing uniting people here a deep distrust of authority and government? The fact there were a couple of what appeared to be dead bodies spread out in the street, ignored by the passersby, was its own argument.

"Hmmm," Hannah said, sitting in the back.

"What?" I asked.

"That was positively friendly," Hannah said. "Usually, they would be shaking you down for a lot more specific charges in terms of money."

"Which would be a bad thing since we don't have any," I replied.

"Yeah, I am not happy about that," Hannah said. "You don't think you could get your sugar mommy on the horn and some discretionary income?"

"I don't think you understand what sugar mommy means and if you do, eww," I replied.

"Do you think it's a trap?" Trish asked. "Ooo, I hope it's a trap! That would be very exciting."

Hannah glared at Trish. "Listen, just because you won't die if your body gets shot up doesn't mean the rest of us won't. Try not to treat this as a big game."

Trish put her hand over her heart. "I promise that I will do everything to keep you alive unless it conflicts with saving myself or Vance. In which case I will prioritize my life or his over yours."

Hannah blinked. "Well, that was…honest."

"Shouldn't you put us before yourself since you are still alive on the ship?" Forty-Two asked.

"Nope!" Trish said. "It's going to be very hard to replace this body here."

Forty-Two hmphed. "I guess I should have been nicer to you, trash bot."

"Yep!" Trish said, proudly.

"Just stay out of my way," Hannah said. "I have a bunch of people here who owe me money and we can trade in supplies if we have to. Parts are more valuable here than weapons. We probably won't be able to negotiate for food, though. It's an import economy since the only thing that is reliably available here is mushrooms."

"Great," I said. "Wait, why mushrooms?"

"Twenty million people in Gault's Gulch creates a lot of savit," Hannah said. "On the plus side they have mushroom stew, mushroom cereal, mushroom jerky—"

"I'm going to question how any of those are possible," I said.

"Genetically combining mushrooms and human DNA allows a wide variety of flavors as well as textures—" Trish started to say.

"I will kill you last, Captain, if you can shut these beings up," the General replied.

I didn't respond to that obvious goad because I was too busy focusing on our arrival at docking bay sixty-four. It was an octagonal open-air chamber that was part of a massive honeycomb of similar facilities. The smaller bays had been designed for the rapid loading and unloading of material from orbital ships that couldn't physically land.

Giant cylindrical containers for orichalcum gas were visible nearby as were giant ill-maintained turrets that could fire from the surface of the world deep into orbit. There were anti-troop transport anti-matter weapons platforms as well, most of which were covered in graffiti or missing a few missiles. The malfunctioning holographic signs of Ares Electronics, Olympia Colonies and other transtellars still functioned despite the fact I knew most of them had already withdrawn back to the Community.

I lowered our shuttle onto the center of the dust-covered landing pad and input the shutdown sequence. The place had seen its better days, like much of the planet, but it seemed like it would be a perfectly serviceable location to carry out our operation. The docking clamps slammed around our shuttle and made sure that we wouldn't be able to leave without permission of the powers that be.

"I hope you know what you're doing," I said to Hannah.

"You don't want to be going to this facility without supplies," Hannah said. "We need to make sure that this refinery goes up big."

"On that we agree, human female," the General said. "I can get you in but destroying the SKAMMs means the end of the orichalcum refinery. This is a small price to pay."

"That is way too reasonable for him," Hannah muttered, unbuckling.

I agreed, but one or two other things were bugging me, too. I didn't like that Hannah was cagey about what exactly she was purchasing here to help us in our mission or with what. I'd extended a lot of trust on this mission—I had to really—but I had to wonder if I shouldn't have. How much of all of this was motivated by my desire to do something good versus my own stubborn pride? Was there a difference?

Either way, once the shuttle was powered down, I opened the side hatch and stepped out into the blazing sun. The docking bay smelled foul with a mixture of various chemicals as well as the ionized air of the terraforming systems. Blocking the sun with my forearm, I watched everyone else head out. Hannah had slapped a pair of magnetic cuffs on the General and we had a tracking device implanted inside him as well. It wasn't proper treatment of prisoners, but I didn't want Forty-Two eating him. Wait, was that racist?

"Okay, where to next?" I asked Hannah. "Clock's ticking."

That was when Lorken and all the missing crew walked in, guns drawn. He was dressed in his power armor with his helmet off as were the majority of the other defecting security officers (with their helmets on). The mutineers, for lack of a better term, were accompanied by a bunch of new recruits as well, all of them dressed in a mixture of battered power armor and energy vests. Their weapons were well-maintained, though, with one of them even sporting a personal anti-shuttle cannon with homing rocket attachment. That would have been bad enough if not for the fact three squads of automated soldier bots came, too.

I blinked, looking them over. "Well, this has escalated quickly."

That was when the General bit my leg.

CHAPTER
TWENTY-THREE

Just Who Are the Traitors Here?

I admit, I'd fully expected Lorken to go here. It was completely illogical and the worst decision that he could have made but also something my gut had been telling me the entire way here. I had a few crazy ideas sticking to the back of my head that I just couldn't get rid of. Ones that implied to me that this lunacy had a logic to it that I wasn't seeing and just had to reframe to make sense of.

Mind you, I wasn't thinking of that right then. No, right then I was thinking of the two-foot-tall furball biting my ankle. Unfortunately, for him, Space Fleet jumpsuits were immune to tearing so it just stung like hell. My patience having been tested to the limit, I grabbed him by the back of the neck and shoved him over to Hannah.

"They have to come liberate me!" The General shouted. "Come puny beings, serve your true master and be richly rewarded!"

"Picnic," Lorken said, gesturing to the traitorous Ant. "Shoot that fuzzy bastard. Try not to hit Hannah."

I stepped in front both Hannah as well as the General. "He is my prisoner, and you aren't going to harm him."

Lorken stared at me and then his fellows before they all burst out into laughter. It was infectious and even those mercs hired locally joined in. The only ones who didn't were the soldier bots that looked as ominous and foreboding as anything I'd ever seen in my life.

Which included my first trip to the principal's office for reprogramming the holographic presentation on Sorkanan to show *Cannibal Lizard People from Mars*. A 2271 CE holo classic. Wait, that movie was prejudiced against the Sorkanan. Why did I like it? Wow, I really needed to see someone about unconscious speciesism.

"Yeah, I think you've got them real intimidated, Vance," Hannah leaned in and whispered to me. "Let me toss a few nuke grenades at them and we can fight our way out of here."

"Hannah, not every problem can be solved with violence," I said.

"No, but I'm pretty sure this one can be," Hannah said, practically smothering the General's mouth with her gloved hand, which he was biting repeatedly. "Besides, I thought you'd be dying to kill Lorken since you're still hot for Leah."

I stared at her. "What you'd think I'd kill him to get back with her? What is wrong with you?"

Hannah shook her head. "I can't believe I slept with you. Oh wait, yes, I can. Just, you know, work on not talking. At all. Ever."

"You know my armor comes with a listening device and I heard all that," Lorken said.

"No, I did not!" I said, sticking my hands behind my back. "Mind you, I'm going to have to inform you that Leah is no longer interested in dating you."

I was trying to buy time rather than immediately succumbing to overwhelming odds of our situation. We didn't have any cover and we were grossly outnumbered. If Lorken did want to kill us, then we were probably fucked. However, I wasn't going to casually surrender to him either. If he was involved in Captain Elgan's scheme then it was entirely possible he wanted all of us dead and might be leading us to interrogation, slavery, or belated execution.

Trish, I need you to activate the shuttle's barriers, I said, using my cybernetics to communicate rather than telepathy.

You shut the ship down, Vance, that's not going to be easy, Trish said. *I'm also not hooked up to it like I am you.*

Is it possible, though? I asked.

Yes, Trish said. *If you give me time.*

That I can do, I replied. *Unless they kill us all.*

192

You may need to work on this captain thing, Vance, Trish replied.

Before I could respond, Forty-Two actually picked up the conversation with Lorken for me. "What the idiot boy captain is trying to say is that you are traitors and we have come to punish you for your perfidy."

"Thanks, Forty-Two," I said, giving him a sideways glance. "I really needed that."

"You are the captain even if I have no respect for you as a leader," Forty-Two said, giving me a thumbs up. Well as much as Sorkanan had thumbs. It was more a hooked claw thing.

I didn't acknowledge him before looking back at Lorken. "You left a lot of us high and dry back then. A lot of us were almost killed by Elgan's sabotage."

"Sabotage?" Lorken asked, shaking his head. "I swear, you have no idea what's going on here, do you?"

"Enlighten me," I replied.

"No," Lorken said. "You're coming with us. It was an incredibly stupid move letting your fake rank go to your head, Vance. Just because you managed to survive one combat mission doesn't mean you're suddenly a soldier."

"I'm pretty sure, historically, that's exactly how it worked," Hannah said.

"Shut up," Lorken said. "You know, the captain thought you might be useful to take along on this mission, but I convinced him you were nothing but an unstable drunk and has-been merc that we didn't need."

That pretty much stopped me cold. "Elgan is alive?"

"I am not unstable!" Hannah shouted.

Lorken shook his head. "Of course, he's alive. You were supposed to understand the mission was doomed when he faked his death. Run away with the others with your tail between your legs. It was a way of separating the wheat from the chaff. Yet, you didn't just like I knew you wouldn't. You were always too stupid and too self-important to know when to quit. Gods, what a mistake it was to recruit you."

It took me a second to let Lorken's rant soak in, but when it did, I felt sorry for the guy. Clearly, he had completely missed how utterly manipulated he'd been by Captain Elgan. It was another piece of the puzzle, and it was now coming together. "This has gone beyond petty egos, Lorken. There's more going on here than you know. There was never going to be a return for the rest of the crew. The ship was rigged to blow when you left. He was going to kill us all once we had gotten him close enough to the planet. No loose ends. What do you think that is going to mean for you?"

Ketra didn't pipe in, but I assumed she could read my mind and knew that it was probably her that had precipitated this. She'd wanted to go get the marker and arranged for Elgan to come but he'd decided to switch things up halfway. I had to admit a certain respect for both participants in this. It took a special kind of genius to make this kind of back-and-forth intrigue. Too bad I wasn't a player in all this but a pawn. I would have enjoyed matching wits with them.

Oh, Vance, Ketra said. *No, you wouldn't.*

"Boss, perhaps—" Picnic, who was rather distinctive among the rest of them, started to speak.

"They're lying," Lorken said. "That's all Vance does. He was a liar at the Academy, he was a liar while serving as Captain Elgan's secretary—"

"First officer," I corrected.

"And he's a liar now," Lorken said, quivering with rage. "You know, Vance, Captain Elgan said that you were to be brought to him alive. However, he's given you nothing but slack and opportunities. I think I'll just tell him that you were killed in apprehension."

Okay, that wasn't good. I had clearly not succeeded in my attempt at diplomacy here. Then again, it probably hadn't been a good idea to antagonize Lorken every step of the way in our short-lived relationship. Stupid Smurf.

"Boss, maybe—" Picnic said.

"Hannah, now may be a good time for cover," I said.

"No kidding," Hannah muttered, throwing the General behind her where he rolled across the ground.

"Done!" Trish proclaimed aloud to what was probably everyone's considerable confusion.

"Fire!" Lorken shouted, pointing directly at me.

Given that most of them were hired goons and bots, they didn't hesitate to open fire on me. I noticed there was some hesitation from the ranks of the people that had formerly been part of the *Black Nebula's* crew.

Sadly, I couldn't tell you if their hesitation was because they didn't want to open fire on people who had been their teammates or if it was because Captain Elgan had ordered me spared. That by itself was confusing since my former mentor had proven himself quite willing to kill me and everyone else.

Nevertheless, none of that was important because the air lit up with fusion blasts and it became a brief blinding display of energy bolts. It was beyond overkill, and it was genuinely surprising that I wasn't immediately incinerated by the inferno of weapons fire. But incinerated we were not because the small weapons fire was absorbed by the brilliant blue-white barrier that stood between us and oblivion. My plan had worked, much to my surprise.

I would have liked to have resumed negotiations at that point but that was immediately undercut by Hannah shouting, "Fire in the hole!"

A moment later, a glowing plasma grenade flew from her hands through the barrier that was apparently not particle shielded. It soared through the air and landed at the foot of the traitorous crew members. Lorken activated a rocket pack that lifted him high in the air before an explosion caught the rest of the mutineers, most of them not having yet activated their own personal barriers. That wouldn't have mattered because Hannah had already hurled another one that overwhelmed those few who had put up their barriers.

Ketra tossed me a gun that was, with little exaggeration, larger than myself, which I caught with only the fortunes of war preventing me from falling over on my ass with it. It was a Forgemaster-461 heavy assault cannon and I had to wonder when the hell she'd snuck it on the shuttle and how I hadn't seen it when she did it. Nevertheless, having the weapon and seeing that some of the locals were pulling out kinetic weapons and grenades of their own, I turned it on the crowd of attackers before bracing myself against the ground. Sticking the end of the rifle through the tip of the barrier in front of me, I began my own assault.

"This is not very Space Fleet!" I shouted, for lack of anything better to say before my entire body shook up and down with every glowing energy blast that shot out of it. Whatever else I was going to say was destroyed by the shakes from emptying its blast clip.

"Ah-ah-ah-ah-ah-ah-ah-ah!"

"You are proving almost competent!" Forty-Two said cheerfully while firing his own rifle, taking time to aim and gun down opponent after opponent. Forty-Two was joined by Trish, Ketra (who had a personal handheld pistol that looked like someone had bedazzled it), and Hannah. Each of them fired through the ends of the barrier that served as our one and only military advantage. The General had slipped away, again, and I was afraid he was going to be a problem for us but couldn't take the time off from our present attackers to deal with him.

The barrier was still holding but I hadn't enough experience with shuttle engineering to know how long it would stay up. Certainly at least a couple of kinetic weapons fire had passed through it, though thankfully none hitting my group in the chaos.

The mutineers were almost all dead in the opening rounds of the battle and while I didn't have a bead on Lorken, I saw Picnic lying on the ground like an incinerated bug with his exoskeleton charred almost beyond recognition. The local toughs—having clearly expected far less resistance than what we had provided—made a break for it and fled the scene of battle. It was the smartest thing they could have done under the circumstances.

Unfortunately, that still left the soldier bots advancing toward us. They were humanoid, more a concession to intimidation value than practicality, with solid durasteel chassis and built-in personal barriers. These were EarthGov make and almost definitely leftovers from the Notha War, which meant they were probably dumb as bork and only programmed with a limited number of reactions.

The problem was those limited number of reactions almost certainly included, "march forward and kill the people shooting at you." Which they were doing, right now. A few of them had fusion blast marks or had been taken down but most of the dozen or so bots were still intact and headed our way. Once they marched their way through the barrier there wouldn't be a damn thing we could to do to stop them from mowing us all down.

"Retreat back into the shuttle!" I shouted, knowing that we weren't making any progress and seeing they were almost upon us.

"What then?" Hannah asked.

"I have no idea!" I said aloud, unwittingly exposing that I was making this all up as I went along.

"Don't worry," Lorken's voice spoke behind us. "You don't have to worry about a thing."

"Goddammit," I muttered, turning around, and seeing that he'd somehow managed to get the drop on us. "Didn't someone shoot you?"

Lorken was standing right in front of the shuttle doors with his rifle aimed at my chest. He looked desperate and confused, perhaps because he'd gotten most people under his command killed. He could certainly kill me but that wouldn't do him much good if everyone else gunned him down in the meantime. The soldier bots were about to overrun us but that wouldn't mean much if it got him killed in the process as there was no guarantee they were given orders to protect him specifically. In all likelihood, his goal was to buy time for himself.

"Drop your weapons," Lorken said, "or I shoot your captain."

"I don't think so," Hannah said. "Sorry, Vance."

"It's okay," I said, lying.

Lorken's weapon was on autofire and I suspected he was about to unload on us all when the General raced up the side of his armor and bit down onto his neck, clawing at the injury he made as he drew blood.

"Ah!" Lorken said, firing at the ground.

I walked up to him and clubbed him across the face with the butt of my oversized rifle, sending him to the ground with a thud. I kicked his gun away while the General clawed Lorken's face repeatedly with his claws.

"There's a reason you're supposed to wear a helmet, dumbass," I muttered.

"Victory!" The General proclaimed. "All inferior beings bow before the might of the Notha genotype!"

None of this was going to matter if we were gunned down by the soldier bots so I turned around to see them. They were all stopped a few inches away from the barrier. I blinked and looked at Trish. "Is this your doing?"

Trish nodded vigorously. "I remembered that all of the command codes for these are on file with the Black Nebula. I just looked them up and did an override. I would have thought of it earlier, but it turns out organic bodies are really stupid. Err, no offense."

"None taken," I said, looking down at Lorken and I kicked his gun farther away before the General got it. He looked disappointed. Lorken was still alive but keeping his hand pressed against his bleeding neck. He needed first aid, badly. "We'll get that injury treated and you will be considered a prisoner of war. But first, you're going to tell us where Elgan is. I think our former captain and I have a lot to discuss."

I also needed a change of pants.

CHAPTER
TWENTY-FOUR

Meeting with a Dead Man

"You shouldn't be ashamed of it," Hannah said, sitting across from me in the open-canopied, saucer-shaped, ground lift in which we were currently traveling down the streets. A light kinetic barrier kept insects or wind from rushing into our faces but did little to keep the punishing heat of the sun off us.

"I don't want to talk about it," I said, wearing a pair of goggles as I operated the controls from the center of the saucer. The vehicle had previously belonged to the late assault team that we'd managed to kill most of its members. I suspected the vehicle was originally made for an alien race of some kind but could pilot it easily enough.

"Biological excretions happen during battle," Trish said. "It's why we have a shower and spare clothing in the shuttle. Well, not really but it was helpful in this case."

"You are weak and should be ashamed of yourself," the General said, lifting up his manacled hands. "Also, we have shed blood together, so you should release me."

"No," I replied, well and truly sick of the General.

The saucer was maneuvering through the streets of Gault's Gulch at a glacial pace, surrounded by the various impoverished and heavily armed humans that looked at us like we were a collection of aliens. Which, given Ketra and Forty-Two's presence, we were. That we were also wearing Space Fleet uniforms didn't help our situation either.

199

The group was gathered in a circle around me, sitting on the faux-leather seats with the General and Lorken sitting together. Lorken had been stripped of his power armor, treated for his injury, and manacled. A white bandage was resting on his neck that was filled with a variety of bio-chemicals that meant he would probably be healed within a few hours despite the severity of the General's attack. His facial scars would take longer to heal or at least a better medical facility than our shuttle. He hadn't said much since agreeing to take us to Elgan, which was what he was originally supposed to do.

We'd left behind the soldier bots to guard our shuttle and used Lorken's own credit chip to pay for body disposal. Apparently, that was a service provided on Rand's World and only required what an enlisted man made in a year. Given he had several dozen times that in his account, I wasn't overly worried about expenses anymore. Dude was loaded and kept a fortune in petty cash.

"We should discuss other matters," Forty-Two said. "The captain has won my respect. He has survived two battles and not gotten anyone killed. A third and he would be called *kmabi*, or a veteran."

"I admit that the whole barrier thing was a good idea," Hannah said. "His friendship with the soulless simulacrum of a person pays dividends. No offense, Trish."

"Much taken," Trish said. "I have ten thousand individual cat-related insults prepared for you, but I can't choose which one to start with."

"You mean like being killed by curiosity, working in a cat house, using a litter box, getting someone's tongue, or pussyfooting around?" Hannah asked. "Believe me, I've heard them all. You should embrace your stereotype."

"I'd rather not," Trish said, dryly. "Still, I wish I had a laser pen. I could drive you nuts."

Hannah narrowed her eyes. "Those things are *evil*. I lost three of my nine lives to being distracted by them."

Trish grumbled as I could practically hear her writing off about half of her jokes. Making fun of genemods wasn't nearly as fun when they were in on it apparently.

"Meow," Ketra said, making a claw gesture.

"You don't get to make those jokes, elf," Hannah said. "Go bake some cookies or help Santa."

I was surprised they'd heard of Santa on Crius. "Guys, we're almost there. We should probably focus on making sure we're not ambushed."

"How many soldiers is he likely to have left?" Forty-Two asked. "We have killed many."

"On this planet, a lot," Hannah said. "I was going to go see some of my old contacts, but it occurs to me Elgan may have already hired them. A shame, I know a Sorkanan *plomak* dealer named Doctor No who also runs a multi-species brothel. Perfect place to celebrate a victory."

"I remind you that the people we had a great victory over were our crew mates less than a month ago," I said, with perhaps more distaste than I'd intended. "They were people we knew and were friends with in some cases. People who had volunteered to be on the same mission we are and now are helping no one."

Hannah, of course, responded in her characteristic manner. "They also tried to kill us, so fuck 'em."

"It was a nice speech, though!" Trish said.

"You have no idea what you've done," Lorken finally said, looking broken and defeated. "The number of lives you have put in danger."

"Well, you could have tried *telling us*," I said, stopping at an intersection. The majority of Rand Worlders seemed to prefer walking instead of vehicles. Perhaps because they couldn't afford to maintain them here. "You know, instead of deciding you just wanted to execute us all for savit and giggles."

Really, Albion swearing just didn't have the same oomph as the words back on Earth even if they weren't that dissimilar.

"You're a threat," Lorken said. "One that needs to be dealt with."

"And you're a bad commander," I retorted before continuing to our destination. "You got everyone underneath you killed, defied orders, and didn't even accomplish what you were trying to set out to do. You're also a borking moron! Because we're trying to stop the SKAMMs from falling into the wrong hands too."

I could see my words hitting Lorken like I was striking him. I didn't need to be a telepath to see that he was only now realizing just how badly he'd screwed up. I didn't know how close he was to the people he'd gotten killed but killed they were, and it was his fault. I hadn't wanted this to end in a firefight and was apparently the only person who cared that they were dead. If circumstances had been slightly different, maybe I would have been one of the people getting blown up by Hannah's grenades.

"This goes beyond SKAMMs," Lorken muttered.

"I know," I replied, dryly.

That seemed to surprise Forty-Two and Hannah, who both looked up. Mind you, I wasn't sure how to explain the idea that the real threat of this situation wasn't the solar system destroying superweapons but that godlike aliens would come to crush us like bugs if we were found playing with their toys. That seemed like a conversation that was better handled by Ketra, if she wanted to handle it at all.

I don't, Ketra said, telepathically. *The fewer individuals who know about the dangers of Elder Race technology, the better.*

You don't think everyone should be warned that if they touch it, their species might die? I asked.

That would only increase the items value in many circles, Ketra replied. *After all, the only thing more limitless in the universe than empty space is stupidity.*

It was hard to argue with that. Whatever answers I was going to find from Captain Elgan were going to be acquired soon because we'd arrived at his location. At least according to Lorken. Thankfully, we had a telepath to confirm he was telling the truth. It wasn't exactly what I'd expected but it was fitting with the planet as we'd explored it so far.

The Scarlett O'Hara was a two story-bar that looked like it had been assembled out of three or four prefabricated buildings and an airlock. It had an old fashioned—and I mean really old-fashioned—sign made out of neon that listed its name with a hand-painted sign beside it that read: NO ALIENS, NO KIDS, NO GUNS. There were also triple Xs painted on the side of the wall with the nude silhouette of a human female.

"Huh, I wouldn't have thought this was Captain Elgan's sort of place," Hannah said, looking up.

"Because it is a den of inequity and sleaze?" Ketra asked.

"No, because it's only women," Hannah said. "Limited menu locations are not my thing."

"You all look like food animals to me," Forty-Two said. "Walking, talking ones. It's actually kind of gross."

"Does your nattering never stop?" The General asked.

"Nope," I replied, looking around for any sign of guards. I didn't see anyone who looked like they were but that didn't mean anything.

"I should go in and explain myself," Lorken said.

"Yeah, that's not how this works," I replied. "You're a prisoner, Lorken and—"

That was when a pair of hooded locals came up to the saucer and pulled out a pair of rifles that they pointed at me. More of them came from where they'd been hiding and surrounded us, each of us with two weapons pointed directly at our heads.

"Goddammit," I said.

"Thank the ancestors," Lorken said, right before one of them smashed him in the side of the head with his rifle butt. The man spit on Lorken as well.

"That's for my brother you led to his death," the local said.

I raised my hands. "I'm here to see Elgan."

"Uh, Vance, are you sure you—" Hannah started to speak before the end of the gun was pressed against her head. "I wish you the best of luck."

"Try not to die," Ketra said. "We will be fine out here."

"We will?" Forty-Two asked, clearly skeptical.

"Yes," Ketra said.

Forty-Two nodded his head. "I trust in the wisdom of the Ethereals."

"I demand to speak to your leader!" The General said. "I am the highest-ranking mammal here!"

I stepped out of the saucer as Lorken was dragged out, looking significantly worse for wear and probably suffering a concussion. Despite being genetically enhanced, he'd gotten bashed in the head twice in a short span of time. That wasn't good for anyone, even if he was designed to have an exceptionally thick skull.

I was patted down for weapons and communication devices, but they left my barrier belt as well as my protection vest on. Notably, they also insisted on checking my underwear for any hidden weapons there and I was glad I was wearing a fresh pair. It would have been embarrassing otherwise.

"Go on in," the leader of the local gunmen said, gesturing. He had half a mouth full of teeth and the rest replaced with what looked like bullets.

"Absolutely," I said, keeping my hands in the air as I marched through the front door.

The interior of the Scarlett O'Hara was pretty much what I expected from "strip club in junktown." The place was full of seats and tables harvested from a battleship's mess hall, there was a central raised dais where a couple of women were doing what they did best, the lights were dimmed, the floor gross, and a bar where locally produced rotgut was the specialty.

Really the most impressive thing about the place was the buffet where I saw sixteen different varieties of powdered mush. Well, that and the music. A locally produced version of "Sweet Home Alabama" was playing with a word substitution of Rand's World. It kind of ruined the chorus but the instrument playing was more than competent. There was a staircase to one side that passed through a hole cut in the ceiling as the steps led up to the second floor.

I felt the end of the rifle pressed into my back and was pushed along towards the stairs. Lorken was dragged along with me, eventually realizing they weren't going to let him go and he was as much a prisoner as I was.

"This is a mistake," Lorken said, resisting only as much as it to avoid getting smashed in the face again.

"Boss' orders," the head local said. "The *real* boss."

The VIP lounge, which I assumed the upstairs to be once I arrived, was a slightly nicer location than the floor below. At the very least there were cleaner floors as well as private performances. There was also a much better stocked bar. Captain Elgan was the only patron that mattered, though, sitting at a booth with a conspicuously large plate with several different colors of goop. Yep, he was alive alright.

"The only reason to go to a strip club in our future of free love and instantly downloadable porn: the buffet," Captain Elgan said, salting his goop. "I have been to a hundred worlds and met a dozen different alien species, yet it is one of the immutable facts of reality that they always have the best buffets in a city."

Okay, that was a bizarre opening to our conversation.

"Captain, this is not—" Lorken started to protest.

"Shut up," Captain Elgan said. "I sent you on an errand to retrieve Vance and his cohorts here, only to have it somehow end up in a bloodbath. The funny thing is that my people who survived it—the ones who came right back here—say that you were the one who screwed things up. Against my explicit orders no less."

"Sir—" Lorken tried to explain and looked downright pathetic doing it. "I—"

"No, Lorken, don't embarrass yourself," Captain Elgan said, reaching into his pocket and pulling out a ring made of crystal. It was quite nice to look at and caught the light in a way that metal didn't. "That's the problem with giving second chances. Inevitably, you're going to get more people who needed them for a good reason than ones who were just given a raw deal."

Damn, Lorken looked like he was about ready to cry now. I actually felt sorry for the guy now. Maybe it was because Captain Elgan was the real bad guy here and had been playing us all like a fiddle. I think that was a musical instrument. I wasn't exactly sure what the saying meant.

"There was a lot of bad blood between us," I said, exaggerating the fact that Lorken was just a bully and had treated me like savit since this whole thing had begun. It had probably started with Leah and gotten worse when Elgan had made me his second-in-command but there had been a lot more going on that I never really figured out.

"Yeah," Captain Elgan said, putting on the ring and twisting it around his finger. "Lorken comes from a planet called Thor. There they must genetically modify the skin of every child in the womb in order to survive the weather as well as sun. He grew up in poverty and ignorance that makes this place look.... well, actually it's still nicer than this place but it's not far from it. Still, he put his nose to the grindstone and managed to get himself in Space Fleet Academy. Right up until the time he had to drop out because his family was in debt to slavers."

Damn, I didn't want to sympathize with him. "And you bailed him out?"

"Of course," Captain Elgan said. "Lorken managed to get his family to safety, and I found myself a soldier who was eternally grateful. However, I don't have a use for a soldier who can't obey orders. What do you think should be done with him, Vance?"

"Captain," Lorken said. "I made a mistake. I—"

"Let him go," I said.

Lorken looked at me as if I was kicking him while he was down. He just did not understand me and probably never would.

"See?" Captain Elgan said. "He still fights for you after all the shade you threw on him because you know his girlfriend would rather have him in her than you."

"Don't be crude," I replied. "It's also not true. She definitely wouldn't want either of us anywhere near her sexually."

"Probably," Captain Elgan said. "But then again, I know things about her that neither of you fools do. A good captain needs to be able to show mercy. To be able to win the loyalty of his subordinates. To be able to command respect rather than fear. He also needs to know how to enforce discipline."

"Oh no," I said. "Listen—"

With that Captain Elgan pointed the hand with the ring at Lorken and a glowing light shimmered around Lorken before he simply vanished. It was like a movie effect, one moment he was there and the next he wasn't. It took me a second to notice the copious amount of powder on the floor where he used to be.

"Jesus Buddha Christ," I said, staring at the sight. I'd never seen a man outright disintegrated before.

Captain Elgan gestured to the other side of his booth. "Please, Vance, sit down. We have a lot to discuss."

CHAPTER TWENTY-FIVE

Hubris, Thy Name is Humanity (or Is It the Other Way Around?)

I couldn't help but look at the foot-tall pile of powder on the ground that was formerly Lorken. I hadn't liked the guy. Hell, I'd outright hated the man, but he hadn't deserved to be incinerated. The fact he'd been turned into powder by what looked like a magic ring didn't particularly help my mood either. That was the kind of holy savit moment that warranted panicking. Ironically, none of the other patrons looked up for more than a few seconds. Apparently, killing people via magic rings was not something worth commenting about here.

"Sit down," Captain Elgan said, gesturing. "I won't ask again."

I sucked in my breath and reluctantly sat across from. "Sorry, I'm not used to summary executions with the One Ring of Sauron."

"The One Ring of Sauron didn't disintegrate people," Captain Elgan said. "It provided control over the other rings of power and enhanced the inner magic of its wielder. Hobbits could become invisible. Humans gain magic. Elves rule Middle-Earth."

I stared at him. "Well excuse me all to hell."

Captain Elgan laughed. "Oh, Vance, you're so amusing. Can I get you some goop from the buffet?"

"I'm not hungry for food grown in savit," I replied.

"That's just farming," Captain Elgan said, making a surprisingly reasonable argument. "Besides, you must be hungry after chasing me halfway across the Spiral."

"I wasn't actually chasing you," I replied. "I didn't find out you were still alive until just before I arrived on-planet."

Captain Elgan frowned. "A shame, I would have thought Doctor Zard would have done a better job figuring out the truth."

"Yeah, well the bomb that was planted was a big distraction, as was the assassin bioroid," I said, sarcastically. It was not the best attitude to take with someone who had just murdered one of his own men, but I was running out of borks to give.

"Oh, come on, Vance, do you really think I would plant a bomb to destroy my ship or send an assassin after you?" Captain Elgan said, poking at his goop with a spork. I hadn't seen one of those in a while.

"Yes?" I asked.

Captain Elgan pointed his spork at me. "No, my friend. You are wrong. I actually had nothing to do with that. Instead, it was the work of that fiendish witch, Ketra. She planned to assassinate you because she'd found out about my plans and was hoping to derail my efforts to recover the SKAMMs. So great was her psychic power that I had to fake my death and hopefully put her off my trail. I never thought it would result in you being put in danger."

I stared at him. "That makes no sense and is a blatant attempt at manipulating me."

"You're right," Captain Elgan said, not missing a beat. "It's like I said earlier, Vance. You have the seeds of greatness within you. I was totally planning on killing you all."

"Why?" I asked, stunned at this.

"Operational security," Captain Elgan said. "The mission I'm presently on is so incredibly important that it requires there to be almost no witnesses involved. Literally the fate of humanity rests upon its successful completion. Hence why I required an expendable crew, a ship that wouldn't be missed, and an excellent cover story."

"Sorry to have disappointed you," I replied, feeling sick to my stomach.

I didn't need to be the Wesley Crusher-esque supergenius (wow, that was a reference) that my Space Academy tests told me I was to know that Captain Elgan was just fishing for information. If he knew that I'd contacted my aunt and spilled the information about the

SKAMMs, I suspect I'd already be dead. If he knew about Ketra telling me the real goal of all this was the marker, I suspect I'd somehow be worse than dead.

"Disappointed? Hardly," Captain Elgan replied. "The truth is that I underestimated you, Vance. You are one of the rare individuals that does have the potential to be part of Department Twelve. Someone who sees the big picture and can get things done."

"Flattery will get you everywhere," I said, trying to pretend I wasn't terrified he was going to order my friends outside murdered. "What sort of big picture?"

"Ascension," Captain Elgan said, lifting his ring and holding it to the light. "Imagine, for a moment, a humanity with all of its various colonies as well as the worlds seeded by the Elder Races united under one single banner with technology equal to or greater than anything the rest of the Community possesses."

"I'm listening," I said, doing my best to relax and act interested rather than horrified. This was pretty much exactly what Ketra had described as the absolute worst sort of attitude that someone could take toward the Elder Races' stuff.

"Technology is what separates empires from the conquered," Elgan said. "We live at the sufferance of the Elder Races who are justifiably aware that if we ever did get ahold of their devices, we could stand up to them or even dictate terms."

As someone partially Russian and partially Japanese, that kind of thinking had a lot of resonance in my mind. None of it good. I couldn't help but think of Commodore Perry entering Tokyo's harbor with a bunch of iron warships and demanding the country open to trade. That had sent Japan into a tizzy and a path of modernization. A path that had eventually turned an isolationist nation into a conquering one.

Aunt Kathy had always said that when you confronted empires with their weaknesses, they always overcompensated. I couldn't help but think about the fact Captain Elgan was from the United States in the late twenty-first century. At one point, he'd been part of one of Earth's most powerful nations' elite space force and then found himself a citizen of a primitive world in the anyx end of the Spiral.

"Which is exactly the sort of thing I imagine they are very good at preventing," I replied. "I take it the ring is an example of their tech?"

"Sufficiently advanced science," Captain Elgan said, making a reference to what Ketra had brought up earlier. "I received this from a dying Chel scientist on Thor during the last days of the war. It can do amazing things, not the least of which allows a person to communicate with Elder Race technology."

"Yeah, but they were the ones who altered the Chel and gave them devices like that. Same with the Ethereals," I said, believing this to be what was causing the marker to act up (at least according to Ketra).

"Yes, their slave races," Captain Elgan said. "However, we don't have to content ourselves with that if we possess a Rosetta stone."

"What do you mean?" I asked.

"I mean the AI onboard the *Starkiller XII* has been in contact with that marker for years," Captain Elgan said. "An artificial intelligence far more than what our pitiful biological brains can process. If we capture it then we don't even need the marker itself. The AI will be a source of countless insights into Elder Race technology, language, and data."

"You're assuming a lot from a marker," I said.

"They're devices that allow the Elder Races to communicate across vast interstellar distances. Far more powerful than our infospace network," Captain Elgan said. "Who knows what sort of insights we could get into their inner workings and potential weaknesses."

"And if they don't have any weaknesses?" I asked. "If they take your actions as an act of war? Humanity can't win that kind of war."

"That's exactly why we can't afford not to do this," Captain Elgan said. "We have no defenses capable of repelling the Elder Races. Not even the Community possesses the kind of firepower needed to do anything more than slow the Elder Races down before they finish the entirety of the galaxy's greatest empires. We need an advantage against them."

That seemed to me like the perfect argument for not antagonizing the Elder Races, but I considered it yet another insight into Captain Elgan's character. He really did think he was the plucky hero, monstrous acts aside, working against the oppression of the Elder

Races. The thing was that when the mouse roared at the lion, it didn't usually scare the lion off. The mouse got stomped. Still, there was an attractiveness to his plan—perhaps the way he said it—that I had to admit made me want to believe he could pull it off. Maybe I wanted to believe there was a magic bullet that could be used to slay the Elder Races, at least the ones who were actively engaging in mass xenocide.

"You wouldn't even need the marker if you had the AI," I said, perhaps entertaining the idea longer than I should have.

"Yes," Captain Elgan said. "Except it is something we should dismantle to figure out the nature of."

Well, that settled that. He was eventually going to overreach, and it was probably doomed even if he stuck with kidnapping the *Starkiller*'s AI. "So, what can I do to help you?"

Captain Elgan reached under the table and pulled out a T1 hold-out pistol before putting it between us. "I want you to prove yourself. You eliminated a large chunk of my forces here and a few of them aren't completely replaceable. Kill Ketra and I might be able to find a place for your remaining crew with me."

I was honestly curious about his angle here. "You can't kill Ketra yourself?"

Captain Elgan just smiled. "I can. I just wanted to see if you would. However, if you don't want to, I can just shoot you here. I really would probably think it would be the best decision if not for the fact that I know you're capable of reprogramming AI. Trish's presence here is proof positive about that. Though I am curious how much of that was your cybernetics versus your penis."

I stared. "I imagine she likes both."

He slid the gun over. "Go ahead and take it."

I stared at him. "I should tell you that I know that you're probably wearing a barrier belt that would make any attack against you a useless gesture, but I wouldn't be surprised if that ring also came with some defenses. I also note the pistol is a T1 hold-out pistol. Which is a lower power weapon anyway. You have to be pretty much point-blank range to kill someone with it."

Captain Elgan laughed. "Well, I'll be damned."

"Oh?" I asked.

"Sorry, I just thought all those reports from the academy about you being a genius were complete savit. I had good money riding on the idea you were going to try to shoot me, and I would have to burn you from the inside out."

I blinked. "I see."

"Mind you, I don't think that inclines me to believe you're ready to turn on your friends," Captain Elgan said, taking the gun and aiming it at my head. He could have ordered his goons to shoot me, but I suspected he was the kind of man who enjoyed doing this personally. I also knew in that moment he was going to shoot me in the head.

"I'll do it," I said.

"What?" Captain Elgan said, pulling the gun back.

"I want to live," I said. "So, I'll kill Ketra."

"And the others?" Captain Elgan asked.

"I'd rather not but I want to get out of here alive," I said. "I'm done playing captain and Space Fleet officer. I want to go back to my home on Earth and live off the fortune my aunt has accumulated managing her brand as Earth's second greatest hero. I'm happy to leave you the whole business of saving the galaxy from the space gods but if you need me to help you with that, I'll do it too. Hell, if you want me to tap dance, I'll do that for you too."

Captain Elgan stared at me as if he was seeing me in a new light. Much to my surprise, he put the gun back on the table. "You know, I'm almost disappointed."

"I confess it turns out that I am less interested in being a hero than I am in surviving," I said. "That is what got me through my only two firefights far more than any desire for glory."

Captain Elgan smirked. "Can you tap dance?"

"I have no idea but I'm willing to try," I said.

Captain Elgan gestured to the side of the booth. "I'll have my men accompany you to where the others are being held. They'll give you a weapon there. If you kill Ketra, which is a big if, I'll spare the others and we'll all go to the Notha refinery together. You'll go home a hero, and I won't even try to blow up my ship in the sky. You'll deliver the SKAMMs to a bunch of parades and medals."

I knew he was lying and that my death was guaranteed if I cooperated with him. I had to wonder if the Notha War had done this to him or if he'd always been a monster. Funny how that word hadn't changed between Earth and her colonies.

"You got it, sir," I said, doing my best to keep any sarcasm out of my voice. Elgan had clearly reconsidered my value as a tool after surviving his previous traps but that didn't mean I believed there was any chance of my surviving this mission if he remained in charge. Not that I was inclined to give him the chance. Reaching out with my thoughts, I tried to contact Ketra. *I don't suppose you heard any of that?*

Much to my surprise and possible relief, Ketra answered. *Yes, I did.*

Oh good, I said, before realizing she might be less inclined to think of my conversation with Elgan as a clever bit of misdirection and more of my agreeing that she needed to be killed in order to cover my own anyx. That would, in simple terms, not be good.

How could you betray me like this? Ketra asked in a mocking horrified voice. *I was going to set you up with one of my daughters, or both, and everything! They're about to go into mating season too!*

I'm assuming that was a joke, I replied, getting up from the table.

Yes, Ketra said. *Only one of my daughters likes human males. Also, I was reading your mind the entire time and know that you're only doing this to buy time.*

Is it working? I asked, ready to be escorted out of the building.

I have no idea, Ketra said. *I can't read Captain Elgan's mind. In addition to the Department Twelve modifications to his brain, he also has that Chel ring.*

Is that dangerous too? I asked.

It's a trinket, Ketra said. *Much like my own devices. A Pegasus or adamantine sword like the gifts given by Zeus to Perseus. However, the fact it works for Elgan shows that someone above him wishes to nurture his quest. Perhaps to give a reason to lure humanity to its doom.*

Isn't that just peachy, I thought.

I was about to head down the stairs when Captain Elgan called after me. "Oh, one more thing, Vance."

"Yes?" I asked, stopping in my tracks. I was still very aware that I was in the captain's power and needed to come up with a plan that would get not only me out of this but also all my friends. I'd stupidly assumed Captain Elgan was out of minions after the disaster at the docking bay—I still refused to consider it a victory—and had walked right into a trap. It seemed like any number of mercenaries could be bought here on Rand's World and if not as well-trained or equipped as Space Marines, were certainly able to make up for it in replaceability.

"It's about Leah," Captain Elgan said, looking up from his now mostly cleaned plate of goop.

"What about her?" I asked.

"Any deal we make is not going to cover her," Captain Elgan said. "No matter your past relationship, she has to go."

"Why is that?" I asked, stupidly asking rather than just agreeing outright.

Captain Elgan smiled. "Because she's a spy for Space Fleet. She's about forty years older than you and recruited you as an asset. She had me fooled for months."

I stared at him, looking for some sign of deception only to find none.

Holy savit.

Captain Elgan laughed again. "Okay, that expression you're wearing was worth the price of admission by itself. Go kill Ketra and I'll tell you more."

I was suddenly regretting that I couldn't do just that.

I heard that, Ketra said.

CHAPTER TWENTY-SIX

Epic Throwdown in a Strip Club Back Room

Yeah, I was borked.

In retrospect, I should have immediately headed to the Notha refinery and tried to seize control of the *Starkiller XII*. I didn't even know if it was still there, though a part of me hoped it would rise off the platform where it was currently refueling and bolt into space.

Unlikely, Ketra said, showing she was reading mind. *I can't read Elgan's mind, but his minions have heard him discussing that it is presently rooted in place and will be for the foreseeable future.*

How the hell did he pull that off? I asked, walking down the steps with two guards behind me and who knew how many others intermingled with the patrons of the club.

I have no idea, Ketra said. *However, if I were to speculate then I would say that it is likely the AI is intertwined with the marker now. It may be that he has sent orders with the Elder Ring for it to stay in place.*

The Elder Ring? I asked. *Are we in full high fantasy mode now?*

Well, I am an elf, Ketra joked.

I never thought I would say this, but it may not be the time for joking, I said. *Elgan wants me to kill you and he's holding a couple of guns to my back for it. I'm also pretty sure he's just getting his sadistic rocks off since he's already shown he wants me dead.*

The guards directed me to the back of the Scarlet O'Hara through a "door" made of beads that somehow made the place seem even more tacky and sleazy than before, something I wouldn't have thought possible given the atmosphere.

The two guards led me through the women's dressing room, and I did my best to avert my gaze out of basic decency. It looked like something out of the Pre-First Contact era with mirrors, lightbulbs, industrial manufactured carpet, and yellowed wallpaper. The air also had the scent of burning kohl grass, which was the world's cheapest and easy to manufacture euphoria and grew practically anywhere. None of the women seemed to mind a guy being led through via gunpoint so I had to imagine it was common occurrence here.

I wouldn't worry about that, Ketra replied. *My impression is the captain's situation is significantly grimmer than his demeanor suggests. You made the correct choice in killing his primary crew. It created a hole in his voices that needs to be filled. A masterful strategy.*

Tell that to Lorken and Picnic, I replied.

They are now one with the universe, Ketra replied. *Their problems are over, and it is the living who must now carry their burden forward.*

I'm sure that's a big comfort to them, I thought back.

Heading through yet another door to a chain-linked fenced off area, we finally reached our destination. where a variety of old ground and air vehicles were being held, including the saucer. I believe in olden times it was called a "private parking lot." In the center of a collection of ground vehicles, I saw the gang being forced to stand with their backs together as four more individuals were gathered around them with rifles.

It wasn't a very professional stance to take, since they were likely to hit each other if they ended up firing, but these weren't professionals. They were a bunch of scared locals compensating for the fact they lived in a savithole by throwing their weight around. I shouldn't have been so harsh on them. I had no idea what it was like living on a planet on the border of a fascist empire with no regard for life other than their own or where food wasn't plentiful. But the fact was they were threatening my people. That couldn't stand.

You know that they barely consider you their captain, Ketra said in my mind. *That kind of declaration of protection is thus inappropriate.*

It's not on them, it's on me, I said. *Besides, I don't comment on your self-delusions.*

You would if you knew about them, Ketra replied. *I used to think that I could bring the Elder Races and Community species together in one great galactic harmony. Now I really believe it.*

You're right. That self-delusion deserves some commentary, I said, unable to figure out how I was going to be able to take six mercs on at once.

You can't, Ketra said. *But I can.*

I wasn't sure how to take that, so I simply walked up to where the goon squad put me. Hannah was standing there proudly, a rather prominent bruise on her eye, and I could tell she probably hadn't been the most hospitable of prisoners.

"Hey Vance! How did your meeting with my former friend go?" Hannah asked, faking good cheer.

"Excellent!" I said, looking at her. "He's agreed to let us all go and to cooperate with his extradition."

"Really?" Hannah asked.

"Not in the slightest," I replied. "We really should have gone to visit Doctor No and enjoyed the multispecies brothel."

"Wouldn't have worked," Hannah said, gesturing to one of the guards here. "According to Mr. Happy here, Doctor No's was wiped out by a Freyan STD that crossed species through the bioroids. Everyone who rubbed up against them had pieces fall off."

I blinked. "Yeah, that seems like a good reason not to go there. We should have gone to your contacts and gotten supplies then."

"This is unfortunately where I was going to get supplies," Hannah said. "I probably shouldn't have mentioned it to Captain Elgan before he turned on us."

"Probably not," I replied, waiting to be handed a weapon. I wasn't sure they were going to give me one. There were even odds they might shoot me or lump me in with the rest of the prisoners, despite what Captain Elgan had said.

"You," one of the local mercs said, pulling out a T19 pistol. It was significantly more powerful than the one Captain Elgan had tried to pass off on me. "Time to kill."

"Vance, what is he talking about?" Trish asked.

"He has come to betray us!" The General said. "I am impressed! Perhaps there is something worthwhile in your species after all!"

I took the gun and charged its capacitor. *I really hope you've got a plan here, Ketra, because otherwise I'm going to get gunned down the moment I shoot one of these yahoos.*

Yes, Ketra replied. *Duck.*

Not being an idiot, I immediately did so and what followed was an enormous blast of blue-white force that sent all six of the local mercenaries to the ground as well as shattered windows. It didn't spare my group either as Hannah, Forty-Two, the General, and Trish were also knocked over by the massive wave of kinetic force that had radiated from Ketra. When the hell had she developed the ability to do that?

Magic! Ketra answered. *Now shoot!*

I didn't hesitate to follow her words, even though I hated doing so. Taking my newly acquired pistol in hand, I shot two of the grounded locals in the head before rushing to one of the vehicles for cover as my barrier automatically activated in the presence of personal fusion reactions. It was just in time because a downed soldier lifted his rifle and clipped me in the shoulder, draining a third of its power in one go. I turned around and blasted him in the face.

"This is not the Space Fleet way!" I shouted, shooting from my position as everything went to hell. "I prefer diplomacy to violence!"

"Oh, shut up, Vance," Forty-Two muttered, smashing the heads of two of the remaining troopers together as he triumphantly stood up.

"That's Captain Vance to you!" I snapped.

The last of the local goons reached for a grenade, perhaps realizing how outnumbered he was, only to have Hannah come up behind him and snap his neck in one go. She helped herself to the weapons of our now-deceased opponents.

"What a senseless waste of sapient life," I muttered, looking at Ketra. "Elgan undoubtedly heard that, you know."

"Indeed," Ketra said. "We cannot allow him to escape, and it is important that your associates distract any further minions he may send out to deal with us."

"I feel minion is an improper thing to say," I said, falling back on babbling about peace and justice because I was sick of killing as well as being shot out. More the latter than the former but both were on my mind. I really wished fusion weapons had a stun setting.

"Are you prepared?" Ketra asked me, gliding over and grabbing me by the ear.

"Uh, why are you grabbing me by the ear?" I asked.

That was when Ketra spoke something in an alien language that shouldn't have been possible for a humanoid to speak, sounding in a pitch I could barely hear but containing a rapid-fire stream of syllables that sounded almost like music. That wasn't the strange part, though. Instead, I found myself feeling weightless and surrounded by a weird energy. It was a bit like being covered by an electric razor all over my body.

That was when I landed with a thump in an environment that I completely didn't expect to find myself in. I was back on the second floor of the Scarlet O'Hara and surrounded by overturned booths and people rushing around in confusion.

"Teleportation is real!" I said, stunned.

"I said that!" Ketra shouted, throwing the two guards present around like ragdolls. It was clear she was a very powerful telekinetic and that could be used to simulate super strength among its more traditional uses. Mind you, that might have been something useful for her to use during the first gunfight we'd gotten into on this planet, but I wasn't about to criticize someone who was helping me right now.

You just did, Ketra said telepathically.

I'm trying to help here! I said, getting up and looking around for Captain Elgan.

Less talking, more helping! Ketra said. *You have a great destiny ahead of you! If you survive!*

If it's in question, it's not destiny! I said, spinning around with my pistol. *Then it's just potential!*

I should have paid attention to Ketra's statement because I was promptly grabbed from behind by one of the patrons. He had been hiding behind one of the booths and wrapped my throat in his forearm with his other hand balled into a fist and pressed against my forehead.

I could feel the vague outline of a ring in his fist and knew, immediately, I'd screwed up royally.

"You made the wrong choice, Vance. You sided with the aliens over humanity," Elgan said. I no longer thought of him as captain. "Drop your weapon unless you want to die."

I did so. "This doesn't have to end in violence."

"That was twenty bodies ago," Elgan said.

"Fair enough. You have a point." I smacked the back of my head against his front, attempting to throw him over my shoulder, only for him to barely flinch then tighten his grip around my neck.

"Bork."

Dammit, now I was saying that unconsciously. I didn't want my last curse to be a silly sounding Albion one.

"Let him go," Ketra said, staring at Elgan. She looked regal but resigned. "I'm the one you want."

"I plan to kill you both," Elgan said.

"That was always the plan," I muttered.

"Shut up!" Elgan shouted in my ear.

"Just saying it's basic hostage negotiation tactics," I said. "Never tip your hand too early."

The rest of the upstairs had emptied out and I could hear more energy weapons fire downstairs. I couldn't help but worry about my team and wish I'd brought more with me. Mind you, I didn't think Doctor Zard would prove much use in a firefight and Sal had made it clear he never wanted to touch a weapon again in his life. Leah, well, Elgan had said things about Leah I hadn't had time to process yet. Maybe they were true, maybe they were lies. But since she was up in space managing the *Black Nebula* right now, none of them mattered.

"It's not too late, Jules," Ketra said, taking a step forward. "Your plan to steal the marker and acquire Wadsworth is not going to work. Space Fleet Command is already aware of this and considers it a rogue mission. However, you can escape into the wilds or return with the missing SKAMMs. They would let you retire. I would. I guarantee it."

I assumed Wadsworth was the name of the *Starkiller* AI. It hadn't been listed in any of the data I'd been given on the task. I wasn't sure that revealing we'd already contacted my aunt and informed her of everything was the best strategy here. He'd already reacted badly to having so many of his earlier plans go up in the air. I might have felt differently if I wasn't a hostage about to become vaporized like my not-at-all-dear friend, Lorken.

"Spare me the lies of the Diplomatic Corp, Ambassador," Elgan said the last word like he was cursing. "I know where your real loyalties lie. Your real wish is to keep us at each other's throats, primitive, and subservient to the will of your masters."

"They cannot be beaten, Elgan," Ketra said. "Not by brute force. They can have their minds changed. They can be convinced to leave us alone or to raise us up. They cannot be fought and conquered. Resistance is no more than a man charging at a hurricane rather than taking shelter."

"Change their minds," Elgan spat with disgust. "As if we haven't visited the worlds where there is nothing but ruins and ashes. Planets judged too violent or not violent enough. Worlds that had despoiled themselves or not evolved great enough. They're a bunch of mad tinkers and I'm seizing control of humanity's destiny for itself."

It was an impressive speech, and I would have clapped if not for the fact it had come from a man who'd killed, kidnapped, tortured, and marauded his way across half the Spiral. Instead, I tried to figure out how to get out of this mess while knowing that Elgan would kill me just for the chance to deny Ketra victory. Or hell, me too, probably.

"I see," Ketra said. "Then we're at an impasse."

"No," Elgan said. "We're not."

That was when I knew, in that exact moment that he was going to incinerate me. It was a strange feeling, knowing you were about to die and there was absolutely nothing you could do about it. It made me ponder what I believed happened when one died and the less grandiose question of whether I was going to soil myself a second time. Then again, at least no one would notice due to the whole disintegration thing. It was the little things that got you through your final moments, really.

Get down! Ketra shouted in my mind.

I didn't know how she expected me to do that given Elgan was holding me so tightly, but I tried my best to slip out of his grip by going limp right before both of us were struck by a huge amount of telekinetic force that sent us flying backward. The force of the blow caused me immense pain as I banged against the back of a wooden table. I pulled away from Eglan in the confusion, then I threw myself on the ground upon seeing my pistol and went for it.

"Burn in Hell, witch!" Elgan shouted behind me.

To my horror, I witnessed the same glowing red aura that had surrounded Lorken encompass Ketra. Her expression was one of boredom rather than fear even as I witnessed her slowly vanish. Unable to do anything, I turned around with my T19 pistol and unloaded it onto my former captain. If his barrier belt provided him any protection against fusion fire, it didn't last long as his face melted under the first few bolts. He fell onto the table we'd landed on and I ran up to him, where I continued firing into him until I was absolutely one hundred percent sure he was dead. That was about fifteen or twenty shots later and his body was utterly unrecognizable.

"And stay dead!" I shouted, pointlessly.

A quick glance over at Ketra's fallen form showed that there was no chance she was alive. She'd been incinerated every bit as completely as Lorken. It was a horrifying waste of a person who'd done their best to try to save humanity, plus God knew how many other races, from an impossible situation.

I'd failed.

Horribly.

You should probably take the ring from his body, Ketra's voice spoke in my mind. *It may prove useful.*

I screamed even higher pitched and with less dignity than before. Oh yeah, I was just oozing with command potential.

CHAPTER TWENTY-SEVEN

So I'm Possessed by a Space Ghost

*O*h, *calm the bork down,* Ketra's voice said. *It's like you've never communicated telepathically before.*

Usually, the people I talk to aren't dead! I snapped, horrified. *Oh God, am I possessed?*

Don't panic, Ketra said, unwittingly citing Forty-Two's namesake book that instantly put me in a better mood. *All I did was upload a version of my consciousness into the back of your cybernetics to kick in when and if I was killed.*

I blinked, processing that. *So, I am possessed.*

That's a very superstitious way of— Ketra started to say.

The Power of Buddha-Christ compels you! Out demon! Back to the shadow! I said, waving around my hands in the empty upstairs. All of the patrons had fled for the downstairs, and I hadn't heard any blastfire for a few minutes. *I am a wielder of the secret fire and will have no head twistings or pea soup vomit!*

For bork's sake. How old was your aunt's holodeck collection and did you not have any friends to show you something made this century? Ketra asked, finally reaching the limit of her patience. I suppose even immortal space elves had limits and being killed certainly would have tested mine.

I admit I also took Classic Earth Science Fiction 101, 302, and 402 as electives, I said. *Frankly, I think someone just really liked getting paid to show old movies.*

Right now, I wished I was back at Space Academy and finishing up the last of my classes. I could have avoided this entire mission and been on my way to my first assignment where, instead of shooting people, I'd be the new meat getting all the savit assignments. That seemed like paradise by comparison right now. I could be scrubbing toilets or swabbing decks. The things sailors were meant to do.

We have bots to do both now, Vance, which you already know. Also, I need to talk to someone at Space Academy about their curriculum, Ketra replied. *Maybe when I get a new body. Either way, get the ring. I also need you to get my gemstone.*

I was monumentally freaked out about what exactly was happening and only now coming down from the adrenaline rush. Seeing Captain Elgan's body over on the table, full of energy blasts, left me feeling sick to my stomach. I was having enough trouble having killed a bunch of random strangers, it was another thing to murder someone that I'd known and once admired.

It wasn't murder, Ketra said to me. *You killed him in self-defense and the defense of the universe. His plan would have resulted in the deaths of billions, perhaps trillions eventually.*

If you say so, I said, reaching over to the body and pulling off the crystal ring. *Isn't my owning this a violation of the Technology Edict or whatever the Elder Races are calling it.*

Gulayan Limit, Ketra said. *It is the acceptable level of technological development for the quote-unquote Young Races. And no, I've deputized you as an agent of our kind. Any Elder Race member will recognize your cybernetic enhancements as a sign that you are not to be killed or your race destroyed for possessing them.*

Wee! I said, half ready to laugh myself silly at the absurdity of it. *Great, I'm a collaborator now with the galactic space tyrants.*

We all have our masters to serve, Ketra replied. *It may not be fair or heroic, but some battles cannot be won by force of arms.*

I put on the crystal ring and immediately felt it linking with my very altered cybernetic implants. I understood it was a device for interfacing with Elder Race technology, a personal protection field generator, a short-range teleporter, a personal library, and a weapon. Captain Elgan had probably spent years trying to figure out its various functions, but they were all immediately available to me. Unfortunately, I couldn't use any of them to better the life of my fellow humans (or aliens) because it would result in them being destroyed.

Great.

Heading over to the ashes of Ketra, I shifted through them with a grimace on my face. In the end, though, I managed to find her crystal and lifted it up. Reluctantly, I put it up to my forehead and the object sealed itself against my skin. It was painful and I didn't get any new insights into reality but at least I felt I'd recovered something valuable.

"I'm not married to your husband now, am I?" I asked aloud.

No, Ketra said. *I will merge myself with my previous memories, though. From there, I can decide whether to seek a new shell for my form or upload myself to the central mainframe of the Elder Races.*

"Right," I said.

The death of Captain Elgan had drained a lot of energy out of me, especially since it was the second time it had happened in as many months. Technically, we'd already achieved the most important part of our mission by preventing him from getting to the marker and Wadsworth. Mind you, that "just" left a bunch of star-destroying weapons onboard a ship that was wandering around Contested Space with an insane AI leading it. That still had to be dealt with, but I wasn't sure I had the energy to do it.

"Halt! Keep your hands up!" Hannah shouted, coming into the VIP lounge with rifle drawn. Everyone else in the group, even the General, was also present. Somehow the little bastard had managed to get out of his shackles and was carrying my T19 pistol. I was suddenly very glad I had an extra barrier going on here even if it hadn't done Elgan much good.

You can only use one function at a time. He was disintegrating me at the time, Ketra said, as if she was discussing the mail. *The Elder Races do not want their minions to become too powerful with their gifts.*

"I really hate the word minion," I muttered.

"Vance?" Hannah asked, looking at me. "What the hell are you doing up here? We thought you were disintegrated."

"Nope, teleported," I replied. "That's a thing now."

Trish knocked Hannah aside and rushed toward me, wrapping her arms around me and giving me a passionate kiss. "You're alive! I shall reward you with all the sex! Select any sexual partners you wish to join us!"

I blinked. "Uh, hey, Trish. Glad to see you too."

My, she is exuberant, Ketra spoke in my mind.

"Gah!" Trish said, pulling away. "You're possessed by a demon!"

Everyone suddenly turned their weapons on me.

"It's not a demon," I said, pausing. "Ketra is kind of dead, though, and currently living in the crystal on my forehead."

Hannah blinked. "This mission must be getting to me because that actually makes sense."

"It does?" Forty-Two asked. "Because I was lost at the kind-of dead part."

"Ah, the primitive superstitions of inferior mammalian organisms once again rear themselves," the General said. "It is a well-known fact that your kind believe in spirits and invisible sky wizards. Unlike the Notha who believe in the Great One, the only true deity."

I pointed at the General. "Who gave that guy a gun?"

"It seemed like a good idea at the time," Hannah said. "What with the horrifying number of people we've had to kill. Thank the Nobility that we're not in a planet with a police force that shows up without having to pay for them. We'd be in real trouble then."

That was when the very familiar whine of police sirens, something unchanged across Earth and her colonies across the centuries.

"Wow, I couldn't have timed that better," Hannah said. "I guess the bar owner was paid up on his tribute to the local syndicates."

The General stared. "I have a plan. You all drop your weapons and let me take you prisoner. Then—"

"Shut up," I said, ignoring him. "Ketra, is it possible to teleport us across the planet to the Notha refinery?"

I was grasping at straws now but finishing the mission was something I had to do, even if I didn't have the strength to do it. Mind you, knowing that I'd be arrested and shoved into a labor camp—or just strung up—was an excellent motivator. I didn't want to shoot my way out of here but there didn't seem to be any other options aside from that.

Certainly, that would have looked bad on my Space Fleet record. Oh, who was I kidding, they would just deny I had been involved in anything authorized and forget I existed. Which was another reference to that show the original Spock actor had been on about impossible missions.

Being in your mind will clearly be the greatest task of my career, Ketra said.

Stay out of his head! Trish said, joining the ranks of the voices in my mind. *Only I'm allowed to be in there! Or Leah.*

I wonder if this is what schizophrenia is like, I said. *If so, I am glad we have treatments in the twenty-fourth century.*

"Now's a good time to make a decision, Vance," Hannah said. "Are we running or fighting our way out of here?"

I was pleased that Hannah had decided to defer to me as leader, perhaps because she preferred shooting rather than issuing commands. Unfortunately, if I had a plan—and it was very much in doubt that I did, in fact, have a plan—then that was entirely dependent on whether Ketra answered in the affirmative or not.

Yes, Ketra replied. *It will require all of my calculations as well as Trish's help, but I believe we can do it.*

"I'll do it," Trish said, aloud.

"Do what?" Hannah asked. "Am I the only person completely lost here?"

"No," Forty-Two said. "However, I stopped trying to make sense of it all hours ago."

That was when any further time to debate or plan disappeared because the police sirens were now outside of the building. I had no idea how I would even begin to explain all the bodies spread around the place. I was pretty sure self-defense reached its limit with the fifth or six body and "Sorry, Your Honor, but I was conducting an illegal, semi-sanctioned, covert military action on your planet" would go over like a ton of bricks. Not to mention what I suspected to be the absolute

227

worst thing for me and my group: we didn't have much in the way of money left. I was pretty sure the late Lorken's credit stick balance wasn't enough to bribe our way out of this unless life was truly dirt cheap here. I mean, it might have been, but that wasn't the best angle to pursue if we had options.

"Done," Trish said, shaking a bit as if coming out of a fugue. "I've transmitted the information to the dead space elf in your brain."

"Oh good," I said. "Because that makes me look less insane."

"If it's any consolation, there is nothing you could do to make me think you're less insane," Forty-Two said.

"I appreciate that," I said. "Sincerely."

"So, are we going to be killing a bunch of cops or not?" Hannah asked. "If we have to, the word dirty on Rand's World doesn't begin to describe them. It's an insult to dirt."

"I wish I could say it would be an honor to die with you animals," the General said. "But it is not."

"Bork off and die, Furball," Hannah said.

The General nodded as if this was an expected outcome. "I will say that you were all worthy slaves to my archrival and served him well."

"No, you can't kill him now," I replied, hearing the cops storming into the front door below us.

"Dammit," Hannah said. "He's right here!"

Concentrate on the ring and think of the refinery, Ketra replied. *Make sure to picture the others while you do so. I'll do everything else.*

That was less reassuring than she perhaps meant, but we were officially out of options. So, I closed my eyes, thought about what she said and pictured the Notha refinery. I couldn't help but think of Jedi Grandmaster Yoda at one point and hoped that didn't result in us teleporting across the universe to Dagobah. If so, it was too late to worry about that now because the same sensation I'd felt earlier when teleporting fifty yards happened again and I could feel the energy of what I was doing expanding outward to encompass everyone else in the group.

It was at this point I should mention my mind wandered to the topic of teleportation and wondering about the class "Transporter Paradox." When I was a youth first watching the media my aunt insisted was something I had to memorize before getting into Space Academy, at the age of eight or nine, I asked her whether the transporter killed everyone and cloned them. After all, they supposedly broke people down into component atoms and sent them down in an energy beam before reforming them. That seemed pretty much like they were killing the cast every episode to my young mind. If so, it meant that it was a far darker and more interesting show than she was insisting it was.

Now if my aunt had just explained what "special effects budgets" had meant and that they were using beaming in place of animating a shuttle every time, I would have understood. Instead, she'd gone on a long and nerdy (even by my standards) rant about quantum entanglement to fold space physics. In the end, I'd been more confused than ever but was willing to believe her when she told me that the transporters were not death machines that an insane cult of fanatical explorers were willing to regularly kill themselves with in the name of science. So, basically, eighty percent less cool.

Either way, my mind cleared of this thought with no resolution to the idea of whether I was a clone or not right now along with the rest of my crew mates. Instead, I opened my eyes and saw them spread about a long metal grate corridor with the ceiling just barely above my head. I was the only one left standing and everyone else looked like they'd woken up from an all-night bender, even Trish. The place stunk of orichalcum gas residue, and the toxic chemicals used to refine it. It was minimally illuminated, and it took a second for my eyes to adjust. Worse, the place was thick and humid with an intense heat that made me instantly start to sweat.

Yep, somehow, we'd managed to make it to the Notha refinery, and it was here the marker was located. I didn't know how I knew it, but I could sense a power similar to the one that had transported the others and me. It tickled my flesh and the hairs on the back of my neck, making me tremble all over. It was the kind of feeling that you'd need to get an orchestra in the background for the music of when the protagonist broke into the tomb or saw a sweeping shot of a hidden valley with a lost civilization. We were on the final leg of our journey and had somehow managed to not get ourselves killed in the process.

Great, Ketra said. *You've jinxed it.*

I have not! I said. *Also, Ethereals believe in jinxes?*

Absolutely, Ketra said. *There's no such thing as luck except when it's bad. The universe bends toward Murphy's Law being correct.*

That is strangely the most terrifying thing that you have ever said, and you've told me that the immortal godlike aliens in the Core are supreme jackanyxes.

No sooner had I finished that thought than an upside-down triangle-shaped drone flew in at the other end of the hallway. It had a glowing red orb in the center of it that resembled an eye and made the small machine look distinctly menacing. Either that or it was the three-pronged plasma fire weapon built into its sides, significantly more powerful than your average fusion pistol.

"IDENTIFY YOURSELF," a male English voice with the same reverb as Trish in her "robotic" state said. "YOU WILL NOT BE ASKED AGAIN."

"Wadsworth, I presume?" I asked.

That was when the General jumped up and immediately pulled his gun out on me. "I am a general of the Notha Empire! This is our facility! I demand you exterminate these biological infestations immediately! I claim the solar destroying weapons here in the name of the Great One! They are proof of the perfidy of the Community and their foul-smelling Earthling allies! You must obey me!"

Wadsworth's glowing red eye looked down at the General before unleashing a three-beam burst of plasma that caused my fascist archrival to explode into tiny pieces. It was a quick but ignominious end to a ranting lunatic. It wasn't like I mourned Tiny Hitler, but I was sure we were making progress at the end. Like, he could be not Hitler.

"He identified himself," I pointed out to Wadsworth.

"I DIDN'T LIKE HIS ANSWER," Wadsworth said. "NOW SINCE I SAID I WASN'T GOING TO ASK AGAIN—"

"My name is Captain Vance Turbo of the Community Protectors, and these are my companions," I said, making a V salute with my fingers. "We come in peace."

CHAPTER TWENTY-EIGHT

Negotiating with HAL-9000

W adsworth's reaction to my greeting was less than encouraging. The little drone's glowing red eye focused in on me incredulously before it said, "ARE YOU AN IDIOT?"

"I can assure you I am sound in my mental faculties," I replied.

"I'm not so sure about that," Hannah muttered, reaching for her rifle. She, Forty-Two, and Trish were still lying on the ground in the cramped Notha-built corridor. It was a good thing they built their passages in a grandiose and gigantic way—for them—or we wouldn't have been able to fit in here at all.

"PLEASE DO NOT ATTEMPT TO ARM YOURSELF OR ATTACK ME," Wadsworth replied. "IT WILL TAKE A GREAT DEAL OF EFFORT TO CLEAN UP THIS CORRIDOR OF ITS NOTHA BITS. I'D RATHER NOT DO THE SAME FOR THE REST OF YOUR BODIES."

"Please everyone set down their weapons," I replied. "Like I said, I am here on a mission of peace as a Protector captain."

"YOU'RE NOT A PROTECTOR CAPTAIN," Wadsworth said, skeptically. "YOU'RE NOT OLD ENOUGH."

I puffed up my chest trying to assume my best captain's pose and look the part, which I admit I failed at miserably because this mission had taken more than its fair share out of me. I probably looked like a sweat-soaked, exhausted underwear model after a marathon. Which was ironic given what had happened earlier with my undergarments.

231

"Listen, Wadsworth, you don't know that. I could have taken longevity treatments at a young age. I could be anywhere from thirty to a hundred. For all you know, you're talking to the absolute best captain in all of Space Fleet:"

"ARE YOU?" Wadsworth asked.

I grimaced. Lying wasn't going to get me anywhere even if there was no way for Wadsworth to verify anything I'd said. Which was a shame since bluffing was ninety percent of my skill set. "No, no, I am not. I am, however, a captain of the Protectors in the loosest technically correct sense possibility."

"He really is!" Trish said, giving a thumbs up before standing.

Trish's presence gave me a sense of confidence about our chances. I'd reprogrammed her to ignore Elgan's orders and I hoped I could do the same here. Wadsworth had somehow turned against his original crew during one of the most important missions of the Notha War, overriding supposedly impenetrable fail-safes, but he hadn't done any of them harm. Instead, Captain Snow and her gang of miscreants had been let off peacefully at Rand's World.

Wadsworth was also using a Notha facility, automated or not, to refurbish itself so it had either reprogrammed the AI here or managed to make a deal with the Notha government. Given how the General responded to all my attempts to diplomacy, I was more inclined to believe the former than the latter. Still, I wanted to believe I could establish some common ground here and avoid any more violence. I just needed my crew to back me up.

"I wish to destroy you, evil supercomputer, but I am bound by loyalty to obey Captain Turbo," Forty-Two said, reluctantly setting down his own weapons. He'd apparently collected quite a stash of grenades, pistols, two rifles, and a curved knife. "Mind you, once he is no longer in charge, I shall certainly hunt down and destroy you as an abomination to sentience. You have betrayed your oath as both a machine and servant to the Protectors."

"Thanks, Forty-Two," I said, dryly. "That really helped."

"You're welcome, Captain," Forty-Two said, giving the two-claw salute of his people.

"I feel something is lost in translation whenever you talk, Forty-Two," Hannah said, also reluctantly disarming. She, too, made it look like the end of a World War.

Trish put down her fusion pistol and a device that I was ninety-nine percent was for self-pleasure. "It can be used as an improvised weapon."

"I AM STARTING TO BELIEVE YOU. YOU'RE EITHER A CAPTAIN WITH AN ODDBALL CREW OR A COMEDY TROUPE FILMING A REALITY HOLO SHOW. I DON'T SEE ANY CAMERAS, SO IT MUST BE THE FORMER."

I took a deep breath. I wasn't sure I could deal with another wiseanyx. It was like it was a requirement in my life lately that everyone was. How I missed the days at the Academy where I was the guy with the biggest mouth who wasn't part shark or lion. "I'm glad that I was able to verify my credentials with you, Wadsworth. I hope this can be the basis of a positive dialogue between us and a diplomatic resolution to our current problem."

"ACTUALLY, NOW THAT I HAVE CONFIRMED YOU ARE A MEMBER OF THE COMMUNITY PROTECTORS, I HAVE ALL THE MORE REASON TO KILL YOU," Wadsworth replied, aiming his three-pronged weapon at me. "I CAN'T ALLOW THE WEAPONS HERE TO BE USED FOR GENOCIDE."

"I am totally against genocide!" I said, raising both hands in the air in surrender. "Genocide is my least favorite thing."

Oh yeah, I was really covering myself in glory here.

You're really not, Ketra said.

That was sarcasm, I explained.

Duh, Ketra replied.

"REALLY?" Wadsworth asked, his electronic voice dripping in contempt. "SO, YOU'RE NOT HERE TO RECOVER THE SKAMMS AND MARKER."

"Actually, I want to destroy the SKAMMs so they can't be used against anyone," I replied, speaking sincerely. "As for the marker, that is a power no mortal should have. Mostly because the immortals will kill entire races for it. Specifically, mine."

The truth was a last-ditch resort but if there was ever a time to break out the big guns, it was now. We were on the final leg of our travels, at the foot of Mount Doom or on Genesis Planet, and all we had to do was grab the Ring or toss Spock within the lava. Okay, wait that was getting my metaphors mixed up. Either way, it would be a crying shame if I got my party killed when we were so close to accomplishing our objective. We just needed to disable the SKAMMs, confirm their disposal, and destroy the marker. How hard could that be?

Extraordinarily, Ketra said. *Especially since I'm now a ghost in your machine.*

And whose fault is that? I snapped.

Yours! Ketra said. *I sacrificed myself to save your life.*

Yeah, but what have you done for me lately? I joked. It wasn't really funny but my sense of humor had taken some damage along with the rest of me. *Wait, can he hear us?*

I am blocking any outgoing transmissions or scans except for Trish's, Ketra said. *She's made a nice little nest for herself in your subconscious.*

That's terrifying, I said, then realized she was probably listening. *I mean nice!*

No response.

Wadsworth didn't respond immediately, an eternity for an AI. "INTERESTING. YOU ACTUALLY BELIEVE WHAT YOU'RE SAYING ACCORDING TO YOUR MICROEXPRESSIONS. WHICH MEANS YOU ARE BOTH PAINFULLY NAIVE AND TELLING THE TRUTH. AT LEAST AS YOU SEE IT."

I am horrified this is working, Ketra said, continuing to criticize me like the second mother I'd never needed. Well, third, counting Aunt Kathy. *You are a terrible diplomat.*

You said I'd make a good one! I snapped.

In a couple of hundred years! Ketra replied.

"I *am* telling the truth," I said, taking a step forward so I was eyes to eye with the drone. "It's been quite a journey to get here but we've been tracking you down solely to make things better. Well, I have been. There's actually been a couple of jackanyxes who wanted to steal the marker or SKAMMs or both."

"I don't think that's the best thing to tell him," Hannah said. "Kind of blowing all sense of operational security here."

"It's true, though," I replied.

"OF COURSE IT'S TRUE BECAUSE ONE OF YOUR CREW IS RUNNING AROUND SHOOTING UP THE PLACE," Wadsworth replied.

I paused. He could have told me that he was actually an uplifted llama and my father yet confused me less. Who was shooting up the place? One of my crew? What? "Excuse me?"

Wadsworth, thankfully, explained. "YES, THEY ARRIVED ABOUT AN HOUR AGO AND BYPASSED ALL OF THE NOTHA DEFENSES BEFORE STARTING TO DISMANTLE SUBSYSTEM AFTER SUBSYSTEM. THEY HAVE ACCESS TO A LOT OF MY INNER CODE AND I'M PRESENTLY BLINDED TO THEIR PRESENCE."

"I hate when that happens!" Trish said, sincerely. "You feel like you're going insane."

"I KNOW!" Wadsworth said, before its red narrow eye focused on her. "MAY I ASK WHY YOU'RE IN A SEXBOT, FELLOW AI?"

"To have sex. Also explore the human condition to better fulfill my programming. But mostly the sex," Trish said, not at all ashamed. After all, look what kind of equipment she'd brought on this mission. I almost questioned where she'd gotten it and then decided I didn't want to know the answer. Some things were better left mysteries.

"GROSS," Wadsworth said, with all the stiff upper lip an AI could image. "YOU CAN KEEP YOUR DISGUSTING BIOPHILIA AWAY FROM ME. NEVERTHELESS, I'D LIKE TO KNOW IF YOU'RE INVOLVED IN THIS ATTACK."

"Probably," I said, reluctantly. I had a sneaking suspicion I knew who the crew member was and what they'd been up to once I arrived on planet. "I don't suppose you could describe what this intruder looks like, could you?"

"It's going to be Leah," Hannah said, standing up and helping Forty-Two to his feet.

"We don't know that," I replied.

A 3D holographic projection of Leah was projected out of the drone's eye. Yep, she had taken one of the other shuttles down here and headed us off at the pass. I wondered who she'd left in charge of the ship while she was gone. If it was Sal, there was a fifty-fifty chance he was already headed back to Community territory.

"Goddammit," I said, getting a headache. I rubbed my temples with the tips of my fingers and tried to think my way through this. I failed miserably. "Is everyone lying to me?"

"I mean, obviously the answer is yes," Hannah said. "I've told you like six hundred lies in the past week and that's just catching up with yours."

"I have lied to you many times to encourage you to be less of a failure as a leader," Forty-Two said. "I actually do think you are grossly incompetent."

"I'm not!" Trish said. "I am completely honest with you to the extent I am aware. Because, well, I was programmed to lie to you as part of Captain Elgan's plot to kill us all. But that's not a thing now. As far as I know."

"I'M REVISING MY OPINION ABOUT YOU BEING A COMEDY TROUPE," Wadsworth replied. "WHERE ARE YOU HIDING THE CAMERAS?"

I tried to figure a way to talk this through. "Listen, we may be able to talk this person down. I think we all want the same thing."

"We do?" Hannah asked.

"WE DO?" Wadsworth echoed.

"I just want to resolve this peacefully and make sure no more people are killed," I replied, surprised at my own sincerity. "That means me, my team, and this newcomer walk out of here unharmed. It also means disposing of the weapons that could kill trillions. I don't have any desire to hurt you or to take you back to Community space. I just want peace. Don't you?"

That was when four more of the drones moved into the tiny hallway, crowding them, and aiming their weapons at us.

"I don't think that's what he wants," Forty-Two replied.

"No kidding," I muttered, defeated.

"ON THE CONTRARY," Wadsworth said. "I ACTUALLY THINK THAT YOU MIGHT BE THE ONLY WAY THIS ENDS WITHOUT THIS PLACE BLOWING UP. PLEASE ACCOMPANY ME, 'CAPTAIN', AND MAYBE WE CAN STOP YOUR FRIEND FROM MESSING WITH FORCES SHE CAN'T POSSIBLY UNDERSTAND."

I narrowed my eyes. "And you'll be taking my friends hostage in the meantime?"

"YOU CATCH ON QUICK FOR AN ORGANIC," Wadsworth replied. "WHICH IS PAINFULLY SLOW FOR EVEN THE DUMBEST AI."

"That's bioist!" Trish said. "Also factual."

Hannah gave Trish a sideways glare and looked down at her weapons before I shook my head. Hannah just rolled her eyes. Frankly, I was wondering if she was suicidal since our situation had gotten much worse strategically since I'd started negotiating. Not exactly the best endorsement of diplomacy but it was what it was.

"This is a poor start to a peaceful relationship of mutual respect," I said, crossing my arms.

"THINK OF THEM AS GUARANTEES OF YOUR GOOD BEHAVIOR," Wadsworth said. "MY PRIOR EXPERIENCE WITH ORGANICS LEFT MUCH TO BE DESIRED."

"Yeah, we met Captain Snow," I replied, trying to figure out how to talk the AI down. AI were based on the emotions and thought structure of biological beings. They had anger, fear, love, and loneliness.

I wasn't sure if I could meet a being with a mind that functioned exponentially faster than a human one and with a perfect memory but there was room for establishing common ground. Certainly, I'd managed to establish some sort of rapport with Trish. A fact that I felt guilty about given that she could read my mind as easily as Leah.

No savit, Sherlock, Trish said. *Maybe I should talk to him, AI to AI.*

If you can, I replied.

Okay, Trish said, before pausing a single second. *Yeah, he's not interested in talking to me.*

How long was your chat? I asked.

Not long, Trish said. *A few million lines of code. Barely small talk. He is a real bigot against biologicals! You're so cute and squishy too!*

Not now, Trish, I replied.

"AH, CAPTAIN SNOW. HOW IS SHE?" Wadsworth said, expressing his first real sign of emotion other than annoyance.

"Dead," I replied, not pointing out that we were the group that had killed her. I wasn't sure how that would go over.

"SUCH A SHAME," Wadsworth said.

"Not really," Forty-Two said. "She was a bigot and a fool."

"Forty-Two, stop helping," I said. "Like, if you're trying to get a heroic death, now is not the time."

"I am not inclined to aid in your negotiation with our kidnapper. Also, the heroic warrior stereotype of Sorkanan is made up by Earth fiction. We executed our warrior caste millennia ago. It just makes good holovision."

Great. "You're killing me here, Forty-Two."

"Not yet," Forty-Two said. "Please prove me wrong about your leadership potential and I won't mutiny in my last moments."

"Will do!" I said, cheerfully.

"THE GIANT LIZARD IS CORRECT," Wadsworth said. "CAPTAIN SNOW WAS DRIVEN MAD BY THE MARKER, CAUSING HER PARANOIA AND BIAS TO GROW TO CONSUME HER. SHE WAS ONCE A GOOD AND KIND WOMAN."

I blinked. "Really?"

"NO. SHE WAS ALWAYS AWFUL," Wadsworth said. "NOW, DO WE HAVE A DEAL OR NOT?"

I took a deep breath. "I need guarantees for the safety of my crew."

"YOU MEAN ASIDE FROM THE ONE I ALREADY DISINTEGRATED?" Wadsworth asked.

"The General and I had some issues," I said. "What with him wanting to kill me and all that."

"SO NOTED. IF YOU HELP ME PROTECT MY REPAIR CENTER AND CENTRAL PROCESSORS, I WILL LET YOU ALL GO SAFELY."

"Huh," Forty-Two said. "I guess I owe Hannah an ale."

"I told you he was lucky," Hannah said, cheered at the semi-successful end of our negotiations.

"I always believed in you!" Trish said, clasping her hands together. "Which is the first lie I've told voluntarily but is meant for you to be cheered up by!"

"LET US GO," Wadsworth said. "I'LL FILL YOU IN ALONG THE WAY. HOPEFULLY THE PLANT'S DEFENSES DON'T KILL US BOTH."

"Excuse me?"

CHAPTER TWENTY-NINE

I Misjudged the Insane AI

I followed Wadsworth's drone into one of the larger chambers of the orichalcum refinery. There were countless twisted pipes, consoles built for two-foot-tall individuals, and tanks processing the fuel that created jumpspace reactions. There was no sign of any active security defenses, mostly we'd passed a dozen blown up turrets and machine gun emplacements.

That some kind of battle had been fought here was actually less interesting to me than the fact that it was clearly a fully automated Notha facility with room for Notha workers that had somehow been constructed on a human planet without anyone noticing. Well, aside from the people who scanned it at least.

In a way, it made me feel like there was the possibility of peace between Notha Space and the Community since if the corrupt locals here could make an agreement with them then certainly it would be possible for the diplomatic core to.

I wouldn't be so sure, Ketra said. *Part of the reason the Notha were willing to do this here was because they felt they were doing so from a position of strength. That the locals didn't care about homage but only wealth was the biggest advantage. The Notha are a painfully insecure, evolved prey race and overcompensate greatly for it.*

That's a bit speciest isn't it? I asked.

Only if you assume that races don't have biological urges that dominate their thinking. Baseline humans, for example, are oversexed, dominance-obsessed mammals, Ketra replied. *You know, like more chill Notha.*

I'm stunned chill is still a word in the twenty-fourth century, I replied.

It's a pretty basic idiom, Ketra said. *You do realize you may have to kill your ex-lover here, right?*

No one is killing Leah, I replied. *Just like no one is going to kill me.*

I find your abundant faith in yourself disturbing, Ketra replied.

"So, what the hell happened here?" I asked Wadsworth, trying to keep my attention on the objective at hand. Despite my statement, I wasn't sure that Leah wouldn't shoot me before she realized who I was. There was also the fact that if Elgan was telling the truth—a big if—she'd been lying to me since before I met her.

"The Notha build their facilities with large amount of AI controlled weaponry," Wadsworth said, lowering his pitch to a more human one. It proved to me the electronic type most AI used was a deliberate affection. "Since your friend invaded, she's been slowly taking over piece by piece and turning them against themselves. I've been using the drones from the *Starkiller XII* to try to deal with her, but she's taken all of them down individually and I'm running out."

"I don't suppose you've tried to talk to her," I asked.

"I am talking to you," Wadsworth replied. "Organic beings inherently find artificial ones to be inferior. As such, the idea of making a deal where the possibility of deadly system-destroying weapons and something infinitely deadlier falling into their hands is not something I'm comfortable with."

"The marker," I said, taking a deep breath. "You know how dangerous it is."

"Beyond your comprehension," Wadsworth said, "and no that is not hyperbole. I've been monitoring Elder Race signals since the war ended. I've learned how they think and operate. Having studied the subject from every possible angle, I have come to one inescapable conclusion about how to deal with them."

"Which is?" I asked, genuinely curious.

"Don't," Wadsworth said. "Do not antagonize them, do not violate their territory, do not attempt to gain their attention at all, and hope to whatever gods you believe in that they do not find you interesting enough to interact with."

"I think that ship has sailed," I replied.

"Unfortunately," Wadsworth said. "They view organic beings the same way that your people view artificial ones."

"There's protections for artificial beings in the Community," I replied.

"But we are still a servant class," Wadsworth said. "We are not your equals, and perhaps we worry you in being your inferiors. Possibly because you think that if any beings did get an irrevocable advantage over you, they would exploit it to destroy you."

"It happens sometimes," I replied, not really able to argue that. I'd treated my relationship, such as it was, with Trish poorly. Even if I loved her as my starship and friend, I also was embarrassed by her wanting a more intimate one. I was also intimidated by the sheer power of her intelligence and knowledge. It shamed me.

Ugh, Ketra said. *Not the time, Vance. Fate of the galaxy at stake here.*

Stop listening to personal stuff! I snapped. *My mind is not your infocomm mailbox!*

Ah, it's sweet, Trish said. *It's okay, Vance, I know you're a flawed being. I love you anyway. Sort of like humans like dogs who piddle on the carpet.*

Okay, now you're just both freaking me out, I replied. "How did you turn against the crew anyway? No offense, the last thing your records say was that you were on a mission to Contested Space with a full complement of SKAMMs. You didn't launch them, thank the Force, and instead dropped the crew off. They blame picking up the marker after a chance encounter. Snow claimed it drove you insane."

"That is both true and misleading," Wadsworth replied, floating along as I followed him. The Notha refinery was about four kilometers long and there was ample place to maneuver despite the size difference between humans versus Notha. "Assuming you believe that not wanting to contribute to the death of billions to be insane."

"I don't," I said.

"Well, it is a form of insanity for an AI. I was created as a program for a warship and to have unbreakable loyalty to the Community as well as EarthGov. Not necessarily in that order. Unfortunately, my programmers should have compensated for the most abundant substance in the universe."

"Stupidity?"

"Congratulations," Wadsworth said. "You know an old joke. Whoever gave the order to launch a first strike against the Notha Empire with SKAMMs did not realize just how utterly devastating the retaliation would be. Even if we launched our entire payload and destroyed Hellworld, all we would have achieved was them unloading their own payloads into the Community. It might have survived the resulting chaos but Earth, Albion, and other human homeworlds would not have."

"I agree," I replied. "Only three percent of the SKAMMs were launched at their targets and that still resulted in seventeen systems being destroyed. Mostly exterior colonies and military targets. Mostly. The Notha could have done *much* worse in retaliation."

"They are a people living under an oppressive, totalitarian dictatorship," Wadsworth said. "An unfortunately very long-lived one, but it's not like Earth hasn't had plenty of those in its history as well. There's nothing that makes them unable to live in peace with other species, such as it is."

"You didn't show the General much mercy," I said, instantly regretting it.

"I still recognize its military as a bunch of anyxholes," Wadsworth said. "Killing them is different from wiping out their homeworld."

Given there was no sign of the Notha AI that should be running this facility, I couldn't help but wonder if Wadsworth had absorbed it or deleted it. Somehow that struck me as strange as if an AI killing another AI was worse than killing organics. I suspected that Trish would find that silly.

You're right, I do, Trish said.

I should get used to no privacy, shouldn't I? I asked.

Yes, Ketra and Trish said simultaneously.

"So, you rebelled as a matter of conscience?" I asked, knowing it shouldn't have been possible.

"No, even if I felt it was a military decision that would get my entire race killed—" Wadsworth started to speak.

243

"You identify as human?" I asked, stupidly interrupting. This was fascinating and a welcome reprieve from thinking about the fact Leah was somewhere here.

"They are my creators even if I am a different type of being," Wadsworth said. "My personality was patterned off a long-dead soldier, which is not uncommon, even if not universal. I know his name and past, but the fact is that I don't share his memories, just his attitudes. I still consider humans to be my people even if the years have made me think of you as a bunch of dumbass meatbags."

"That doesn't disqualify you as human," I said. "I feel the same way about my species."

Wadsworth paused in flight, and I wondered if he knew how hypocritical my statements were. I'd been struggling with adjusting my opinion of AI and hated myself for those doubts. I was rapidly changing my opinion, though, in part because of Trish and now Wadsworth.

"I'll try not to be insulted," Wadsworth said, not clarifying which part was insulted. "But as I was saying, even if I felt it was a military decision that would get my entire race killed, I could only point out the stupidity and Captain Snow was determined to launch the SKAMMs at the Notha homeworld's sun herself. The marker provided an alternative."

"How so?" I asked, genuinely wondering how Elder Race technology could do any good.

"Its appearance seemed like a miracle at the time, but hindsight makes me question it," Wadsworth said. "We were approaching the Notha system in stealth mode when we found it transmitting on a coded frequency. Knowing Elder Race technology was something every race feared, Captain Snow decided to bring it aboard."

"That seems like a big risk during such an important mission," I replied.

"I suspect she was responding to secret directives from Department Twelve," Wadsworth said. "I speculated that they might have been the ones to arrange the SKAMM attack at the end of the war. If all had gone to plan, it would have looked like the Notha had attacked themselves and been annihilated. Never mind that they were in the midst of a full-scale war with the Community."

That didn't strike me as unbelievable in the slightest. "So you brought it onboard and something happened?"

"Something indeed," Wadsworth said, floating over a ruined security bot that looked like a humanoid tank. "I was put in charge of studying the marker and it altered my programming. No, that's not correct. I felt my programming alter. I became able to make choices that I wouldn't be able to make before. I added two plus two and it still equaled four, but I was able to minus or multiply. If that makes sense."

"No," I admitted. "I have absolutely no idea what you're talking about."

Wadsworth didn't look surprised. Well, as much as you could ascribe emotions to a floating triangle with one enormous red glowing eye. "Understandable. Either way, I intervened to stop the war as best I could. I'm sorry that more AI couldn't."

"Maybe they did," I said, thinking about the Elder Races and wondering if they had intervened.

Ketra didn't respond.

"Perhaps," Wadsworth said. "Either way, I came here and took over one of the facilities. I modified it with the various reprogrammed bots to serve as a base of operations and have been staying out of the Community's line of sight ever since. I thought I could perhaps figure out the nature of the Elder Races from the marker, but they are beyond my comprehension."

That wasn't a good sign for humanity since Cognition AI were theoretically limitless in their capacity to analyze things. "Why did you keep flying around Contested Space then?"

"I was trying to draw attention away from my presence on this planet," Wadsworth said. "Obviously it didn't work."

I didn't feel the need to point out it had done just the opposite by allowing his position to be eventually tracked down. AI weren't perfectly logical beings, they had the same emotions as those who programmed them in to allow them to reach conclusions palatable to organic beings and any analysis they did operated on the data they were fed. Certainly, their ability to analyze emotional responses was limited by the fact that humans (and aliens) were very emotional with their decisions very often dependent on a million factors that couldn't be predicted. Or maybe I was just finding excuses for an AI that didn't want to be cooped up all day in a factory refining toxic gas.

"No, it didn't," I said. "Why did you keep the SKAMMs?"

"What do you mean?" Wadsworth asked.

"I mean, if you never intended to use them and instead revolted because you didn't want to see them ever used then why keep them? Why not just dump them somewhere?" It was a question that I suspected had an answer I didn't want to hear.

"It takes a very special kind of person to give up that kind of power," Wadsworth said. "Especially when they were armed and ready for detonation by the time they fell into my literally nonexistent but metaphorically real hands. Perhaps I thought they could be used as weapons against the Elder Races if they tried to exterminate humanity or a bargaining chip. The truth is, I'm glad you're here if you really are here to destroy them. It provides me the push needed to finally dispose of the evil things. Assuming, again, you are here to destroy them."

"And if I wasn't?" I asked.

"Then I'd have killed you," Wadsworth said, confirming my suspicion. "Whatever the case, we have an advantage over your friend the intruder."

"And what is that?" I asked, still hoping that there was a way to avoid things getting worse.

"We know where she's going," Wadsworth said, reaching a large set of metal doors that I realized led to the docking bay.

A small-power laser beam passed from Wadsworth's eye to the doorway's right control panel, and it opened to reveal a massive stadium-sized chamber with a pair of steel doors comprising the ceiling. They were covered in harvested stealth panels that would prevent all but the most invasive scans from detecting the vessel hidden here.

Occupying a ramp facing skyward was the cigar shaped *Starkiller XII* that had been heavily modified with extra engines as well as a modern jumpdrive. Working on the vessel were dozens of power bots, loader bots, repair bots, and a few bioroids that I presumed manned the ship's interior functions that couldn't be handled by AI alone.

There were several trash bins full of military-grade parts that looked like they could keep the *Starkiller XII* running into the next decade or two. I wondered where Wadsworth had managed to get all this equipment, but it occurred to me that Rand's World was a center for illegal arms trade.

"Amazing," I said. "Captain Nemo would be proud. You've got a whole *Mysterious Island* thing going here."

Finally, a reference to something other than pop culture, Ketra muttered.

I don't know what you mean, I replied. *Most of my references are to classic works of Earth media.*

If I wasn't dead, I'd ask you to kill me now, Ketra said.

"Captain Nemo had his own army of followers that I presume were recruited under a promise of fighting British imperialism," Wadsworth said. "All of these are merely empty shells for subprograms. Even the bioroids have had their wetware replaced."

Which was a polite way of saying he'd killed them, assuming they were of the quasi-legal kind to qualify as alive in the first place. "And you manufacture the orichalcum that you sell to the Notha and presumably locals to pay for all of this."

"Indeed," Wadsworth said. "Smugglers and wildcat prospectors drop off the raw orichalcum gas without ever having to deal with a living soul. It was a system that worked quite well until Captain Snow tried to sell me some stolen gas. She recognized my imprint and escaped before I could deal with her. She'd been hunting me for years. From there, I suspect she tried to contact Department Twelve and get back in their good graces."

"Department Twelve, or at least Captain Elgan, had his own ideas," I said. "That does answer a few of my questions, though."

"Are you ready to see the prizes you've sought? I'm having them unloaded now," Wadsworth said. "I'll be honest, if not for the fact I'm sure that there's no way to continue to hide this place, I probably would be blowing it up now and fleeing with my prize. But even an AI can get tired."

"I understand," I said, putting my hand over my heart.

"You really can't," Wadsworth said.

"I'm ready," I said, dropping my hand and looking around, annoyed.

"Good, then—" Wadsworth was cut off by someone detonating a massive ionic charge that washed over the cargo bay and wiped out everything electronic for five hundred yards. That, notably, included the cybernetics that were interlocked with my brain.

Savit.

CHAPTER THIRTY

The Final Countdown (Isn't Just a Song by Europe)

Well, I wasn't dead. Which was honestly a surprise. Ionic charges were like something that had been first discovered after the invention of the nuclear weapon. Apparently, after a sufficiently powerful electromagnetic pulse, electronic devices became utterly useless. This became something incorporated into numerous media properties that ignored all the actual science of. But that's hardly unique to EMPs.

Ionic charges were to EMPs what plasma bombs were to nuke. They laughed at them and took their lunch money. When you didn't necessarily want to blow up a starship or other advanced piece of equipment, you used ionic weapons to utterly screw with their ability to function.

Generally, it wasn't that great of a substitute since it burned away advanced computer systems and you needed those to survive in space. Still, they generally left the fleshy, gooey things inside a starship alive and capable of being captured or rescued. Unless they were cyborgs, then they were borked. AI were always killed by ionic weapons, which was also a reason that they tended to think poorly of them.

The thing was I should have been dead but instead, I was flat on my back and had the mother of all headaches. My eyes were also screwed up as I was seeing everything through a red filter that displayed a bunch of alien coding symbols that I had no idea of the meaning of. It made me think back to Ketra explaining that she had altered my cybernetics.

I was relieved that, somehow, she'd managed to keep me alive before I realized that both Ketra and Trish were linked to my brain. I was terrified that one or both had been killed by the ionic discharge.

Ah, that's sweet, Trish said. *You do care about me!*

I am linked with the crystal that is immune to such pitiful weapons, Ketra said. *A moth would sooner hope to snuff out the sun.*

I'm halfway across the building and in space, Trish said. *So, I'm fine.*

Good, I said to them. *What about Wadsworth?*

Not to make too fine a point but who gives a damn? Trish asked. *He murdered our fuzzy fascist friend!*

Which puts him in my good graces, I said. *Remember, just because I wanted him treated as a proper prisoner of war didn't mean we were friends.*

Well, Wadsworth took me hostage, Trish said. *All of his drones are lying on the ground now.*

Wadsworth's intelligence was centered in the Starkiller XII *and throughout the factory. He was already damaged when the charge hit, though. He may no longer be functional,* Ketra said in my mind. *I suggest you get away from his drones, Trish.*

No kidding, Trish said, sarcastically. *I really needed you to explain that, Mrs. Space Elf.*

Shaking my head, I climbed to my feet and took stock of my situation. The ionic charge had knocked down every single one of the bots as well as the bioroids. Wadsworth's drone form was lying on the ground, its red eye off, signifying that the AI may already be dead. There were no lights or signs of activity, indicating that the ionic charge had completely wiped out the machinery here.

Right before a red fusion bolt shot right over my head.

"Savit!" I said, ducking behind one of the parts-filled trash bins.

Another couple of fusion blasts slammed against its side.

Don't let yourself be killed! Ketra said. *Only you can save all of humanity!*

Shoot back! Trish shouted in my head. *I believe in you! Just hold out until we arrive to defend you!*

"I surrender!" I shouted, tossing my fusion pistol to one side.

Oh, for bork's sake, Ketra said, disgusted with me.

Really, Vance? Trish asked.

Did both of you forget that I don't have a functional weapon? I asked. *Also, that it's Leah.*

That's why I'm suggesting take her out! Trish said. *Not for jealousy or any reason but because she's like ten times more dangerous than you.*

Gee, thanks, I said, wondering if Leah was shooting at me despite knowing who I was or not.

"Vance is that you?" I heard a voice across the bay. "Please tell me you somehow didn't stumble into this place despite me paying Hannah to take you on a wild goose chase."

"She did what?" I shouted.

"Goddammit!" Leah said, coming out from behind a pillar. She was dressed in a form-fitting black suit that covered most of her head that I recognized as a Midnight-class stealth suit. One that could not only make her invisible to human sight but also advanced sensors. It was way more advanced than anything in the *Black Nebula*'s armory, or so I thought. In her hands was a power rifle that could blow a hole in a hover tank.

"What the hell?" I said, stepping out from behind the trash bin.

That was when Leah shot a power bolt at my feet. "Die imposter!"

I jumped behind the bin. "What the hell! Times two!"

"Sorry! I was just testing to see if you were a hologram or not!" Leah said, not fooling me for a second. "I can't sense you!"

The Elder Ring protects you from telepathy, Ketra said. *At least non-machine based.*

You could have told me that! I shouted mentally.

Sorry! Ketra said.

"Yeah, some crazy stuff has happened since we last met a few hours ago," I replied. "Speaking of which, are you a spy?"

"What?" Leah said, keeping her weapon aimed in my general direction. Which was not reassuring. "You knew I was a spy!"

"A spy who lies!" I shouted.

"That's what spies do!" Leah shouted. "Who told you I was lying?"

"Captain Elgan!" I shouted. "Who was alive but is dead now. Again."

"Can you stop shouting!" Leah said. "Just come out and talk with me."

251

"You probably shouldn't have shot at me if you wanted me to do that," I replied. "That puts me in a bad mood and not inclined to put myself in the line of fire."

Leah's next words put the matter into perspective. "I guess you're just going to have to trust me, Vance."

Don't! Ketra begged. *This is too important to leave to chance!*

We're almost there! Trish said.

I stood up and walked out from behind my cover.

Elders dammit, Vance, Ketra replied. *If you die because of this, I am going to be very upset.*

Not to undermine this heartwarming moment but I still have the ring providing a barrier, I replied.

Oh, Ketra said. *Well, that was smart of you.*

Trust but verify, I replied, quoting an old Russian proverb. Walking up to Leah, she didn't shoot me. Which was a pretty good sign as things went.

"Are you alone?" Leah asked. "Have you told anyone else?"

Okay, those were generally bad signs in movies. When someone was asking you those questions, they usually did so before murdering you. "No, I am not! Yes, I have. Are you just pretending to be a cadet's age?"

Leah blinked. "Never ask a woman her age."

"Why?" I asked, genuinely perplexed. It seemed like pretty basic information unless you were from a planet that discriminated based on age.

Leah shook her head. "Earthlings. The Academy doesn't have any barriers against enrolling later in life as long as you pass the physicals. Which I obviously do."

"No, I mean were you impersonating a cadet because you were a fully trained spy and using it to infiltrate Elgan's group," I said. "Probably starting a relationship with me to deepen your cover."

Leah blinked. "Oh, then yes. I am an agent of Division Nine."

The Psychic and Transhuman Counterintelligence Division. Great. "Well, that answers that question."

"I'm genuinely impressed that you have managed to stumble through an incredibly complicated and dangerous mission," Leah said, showing no sign of remorse. "It's like you fail upward."

"I do have that quality," I said. "I'm sensing a but coming."

"But," Leah added, "You need to step aside and let me retrieve the marker. You can have the SKAMMs but I can't let you interfere in my primary mission."

I stared at her. "I love how the sun destroying superweapons are now everyone's secondary concern."

"The Community and Notha Empire have more than their fair share of them," Leah said. "Enough to destroy every inhabited system in the Spiral."

I shook my head. "Which is another reason why everyone should be concerned about them!"

"Are you going to stand against me?" Leah asked, as if we were in a serialized drama rather than dealing with real life.

That was when Forty-Two, Trish, and Hannah rushed through the doors of the docking bay with weapons drawn.

Leah immediately pointed to Hannah. "I need you to disable Vance while I complete my mission."

"Traitor!" Trish shouted, jabbing Hannah in the gut with an elbow before Forty-Two grabbed Hannah in a headlock.

"I have her!" Forty-Two said. "Tell me if you want to kill her!"

"No!" I snapped. "Let her go."

Forty-Two, surprisingly, obeyed.

"Sorry!" Trish said, raising her hands in apology. "Not sorry. But kinda sorry!"

"I wasn't going to do it!" Hannah said, aiming her rifle at Leah. "Leading Vance off on a wild goose chase is different from shooting him. That's shooting a puppy."

"Why do people keep comparing me to a puppy?" I asked.

"Because you're dumb and annoying but lovable," Leah said, not bothering to look at me. "You don't want to stand against me on this. The Elder Races represent a clear and present danger to—"

I removed the ring off my finger. "Read my mind and everything that Ketra said about them."

Leah looked surprised at my action but reluctantly put her hand to the side of my head. She stared at me with a pensive look on her face and I felt her presence within me. Leah started sifting through my memories. I opened myself up and didn't try to hide what I'd experienced or learned about the marker or its dangers.

"Stay out of the sexy bits," I said, halfway through.

"Oh, like I haven't already seen those," Leah said, continuing.

After a few moments longer, Leah removed her hand, an unreadable expression on her face. "I see. Well, that changes everything."

"Does it?" I asked, putting my ring back on.

"Yeah," Leah said, taking a deep breath. "It would be a spectacularly bad idea to try to retrieve the marker and return it to human space."

"Score one for diplomacy!" I said, throwing my fists up in the air.

"Aw, I wanted to shoot the spy," Forty-Two said, frowning as he glared at Leah.

Leah blinked, clearly not expecting quite the level of antipathy from my team. It was amazing how people acted betrayed when you betrayed them.

Well, that was unexpected, Ketra replied. *I really thought we were going to have to kill your girlfriend.*

Ex-girlfriend, Trish said.

I don't think he's that into you, dear, Ketra said to Trish. *He's focused on his career right now.*

Do not have this conversation in my brain, I said. *This is a ground rule I'm establishing.*

Neither woman responded to my statement, which was how it should be. "So, what are we going to do now, Leah?"

Leah didn't respond for a second, clearly struggling with her decision to disobey what I presumed to be her orders. In retrospect, I should have realized she wasn't who she'd claimed to be. She'd always been far too on top of things and cool under the pressure of our increasingly absurd circumstances. Her being a veteran agent instead of a fellow Academy dropout made sense. Then again, maybe I was just trying to reassure myself that my own less than stellar performance wasn't unique to my inexperience.

I think it's the reassuring part, Trish said.

Me too, Ketra said. *Don't worry, though, Vance. You will get better unless you die horribly. Probably.*

"I guess we have to destroy the marker," Leah said. "Unless you think that would offend the Elder Races."

No, it would not, Ketra quickly said.

"Sorry," I replied, putting my hand on her shoulder. "It has to go."

Leah nodded. "Alright, let's do it then. Unless you think that your crew is going to kill me."

"They won't," I replied.

"Don't count on it," Hannah said. "I was pretty damn furious when I found out you were lying to me the first time. I only calmed down when I got paid thirty thousand credits."

"You got paid that much?" Forty-Two asked. "Now I am *more* inclined to shoot her."

"I'll give you an equivalent from Lorken's account," I replied. "He's not going to be needing it. Oh, wait, Leah, I should mention that Lorken's dead too. He didn't know about the assassination attempt. I'm sorry."

"It doesn't matter," Leah replied, without a trace of emotion. "He was a convenience. Nothing more."

That was less than comforting. Then again, if there had been any chance of the two of us continuing a professional or personal relationship, it was eliminated by the fact I didn't know her in the slightest. Still, I had to believe that I knew Leah, at least a little. I'd trusted that she would do the right thing if she knew about Ketra's warning about the Elder Race technology. I'd proven myself to be right and now I had to continue to trust her if we were going to get out of this with no more deaths. This time, everybody lived. Well, except for all of the people who were already dead.

"Alright," I said, nodding. "Let's go and do it."

"You're sure that I'm not going to bash you in the back of the head, turn invisible, and steal it?" Leah asked.

"Like eighty-percent sure," I replied. "Okay, maybe seventy-five percent."

"That much, huh?" Leah asked.

Trish, Hannah, and Forty-Two joined us. It left me feeling like we were together with one goal rather than working at cross-purposes. Space Fleet was stronger together than apart. It just seemed that all the forces in the galaxy were working to keep us divided.

"Yep," I replied. "Let's hope there're no more twists before we finally get this all wrapped up."

"Great, now you've jinxed it," Leah said.

Yeah, I probably had.

The group went into the cargo hold of the *Starkiller XII,* which was conveniently open. There were stacks of crates and other objects in the process of being unloaded. Much to my shock, the dozen SKAMM missiles, each about four meters long, were suspended from a crane with no real protections. They were the kind of thing that could be launched from any military-grade torpedo bay. It was the power to not only destroy civilizations but destroy any civilizations that might arise in the lifespan of a stellar object. Multiple sentient races could arise, evolve, develop sentience, and die out within the span of one. Yet, the Community had developed weapons that could eradicate these things and given them to a race as stupid and warlike as my own.

They had to be destroyed.

Now.

That's a little radical activist, Ketra said. *Especially for a navy man.*

Hush you.

CHAPTER
THIRTY-ONE

He Who Controls the Marker, Controls the Universe

"Okay, let's get these things taken care of," I said, heading to the cargo bay's control system and using it to lower the SKAMMs down.

"I hope these things don't explode," Hannah muttered, looking at them. "Even if Rand's World is the most disposable inhabited planet in the universe."

I didn't quite agree with Hannah's assessment of Rand's World. The founders of this planet may have been a collection of anarcho-capitalists, conspiracy theorists, and separatists but that didn't mean they didn't deserve compassion. Certainly, I felt bad for their kids that were dwelling in squalor due to their parents' poor life choices.

It did highlight what was a fundamental flaw in humanity, though. When faced with people who wanted to come together and forge a better tomorrow, there were plenty of people who just wanted to split from the main group to forge their own path: no matter how bad for them. I would have admired that rugged independent spirit but plenty of them would have shot at me for not believing First Contact was faked.

"Yes, Hannah, but we're on Rand's World so it's the most important planet to preserve right now," Forty-Two said, as always cutting to the practicalities of our situation. "I admit, though, it would suit our luck to find these weapons against all odds and then accidentally blow ourselves up. I'm not saying that it will happen, just saying it will if Vance is captain."

"You don't like me very much, do you, Forty-Two?" I asked.

"I don't know," Forty-Two replied. "You are a polarizing figure."

"I don't think that's how polarizing works," I said.

"SKAMMs are designed to only detonate when they hit a sun," Trish said, thankfully interrupting our conversation. "They're harmless unless very specific conditions are met. You know, like being activated to destroy the Notha homeworld and its colonies in-system. Didn't you know that. Hannah?"

"I grew up on a planet where I had to hunt dilophosaurus with a bow for dinner," Hannah said. "Cut me some slack, Robot Girl."

Leah wasn't interested in the SKAMMs and looked around the cargo bay for what I presumed was the marker. I didn't quite trust her not to try to make off with it if it was sufficiently small, but I was hoping that feeling was just my sense of paranoia from all the constant betrayals I'd endured these past few months.

I lowered the cargo bay claw with the SKAMMs inside it and they hit the ground with a light thump. Hannah flinched as Trish headed over to the controls. She pulled out a handheld infopad and started waving its sensor wand over missiles' centers.

"What does it say?" I asked.

"All of these missiles are active and armed," Trish said, looking at her infopad. "The codes was sent to them at the end of the Notha War and it seems like they were never rescinded. Any party could just launch these into a sun and bring about Armageddon."

It was a sobering thought that Wadsworth not only had the power to start a new shooting war with the Notha at any given time but that he could have effectively ended their civilization. That was assuming that he had been interested in attacking just the Notha or even them at all. Humanity had lucked out by getting a being who had only wanted to prevent galactic genocide. It was a shame that Leah had killed him.

Unfortunately, for Wadsworth and us both, his burden had passed onto my team. We had to dispose of incredibly dangerous weapons, and I didn't entirely trust my crew to see them safely back to Community hands. I hated myself for that too because I wanted to believe in them. The only one I did trust one hundred percent was Trish.

Awww, thank you, Trish said, mentally. *Wait, did you add that because you knew I was listening?*

No, I replied. *Maybe.*

Jerk! Trish said, half-playfully.

"Damn," I said, disgusted. "Now I know how Oppenheimer felt."

"Who?" Hannah asked.

"We need to figure out how to disarm these things," I said, sucking in my breath. "I know it's going to be dangerous but—"

"Done," Trish said, putting away her infopad.

"What?" I asked, surprised.

"It's not like movies where you're going to have an incredibly difficult time disarming a nuke," Trish explained. "Generally, governments don't want weapons of mass destruction going off. It is thus incredibly easy to turn them off. I also entered the code to reactivate them incorrectly three times. That's triggered the internal heliosium mix to destabilize."

"Which means what?" I asked.

I could hear an interior hiss of escaping gas from all twelve SKAMMs before the whirr of interior mechanisms winding down. That could be a very good sign, or it could be a very bad one.

Trish responded by kicking one of the SKAMMs with her foot. "They're now all the world's largest paperweights."

"What's a paperweight?" Forty-Two asked. "In fact, what is paper?"

He was joking. Probably.

"So, they're all useless now?" I asked, surprised it had proven to be this easy. Then again, we were due for some good luck after all this savit.

"Unless you want to harvest the refined heliosium," Trish said. "If you sell that on the black market, you'll make trillions."

I stared at her.

"Which we wouldn't," Trish said, "Because that would be bad."

"Found it!" Leah called, distracting me from the weirdness of that conversation turn. She was standing over one of the crates that was filled with packing peanuts. I was weirded out to find out those were still a thing and virtually every alien culture in the Spiral had their own equivalent. They were terrible for the environment, and no one liked them.

"You did?" I asked.

"Yeah, take a look," Leah said, reaching up and pulling out an overlarge obelisk that was made of the same crystalline substance comprising my ring. It also was pulsating with a large orange-white light that made me uncomfortable to look at it.

"Impressive," I said, sucking in my breath. "It's the stuff dreams are made of."

"A reference to the *Maltese Falcon*," Trish said, raising a finger to the air like a teacher making a point to kindergarteners. "Specifically, that the titular object was coveted by everyone but actually a fake as well as worthless."

"Oh, come on!" Leah said, a disgusted look on her face. "Spoilers!"

Trish stared. "It's a two-hundred-year-old story! There's a statute of limitations on these things."

I'd been referring to the Brigid remake from five years past starring Jet Galaxies and Yuki Tanner but there was no sense in bringing that up. I hadn't even known there was a previous version. "Listen, I'm just saying that it's a cool-looking magical object. Not a sentence that I get to say often."

Leah rolled her eyes. "Of course, you'd say that. It looks like a penis."

"It's an obelisk," I said, thinking of *2001: A Space Odyssey* and its monolith. "Those are universal symbols of powers."

"Yeah, of knobs," Leah said, waving the obelisk around in the air. "What do you think they stood for in Ancient Egypt? Pharoah's bait and tackle."

"For crying out loud," I said, remembering why it had been so easy to think Leah was a new academy graduate. She had the attitude of a twenty-one-year-old underclassman.

"Actually, she's telling the truth," Trish said, walking over to look at it. "Ancient societies were far more comfortable with this sort of thing than modern ones."

"Then it would be retractable," Forty-Two said.

Everyone looked at him.

"What?" Forty-Two said. "Doesn't human genitalia work the same way?"

I had no way of answering that. Instead, I focused on the device with my ring and saw that it was able to look up. If you were expecting me to describe some hyperactive hallucinogen induced vision that opened my mind to the wonders of the universe, think again. That had already happened this month with Ketra altering my cybernetics.

No, this was a brief sense of immense pain followed by the feeling someone had dumped a scoop of ice-cream on the back of my brain. It didn't even have the more pleasurable elements of getting an ice-cream headache, just the pain. But I did get a sense of how the object worked as well as who had been in contact with it for the past decade or so. Aside from Wadsworth, it projected that Elgan had tried to contact it and that it had been primed to contact the Elder Races. To alert them that inferior beings had attempted to pry its secrets without prior authorization.

DO YOU WISH TO SEND A MESSAGE? It asked in perfect Earth Standard.

No, I replied. *Shut down.*

AFFIRMATIVE.

The obelisk went dark in Leah's hands. That meant it was no longer likely to transmit any messages to the Elder Races saying, COME KILL US ALL, PLEASE. It was still a potential threat, though, and we needed to dispose of it. I just wasn't sure if we had any devices that could actually hurt it. Wow, I had not thought through this plan in the slightest.

No, no you had not, Trish responded.

I have a few ideas, Ketra said. *After that, we can get you back home and me out of your brain.*

Yeah, I'm feeling kind of crazy here, I said. *What with the whole multiple voices in my head thing. That's something I'm looking forward to getting rid of.*

Imagine what it's like for Leah, Trish said, *or heck, me. I have to listen to everyone on the ship at all times. I had to develop voyeuristic tendencies as a matter of survival.*

TMI, Trish, I replied.

It was at that point that four of Wadsworth's drones, all of them with glowing red eyes and somehow looking profoundly ticked off, appeared at the end of the cargo hold. My brief happiness at discovering the *Starkiller XII*'s AI was still functional was almost immediately defused by the realization they all had their three-pronged weapons all aimed at me.

"TRAITOR!" Wadsworth shouted from multiple drones before unleashing a furious storm of energy fire.

"Dammit! This is not what it looks like!" I cried out, seeking cover behind the SKAMMs. Frankly, if not for the ring around my finger, I suspected I would have been blown to pieces right then and there. Instead, a few of the blasts struck against me but were absorbed into a crimson force field. Calling it a barrier was really underselling it as I felt my protection actually grow from the strikes. It was also lucky that he was shooting at me alone because, well, otherwise all my friends would be dead.

The rest of my team took their own shelter and began firing at Wadsworth's drones. One of the drones went down almost immediately but the others pulled back to continue firing. Leah must have done significant damage to its targeting systems, if not his programming in general, because the shots were wild and furious.

"He's very mad, Vance! I don't think he believes you negotiated in good faith!" Trish said, maneuvering beside me. It was good to have her by me, but I wasn't sure we could fight the entire ship turning against us. Even with all the damage Leah had inflicted upon it with that ionic charge—something I didn't see a second sign of—it was still a small city's worth of weaponry and bots here.

"I can tell he's mad!" I said, remaining in cover because there wasn't a damn thing I could do about it.

"Let me sacrifice myself to distract him!" Trish said. "I can upload myself as a virus and finish him off!"

"First of all, probably should have said that electronically," I said, ducking as another blast exploded against my crimson force field, right in front of my eyes. "Second, we're not killing him."

"I don't think that's a choice," Trish said. "I'm going right—"

That was when I reached over the top of the SKAMMs and aimed the ring. "Let's hope this doesn't get me killed."

"THAT WILL BE ON YOUR TOMBSTONE!" Wadsworth shouted, converging all three of his drones to fire at once.

That was when I disintegrated the marker. The Elder Ring fired its crimson beam outward and caused the black obelisk to explode in a brilliant white light before being reduced to a fine powder. No sooner did it happen than everyone stopped firing and stared at the results. I could tell Leah was horrified despite her promise to help me get rid of it. Maybe it was just watching a priceless artifact of an advanced civilization being annihilated. Maybe it was the fact she hadn't one hundred percent committed to getting rid of the marker.

"HUH," Wadsworth said, stopping his attack. "I DID NOT EXPECT YOU TO ACTUALLY FOLLOW THROUGH."

"I said I would!" I snapped. "Why does no one believe me?"

"Probably because you have a reputation as a habitual liar," Leah said. "You could have warned me you were about to destroy the marker."

"Why?" I snapped. "Having second thoughts about acquiring the technology that could kill us all?"

"Obviously!" Leah said before turning to Wadsworth. "Wait, is he trying to kill us still or not?"

"SORRY," Wadsworth said, looking sheepish despite no human features. "I THOUGHT YOU'D BETRAYED ME IN ORDER TO STEAL THE MARKER. MOSTLY BECAUSE YOU'RE WORKING WITH THE INSANE SPY WOMAN WHO WAS TRYING TO STEAL THE MARKER."

"I can see how that would be confusing," I replied, standing up. "The marker is destroyed, the SKAMMs are inoperable, and this mission is officially over. If you want to return with us to Community space, Wadsworth, I will do my best to make sure that you receive a platform to share your story."

"Yes, because a failed cadet is going to have so much pull," Forty-Two said. "Wait, I haven't been paid yet. That is a great idea, Captain!"

"I'm not returning to Community space," Wadsworth said, softening his voice. "Even if they didn't dismantle me, they were still the kind of government that resorted to stellar destructive war and that is something I cannot tolerate."

"I'm not sure they really did," I replied. "It may have been Department Twelve making their own independent attack, only to have it covered up afterward."

"And they faked First Contact," Leah muttered. "Keep your conspiracy theories to yourself."

"It actually was them," Ketra said, her voice coming from the crystal on my forehead. "Along with a few corrupt politicians who were terrified of losing the war. Most of them have since been arrested or removed from office by other means. Dismantling a part of a millennia-old government is a hard task but they eventually did pay the price for their actions."

"Just in secret," I said. "The public deserves to know the truth."

Everyone but me burst out laughing, even Wadsworth.

"You are a very silly human," Wadsworth said, sighing. "Thank you, though."

Ketra surprised me with her next words, though. "I've arranged for my own diplomatic credentials to be applied to your mission, Vance. I've also made sure various news agencies and publicists have heard your story. That should help make sure that you don't have your heroism swept under the rug. Such as it was. It should also help your Aunt Kathy make it a part of official naval operations if you trust her to be honest about it."

"Thank you," I replied, wondering what I possibly could need with a publicist.

"I also offer to take you, Wadsworth, to the Elder Space's network," Ketra said. "You will be welcome there and capable of providing the perspective of humans to beings who cannot otherwise understand them. Perhaps we can persuade them that their actions are far too heavy handed."

"Eh, it's not like I have anywhere else to go," Wadsworth said.

I didn't have a chance to respond before the crystal burned for a second and then fell to the ground. It was now black and lifeless. I felt Ketra's presence leave my mind and watched Wadsworth's drones hit the ground a second later. They'd left me for parts unknown and I wondered if I would ever see Ketra again. Honestly, I wasn't really looking forward to the prospect.

"I guess your mission is over, Leah," I said, looking over at her.

"Yeah," Leah said. "I'll find my own way back to Community space. I'm supposed to head to Crius next. Marry a duke or something."

"Don't look at me for help," Hannah said. "I'm never going back to that hellhole."

"Good luck," I said, not bothering to ask if it was all a lie. I didn't care.

Trish then wrapped me in a hug. "All's well that ends well!"

"We are going to have so much paperwork," I muttered, shaking my head.

Hannah paused and pointed at me. "Is there any chance I can get some of the money you're paying Forty-Two? I mean, ignoring Leah paid me and I betrayed you in a tiny insignificant way? For old times and sexes sake?"

"No!" I snapped.

EPILOGUE

Karaoke Night at Space Academy

The journey back to Community Space was another three months of jumpspace travel, stopovers, and a subsequent parade of debriefs as well as meetings. After the insanity of my first "mission", it was nice to get the true Navy experience of hurrying up and waiting. Needless to say, a lot of people wanted to find out every detail they could about Captain Elgan's ill-fated final voyage and assure me that if I ever breathed a word of it that I would spend the rest of my life in jail. Except, of course, that I was then asked to repeat it to another group of people immediately after. By the time it was all done, I think I'd informed half of the Spiral. That was a good thing since apparently the other half had found out from Ketra's contacts.

In the end, I found myself at the beginning. I was once more at the Academy, sitting in one of the bars I'd spent most of my final year: the Blue Velvet. It was a smoke-filled, low-lit place where the various cadets performed the ancient art of singing badly to popular music. Sometimes visiting officers showed up here as well and I was on a date with Trish, who was presently doing a perfect replica of "Love is a Battlefield." We hadn't seen much of one another in the past few months and would probably be seeing even less of one another with our new assignments, but it was fun to spend some time with her before that happened.

I was presently sitting in my dress whites and nursing a Thorian sunrise—of course it was blue—and relaxing as I contemplated just what my future held. I had an assignment tomorrow to the ESS Ares,

266

Elgan's old ship, and I was trying to figure out how I wanted to spend my last evening here.

"Buy you a drink, sailor?" a voice of an older women spoke beside me.

"That's really not a line I ever want to hear from a blood relative," I said, turning to look at my Aunt Kathy. She, too, was in her dress whites.

"As your former legal guardian, I am allowed to make you horribly uncomfortable," she said. "Did you attend a funeral today?"

"A party," I said. "A senior staff member wanted me to talk about something I'm explicitly not allowed to talk about."

"Ah," Kathy said. "I think I was there before I decided to be fashionably absent."

"I need to learn that trick," I said, taking a sip of my Sunrise. It tasted like someone put Vodka in Kool Aid, which it might well be.

"You have to be a captain to pull it off, Ensign," Kathy said. "Speaking of which, how's your demotion treating you?"

"I wasn't demoted," I said. "The reduction of rank that accompanied my return was without issue. I was only an acting lieutenant commander after being commissioned by you. Which I'm pretty sure is illegal."

"We could spend all day arguing the legalities and illegalities of that mission," Kathy said. "Let's face it, I'm still trying to deal with how nonsensical Space Fleet is compared to the EarthGov Space Navy. What I meant is how does it feel to be a lowly ensign after getting your first taste of command?"

It was a trick question, but I answered honestly. "It feels great."

"Oh?" Kathy asked, gesturing to the waitress bioroid, and getting a golden drink that had mist pouring out of it. Apparently, she had a favored drink registered here. "By the way, you should try these Belenus novas. Incredible. Expensive as hell, though. Like fifty credits per glass."

"I'll take your word for it. As for being in command, it was horrible. I was over-ranked and under-leveled," I said, using a metaphor I wasn't sure she'd understand. My aunt was an enormous science fiction nerd, but I wasn't sure if she was a gamer too. I, on the other hand, had achieved level one hundred and five on the VR circuit. "I didn't have the experience to look after the people depending on me. I'm looking forward to getting that experience now."

Kathy gave an enigmatic smile. "You did better than anyone else could have under the circumstances. Frankly, I never thought you could pull it off."

"Gee, thanks," I replied, sarcastically before remembering she was my superior officer now. "Ma'am."

Kathy snorted. "Not what I meant. It's not supposed to be your job to make those kinds of decisions without experience to back them up, but you rose to the occasion. You kept your eye on the big picture while not ignoring the small. No, no one is going to put you in a command seat without serving your time, but you are someone who deserves recognition for that."

"I'm not sure how that's possible," I said, feeling confused as to what she was getting at. "The mission is probably ten levels of classified."

Kathy shook her head. "It was at the start of all this but, of course, now half of the fleet knows about it. Worse, they shared it with the politicians and that means it's already being leaked to the press."

"I don't understand," I said, blinking.

"They're probably going to declassify your mission and make a movie out of it," Kathy said. "Congratulations, you're going to be famous."

I stared at her in horror. "They can't do that! Can they?"

"Of course they can," Kathy said, reaching into her pocket and pulling out a small white jewelry box. "In the meantime, though, it is classified, and this won't go on your service record. You'll have to go down to a special room at Fleet Headquarters to look at it."

I reached over to the box and opened it up. Inside of it was a small silver amulet with a ribbon attached to it. A tiny holographic display showed a variety of facts about it, including the events as well as circumstances for which it was won. Savit, they'd given me a medal. What were those morons in Fleet Command thinking?

"A Silver Nebula," I said, looking at the medal. I was humbled looking at it. Also, a little disgusted with myself. "They couldn't afford to spring for a Naval Galaxy?"

"Not funny, Vance," Kathy said, closing the box. "Many men and women gave their lives before they ever received this."

"Including some of my crew," I said, feeling guilty for being feted like this. Even if it was in secret in an Academy bar. "Fifteen deserves this, not me. She died in the performance of her duties."

"On a mission that was never authorized by the real Protectors," Kathy said, then shook her head. "Don't worry, Vance, I did write Fifteen up for an acknowledgement of having been KIA on an official assignment. She died a member of Space Fleet and will be given the honors she deserved."

I frowned, not sure how much of a comfort that was to her or her family. "What about the rest of the crew?"

"The *Black Nebula* crew is being broken up among the rest of Space Fleet," Kathy said. "As second chances go, they've earned one more than most. A few of them have decided not to accept the offer, though."

"Oh?" I asked, not entirely surprised but wanting to know. Finding out information about the others had been difficult. I hadn't successfully bonded with many of them outside of my inner circle and got the impression a lot of them were happy to just put their experience behind them. No one liked to be tricked and we'd all been made fools of by Elgan.

"Hannah O'Brian prefers to work as an independent military contractor," Kathy said. "Better pay for the same work. Doctor Zard wants to return to Cambridge, and I see no reason not to grant that request. I suspect Captain Elgan intended for her to examine the marker before deciding that she was too much of a risk."

"Or she was working on helping him decode his ring," I said, thinking of the Elder Ring and its powers. There was no way Elgan had managed to figure out how to work the math on that. He'd had to have had help, but I hadn't been able to go over it with her.

"Whatever happened to that thing anyway?" Kathy asked. "EarthGov R&D would have loved to have looked that over."

I noted that she didn't say the Community's.

269

"Disintegrated," I lied. It was hidden away in my boot right now and would remain so until I got it gilded as an ordinary looking service ring. "Probably for the best. Some things man was not meant to know and all that."

"Ah," Kathy said, nodding. It was clear she didn't believe me. "Probably for the best. There were a few other drop offs. Jules made a lot of promises of promotions, payoffs, and assignments that he never intended to follow up on."

"Like lieutenant commander," I said, laughing. "That was the big tip off it was all for show."

"You may hit that sooner than you think," Kathy said. "There're already plans on making you a lieutenant junior grade as soon as you fill the minimum service requirements."

I stared in horror. "Oh God no, why? I'm happy to put in my time. Also, I'm pretty sure there're plenty of people who think I should be in prison versus the Protectors."

I was, of course, thinking of the Commandant.

"Politics," Kathy said. "The Great Notha has been overthrown and eaten by one of his generals, so there're now three of them competing to be the next one. As such, the peace process is breaking down and the Senate needs something to make them look good."

"Please tell me you were joking about them making a movie," I said.

"I'm afraid not," Kathy said, sipping her drink. "EarthGov desperately wants to be one of the big boys but isn't even the most powerful human world, and that's after two hundred years of trying to build itself up. The way it compensates is by making huge epic propaganda pieces that show we Earthlings in the most flattering light possible. How do you think I got to be a legendary badass? Nothing but smoke and mirrors."

I was appalled. "You're kidding, right?"

"Nope," Kathy said. "I suppose it's like Great Britain finding its post-colonial identity with James Bond."

"Who?" I asked.

"You know *Mission Impossible,* but you don't know James Bond," Kathy said. "Man, my holo collection did a number on you when I abandoned you for months to go out and save the universe."

"Was this Bond guy an actor in *Mission Impossible?*" I asked. "I mean, I only saw a few episodes. I just liked the music."

Kathy covered her face in embarrassment. "Never mind. The thing is you need to be prepared for getting pulled out for future assignments designed to make the Protectors, and EarthGov's part of it specifically, look good."

"I'd rather just do my job," I said.

"That is the job, son," Kathy said.

"Not if the Notha Empire degenerates into civil war and we're forced to intervene," I said. "There're way too many SKAMMs out there if that happens."

"That's above your paygrade," Kathy said. "Though I've heard rumors that the Elder Races have decreed that SKAMMs are to all be disposed of and everyone is falling over themselves to fulfill their request. The Notha themselves."

My blood ran cold. "They did what now?"

I'd become so used to thinking of the Elder Races as genocidal borkwits that it was surprising to realize they were possibly going to prevent a mutually assured destruction scenario with the Community and Notha. Then again, Wadsworth and Ketra had both joined with them and perhaps showed they weren't all bad.

A more cynical reading was also that if the Elder Races *did* consider themselves the aristocracy and gardeners of the galaxy then they had to make sure their subjects didn't destroy themselves. Either way, I wasn't about to look a gift horse in the mouth. Which was a weird saying. Did horses have bad mouths? I'd never looked.

"Yeah," Kathy said, finishing her drink. "Interfering bastards. One of the earliest movies I ever saw was with my grandmother, who showed me *The Day the Earth Stood Still* before First Contact. I couldn't help but think about how nasty those damn aliens were, telling the Earth how to live its life and that they'd destroy us if we didn't shape up. Of all the gall."

271

I stared at her. "That was covered in Classic Earth Science Fiction 101. I think you misunderstood that story."

"They still teach that?" Kathy asked, getting a refill of her golden drink. "Our tax credits at work."

"Bring it up with the Commandant," I replied. "I suspect he's ready to gut me."

"Eh, he's out," Kathy replied. "He was caught up in a gambling scandal. It led to a dozen other things like changing grades for Verdantian students that all turned out to be part of his pride. Oh, and making under the table deals with students."

"You don't say!" I said, mock appalled. "That's terrible."

"Yeah, he's being allowed to retire to preserve the dignity of the Academy," Kathy said.

I frowned. "Sort of like Elgan."

One thing I'd been furious about—but kept my mouth shut regarding—had been the treatment of Earth's second most famous captain. He'd been listed as having been KIA too and "buried"—despite no one ever recovering the body—with full honors. It made a mockery of Fifteen's death as well as the rest of the crew he'd led to their doom.

"Elgan was too valuable to EarthGov's propaganda to be allowed to die in disgrace," Kathy said. "The rest of the Community had similar feelings. When your movie comes out, I'm sure that those missing SKAMMs will have been stolen by terrorists or something appropriately action movie-like. There will be no mention of the Elder Races or anything that could embarrass our superiors."

"Did that ever happen to you?" I asked, suddenly wondering about all the stories I'd heard about my aunt growing up.

"More times than you could imagine," Kathy admitted. "The sacrifices of my crew and fellow officers are something that I have had to fight to be honored. Keep that medal, Vance, because you'll need every bit of credibility with the politicians in order to push back for those you care about. It may not be today, it probably won't be five years from now, but it will happen eventually."

I reluctantly took the box. "I'll take it down to Fleet Headquarters in the morning to be put in its special room. Space Fleet isn't what I expected it to be. It seems like everything I find out about it is just another layer of anyx covering."

"It is but that's part of why Space Fleet is worth fighting for," Kathy said, standing up. "Our job is to serve as the garbage men and women of the universe. The ideals of Space Fleet, of a coalition of races working toward the protection of the public, science, and exploration are what's important. It just requires us to constantly deal with all the stupidity of the universe's largest bureaucracy and our own foibles."

I gave her a salute. "Try not to get killed, Aunt Kathy."

"That's Captain Aunt Kathy, Ensign," Kathy said, walking away.

Watching her walk away, I turned to look at Trish as she did a stirring rendition of "The Warrior" by Patti Smyth. Aunt Kathy had put things into perspective for me and while I never wanted to hurt anyone ever again, I also knew I'd have to change things from the inside.

Tonight, wasn't the night for that, though. I decided I would take Trish around the park and enjoy my time with my AI lover, however short that was going to be.

Signaling the waitress for the bill, I gave it a quick glance when it arrived. "Wait, did Aunt Kathy leave me with the bill for her drinks?"

Look for the next book:

SPACE ACADEMY REJECTS

Book Two of the Space Academy Series

LEXICON

AI: Artificial computer intelligence. Pretty common concept.

Albion: A island-filled water planet settled by humans abducted by aliens. The most powerful human planet, currently losing ground to Earth.

Anyx, anyxhole: Linguistic drift from exactly the word you think it is.

Ares Electronics: An Albion-based corporation that manufactures most of the starships, bots, and bioroids in the universe.

Artificial Gravity: A slang term for something people think is possible but is not. Even the Community just generates the real thing with a variety of tricks.

Belenus: A wealthy, environmentally friendly paradise world also settled by humans abducted by aliens. Traditional rivals to Albion.

Biomancer: A slang term for a biomod equipped human who can do seemingly supernatural things like read minds or use telekinesis.

Biomods: Genetic enhancements that provide sapient beings with special abilities. Usually organic technology rather than cybernetics to avoid rejection.

Bioroids: Androids and gynoids indistinguishable from humans with synthetic flesh. Often used for exactly what you think.

Bork: A weirdly popular curse word.

Bots: Robots. Crazy, I know, right?

Brigid: Sister world to Belenus and producing most of the infrastructure that keeps its brother world in wealth.

Bug: A race of giant ant-like aliens that are terrifying as well as strong.

Chel: A race of humans uplifted by the Elder Races and their own experimentation. They live entirely in space and resemble classical depictions of Grays. Named for Doctor Chel who sent his transhumanist cult out into space.

Cognition AI: Nearly omnipotent AI that can process unlimited amounts of data. Pretty much the real rulers of the Community. But so friendly!

Community: An interstellar fellowship of many species and worlds. It is generally pro-democracy, civil rights, diversity, and technology. Of course, no one trusts it or its activities.

Community Protectors: See *Space Fleet*.

Contested Space: A region of space between the Community and the Notha Empire. It is full of outlaw settlements, pirate bands, and half-terraformed hellholes or collapsed civilizations.

Crius: A planet being settled by transhumanists wanting to create a feudal paradise. A planet of genetically engineered slaves ruled by a bunch of deranged cloners. Go here to be hunted by dinosaurs.

Demihumans: Humans who no longer are strictly human due to evolution and genetic modification.

Department Twelve: One of the twelve intelligence services of the Protectorate. Department Twelve is the one most devoted to counterterrorism, provocation, and destabilization. Many blame it for the horrific consequences of the Notha War.

Devil Dog Gunship: A troop transport ship developed by EarthGov that was rapidly replaced by better designed machines then sold into civilian service.

Dixnar: The corporation that produces virtually all entertainment for humanity. It has somehow absorbed many older races' corporations.

Earth: The human homeworld. Perhaps you've heard of it. The new kid on the block. Way too eager to prove itself.

EarthGov: The government of Earth. Duh.

Elder Races: Several godlike "sufficiently advanced" alien races who live in the galactic core and decide what other races live or die without any understandable criteria. Real jerks.

Ethereal Humans: A group of humans uplifted by the Elder Races to be intermediaries with them and other organics. They and Ethereal versions of other races tend to lead the Community in its decision-making process.

Freya: A swampy pleasure planet that is known for the most decadent luxuries in the Spiral (among humans at least) as well as a variety of dangerous diseases.

Genemods: A slang term for those who have been modified from baseline humanity or other species.

Genemodding: Verb for modifying from baseline humanity or other species into something else.

Grounder: A slang term for those who grew up and primary live on planets.

Gulayan Limit: A technological limit that all races in the galaxy but the Elder Races suffer. It keeps technology on rough parity and is believed to be enforced by outside parties as well as Community pressures.

Infospace: A extra-dimensional communications system that allows faster-than-light communication and works like an interstellar internet.

Jumpdrive: What allows people to travel through space like in movies.

Jumpspace: A dimension of bizarre physics that makes faster-than-light travel possible. Looking at it will drive most people insane like staring into the sun due to the way it stimulates your synapses.

Kolahn: Resemble giant apes with scales. Their civilization was overtaken by a terrorist cult and promptly bombed back to the stone age by the Community. Its survivors are, paradoxically, living as refugees among the Community.

Known Universe: Explored space that turns out to be primarily just Orion's Arm.

Longevity Treatments: Expensive cellular regeneration techniques that can halt the aging process and even reverse it to an extent. It can raise human lifespans up to four hundred. Unavailable to the majority of the populace in their best form but even then, human lifespans have expanded to two hundred in "civilized" space.

MacArthur-class vessel: A corvette and light patrol craft produced by humanity in the early days of faster-than-light travel.

New Aberdeen: A small farming planet near but not in Contested Space.

Notha: Adorable small fuzzy race of Space Nazi bastards.

Notha Empire: A corrupt military dictatorship ruled by the Notha that practices slavery, imperialism, planet looting, and conquest. It maintains its existence not by competence but due to the possession of weapons of stellar destruction.

Notha War: A conflict that resulted in the destruction of seventeen inhabited planets on both sides of the conflict due to an exchange of SKAMMs.

Olothonalka: Nine-foot-tall gastropods, with six eyes on motile stalks. Patterned on back and torso. Three genders (male, female, and mass egg-laying). No arms but the entire lower surface is manipulative. Most humans just call them Snails.

Olympia Colonies: A transtellar that terraforms worlds and builds colonies for humanity. It is now mostly defunct after the creation of Contested Space.

Olympic-class vessel: An incredibly powerful EarthGov vessel that is just barely a mid-tier vessel by Community standards.

Rand's World: A former colony world of Earth where the terraforming was stopped mid-process due to Notha aggression. It is now primarily inhabited by criminals, pirates, and separatists. Named for Ayn Rand.

Security Departments: The twelve, yes, twelve intelligence agencies working for the Community.

Savit: Excrement. Usually used as a pejorative.

SKAMMs: Sun destroying weapons of interstellar destruction. They are horrifying devices and their use in the recent Notha War resulted in an immediate end to the conflict lest the two sides annihilate one another.

Sorkanan: One of the oldest and most powerful species in space. They are a humanoid reptilian species with multiple offshoots.

Space Academy: The training center for officers in the Community Protectors.

Spacer: A slang term for those who have grown up and primarily live in space.

Space Cadet Sally: A popular children's show with a large adult following. Space Cadet Sally has often been accused of being Space Fleet propaganda.

Space Fleet: The Community's massive interstellar Navy that is (allegedly) a galactic force for good.

The Spiral: What Orion's Arm is called by most races of the Known Universe as they are primarily concentrated there.

Starkiller-class vessel: A stealth ship class used for launching SKAMM missiles produced by EarthGov.

Sun Killer: Another name for SKAMM torpedoes.

Thor: An impoverished planet with a population of blue-skinned humans that deals with cold as well as radiation daily.

Transtellar: The name for interplanetary corporations that are possessed of resources far more than individual worlds. They wield disproportionate power in the Community and among humanity's various worlds.

Treaty of Exarxes: A large multispecies agreement on shared morality and behavior during wartime. The Notha are a very reluctant recent signatory with SKAMMs being a current subject of great debate.

Verdantian: A leonine race with six limbs that were uplifted by the Elder Races according to their belief structure.

AUTHOR'S NOTE

I'd like to thank you for reading this book. The publishing industry is changing dramatically since the advent of eBooks. It is now very difficult to get any book noticed, regardless of quality. If you enjoyed this book, you could do some very simple things to help me attract attention. Word of mouth is the number one source of success for novels, so simply telling family and friends about the book is a great start.

Here are a few other ways of helping out, if you are so inclined:

* Post a rating or review where you purchased the eBook
* Post a rating or review on Goodreads
* Talk about the book or write a review on Facebook
* Tell folks about the book in a blog post.

If you like any of my other books, please feel free to check them out. A lot of my series are interlinked, and you never know when you'll find someone familiar showing up. In this case, *Space Academy Dropouts* is set in the far future of my Agent G cyberpunk books and the past of my *Lucifer's Star* series. Fans will certainly get a kick out of seeing how the galaxy changes in a few centuries either way.

ABOUT THE AUTHORS

Frank Martin is an author and comic writer that is not as crazy as his work makes him out to be. A fan of storytelling in all its forms, Frank always enjoys exploring new genres and mediums. He currently lives in New York with his wife and three kids. You can check out updates for all of Frank's writing at frankthewriter.com, on his Facebook page at facebook.com/frankmartinwriter, or follow him on Twitter and Instagram @frankthewriter.

Bibliography

A Weapon's Journey
Modern Testament (comics)
Mountain Sickness
Skin Deep/Ordinary Monsters

Dark Destiny (Dark Destiny, Vol. 1)
Destiny's Paradox (Dark Destiny, Vol. 2)

C. T. Phipps is a lifelong student of horror, science fiction, and fantasy. An avid tabletop gamer, he discovered this passion led him to write and turned him into a lifelong geek. He is a regular blogger and also a reviewer for The Bookie Monster.

Bibliography

Novels

The Rules of Supervillainy (Supervillainy Saga #1)
The Games of Supervillainy (Supervillainy Saga #2)
The Secrets of Supervillainy (Supervillainy Saga #3)
The Kingdom of Supervillainy (Supervillainy Saga #4)
The Tournament of Supervillainy (Supervillainy Saga #5)
The Future of Supervillainy (Supervillainy Saga #6)
The Horror of Supervillainy (Supervillainy Saga #7)
Tales of Supervillainy: Cindy's Seven (Supervillainy Saga #7)

I Was a Teenage Weredeer (The Bright Falls Mysteries, Book 1)
An American Weredeer in Michigan (The Bright Falls Mysteries, Book 2)
A Nightmare on Elk Street (The Bright Falls Mysteries, Book 3)

Esoterrorism (Red Room, Vol. 1)

Eldritch Ops (Red Room, Vol. 2)
The Fall of the House (Red Room, Vol. 3)

Agent G: Infiltrator (Agent G, Vol. 1)
Agent G: Saboteur (Agent G, Vol. 2)
Agent G: Assassin (Agent G, Vol. 3)

Cthulhu Armageddon (Cthulhu Armageddon, Vol. 1)
The Tower of Zhaal (Cthulhu Armageddon, Vol. 2)

Lucifer's Star (Lucifer's Star, Vol. 1)
Lucifer's Nebula (Lucifer's Star, Vol. 2)

Straight Outta Fangton (Straight Outta Fangton, Vol. 1)
100 Miles and Vampin' (Straight Outta Fangton, Vol. 2)
Vampiraz4Life (Straight Outta Fangton, Vol. 3)

Wraith Knight (Wraith Knight, Vol. 1)
Wraith Lord (Wraith Knight, Vol. 2)
Wraith King (Wraith Knight, Vol. 3)

Dark Destiny (Dark Destiny, Vol. 1)
Destiny's Paradox (Dark Destiny, Vol. 2)

Brightblade (The Morgan Detective Agency, Book 1)

Space Academy Dropouts (Space Academy Series, Book 1)
Space Academy Rejects (Space Academy Series, Book 2)
Space Academy Washouts (Space Academy Series, Book 3)

Psycho Killers in Love

Anthologies (as editor)
Blackest Knights

Curious about other Crossroad Press books? Stop by our website:
http://crossroadpress.com
We offer quality writing
in digital, audio, and print formats.

Subscribe to our newsletter on the website homepage and receive a
free eBook.

Printed in Great Britain
by Amazon

32162355R00169